Acknowledgements

Ed Mooney. Who is he? He was my English teacher at Father Judge High School. He made books seem interesting even when we were certain that they were the cure for insomnia. He had a natural love that all good English teachers possess . . .

A love for the written word.

If anyone deserves an enormous amount of credit for this novel it's him.

I had been writing since I was seven-years old. It began as badly drawn comics then at fifteen I wrote my first full-length novel.

I shopped my manuscript (that I was sure was going to rock the world) to some of my other teachers, and had gotten the same reply from all of them.

"Needs work."

Then I ended up in the class of Edward Mooney, literature and grammar's best friend. In his class I learned the fine art of symbolism and, when used properly, how to disguise it.

He taught me that symbolism, when used properly, was like writing two books at once. On one hand, if one only cared to look at the surface, they would be entertained. On the other hand, if one cared to look deeper, they would find a different, deeper, story.

A few years after I'd left the hallowed halls of Father Judge, I'd taken up writing again. Upon the completion of my first short story The Reunion, I returned to my alma mater and found Mooney. I humbly asked him to read it and tell me what he thought.

My stomach tied in knots until he finished.

Here it comes . . .

Needs work.

"This is great," he said with all the enthusiasm he held for the novels he'd given us. "You've got real talent. Don't give up. Keep plugging away, it'll happen."

If you ever want to be a writer learn to plug away.

Learning how to live off bologna and cheese doesn't hurt either.

That day meant a lot to me. I had gotten encouragement from someone I had, and still do have, a vast amount of respect for. I had youth, I had drive, I had ideas, I had everything but what a writer needs most.

Life.

Until you've lived, you have no real foundation to draw from.

That was about to change. I never went to college. I taught myself to write fiction. I refined my skill as best I could and I started . . . ugh . . .

Plugging away.

And eating bologna and cheese.

Hemmingway said it best when he pointed out that a writer's life is a solitary life at best. It consists of countless hours of fruitless key and head banging. It consists of a small group of friends and being counted out as slightly off-center because you're not wired for "normal life."

It's living with a vision sometimes only you can see, and if you're as lucky as I am, you'll have friends who will see your vision even when you can't. It's the greatest gift you could ever be cursed with.

And it will get you banged up whether you like it or not.

Getting banged up gives you experience.

Experience is life.

Before we go forward. I would also like to take this time to thank everyone who backed me on my journey: People who, at times, had more faith in me than I had in myself: My father, my brothers and sisters: Betty, Nan, Mary, Anthony and Jim. Bess Trotman, John Trotman, Maryanne Trotman, My friends: Sean and Rita Gallagher, Joe Moore, Larry and June Madden, Joan, Joey, Eleanor, Joanie, Cindy, and Howard Cameron, Charles "Rock" Robertson, Luke and Barb Getter, Marie Ford, Colleen Moore, Irene Bouda, Renee Cendrowski, Marie and Tom McCracken, Ed Gallagher, Glen Reed, Tony Baratta, Teddy Barrett, Jack Thompson, John McGinnis, Dave, Lisa and Sean Behrle, John and Mabel Riedel, Frank and Cass Fanelli, Sharon Hale, Tom Brown, Bill McLaughlin, David Cardinal, Bill and Sally Canna, and Joe Kincade. I'm sure Joe doesn't even know I'm a writer, but the man just deserves recognition.

If you knew him, you'd know why.

I would also like to take this time to acknowledge the ones have gone on: Howard Cameron Sr. Frank Murphy, Cathy Krueger, Joseph "Pop"

Jack

Merry Christmas

M. A. Hertzler

Timothy W. Burger

2003

Moore, Frank Bouda, Andrew Condron, Joseph Condron, Peter Trotman. Pete Trotman Jr., Joe Graham, Don Johnson, Matt McClure, Helen Urban, Sheila McGinley, Helen Heisler, Tony Kulikauski and Bob Mattai.

We miss you all.

A special thanks goes to the team: Tim Krueger for his patience with all my changes on the cover art, Sean Gallagher for his unrelenting patience with revisions to text, and to my brother Anthony for finding a way to make me look good.

Thank you, brother. Appreciate it.

Last, but by no means least, a very special thank you to Steve Jobs and the people at Apple Computers. Three of these stories were written on a Mac Plus, two on a Mac Performa, and the book was finished up on an iMac G4. Believe it or not, I really miss that Mac Plus. Thanks to all at Apple for making this writer's life a whole lot easier.

I know you all work hard for your money. I'm honored you bought my book. I hope you find it money well spent.

From me to you,
Merry Christmas.

Take Care,
God Bless,
Breathe Free.

W. A. Heisler

Philadelphia
2003

To My Father
Wayne R. Heisler
Merry Christmas, dad,
May you have many, many more.

In Memory of my Mother
Rita T. Heisler
For the many things left unsaid.

An American Christmas

By

W. A. Heisler

The Tradition

1

Jennifer Dugan sat silently at her dining room table sipping eggnog as she eyed her husband who sat sullenly at the other end.

Timothy Dugan sat there quietly for an hour, occasionally looking up from the table to check the time on the wall clock hanging above the buffet table.

Taking a long drag on his cigarette, he glanced at the clock. It read: 11:45 P.M.

Almost time to go.

Jennifer sighed knowing that the argument was coming. The same argument took place every Christmas Eve.

She looked into the living room at the large tree in the corner with its flickering lights reflecting off glass balls of assorted colors.

Beneath it lie a pile of boxes wrapped in bright holiday paper, each crowned with a bow.

In another corner stood a bicycle on training wheels. On its handlebars were tied strands of red and green ribbon.

Garland and lights snaked up the stair's banister. Below them, held in place by thumbtacks, hung three red and white Christmas stockings. The largest had Bobby lettered on it with a mix of red and green sparkles.

The house shone with holiday decorations. Although Yule Tide ornaments glittered and glistened throughout the house, there would be no cheer tonight. The argument was coming. It always came.

It was a holiday must for them.

Looking across the table at him, she decided now was as good a time as any to start. "You're going there again this year, *aren't you*?"

Timothy Dugan tapped his cigarette into the full ashtray. "Yes," he said, not looking up.

Jennifer leaned forward on her elbows, "But why, Tim? Why do you do this to yourself? Every year it's the same thing: You go see him and come back in a bad mood. And what about your mother? She comes over every year to have Christmas dinner with us and she has to see you like this. Tim, she's not *blind*. She knows where you were. She knows you went to see him. Think of her and how *she* feels. Why do you do this? Why?"

Dugan looked up from the table, "Because I have to. I want to let him know it's Christmas. I want to thank him for all the merry Christmases he gave me. I want to let him know how much they meant to me."

Jennifer shook her head, "And what about Bobby? Tim, don't you think this is affecting him? He's only five, but he can sense when something's wrong. Think of what this is doing to him. Why now? Couldn't you at least wait and go see him in the morning. Does it have to be in the middle of the night?"

Dugan looked up at the clock.

Midnight.

Crushing his cigarette in the ashtray, he stood up. "I'll be back in an hour or so," he said walking to the dining room closet and retrieving his overcoat.

"Please, Tim, I'm begging you don't go," she pleaded following him passed the sparkling tree to the front door. Cold December air gusted through the door as he opened it.

"Tim," She begged in a final desperate attempt, "Please don't go. Couldn't we have a nice Christmas for just one year?"

Dugan took a pair of gloves from his coat pocket and pulled them on. "We'll talk about it when I get back," he said quietly.

Frustrated, she watched him walk down the steps and cross the pavement to their Buick.

She knew there would be no talking when he returned. And tomorrow, he would sit in his recliner in front of the television like a statue.

That was the way of Christmas.

2

Timothy Dugan maneuvered his '87 Regal through the barren streets to his destination. Dugan would think of him and his teeth would clamp tight. He hated him. He hated him for what he had done.

In twenty minutes, he was there.

The Buick rolled to a stop at the curb. Parking was easy here. This side of the street was always vacant at this time of night. Dugan stepped out of the car slamming the door shut.

He walked around the car, onto the pavement, and up to the metal gate. For a few moments he looked beyond it, then pushed it open.

The gate opened up onto a path lit only by moonlight shining on a silver-blue world.

Digging his hands into his pockets, Dugan walked twenty yards up the path. Veering off the path to his right, he walked ten steps and stopped. Turning, he looked down. “Merry Christmas,” he said angrily. In front of him sat a stone.

On it read:

Timothy Dugan Sr.
July 11, 1930 - December 25, 1972

In an instant his mind wandered from the dark cemetery to another place. A far away place filled with more innocent thoughts.

He was six then, lying beneath his warm quilts in his second floor bedroom. He had lain awake the entire night. Waiting.

Waiting for Santa to come.

Christmas mornings in the Dugan household were a tradition to young Timothy. He would wait until daybreak, then he would rise. Tiptoeing down the hall and passed the stairs, he would make his way to the closed door of his parents’ room.

For a moment, he would stand there smiling, then he would throw open the door. He would run to the bed and jump on the lump beneath the covers nearest the door.

His father would sit up and look around, acting surprised. “Wha-who’s there?” His father would look at him, and shock would fall over his face. “Why, it’s you, Tim,” he would exclaim. “And what gets you out of bed so early in the morning?”

Young Timothy would look at his father and laugh, “It’s Christmas, daddy! Merry Christmas!”

His father would let out a goodhearted laugh, “Well so it is.” His father would then throw his arms around his boy, and give him a kiss on the cheek. “Merry Christmas, Tiny Tim,” his father would always whisper to him.

His father then pulled back from him, and gave him a big smile. “Are you ready to go see what Santa's brought for you?"

Timothy looked at him through huge, wondrous eyes, "Did he come? Did he really?"

His fatay the same thing he always said. "Sure did," he would say, "let 'im in myself. He asked me if you were a good boy this year and I said yep. They don't come any better than my Tim."

"Did he take the cookies?"

"Sure did. All of 'em."

"Even the one *I* decorated?"

"Ate that one first," his father grinned.

Timothy then shook his father excitedly, "C'mon, daddy! C'mon let's go see!"

His father laughed, and ruffled his son's already disheveled hair, "Okay, son, but let's get your mom up so she can see too."

His father put a gentle hand on the lump of blankets beside him, and give it a soft shake. "Come on, mom," his father called to her, "let's go see what Santa brought for us."

His mother sat up with a groan and wiped her eyes.

Timothy could remember how she always looked the most beautiful on Christmas morning, with her slightly mussed hair, and dressed in her red flannel Christmas nightgown.

Sleepily, she turned and looked at her husband. "Merry Christmas, Mr. Dugan," she bade in her light melodic voice.

Putting his large arm around her neck, Tim Dugan gave her a kiss. "Merry Christmas, Mrs. Dugan," he said with a smile then asked. "Did you get enough sleep last night, Mrs. Dugan?"

This made her laugh as she kissed him. And her reply was: "More than enough, Mr. Dugan. More than enough."

"Let's go," young Tim yelled, pulling at his father's arm.

His father would get out of bed holding onto his wife's hand. Together like a train, the Dugan family made their way, hand in hand, down the steps. . .

To begin the magic of Christmas.

Sitting on the sofa, his father would look approvingly at everything young Timothy had been given. While he would rip open his presents at a feverish pace, his mother would be busy in the kitchen fixing breakfast. As he tore madly at the festive wrap, the smell of bacon and eggs filled his nose.

Every once in a while, when he yelled extra loudly, his mother would call into the living room, "Ooh what is it, Tim? Come here and let mommy see!" Tim would grab what he had gotten and run it into the kitchen, but not before he had to promise his father to steal him a slice of bacon.

They would all sit at the dining room table and eat their breakfast, and his father played his favorite record of Christmas carols. He remembered his father playing *Joy to the World* over and over again, and his mother humming to it as she put the food on the table.

"This one's my favorite, Tiny Tim," his father always said. "Best version of it in the world. All the others are ka-ka at best."

Tim listened as the booming voices of the choir filled the house. To him this was Christmas.

He was six then.

Now at seven he stood in front of his parents' door. Waiting. Finally he decided it was time and threw open the door. With a smile he jumped onto his father.

The lump didn't move.

"Dad," Tim called, as he shook his father. He looked at his face, and it didn't look right to him. His father's lips had a purplish color to them. His closed eyes looked a bit swollen to young Tim. Alarmed, he shook his mother furiously. "Mom," he yelled. "Mom get up! Something's wrong with daddy! *MOM!"*

Sitting up, his mother rubbed her eyes, "What is it, Timmy?" He watched confused as his mother looked down at his father. He saw the look of horror and pain slowly dawn on her face.

She said no repeatedly under her breath as she put a finger to his neck. She had begun crying as she put her ear to his father's chest.

"What is it, mom," he asked her.

She looked at him and donned her calm voice. "Go downstairs, Timmy. Mommy has to - has to make a few phone calls. Go downstairs, please."

Timmy walked backward to the door. "But mom-"

All calm left his mother's face as she began crying, "Timmy, *PLEASE*!"

Running to the top of the steps, he turned and looked back.

Down at the end of the hall, through the open door, he could see his mother with her head on his father's chest. Her shoulders were shaking, her tears uncontrolled.

Young Tim sat at the bottom of the steps looking at presents whose shine had somehow been stolen overnight as he listened to his mother place her calls upstairs.

In an hour, the house was full of strangers. Strangers, who whenever they passed him would stop and say they were sorry. Timmy watched in confusion as men in white jackets hauled in a stretcher through their front door and went directly up the steps.

He could see his mother sitting at the dining room table, tissue in hand. Her eyes were red and swollen, and she tried to smile as she talked to a man in a black suit.

Turning around to face the steps, he saw the men in white appear at the top.

Slowly, they negotiated the stretcher down the steps and lifted it up over the banister. Tim could see his father had been strapped to it and the sheet covering him had been pulled up over his face.

Timmy tugged on the jacket tail of one of the white coats. "Where are you taking my dad? Where's he going?"

The man in white didn't answer.

"Where's my daddy going," he demanded.

A soft hand fell on his shoulder. Tim spun around to see his mother. She knelt down in front of him and took hold of his shoulders. "Daddy has to go away, Timmy."

"Will he be back?"

"No." She said, her eyes filling with tears.

"But why?"

Tears and a hug were her only response.

Quietly, he stood alongside his mother at his father's viewing. It snowed the day they buried him. Tim stood there shivering beside the closed coffin as people, half of whom he didn't know, shook his hand.

Looking at his father's casket he filled with hate.

He hated his father for leaving the way he did. He hated him for not saying goodbye. He hated him the same way he had ever since. That was why he never cried for his father.

You don't cry over people you hate.

But that was long ago. The boy was a man now and the shining mahogany casket had long since been buried. Dugan looked at the stone red-faced.

"Well here we are again," Dugan snorted. "Another great Christmas in a long line of great Christmases. You've made it a very memorable occasion for me. I came here to thank you for that. I hope you can hear me, wherever the hell you are."

"I can hear you just fine, boy," a voice answered from behind him.

3

Dugan spun around, his heart racing. On the path stood a figure in a navy-blue three-piece suit. Outlining the tall shape pulsated a glowing white aura. Dugan gawked at it, his mouth hung slack. His eyes met the eyes of the figure, and recognition set in. He knew that face.

It was the face of his father.

Dugan began backing up, unable to take his eyes off the figure. He took three steps and banged up against his father's gravestone.

Staying on the path, the apparition walked up to the row of stones, Dugan's eyes followed its every step. His father looked at him and smiled. "Whatsamatter, boy? You look like you've seen a ghost."

Dugan tried to speak, but could only manage a thin whimper.

His father threw back his head and laughed.

"No," Dugan said shaking his head. "You *can't* be here. It's impossible. You're dead."

His father nodded, and shrugged, "Well, can't argue with you on *that* one."

Dugan's mouth went dry, "Then how-I mean if you're dead-"

His father shook his head sadly, "Son, if you want people to understand you, you've got to get that *knot* out of your tongue. Until then," his father said gesturing to Dugan's feet, "do you mind?"

"M-mind what?"

"You're standing on my head."

With a disgusted yell, Dugan jumped off the grave and stumbled to the path. Shakily he looked at the grave then turned back in the direction of his father. His eyes widened, as he found his father nose to nose with him.

He screamed again.

His father gave an amused grin, "Don't worry, boy, I'm not going to hurt you. I just came to talk to you." Timothy Dugan Sr. watched his son shiver in the biting December wind. "You cold, son?"

Dugan shook his head.

His father smiled, "Liar."

With a wide arc of his right arm, Timothy Dugan waved his hand over his son. From his fingertips shot thousands of tiny lights. The sparkling objects fell over his son and formed a glowing outline. Timothy Dugan looked at his father open-mouthed as he felt the cold disappear.

His father smiled broadly at his son's expression. "Pretty neat trick, eh boy," his father laughed. "Just think of the fortune I could've saved on gas if I coulda done that when I was alive."

"That's not funny!" Dugan roared.

"Sorry, son." His father apologized.

"What are you doing here, anyway?" Dugan asked.

"I've come to talk to you, son." He father replied.

Looking around, his father's eyes fell on a bench further up the path. "C'mon, boy," his father said gesturing to it, "Let's sit and talk for awhile."

Dugan backed away.

His father rolled his eyes, "You still don't believe I'm here, do you? What do you want me to do? Rattle *chains*? Don't carry them with me. Too heavy. Show you my wings? Son, I was good, but I wasn't *that* good."

Dugan eyed him warily.

His father rolled his eyes again, "Will ya just sit with me for awhile, please? Ten minutes, tops, then you can go." Timothy Dugan Sr. then crossed his hands over his chest, closed his eyes, and added, "Corpses honor."

"*STOP THAT*!" His son bellowed.

"Sorry," his father apologized again. "You were too young to know about my sense of humor. And apparently you didn't in*herit* any of it." His face grew serious, "Son, please. Just for a little while."

Slowly, Dugan followed the apparition to the lone bench and they both sat down.

"Well, what are you doing here," his son grumbled.

His father rested both arms on the back of the bench and looked out over the stones, "Son, why are you here? I mean, everyone else's families come here during the *day* to leave *flowers*, but not *my* son. *Nnnnooooo*! *My* son has to stop by once a year to bawl me out. Why?"

"I hate you." Dugan replied.

"I don't hate *you*."

"You left me! You left both of us! On *Christmas*!"

His father sat up, shocked, "Son, I didn't want to go. You have to believe that. Son, I had a bad ticker. I didn't want to leave you like that, but when He wants you up there, you gotta go. My pump just gave out. It's a common heart ailment. It's hereditary. So why don't you go 'cross town to your grandfather's grave and pick on *him* awhile?"

Dugan stared at the ground, not saying a word.

"You know Christmas has always been a special time for us," his father said with a smile. "I proposed to your mother on Christmas eve."

"I didn't know that," Dugan mumbled.

"Yep," Timothy Sr. grinned, "right under the mistletoe in her parents' home. That was in '52. Mind you, your mother was a heck of a lot younger than me. Here I was, a thirty-two year old man courtin' this little twenty-three year old slip of a girl.

"Of course, I always looked a lot younger than I really was. Her parents didn't even know how old I was until after we tied the knot.

"I remember walking in with presents for her and her parents. She looked upset, almost to the point of tears.

"I sat her down on the sofa and asked her what was the problem. Always hated to see her cry. She looked at me and told me that she couldn't afford a present for me. That made me laugh. She was a waitress at a diner when I met her and I knew what kind of money she made. To tell you the truth, I didn't *expect* to get anything from her.

"Well it was enough to set her off, and that was that. You know how it is, son. Christmas
comes and everyone wants to play Santa. So I told her if that was the problem, that I had the solution. I took a bow and ribbon from one of the gifts I brought her, and plopped it on her head. Smack dab in the middle.

"She looked at me honestly confused. I took a look at her with her long brown hair, and those big chestnut eyes, and that ridiculous looking bow on her head, and my heart melted. One smile from your mother could melt an iceberg, son.

"Then, I told her that she was the greatest present I could ever hope for. And she was, son. I didn't know what happiness was until I found her. Well, don't have to tell you what happened *then*. The dam broke, and it was tears *everywhere*. She cried so hard that her parents came in from the kitchen thinking we'd had an argument.

"While we assured her parents that nothing was wrong, she turned back to me and smiled. 'I'm no present,' she said. 'That's not enough for what you've given me, Tim.' And I said she was right. I pulled a little black box from my pocket, and gave it to her.

"While she looked at it, I got down in front of her on my knee and took her hands in mine. 'Maggie,' I said. ' I would be honored if you would share my name and my life with me. Maggie will you marry me?

"I tell ya, she almost choked the life right outta me with the hug she gave me. She starts bawlin'; your *grandmother* starts bawlin', what a picture. There's me and your grandfather in a room with two hysterical women. What a sorry sight *we both* were.

"Then from behind me, I hear her father clear his throat. I turned to him, and he says to me, 'You gonna marry my daughter without asking for her hand proper like?' Understand, son, he was from the old-school where you asked the father's permission before you asked his daughter to marry you.

"I stood up and walked over to him. I was pretty nervous. Even at my age, a father was a father. I looked him in the eye, and said, 'Mr. Cullen, I would like permission to take you daughter's hand in marriage, sir. I'll take good care of her, and give her the best I can. Do I have your permission?'

"Instead of answering me, he points to the gift with his name on it. 'That for me, boy?' I nodded. 'Well give it here,' he grumbled. I picked up the box, and I don't mind tellin' you I was nervous.

"He takes the present from me and looks the box over. And he was a tough man, your grandfather. Gave the box a thorough exam. And I'll tell ya son, the room went *silent*. Everyone was looking at him. And never once did his face soften.

"All eyes where on him and we figured if he didn't like what I had gotten him, I was outta luck. After a few minutes of looking me straight in the eye, he pulled off the bow. Before I knew what was going on, he smacked it onto my forehead. He put his arm around your grandmother and said, 'Well, Barbara, it looks like we got ourselves a son for Christmas.' Then he shook my hand with a big smile, and said, 'Welcome to the family, Tim.'

"And I'll tell ya, son, me and your grandfather handled Christmas Eve like two fine upstanding Irishmen. While your mother and grandmother were busy calling everyone and their uncle with the news, we sat in the kitchen and got snookered on Irish whiskey."

Dugan's father burst out laughing at the memory.

"Mom never told me about that." Dugan said.

"Ask her. Oh she'll remember it all right."

His father's laughter slowed, as he watched his son stare morosely at the ground. Timothy Sr. gave him a light hit on the shoulder, "What's wrong, Tiny Tim?"

Dugan looked at him, "Don't call me that. I haven't been that since-since-."

His father nodded, "Do you remember how you got that name, boy?"

Dugan shook his head, "All I remember is strangers in our house and the undertaker. And you on a stretcher."

His father nodded solemnly, then added, "You were almost three at the time. Christmas was rolling around, and we were watching *A Christmas Carol*. You were sitting on my lap on the sofa,
when that part of the movie came on where Tiny Tim says, 'God bless us; everyone.' And out of
nowhere, *you* said it too.

"It shocked the bugger out of me! I yelled for your mother, and she came running in. It took a little coaxing, but I got you to say it for her too. The next thing we know, you're running around the house yelling, 'God bless us; everyone!' It was like having our own little Tiny Tim in the house. So, every Christmas after that, you were our Tiny Tim."

"I don't remember that." Dugan mumbled.

"Course not. You were just knee-high to a grasshopper then."

His father looked out over the stones again. "Do you remember the light bulb, son?"

Dugan looked at him questioningly. "Light bulb?"

His father nodded, "Yeah, the light bulb. When you were five and decided you were big enough to help daddy with the decorations, we went out on the porch to hang the lights together.

"And what a sight you were. Daddy's little helper, all rosy-cheeked and ready to go. So there we were stringing up lights, me in my lumberjack jacket, and my right-hand man in his jacket, cap and mittens.

"I remember saying, 'Okay, Tim, your job is to hold the spare bulbs while I hook up the string.' And you smiled up at me all proud, and said, 'Yes, sir.' Sounded just like a little soldier.

"After we had them all hung, I threw the switch and they all lit, except, for a red one in the middle of the line. So I said, 'Okay, Tim, you pick me out a good color to replace that one with.' And you looked through that box for five whole minutes until you found one you liked. A blue one.

"You handed it to me and I took the bad one out and screwed the good one in. Then you asked me what I was going to do with the bulb I had replaced and I told you I was going to throw it out.

"You didn't like that at all. You asked me if you could keep it. When I asked you why you said that you felt bad for it. Said you didn't like the idea of it being in a trash heap somewhere for Christmas.

"The thought struck me as odd, but then I thought about it. And I couldn't hold having compassion against my Tim. It's a good trait to have. Even if it was for a *light bulb*.

"So I gave you the little bulb and you looked at it for a moment, then you stuffed it into your pocket. Then on Christmas Eve, you put it under the tree. When I asked you why, you said, 'Santa can fix it. I know he can.'

"After you told me that, I went out and looked for three hours for a light bulb just like that one. In a foot of snow yet! Try and find decorations on Christmas Eve sometime. It's like sorting through other people's *trash*. But I found it just the same. And when you went to bed, I put the good one in place of the bad one, just where you had left it.

"And on Christmas morning, you made me go out, and screw it back in. I said, ' Cross your fingers, Tim. Let's see if Santa fixed it.'

"And you said, 'I can't! My mittens are too tight!' And then you made me promise to cross mine on *both* hands instead.

"And when I hit the switch and that bulb lit up, you went crazy. You were jumping up and down and clapping your hands, like it was the greatest thing you'd ever seen. Seeing you so happy was the best part of that day for me.

"And for the rest of the day, you would stop playing with your toys every once in a while to look out the window at it. I'd be sitting in my easy chair, and look up from my paper and ask, 'Still lit, Tim?' And you'd look at me with a big smile, and say, 'Yeah! Santa fixed it *real* good!"

"What ever happened to the first bulb?"

"Does it matter?"

"No," Dugan huffed.

Dugan sat up, pulled a pack of cigarettes out of his pocket, and lit one.

"You shouldn't smoke, son," his father warned. "Those things'll kill ya. Take it from me. I know. I'm *dead*. We have a lot of *black-lungers* up there."

"Save it." Dugan grumbled.

"Do you remember the angel, boy?" His father asked.

"Angel?"

His father grinned, "Yeah, the angel. I remember you and your mother and I were out shopping on your fourth Christmas. We went looking for a tree, and finally found a lot with trees that looked like they hadn't fallen off the back of the truck.

"And the guy at the stand had decorations at the counter. And one of the decorations was one of those new angels holding two candles. And the candle flames were lights. Remember?"

Dugan nodded.

"Well," his father began again. "You saw the angel all lit up, and you start tugging on my coat. 'Look at the angel, daddy! Look!' And I bent over to you, and said, 'Do you think we ought to get one of those for the tree this year, Tim?' And you nodded so hard I thought your little head would roll *right off*."

Dugan smiled in spite of himself.

"So we took it home," his father began again, "and set up the tree so the branches would fall overnight.

"The next night, you, and your mother and I, decorated it. Then when it was all done, I leaned over to you and said, 'All right, Tim, go get your angel for the top.' And off you went, running to get your angel.

"When you came back, I hoisted you up on my shoulders and let you put it on the tree. Then when we lit the tree, the angel lit up with it. I remember how the sparkles on his red and white gown, and gold halo caught the twinkling lights. What a sight it was. The most beautiful ornament on the tree, it was.

And when I set you down, I said, 'Okay, Tim, that's your job every year. It's your job to make sure the angel gets put on the tree. Now don't you forget.' And you shook your head to confirm that it would never slip your memory.

"And it didn't. Every year you would run downstairs and get your angel out of its box and would put it on the tree after it was all decorated. It was our little tradition. Do you still have it?"

"Mom gave it to me when I got my house."

"Ever use it?"

"No. It's in a box somewhere."

Timothy Sr. looked up at the stars, "I love Christmas, boy. It's a time for miracles. You know, you were a miracle baby, son?"

Dugan looked over at him, "A miracle baby?"

His father nodded, "You sure were. After your mother and I were married, we tried for three years to have children, but nothing happened.

"We went to doctors, and they told us we couldn't have any. Your mother and I were heartbroken. We wanted so much to have a family, she and I. And here are these doctors saying we couldn't. But that didn't stop us. No sireee.

"One day I came home from work and found your mother crying in the dining room. I knelt down beside her and asked her what was the matter. She looked at me and told me that she had seen the doctor that morning. I asked her what he had said, and she looked at me and said, 'Do you want a boy or a girl?'

"I remember I just knelt there with my mouth open. All I could say was, 'A baby? We're gonna have a *baby?'* I don't think I could have loved her any more than I did right then and there, son. I put my ear to her stomach to see if I could hear you, then I looked at her with a smile and said, 'Yep, Maggie, he's an Irishman all right! He just said: Whaddaya mean all I get to drink is milk!"

Dugan looked at the ground his face unchanging.

"But you were no easy birth, let me tell you. You arrived two months premature, and were extremely underweight. The doctors told us when you were born that your chances for survival were slim. They had you in an Intensive Care ward and wouldn't even let me in to see you. They said that if you lived for forty-eight hours, that there was hope for you.

"And for forty-eight hours I was on my knees in the hospital's chapel. I wasn't about to lose you, son. I had just gotten you, for cryin' out loud. I remember kneeling in front of the altar, and
saying, 'Lord, I'm here to talk to ya about my boy. They say he's too tiny to live. I don't believe

that. You can save him I know it.

"They won't even let me see him. Lord, he's my son. Please help him I'm begging you. If you need someone, take me, not him. He's so little and defenseless. Please Lord. Lord, I'd give you my life, if I could just hold my boy. Just for an hour. Please?" Timothy Sr.'s voice softened to a whisper, "Just one hour with my son."

Dugan felt tears welling in his eyes, but refused look up.

"He heard me, Timothy Dugan Sr. nodded. "But He gave me more than an hour. He gave me seven *years*. Seven years to enjoy you. And every night for those seven years, I thanked Him for you. He gave me something that was worth *more* than my life: He gave me my son."

"*STOP IT*!" Dugan screamed, as he threw his hand over his face. "Oh, God, just *stop it*! Leave me alone! Why can't you leave me alone! Why are you here!"

His father stood up, walked three steps, and turned, "I'm here because you're in pain, son. I couldn't bear to see you like this any longer.

"I've got to go now, son. You won't be seeing me anymore. This was a privilege I was granted, one time and one time only. But even though you won't be seeing me, whether or not you *feel* me is up to you.

"Think of me what you will, but always remember; I love you, boy. I always have and always will. And, for me, Christmas will always be our *special* time.

His father lowered his head and began walking away.

Dugan looked up at his father through a film of tears. *You don't hate him, dammit,* a voice in his head roared. *You hate the fact you never got the chance to say it to him! He's here now! Say it to him before he goes! You've waited all these years now say it! Hurry! Say it! SAY IT!*

"*Dad*!" Dugan screamed in a tone of desperation.

His father turned back to him.

Dugan mouthed the first word, but the tears had constricted his throat making it hard to speak. "It's-," he choked out. "It's Christmas, daddy." He closed his eyes for a moment, then opened them, "Merry Christmas," he pushed the words out just before he fell into tears.

His father looked at his son with a loving smile. "Merry Christmas," he replied as a sparkling diamond formed in his eye and ran down his cheek, "Tiny Tim."

Through the rain in his eyes, Dugan could see his father wave a last goodbye.

Then he was gone.

The glowing aura around him disappeared, and he could again feel the December winds. Still sobbing, he looked to the East and found the sky brightening.

Burying his face in his hands, he released himself to grief. To missing. There he sat alone in the cold. As the wind whipped around him, he felt nothing. For Timothy Dugan was enveloped in warmth.

A warmth no flame could ever match.

4

Carefully, Timothy Dugan pulled his Buick to a stop in front of his house. He drew in a deep breath and dabbed at his eyes with gloved fingers.

He stepped out into the early morning, which was still a shade of purple and closed the door. Looking at his house, with its lights still shining and flickering, he had to smile.

Walking up to his door, he slid his key as quietly as he could into its lock. Gently, he turned it and slowly pushed it open.

Dugan took off his coat as he walked into the living room. On the sofa, his wife lay sleeping. Trying not to disturb her, he slowly sat on the edge of the couch. Looking down into her peaceful face, framed by flowing auburn hair, he realized how lucky he was.

He turned and looked up the steps.

Up those steps, lying in his bed was a miracle of his own. A miracle he could share things with. The way fathers do with sons. He turned back to his wife running a gentle hand through her hair.

She stirred then opened her eyes. "Oh," she muttered sleepily, "I didn't hear you come in." She searched his face. On his lips rested a peaceful smile, in his eyes: shining tears.

She sat up on her elbows, and ran her fingers through his hair, "Honey, are you all right?" A sob escaped his lips before he could pull it back. "Tim, what's wrong," She asked concerned.

Wrapping his arms around her, he pulled her tight. "I'm so sorry, babe," he whispered in her ear. "Please forgive me for acting this way. I'm so sorry."

Jennifer Dugan held him close as he cried into her shoulder. "It's all right," she whispered. "It's okay."

He pulled away, below his glistening eyes, a wide smile, "Let's get Bobby up."

She looked up the steps, then back to him, "Honey, I don't think he's awake yet."

Dugan looked up the steps then back to her, "Wanna make a bet?"

"Hey Bobby!" Dugan yelled, not taking his eyes off his wife. A small voice came back down to him, "Yeah, dad!" Dugan and his wife looked at each other and laughed. "Come down here, boy," Dugan yelled back, "and see what Santa's brought you!"

Hooray was yelled from somewhere upstairs followed by the sounds of little feet running to the steps.

"I'll make us some coffee," Jennifer said rolling her eyes and giving him a kiss.

A blond-haired boy raced down the steps, dressed in pajamas adorned with cartoon characters. His eyes lit up at the sight of all the brightly decorated boxes. Then his eyes fell on something else. "A bike!"

"Wait," Timothy Dugan screamed. "Nobody move!"

Jennifer walked from the dining room back to him, "What is it?"

Bobby walked up to him and tugged on his pant leg, "What, daddy?"

"We forgot something," Dugan exclaimed. He turned and ran up the steps.

Dugan threw the door to the attic open with a loud bang. Skipping every other step, he ran up the stairs. With a hard yank, he pulled on the ceiling light's rope switch.

As the light swayed back and forth, Dugan looked around wildly. He ran to the back of the attic and began throwing boxes over his shoulder.

Finally, he reached the one he wanted.

Ripping open the now yellowed tape, he threw back the flaps of the carton. Digging furiously, he threw his yearbook, varsity letters and old photos onto the floor. He could feel it now; a smaller box.

Pulling the box out, he gently opened its lid. Inside lie his angel with its two candles and peaceful smile. Carefully, he took out the ornament, and found something else lying beneath it . . .

A single red Christmas bulb.

Gently, he held it up and gazed at it.

Still lit, Tim, a warm voice called from the past.

"Yeah," he whispered, wiping his eyes. "Santa fixed it real good."

He took one last look into the bottom of the box. "Good Lord," he breathed with wide eyes. Lying flush with the bottom was a record. "God bless ya, mom," he said as he lifted it from the carton.

The picture on the cover now growing white with age was almost unintelligible. But in the right upper corner he could still see what was written on it in his father's scrawl:

Tim Dugan Sr.
HANDLE WITH CARE!

Jennifer looked at her son, as he reflected the same confused look up at her. From above them she could hear the thunder of her husband running back down the steps.

In seconds, Dugan rounded the top of the steps and darted back down into the living room. He stood in front of his family holding an angel, and a record placed in the nook of his armpit. His other hand was balled into a fist.

He put his fist up in front of his face, and opened it. In his palm, sat the bulb. Jennifer walked up to him and wrapped an arm around his neck. She regarded the bulb for a moment then asked, "Is that one of ours?"

Dugan shook his head, "No. It doesn't even work."

She looked at him with her brow pulled together in question, "Then why keep it?"

Dugan gave her a kiss then turned back to the bulb. "Because," he said softly, "someone searched for three hours in the snow so I'd think it did."

Stuffing the bulb into his pocket, Dugan knelt down in front of his son. "Well, Bobby, what do you think," Dugan asked handing over the angel.

His son took the angel and examined it. He ran his hands over the white furry material that traced the bottom of the robe then ran up the center to form a fluffy collar.

He felt the red velvet of the robe that had on it little doves made of red, green, and gold glitter. Then he ran his fingers over the large dove-like wings, made of white silky material and outlined in gold glitter.

The boy then touched the gold silken hair that ran to the angel's shoulders. His eyes ran over the golden halo, which circled the angel's head.

And finally he looked at the little angel's face. His cheeks where slightly pudgy and his blue eyes made of glass sparkled. Bobby looked at the angel's smile. It was a smile of peace and serenity. Of joy and love. And it seemed to him that the little angel was smiling up at him.

And he smiled back.

Dugan looked at his son expectantly, as the boy looked back up at him.

"It's nice, dad." Bobby said quietly.

Dugan smiled, "It's yours if you want it."

The boy looked up at his father in disbelief, "Really?"

Dugan laughed, "Really. But you have to take care of him. You have a special job now, Bobby. It's your job to make sure he goes on the tree every year. Now you won't forget, will you?"

"No, dad," he said looking at the angel, "I won't forget."

Handing the record to his wife, Dugan unfurled the cord from the bottom of the figurine. "Go turn out the lights on the tree, Bobby," Dugan said, taking the record back from his wife.

As his son flicked the switch that turned the tree lights on and off, Dugan walked over to the stereo, flipped up the lid, and pulled the record from its cover. Carefully, he slid it out of its thin white sleeve and laid it on the turntable. Standing there looking at it, he wondered if it would still play.

"Ready, dad," his son yelled.

Jennifer watched as her husband hoisted their son onto his shoulders. "Okay, Bobby boy, take the star off the top and hand it down," Dugan said maneuvering his son closer to it.

His son took the plastic star, studded with lights, off the tree's tip, and handed it to his father. Dugan unplugged it from its outlet in the line, and replaced it with the angel's. "Okay, Bobby," he said letting go of the wire, "all set. Put him on."

With a grunt of determination, the boy leaned over and placed the angel where the star had been, pressing it down hard to make sure it wouldn't fall off. He was then lowered back down.

"Okay, Bobby, turn 'em on," Dugan said with a smile.

Bobby flicked the switch and ran back to his mother and father. He turned and his mouth hung open. "Wow," he breathed. "Look at 'im, dad!

Mom, look at 'im!"

His mother smiled, not taking her eyes from the tree, "I see him, honey. I see him."

Bobby moved up to the tree craning his neck to see his angel, whose wing's tips touched the ceiling. To him it looked like his angel was sitting atop a mountain of lights with his two candles burning bright, his robe changing colors with the flashing of the multicolored bulbs below.

Bobby looked at the other ornaments, then back up to the top. There his angel stood alone, like a
sentinel for the season. The angel was best part of the tree, Bobby thought. And he liked it even more because it was his.

His father had told him so.

Dugan left his wife's side and returned to the stereo. With a press of a button, he turned the power on. He switched the needle setting to automatic, and returned to her.

The arm of the turntable rose from its cradle.

"He *is* beautiful, Tim," Jennifer Dugan said looking at the angel on his perch. She turned from the tree to her husband, "You've never used him before. Where did you get him?"

Dugan's eyes began to glisten reflecting the colors coming off the tree as he answered, "My father bought him for me."

The arm moved over the record and hovered in place.

On his shoulder, Timothy Dugan could feel an unseen hand come to rest. In its touch, he could sense a feeling of love.

Of joy.

Of family.

Of togetherness.

Of someone special who had come home for the holidays.

The needle lowered and came to rest.

The sound of huge banging chimes filled the house. Through every room the thunderous melodic tones echoed. Then the booming, spirited, voices of the choir joined in . . . .

"Joy to the world the Lord has come, let earth receive her King!"

Stille Nacht

1

December 24, 1943.

Somewhere in the French countryside.

11:01 P.M.

I'm going to die tonight, Pvt. Daniel Raines' mind screamed as he scrambled madly across a clearing in the French forest. Around him the explosions of heavy artillery fire echoed through the overcast night, complimented by the sound of whining planes and the blasts of their dropped cargo.

Raines' division had gotten word from British Intelligence that the German forces had planned a mass insurgence into the area and were sent out with two thousand other men to meet them.

They were now saying hello.

Raines had been sent back to gather incoming data from U.S. Air Reconnaissance with another soldier when his jeep ran into a troop of German soldiers. The other soldier, Corporal Eddie Warren took three rounds on sight. Raines had somehow managed to escape into the woods with his rifle and his pack.

Now he was lost.

The Army Air Corp. arrived in the area at 2200 hrs. (10:00 P.M.), and had immediately begun to pepper the perimeter with shells. Raines spotted an explosion from one which was followed directly by a series of other explosions, which made him sure that a fuel convoy had been hit. That was at ten-thirty

Right about the time he began to lose feeling in his legs.

Here I am, he thought panic-stricken, *twenty-five years old and I'm going to die in some god-forsaken part of France.*

A whistle cut the air.

Raines could tell by the pitch that it was close. *Too close.* With a grunt, he forced his legs, which somewhere along the line had lost their ability to bend, to move faster.

Fear reached deep into his chest, grabbed his heart, and began to squeeze as he trudged through the knee-deep snow.

Thirty yards behind him, the shell erupted in a massive upheaval of flames, snow, and ruptured earth.

The blast slammed Raines face down in the snow. Pain shot through him as the white powder instantaneously melted then froze to his face.

With great effort, he rolled over, his left leg sticking grotesquely into the air as he did, almost rigor.

Raines looked into the European sky now clouded so badly that celestial navigation was impossible, and searched frantically for a part of his body that he could still feel. He could still move his fingers, but the movement was minimal.

Snow fell silently onto the ice that had formed on his cheeks.

The temperature had plummeted below freezing as soon as the sun had set and it was still going. *Christmas Eve, and I'm going to die. Die because we're out here fighting in weather not even fit for animals. Fighting on Christmas Eve. It's inhuman. But who ever said the Nazis were human. Damn Germans.*

Raines closed his eyes and flinched at the pain of the million tiny pins that pierced into every inch of his skin.

He was ready to die.

His dazed mind reeled with fatigue and exhaustion and it now hurled him backward.

Twelve months backward.

It wasn't snowing in January of '42 when his number came around. Emotions all across the nation now ran at a fever pitch.

Emotions and *rage* over the unforgivable attack of the previous December.

America had now been attacked personally. An attack she now planned to respond to in kind. She now found her fists clenched and was pounding them with all her might.

One hammering Germany; the other Japan.

Daniel Raines stood in the train station with a group of other draftees in Evanston Illinois waiting for his ride out.

On one of the Walnut benches lining the waiting area he sat with his four-year old son on his lap and talked with his wife.

Anne Raines sat in her best outfit and hat, with her dark hair pinned up, chatting with him as though he were only taking a trip to town instead of Europe. "Dan, how long do you think you'll be gone," she asked.

"Until it's over, sweetheart," he replied as he bounced his son on his knee.

"How long do you think that'll be," she asked again.

"Couple months. Tops," he answered, trying to sound optimistic.

The conductor called out the number of his train.

"Here," Raines said letting the boy down, "you take Danny."

Raines grabbed his suitcase, and the three of them stood up.

"Well, it looks like it's time to go," Raines grinned weakly looking for words.

"Yeah," Anne said in a low voice. "Well you be careful. And remember to write us every day. And don't worry about us, if we need anything our folks are around." Her eyes began to shine under the hanging lights.

"And remember to dress warm," she began as a tear ran down her cheek, "I hear it gets cold over there." Her words became jagged, "And remember we love you. And-and we'll miss you." She put a hand over her mouth as the tears began to rush down her face. "Hurry home," she said in a high strained voice through wet pleading eyes.

Raines pulled her to him and held her. "It's all right," he whispered. "Everything will be fine, you'll see. We'll get the job done and I'll be right home. Honest." He tried to make the words sound believable, but he knew that there was no way of telling.

"Daddy," a little voice called.

Raines looked down at his son, all wrapped up in his hat and mittens. He knelt down on one knee in front of him and smiled, "Yeah, champ?"

"You going away," the boy asked.

"For a little while," Raines answered.

"But I don't want you to."

"I have to, Danny. There's something I gotta do."

"But who'll read to me at bedtime?"

"Mommy can."

"No. I want *you* to."

"I can't, son. I've got to go."

"But I don't want you to go," his son said as tears formed in his eyes.

The conductor called out his train again.

"C'mon, give us a hug before I go."

Raines wrapped his arms around his son and squeezed him tight. "You're the man of the house until I get back," he whispered in his son's ear. "You take good care of your momma until I get back. I'll be home soon."

I'll be home soon.

I'll be home soon.

I'm going to die tonight.

"NO," Raines screamed into the cloudy smoke-filled sky. Pain running the length of his body, he pulled himself to a sitting position. He felt for his rifle, threw its strap over his shoulder, and fought his way to his feet.

Grunting as he pushed his legs that were now no more than stilts made of flesh and bone, he made his way to the edge of the clearing. *Got to get out of this cold. Got to find warmth or I'll die for sure.*

Raines covered the span of the wooded area and came out onto a snow-covered back road. Not wanting to travel the woods where the drifts had grown waist-high, he decided to follow it.

Raines traveled the road for another twenty minutes when he noticed a smaller road leading off to the right. *Too narrow to be a road,* Raines thought. *It's a driveway! It has to be!* Raines made his way along it. Where there is a driveway there is a house.

And where there is a house there is warmth.

He followed the drive for fifteen minutes, to where it rounded a bend. As he turned his eyes fell onto a palatial country home.

People must be rich, he thought as his eyes regarded the size of the house. Looking up to the roof, Raines noticed a line of smoke coming from the chimney, but looking back to the house he noticed all the windows were black

They must have the blackout shades down, Raines thought as he moved to the home's large front door.

The soldier gave the door two raps with his fist, which immediately sent a wave of pain up his right arm. No one answered. *They must've run when the shelling started,* he reasoned. He tried the knob and found the door unlocked.

The ground rocked as another bomb tore into the countryside.

Raines stumbled slightly as his feet shifted on the ice beneath him. Steadying himself, he pushed open the great wooden door.

His eyes fell onto a vestibule, its doors on the other end ajar. Beyond the doors stretched a long corridor. As Raines' eyes became used to the darkness, he could make out three doorways on the right, two on the left, and a darkened doorway at the end facing him. The second one on the left was the only room emanating light. From the second doorway on the left shone a soft flickering orange glow, complimented by the warming sounds of crackling wood.

Raines breathed a soft sigh of hope as he forced his legs to bring him inside. He was sure it was a miracle that he had found this place in this vast countryside. He was also sure now that if he had made the decision to stay on the road, he would have been found come sunrise frozen to death.

As he moved down the still hallway he kept his stinging ears open for the slightest sound. In response to his alertness, he heard only the silence of an empty home. As he neared the glowing doorway, his face began to grow moist with the melting ice on his cheeks.

Raines reached the threshold and peered in.

Against the wall opposite the doorway a large hearth blazed, a stack of cut wood beside it. On either side of the wide chimney and large mahogany mantle sat two windows which stretched from the just below the ceiling to right above the floor. Both were covered in the familiar black cloth used when bombings took place.

Directly in front of the inviting fire lay a large Oriental rug, which covered the hard wooden floor of the room leaving only a foot of wood showing near the walls.

Raines' eyes wandered to his right, where they fell on a long sofa set flush against the wall

"Gonna make a swell bunk," Raines said to himself, wearily.

Slowly, he made his way into the room, his tired eyes transfixed on his chosen bed for the night. Tomorrow he would get up and find his way back to his unit, but for now he took comfort in the fact that he wouldn't have to freeze to death.

A loud click from behind cut through the silence.

Instinctively, Raines grabbed his M-1 and swung around. His eyes met with the eyes of a German soldier who had been standing in the corner of the room. The soldier, whom to Raines looked to be around the same age, had his rifle up and Raines knew it was now a matter of who could pull their trigger faster. Unable to feel his fingers, Raines felt sure he had met the end of his military career.

Silently, the two men stared into each other's eyes.

Must've heard me come in. He heard me then just waited, *Raines thought*. And I walked right into it. Gotta bluff him. Gotta stall until I can get some movement in my hands.

"Drop it, Kraut, or I'll blow your head off," Raines rumbled.

The German's stony jaw stiffened at the insult. His cold ice-blue eyes lowered to the American's weapon. His jaw softened and he began to laugh.

Raines looked down at the M-1 in his hands and saw the muzzle had been bent. *Must've happened when that blast threw me*. Raines looked up, rage covering his face. The bend in the rifle was small, but it was enough.

And the German knew it.

The German soldier motioned to Raines' rifle with his own. "If you wish to blow off your hands," the soldier mused in a thick German accent. "You are more than welcome to pull the trigger. Although I assure you that it will make no difference to my head either way."

Raines fumed at his enemy's arrogant confidence.

"Drop it slowly, Amerikaner." The German ordered with a nod, "Here at my feet."

Raines boiled indignantly. He knew it was a mistake to enter the room without checking it all out first, and he knew that getting caught off-guard was his fault. He knew he had no choice in anything anymore.

For him the war was about to end.

2

Raines angrily did as he was told.

"Go ahead." he seethed. "Kill me. If you're waitin' to see me beg, you can forget it. I ain't gonna crawl. Especially not to you. So don't bother holding off. Just do it, and get it over with!"

Never taking his eyes from his prisoner, the German knelt down and picked up the rifle. Raines watched as the German inspected the weapon, dislodged the clip, and threw it back onto the floor.

Stuffing the clip into his pocket, he looked at Raines and sighed. His hard eyes softened slightly. The soldier took his eyes off Raines and looked at the fire.

A far away look covered his face.

"No," the German soldier said in a distant tone. "No, I will not kill. Not on this night. No, this night of all nights I will not mar."

As though he had forgotten Raines was there, the soldier turned, gently set his rifle in the corner, walked to the fireplace and sat down.

Raines looked at the German incredulously.

He forced his legs to carry him to the corner. He grabbed the German's rifle and raised it. "That was stupid, Max," Raines said taking aim on the back of his head. "What's to keep me from killing you right now?"

The German pulled his knees up to his chin and wrapped his arms around them. His blue eyes looked deep into the fire. Not once did he attempt to turn toward the American. "You do what your conscience dictates, Amerikaner. And I will do as mine. This is a time when we must remind ourselves we are all human."

A bomb exploded in the distance.

"There will be time to act like animals later," the German finished.

Raines wrapped his thawing fingers around the trigger. He hated this German for taking him by surprise. He hated this German for pulling him away from his family. And most of all, he hated the fact that he agreed with what the German had said.

"There *will* be another time," Raines assured. "I'm waitin' for daybreak out in the hall. Make any moves and that *time* will come sooner than you think."

Raines began to move his legs towards the doorway.

The German looked around. "You are frozen, Amerikaner. You should sit by the fire," the German said.

"No thanks," Raines grunted.

"As you wish," the German replied turning back to the fire.

Raines left the warmth of the room and made his way back to the inner door of the vestibule. The soldier cradled the rifle in his arms as he blew into his frozen hands. With a quick rub of his palms, he turned his eyes warily to the flickering orange doorway.

Silently, the German soldier sat in front of the roaring fire, his eyes glued to the flames, but their gaze was somewhere else. "It is Christmas,

Elena," he whispered softly into the fire. "Remember to say your prayers tonight and give your momma a kiss for me."

The German put a hand into the left breast pocket of his jacket, and pulled out a piece of paper which had been folded into fours and opened it. He regarded it with a look of deep longing.

His eyes looked away as another explosion roared off in the distance. He pulled the paper to his chest and held it tight. Closing his eyes, he drew in a deep breath, "Stay safe."

An agonized scream echoed through the house.

The German snapped his head around in the direction of the doorway. The soldier dropped the paper to the floor and darted to the door. Looking down the hall, he found the American lying on his side as if he had fallen. The American screamed through clenched teeth grabbing wildly at his legs.

The German ran to his side and knelt down.

"Get the hell away from me," Raines warned.

The German took no notice. Instead, he pulled the American's pant leg out of his boot. As the cloth rose above the boot's top, the German could see the flesh had turned blue and red.

Raines watched the German rise and run down the hall. He stopped at the last door on the right, opened it, and disappeared. Raines could now hear the hurried footfalls of boots running up steps.

As they reached the top, Raines could hear them run down the second floor hallway. Every few steps they would stop as though the German were looking into each room. After a few moments, the boots returned back to the top of the steps.

The German again appeared in the hall and ran back to Raines' side.

"You are thawing," the German told him looking at the leg. "We must go quickly."

"I ain't going anywhere," Raines replied grabbing the gun.

The German grabbed the rifle and threw it into the vestibule. Grabbing Raines by the collar, he shoved him against the wall. The German looked hard into the American's eyes. "If you do not move *now*," the German warned. "You will lose them *both*."

Before Raines could answer, the German grabbed him under the arms and pulled him to his feet.

Raines found the strength in his legs gone. Pain was now all they had to give him.

The German slung the American's arm over his shoulder and half walked, half dragged, him down the hall to the door leading to the steps, which sharply ascended to his left.

"Grab the rail," the German ordered as they began to climb the steps.

For what seemed to Raines as an eternity, they made their way slowly up the staircase. Finally they reached the top where another door sat closed. The German grabbed the knob and threw it open.

He dragged the American out into the hall. When they had reached the first door on their right, the German stopped. "In here," he said.

Raines looked into the room to see the house's bathroom, lit by a decorative fixture hanging from the ceiling.

"What are we doing he-" Raines began.

"Just move," the German answered.

Silently, the German led the American to a large cast-iron bathtub. "Get in," the German ordered him again.

Leaning on the German's shoulder, Raines gritted his teeth, and lifted one leg over the side, then the other.

A muffled scream escaped through Raines' clamped teeth as the German forced him down into the tub. Looking around furiously, the German's eyes fell onto a wall rack, from which hung large towels.

Grabbing one, the German knelt down beside the tub and forced as much of it into the drain as he could. He then patted his jacket until he found the clip he had taken from the American. He gave it back to Raines, "Put this between your teeth."

Raines stuck it in his mouth and clamped down hard.

Above the shining brass spigot of the tub sat two brass levers. The German pulled the one on the right, sending cold water gushing into the tub.

On contact with the water, the stinging pain in Raines' legs increased to the point that the American's back arched in an attempt to hold back the scream. The German sent his hands into the Americans mid-drift, and pushed him back into the water.

"Bite," the German ordered.

Raines bit down hard on the steel casing of the clip as the veins in his neck throbbed.

After a few minutes, the water had reached Raines' chest. The German turned off the spigot and reached down into the water. Grabbing the towel, he yanked it out of the drain.

Absently, he threw the towel to the side and turned on the hot water. At first, he let the water run out slowly, then steadily increased the flow to slowly raise the temperature.

Raines started to breathe easier as the pain in the lower half of his body decreased. After fifteen minutes, he could feel the sensation of water against his legs, mixed with the tingling feeling of the circulation beginning again. He took the clip out of his mouth.

The German reached for the towel again and shoved it back into the drain. He mixed cold water into the hot until the temperature was lukewarm. After a few moments, he stood up and looked at Raines. "You were lucky, Amerikaner. *Very* lucky."

The German then fell silent and left the room.

Raines eyes stayed on the door long after the soldier had left. As he listened to the boots make their way down the steps, his mind flew into a state of utter confusion. He now faced a circumstance he had never prepared himself for. He had met the enemy . . .

And the enemy had come to his aid.

3

A half hour had passed. A half hour the German spent looking into the fire moving only to stoke the flames or throw on another log. A creak from behind snapped him out of his trance. He turned to see the American standing in the doorway, his clothes soaked.

"Now," the German began, "if you do not wish to die of pneumonia, I suggest drying off by the fire."

Raines moved slowly over to the fire and sat down in front of it.

The German turned back to the paper he had unfolded and stared at it. Raines looked over at it. On the paper were the words, "Vater, gefallen kommen heim bald. Ich liebe dich sehr viel. Elena." The words were scrawled in pencil.

It was the unmistakable scrawl of a child.

"I suppose I should thank you," Raines muttered.

"I need to hear nothing from you but silence, Amerikaner," the German replied.

"You speak the language very well," Raines observed.

"It is part of my job."

"Your job?"

"I translate all captured intelligence reports for my unit."

The German fell silent again, his eyes on the paper.

"What's it say," Raines asked, unable to help himself.

The German looked over to him, his face still, then back to the paper. "It says," he began. "Father, please come home soon. I love you-," the German's voice cut off sharply, as he swallowed hard. "I love you very much. Elena."

"Your daughter," Raines asked.

"Da," the German replied.

The German reached into his breast pocket and produced a wrinkled photograph. He looked at it with a warm smile and handed it to Raines. "She is my little angel, Amerikaner," the German added as Raines took the picture.

Raines looked at the photo and saw the German was dressed in a white woolen sweater, his hair neatly combed. Beside him stood a woman with long dark hair, a wide smile on both their faces. The woman held a little girl in her arms dressed in a light colored dress, with blonde hair tied into ponytails.

Raines found his own heart pulling at him. He thought of his wife and son back in the states. He wanted to be home now, setting up the tree, wrapping presents, being with his family.

But he knew that wasn't to be.

"You have a beautiful family . . ." Raines faded.

"Peter," the German finished taking back the picture. "Thank you, Amerikaner. You have a family? A wife? A child?"

Raines nodded and reached into his breast pocket. Pulling out a photograph, he handed it to the soldier. "That's my wife, Anne and my son Daniel," Raines offered pointing to the picture, not knowing why he was offering the information at all.

"A good looking boy," the German nodded. "He resembles his father."

"Everyone's got a cross to bear," Raines said dryly.

The German looked at him confused, then smiled and began to laugh. It was a deep hearty laugh. It was one of those laughs that would be contagious to anyone who heard it. Raines was no exception. Raines forced himself to stop when his thoughts reminded him that he was sitting with the enemy.

"How old is he, Amerikaner," the German asked.

"Five."

"Ah. My Elena will be five in the spring."

Another bomb blast ripped apart the silence of the night.

"The German looked up into the direction of the explosion. "She hates thunder," the German said aloud to himself.

"What's that," Raines asked.

"My little one," the German said. "She is a afraid of thunder."

Looking into the flames, the German's mind wandered back in time. A time when he was merely Peter Werner and not just a number in the German war machine.

His thoughts came to rest in a time in the late spring two years ago. Werner and his wife resided at 12 Oben Strasse just outside Luxembourg.

He had put his little girl to bed, and was now sitting in the small living room of his home, listening to his wife Elsbeth play on their worn stand-up piano. She was a petite quiet girl, and Peter supposed that was the reason he had fallen in love with her.

She spoke in mild tones and had a shy girlish smile. A smile his daughter now showed. Elsbeth's greatest gift was the piano. She had the touch of an angel when she played. Her favorite composer, as was his, was Wolfgang Amadeus Mozart. And to Werner, she played it in such a way that would make Mozart himself envious.

Over the music, came the sounds of a spring storm.

A loud clap of thunder shook the house. Werner jumped to his feet as the sound of a terrified scream rushed down the steps. "Poppa," his daughter screamed in tears.

"I'll get her, Elsbeth," Werner told his wife as he ran to the stairs.

Werner ran into his daughter's room to find her huddled in the corner shaking with fear, clutching onto her blanket. She looked up at him, her eyes wide with terror. Werner ran to her and knelt down, "What is it, little one? What is it?"

Another burst of thunder shook the house.

Elena jumped into Werner's arms and buried herself in his chest, looking with horror out her window at the storm. Werner looked out the window at the rain that beat against the pane then back to his daughter.

"Come, little one," he said lifting her up. "It is time for all little girls to be in bed." As Werner walked her over to the bed, a quick flash of lightening filled the room, followed by another explosion of thunder.

Werner's daughter grabbed his neck, and squeezed. "Get me, Poppa," she cried frantically. "Get me, Poppa!"

Instead of putting her to bed, Werner instead walked to an old rocking chair in the corner of the room. Sitting down, he wrapped his daughter in her blanket. As she laid her head against his chest, Werner began to slowly rock.

Gently, he stroked her long hair as she cried. "It is all right, little one. It is only thunder. I won't let it get you. I promise." He kissed her lightly on the crown of her head and rocked her slowly until her tears ceased and she drifted off to sleep.

But now so much had changed.

Now not even the thunder was the same. Now, instead of it leaving a rumble in its wake, it left twisted metal, shattered brick and carnage.

Now the thunder had indeed become something to be feared.

Werner remembered seeing pictures of the "London Blitz", distributed to papers as propaganda to fuel sentiments for the war. One picture caught his attention above all others.

It was a picture of children playing among burned-out cars and rubble of what used to be buildings. To him, there was nothing the Fuhrer could say that would justify this. What Werner looked upon, he looked upon as an atrocity.

The atrocity of innocents forced into the middle of madness.

His mind flashed to his daughter huddled in her mother's arms in the basement of 12 Oben Strasse. He could hear her screaming for him as the steel thunder rained down around them.

Was she even alive, he wondered? Was she shaking with tears, holding onto the promise he had made her so long ago? Did his words ring over and over again in her ears, as the man-made thunder ripped away humanity? Would she still be trusting in his words to her, even as their home caved in on her?

Would they find her in her mother's arms?

Tears of agonizing frustration ran down Werner's trembling face as he stared at the paper. Shaking with rage, he thought of the one who had sent his country into upheaval. One who was not even German. One whose insanity was destroying his home.

Werner's body flinched as a bomb landed close to the house.

"It is only thunder, little one," Werner whispered into the flames. "I won't let it get you." The German clenched his hands into fists and lowered his head until his chin was on his chest. "I won't let it get you."

Raines put a hand on the German's shoulder, "Hey, take it easy. I'm sure they'll be all right."

The German composed himself. "I pray you are right, Amerikaner," Werner said softly. "It is not their war. You know that he is not even German?"

"Who," Raines asked.

"Hitler."

"No," Raines asked.

Werner shook his head, "No. He is Austrian. It is odd, Amerikaner, how things work. If he had stayed in Austria, we may have been allies, you and I."

"Maybe," Raines agreed.

"He is insane. He is insane with hatred," the German said darkly.

"Then why are you fighting for him," Raines asked.

"It is not like your country, Ameri-," the German began.

"The name's, Dan, Kraut," Raines corrected him lightly.

"The name is, Peter, Ameri*kaner*."

"Deal," Raines nodded.

"It is not like it is in the United States," the German went on to explain. "If you do not fight, you are labeled a sympathizer, or an enemy of the state. I have seen men labeled in such a way. Men I have never seen again. Men who disappeared over night with their families. Men that the state has taken care of. I was not about to see my family harmed."

Raines handed the German an understanding nod.

"But," the German said in a hopeful tone, "it will not last forever. Hopefully it will be over soon, and we will be with our families again."

"Sounds good to me." Raines agreed in a weary tone.

"Yes," the German said in a far away voice. "Yes, it does."

"You hungry?" Raines asked.

"Was?" Werner asked.

Raines stood up. "Be right back," he told Werner as he walked out of the room.

A few moments later, he returned with his pack. Kneeling down in front of the fire, he opened the top flap and put his hand in. Raines pulled out a can and set it on the floor. "Spam," he told Werner as he put his hand back in the bag.

Raines pulled out a can and set it down beside the Spam. "Beans," he announced as he sent his hand back into the bag. He pulled out his hand and held up two bars wrapped in brown paper. "Chocolate bars. Now if that isn't a Christmas dinner, I don't know what is?"

"And to drink," Werner asked.

"Water," Raines exclaimed as he pulled out a metal can.

"Wasser," Werner asked incredulously.

"Yeah," Raines said defensively. "What's wrong with water?"

"Ach," Werner muttered with a roll of his eyes. "You would celebrate Christmas with wasser? I do not even *know you*, and already I am ashamed of you."

Werner stood up, looked around, scratched his head and looked at Raines. "Come," he said looking out into the hall. "This is a house for the rich. And the rich must have a cellar."

"A cellar," Raines asked.

"A *wine* cellar," Werner nodded.

"I *hate* wine," Raines grumbled.

"Not tonight," Werner replied. "Now on your feet. It is here somewhere."

Raines watched the German walk to the doorway. Werner turned and regarded him dully. "We will not find it sitting here. Now on you feet."

"Stubborn *Kraut*," Raines mumbled pulling himself to his feet.

"Pig-headed Amer*ikaner*," Werner replied as he walked out into the hall.

4

The two soldiers looked down the hallway to the door at the end. "We must find the dining room," the German said walking to the end of the hall.

Raines followed, a questioning lock fell over his face.

"Why the dining room?"

"There should be two entrances and one should be there."

"That room," Werner said pointing to the closed door near the door to the stairs. "If I am correct that is the largest room from what I can tell. That should be it."

Werner grabbed the knob, gave it a turn, and opened the door onto the darkened room. Fumbling blindly with his right hand, Werner found the wall switch and flipped it.

The two men found themselves blinded as the room flooded with light.

"Jesus," Raines breathed looking around at the room. In its center sat an extended mahogany table, lined with five chairs on either side and one at each end. In the center sat a large gold candelabra shining in the light, white candles sprouting from its stems.

Fine paintings adorned the walls, and beneath them fine silver serving sets sat on finely
crafted mahogany buffet tables.

The soldier's eyes fell on the most elegant piece in the room. Above the dining table hung the room's chandelier. Raines stared slack-jawed at what looked to be a thousand diamonds all aglow.

"Beautiful, no," Werner asked.

"It's somethin' all right."

Raines found his words punctuated by another bomb blast.

"We had better get to the cellar, before there is no cellar left," Werner nudged.

The soldier's eyes fell on two doors, one on either side of the room. "You take that one," Werner instructed pointing to the one on the right, "I will try the other."

Raines walked around the large dining table and to the closed door. With a turn of the knob, he pulled it open. In front of him hung a length of ball-chain. With a tug the space filled with light. He stood speechless, staring into a large walk in closet filled with fine crystal dining ware, and gold settings.

"Here," a voice called from behind him.

Raines turned to Werner, who stood inside the doorway across the room, looking down a flight of steps. "We have our cellar," Werner announced.

Raines took one last look into the closet and closed the door. "I hate wine," he muttered walking to the German's side.

Slowly, the two made their way down a flight of wooden steps. The smell of must and mildew filled their nostrils.

Reaching the bottom, the two soldiers looked around at rack upon rack of black bottles, which lined the cellar's walls. "We shall find a good wine, and celebrate," Werner said walking to the racks.

Raines walked across the damp dirt floor to the wall of bottles. Pulling one out, he took it to Werner. "Here," he said to the German, holding the bottle out.

"No," Werner said with a shake of his head.

"Why not?"

"Not enough dust on the bottle. Put it back."

Werner looked around until his eyes fell on a rack of bottles, which had turned white with dirt. With a smile, he walked over to them and pulled a bottle from its perch.

Rubbing away at the dirt with his jacket sleeve, Werner read the label. "Chateau Briard, 1912," he said aloud. "We will take these."

Werner pulled out three more bottles of that year, and the two men headed back to the fire.

5

The field rations had gone down well, and the beans cooked over the flames of the hearth were welcomed by both men, who ate them eagerly off bone-china plates with silver forks.

Raines found the taste of the wine bitter at first, but as time went by, he found himself enjoying it. The wine began to taste especially good after his face went numb.

The two men now sat cross-legged in front of the hearth, working on their second bottle.

"I think I'm drunk," Raines announced.

"You have to think about it," Werner asked with a slight sway.

"No," Raines corrected. "I'm drunk."

"I wish I were home," Werner said taking a solemn drink of wine.

"Yeah, me too," Raines nodded, a look of sadness falling over his face.

"Tell me of America," Werner said quietly. "How do you spend your Christmas?"

"Well," Raines started, his voice brightening. "Christmas was when all of our family would get together. I came from a family with five children. We didn't have too much, but on Christmas we spared nothing.

"The week before Christmas the house would be filled with the smell of baking pies and cakes. It was great." Raines looked into the fire, his eyes looking at another time. "We would all scurry around decorating. We didn't have money for decorations, so my father would give us his old newspapers he had saved and some glue.

"'Here ya' go,' he would tell us. 'Make it nice, so Santa can see it when he gets here. And off we would go. We would cut the paper into strips, then glue the ends together, then we would wrap the next strip inside that one, and so on. We would keep doing that, until we had paper chain that my father could hang all the way around the living room.

"'Oh', he would say standing in the center of the room looking around at what we had done. 'You all did a good job on this one. It looks better than the one we had last year. I think Santa's really gonna like this.'

"My little sister, Christine, was only about five then. Well, anyway, she runs up to my father, and grabs his arm. 'Is he coming soon, daddy,' I remember she was so excited.

"My dad looked down at her with a big smile, and picked her up. 'He sure is, honey. Why, as a matter of fact I think he's coming tonight. And he's going to say, 'And were all you children good this year, Mr. Raines?' And I'm gonna say, 'You betcha, Mr. Claus. All my children were very good this year.'

"And my little sister would get so excited she would run around all day. Then while we were sleeping my father would dress in this Santa outfit that my mother had made for him. Pillowed belly, beard, the whole thing.

"My mother would wake us up, and say, 'Come on, get up. There's someone downstairs who wants to see you.'

"We would all run downstairs, and there my father would be, with a sack.

"He would ask us all if we had been good, and of course we said yes. And he would laugh, and hand out toys. One for each of us. Toys he had bought one at a time over the year. He would save a nickel here, a dime there, just to make sure we had our Christmas. He would work at a farm for six months on top of his other job, so he could have a turkey for us.

"Then as we grew up," Raines pointed out. "I was the third from the oldest. My two brothers and I took jobs after school. Shining shoes, paper routes, that sort of stuff. We would take our money, and help buy food for the dinner, and presents for the younger ones.

"We always had a tree, food, at least one gift for each of my brothers and sisters. Y'know, looking back on it, I don't know how my parents did it. So many mouths to feed, so many backs to clothe, but still they found a way to make Christmas special for all of us. It was growing up that I learned an important lesson. There's a difference between not having money and being poor.

"My mother and father let us know that we couldn't have all the things we wanted, but all the time growing up, we never felt poor. And thinking back, I don't think we ever were.

"My father gave me his Santa suit when my son came along. He didn't really get excited over it until he reached three. Now I know why my father did it. I loved looking down into his little face all lit up with excitement.

"He would come running to me on Christmas morning yelling, 'Santa, Santa!' He would sit on my lap, and I would ask him if he had been good, and he would try to tell me. Back then, his vocabulary was: Mommy, Daddy, and Max that's our dog.

"He would jump up and down, and look up at me when I gave him his presents with the biggest smile. Got a million-mile smile, my kid. Just like his momma." Raines looked deeper into the fire, his eyes beginning to glisten as his memories played in his head. "I'm sorry, boy," he whispered, taking a gulp of wine. "It doesn't look like Santa's gonna make it this year."

"Easy," Werner said softly, putting a hand on his shoulder. "You will be home soon. This cannot last forever."

"Yeah," Raines replied huskily. "And what about you?"

"Me," Werner asked.

"Yeah. What were your Christmases like?"

"Ah," Werner said with a nod. "When I was growing up, it was very much a special time. It would begin for us early in December."

"Yeah," Raines asked.

"Oh yes," Werner nodded. It would begin on December fifth. On that day, St. Nicholas would visit all the homes in my village. When I grew older, I found that it had been my father. He would dress in a red robe fringed with white, with a long brown beard, and a long brown hairpiece.

"He would come into the house, and gather all the children around him. My brothers and sisters and I would look at him in awe. St. Nicholas, the one we had been waiting for all year, had finally come.

"There he would sit, and ask us if we had been good, and like you said, of course we said yes."

Raines laughed.

Werner gave a reflective smile, then continued, "Then my father would tell us the story of the infant Jesus, and we would all sit there still and silent until he finished. My father would then stand, and hug each of us, and wish us a joyous holiday. Then on December sixth, the feast day of the saint, the Christ Kind would appear."

"Christ Kind," Raines asked.

"Yes," Werner answered. "In English, it would be Kris Kringle."

"Oh," Raines smiled recognizing the name.

"And on the sixth, he would appear, dressed in white satin robes, a golden halo, and great golden wings. He was the one who left presents for all the good children of the world.

"But the celebration was not over. My mother would spend weeks in the kitchen cooking and baking, preparing for the day of days. She would bake pies, and cakes, and cookies.

"I remember when I was no older than your boy, standing on a chair in our kitchen, stirring batter. It was heavy batter, used for baking Springerle cookies."

"Springerle," Raines asked quizzically.

"Yes," Werner replied. "Springerle are hard cookies. It was tradition that every member would take turns stirring batter and cutting the Springerle. We would cut the cookies into different shapes before baking. We would make stars, and sleighs, and angels, and hearts. We would then decorate them with sprinkles of sugar and nuts.

"Then before they went into the stove, my mother would poke holes in them near the top, then bake them. And when they were finished, my mother would string the Springerle with red ribbon, and we would all hang them on the tree for decorations.

"I remember stirring and stirring the lumpy batter, trying to get it smooth. Once I looked up at my mother who was busy at the stove, and saying, 'Momma, my arms hurt.'

"She looked at me with a smile, walked to me and gave me a hug. 'But, Peter,' she said in her sweet voice. 'We must have the batter for our cakes, and for the Pfefferkuchen.'

"'Pfefferkuchen,' I yelled happily at the thought of them. Just thinking of them took the pain from my arms, and I stirred like never before. And my mother went back to her cakes, the sounds of her humming filled the kitchen."

"What's fef-fef-," Raines asked.

"Pfefferkuchen," Werner finished. "Pfefferkuchen are cookies. My favorite, and my mother knew it. She would take thin cookie dough, and cut it into squares. Then she would make a line of fruits and walnuts diagonally from one corner to the other, and cover them with fruit preserves. After she did that, she would fold the other two corners over them, to wrap them together. Then she would sprinkle the tops of them with sugar."

"They sound good," Raines smiled.

"Good," Werner said indignantly. "Ach. If you could taste *one* of my mother's Pfeffekuchens you would *defect*."

"That good, huh?"

"Like heaven," Werner nodded. "My mother made them only on Christmas. I can still remember the smell of them baking. It would not be Christmas without them." Werner's face grew somber as he turned to the fire. "No," he repeated in a low voice. "It would not be Christmas without them."

"Hey," Raines blurted, slapping Werner on the shoulder. "We should have a tree."

"A tree?"

"Yeah," Raines said with a nod. "We got our feast. We got wine. But we got no tree. It's Christmas, and we have no tree."

"Well, some things cannot be helped," Werner sighed.

As the last word left his lips, a sound appeared off in the distance. It was a high whirring sound, the whining growing increasingly louder. The whine turned into a roar as it passed over the house. When it disappeared, another sound took its place.

A whistling noise.

Raines looked at Werner and found the German's expression mirrored his own. In that brief moment of silence, every thing that needed to be said had been.

The two soldiers threw themselves onto their stomachs and covered their heads. The house rocked as another bomb fell onto French soil.

Plaster fell like snow onto the two men as the ceiling cracked from the vibrations that rampaged through the home's structure. From the other room, Raines could hear the shattering of glass, and the splintering of wood, as the windows in the front of the house were blown out of their frames.

Then nothing.

Raines looked over to Werner, "That was clo-."

Werner put up a silencing finger.

There they lay, covered in chunks of plaster and dust, listening. It was a soft sound, barely detectable at first. As it grew louder, Raines could make it out as the sound of breaking wood. The creaking grew then stopped. In a few seconds, it was followed by a swishing thump.

Werner looked over at Raines with a drunken grin, "I think we have found our tree."

6

The two soldiers dragged themselves to their feet and brushed themselves off. "Can you walk," Werner asked, with a slight sway.

"Nope," Raines answered with a wide boyish grin.

"Good. Let us get our tree."

As they stumbled into the vestibule, now cold with wind and snow rushing through the broken glass of the windows on either side of the door, Raines felt something under his boot.

Looking down, he found the rifle lying where Werner had thrown it. He bent down and picked it up. He and Werner stood there silently, staring at the crude reminder of who they were, and what had brought them here.

Werner looked over at Raines, not saying a word. Raines reciprocated the look. Quietly, he propped the weapon in the corner. "How many times do I have to tell you," Raines asked Werner in a stern voice. "Pick up your toys when you're done with them."

"I shall try to remember that," Werner laughed.

"You do that," Raines huffed, opening the door.

"Oh no," Raines exclaimed as he looked at the tree. The blast had caught an eight-foot Pine tree, the force of the explosion severing the trunk at ground level. The tree now lay on its side about twenty feet away from them, its exposed side on fire.

The two men half ran half stumbled through the snow to it. As they reached the fallen tree, they took off their jackets and beat out the flames.

In a few moments the flames were gone, leaving only burnt branches behind. "It's burnt," Raines moaned, sounding like a disappointed child who had just opened his present and found it broken.

"Well," Werner said in an optimistic tone, "at least we know which side to put against the wall."

Raines shot him an amused look, his one eyebrow cocked. "Got a good point there," he smiled.

Huffing, puffing, slipping, falling, the two men dragged the tree through the door. "This reminds me of when my father and I would go out to the woods to cut down our tree for Christmas," Werner said as he pulled the trees top through the doorway of the fire-lit room.

"We bought ours," Raines puffed.

"Over there," Werner said nodding to the corner of the room opposite the hearth.

The two men laid the tree on the floor, grabbed it by the middle and lifted it upright until it stood propped against the wall. Taking a few wobbling steps back they inspected it.

"It looks pretty pathetic," Raines observed.

"Yes, it is lacking, that I will grant you," Werner agreed.

Quietly, they looked at the tree, their minds searching for ideas. Simultaneously a singular thought struck.

7

"Careful," Werner warned pulling Raines up onto the dining room table. Werner gently took a crystal from the chandelier and detached it from one of the several metal rings which made up the fixture.

The crystals, a small octagon crystal from which dangled finely carved long diamond shaped crystals, were fastened to the rings by brass hooks. "Perfect," Werner smiled with a satisfied nod.

Raines ran the series of events leading up to this moment through his mind. *Here I am standing on a dining room table somewhere in France, with a German soldier who managed to get as drunk as I am, plucking crystals off a fancy chandelier. Why? So we can decorate our half-burnt Christmas tree, that's why.*

"Why are you laughing," Werner asked, looking confused.

"No reason," Raines replied, sticking crystals in his pockets.

In twenty minutes, the skeleton of the chandelier hung naked as the two soldiers jumped off the table, their legs almost buckling under the weight of their cargo.

8

His last crystal on the tree, Raines walked back to the fire, took two pieces of wood from the dwindling pile and threw them in. On his way back to the tree, he picked up the two wine bottles.

"Here," he said, holding one out to Werner, who still had one crystal left.

"Just a moment," Werner said taking three steps back away from the tree. Scratching his chin thoughtfully, the German eyed the tree. "Ah," he exclaimed. Walking back to the tree, he placed his last crystal gently on a branch.

"Now, let us see," Werner said walking to the hearth, Raines behind him.

The two men turned, smiles dawning on their faces.

The tree shimmered with a thousand tiny stars made by the light of the fire bouncing off the cut stones. Occasionally, a blue or red star would flicker, as the light ran through the thousands of tiny prisms in the makeshift ornaments.

"Now, it is Christmas," Werner breathed.

"Uh-huh," Raines replied, taken by the tree's beauty.

Each of them stood silent, engulfed in thoughts of family and friends they had left behind. Thoughts of wives who were preparing presents for their children to open.

Thoughts of their children whose faces would light up with excitement come morning.

Faces they would not be there to see.

Raines lowered his head and closed his eyes. He felt a hand rest on his shoulder.

He lifted his head and looked at Werner who had put his arm around his shoulders his own eyes glistening orange in the firelight. "Our families would be proud of us," he smiled. "We have kept Christmas well."

"Yeah," Raines replied softly. He raised his bottle to Werner. "Merry Christmas, Kraut," he said with a smile.

Werner laughed and bumped Raines' bottle with his own. "Merry Christmas, Amerikaner."

The two men drank to each other and turned back to the shimmering tree.

Werner's mind wandered back to his childhood when his entire family would gather around the tree on Christmas night. His parents would have a glass of wine, and the children would each have a cup of warm cider.

There they would sit together and sing the songs of Christmas.

The tradition of his family always ended in the same way. Everyone would make sure their cups were full, and they would all sing a carol that had been written by a German priest named Fr. Francis Mohr.

In a lilting tone, Werner began to sing, knowing he could not bear the thought of breaking the tradition that had carried on to his own family. "Stille nacht," he sang softly, "Heilige Nacht . . ."

Raines looked over to him with a grin. He couldn't understand the words, but he knew the melody. And he joined in, "All is calm, all is bright. Round yon virgin, mother and child. Holy infant so tender and mild . . ."

The two men stood alone, singing in two different languages. Two different languages with one sentiment. One sentiment sent out for One to hear.

The One for whom the day was celebrated.

9

"Wake up," Werner coaxed giving the American's shoulder a push. Raines' eyelids fluttered then slowly opened.

"Come on, get up," Werner said in a whisper, "It is morning."

Raines sat up slowly, squinting as he looked around. The fire was now gone, and an empty bottle lay at his feet. He looked at Werner, who now had his jacket zipped to his neck, and a pack, slung across his shoulder along with his rifle.

"What time is it," Raines asked half conscious.

"It is time to get up, that is what time it is."

With a roll of his eyes, Werner grabbed Raines' hand and pulled him to his feet.

"Come," the German motioned in the direction of the doorway, "I have something to show you."

Raines followed Werner to the dining room.

On the table, beneath the skeletal remains of the chandelier, Werner had spread out a geographical map of the area. Werner pointed to a spot on the map, "We are here," he told Raines. He then moved his finger a half-inch to the West, "We recorded allied troop movements here. If you keep going in that direction, you should meet up with friendly forces. Do not go east, do you understand. We have that region heavily populated. Stay true to the map, and you will do fine."

"Thanks, but if I've got the map, how-" Raines began.

"I will be fine," Werner assured. "Here," Werner blurted as one does when nearly forgetting an important point. Pulling his pack from his back, he flipped open the top, and put his hand in.

Raines watched him pull his hand out, in it a silver object. An object Raines immediately recognized as the Mauser pistol called a Luger.

Werner held it out to him. "Take it," Werner told him. "Take it, and remain aware of your surroundings until you find your people."

Raines took the pistol.

"It has a full clip. That is all I can do for you."

"Thank you," Raines nodded putting the gun in his pocket.

As Werner turned to fasten the top of his pack, Raines noticed a red and black patch on his sleeve. The patch was in the shape of a shield bordered by black. In the center of the shield was the black silhouette of a wolf in a prowling position against the red background. The wolf, with its head low, held its jaws open wide, fangs sprouted from its mouth.

"What's the patch stand for," Raines asked.

"It is the Iron Wolf. My regiment."

Raines folded up the map and returned to the other room to retrieve his pack. Bending over, he grabbed the straps of the bag, which still lay in front of the now dim hearth.

He stood up and turned to leave, when he noticed Werner standing silently in front of the tree, his hands in his pockets.

Raines walked up behind him, and slapped him good-naturedly on the back. "Helluva Christmas," he said looking at the tree.

"Yes, " Werner agreed, "but we have forgotten one thing."

"What's that," Raines asked honestly puzzled

"Gifts," Werner replied.

Gently, the German soldier reached out to the tree and plucked a single crystal from its perch. With a smile, he held it out to Raines. "To you, from Elsbeth, Elena, and myself."

Raines handed him a stunned expression, which turned to an appreciative grin. He took it, and quietly put it in his breast pocket.

Gently, the American soldier reached out to the tree, and plucked a single crystal from its perch. With a smile, he held it out to Werner. "To you, from Anne, Danny, and myself."

"Danke schon," Werner grinned, taking the ornament, and putting it in his breast pocket.

The two men walked to the doorway, took one last look at the tree, and walked out into the hall.

The sound of crunching filled the vestibule as the soldiers walked over the broken glass.

Raines opened the door. Both had to squint from the glare of the sun bouncing off the freshly fallen snow.

The two soldiers walked out into the light of the sunny Christmas morning.

They found themselves staring at each other in silence. It was time to go back to war, but both knew that in some way, they had been changed.

"Listen," Raines began, breaking the silence. "You know that if I see you again, I'll have to-," Raines stumbled, not wanting to say it.

"I understand," Werner nodded. "I shall have to do the same."

"I'll shoot high and to the right, so stay low and to the left. Okay?"

"I will do the same," Werner replied.

"Goodbye, Peter," Raines said extending his hand.

"Goodbye, Daniel," Werner replied shaking it.

Simultaneously they turned and headed into opposite directions. As they both reached the tree line, Raines turned. "Hey," he called after the German.

Werner turned.

"My last name is Raines," the American shouted across the clearing. "When this is all over, and you ever find yourself in the States . . .!"

"My last name is Werner," the German shouted back. "If you ever come back to Europe, your family is welcome!"

Raines watched the German turn; in a few steps he reached the trees.

Then he was gone.

10

December 25, 1953
1522 Rayburne St.
Evanston, Illinois.

"And that's how I spent my Christmas eve in 1943," Raines finished sitting at the end of his dining room table, dressed in a white sweater adorned with brown trees woven into the material. On his face a grin of remembrance, in his hand, a glass of wine.

"Wow," exclaimed a red-haired boy who was sitting next to him. His name was Kevin Closky, a friend of his son Danny from next door. Beside

Closky sat Danny, his shoulders now wide, his height shooting toward six feet, his voice grown deeper, his features now becoming those of a man.

On the other side of the table sat Raines' seven-year old daughter Kimberly, with her long brown hair tied in a ponytail. She stared at her father through wide, deep, brown eyes, still engulfed by the story.

Anne Raines sat at the other end of the table, their two-year old son Gary on her knee.

"I told ya' it was a neat story," Danny said nudging Closky.

"That *was* neat, Mr. Raines," Closky said. "My dad tells me stories from the war, but they always end with him saving all the men in his squad from a hundred German soldiers with one bullet."

Raines looked at his wife and all of them laughed.

"Do ya' think the German guy made it," Closky asked.

"I'm sure he did," Raines replied taking a drink of wine.

Raines had told this story to his family when he arrived home in '46, and every Christmas since. At the end of the story, if anyone new was listening, they would ask that very same question, and Raines would give the same reply. That was the only part of the story he hated.

He knew he was lying.

He left out the ending. He never told them how he was picked up by a British convoy and returned to his unit.

After his arrival, a medic checked him over then he was sent to the Commanding Officer. He was asked what had happened. He told them of the death of his partner, and the trek to the house, where he spent the night. Never once did the German come up in the course of the story.

He smiled as the officer welcomed him back.

Later that day, two friends of his from the unit, Pvt. Gus Horton, and Corporal Marty Jenkins met up with him as he was walking to his tent, both grinning and laughing.

"Hey, Danny, thought we lost ya', pal," Horton yelled slapping him on the back and shaking his hand.

"Yeah. Welcome back, Danny boy," Jenkins laughed.

"Thanks, guys. Nice to *be back,*" Raines grinned.

"Hey, guess what happened to us today," Horton tempted.

"I give," Raines conceded.

"Well," Horton began, obviously anxious to tell the story. "Jenkins and me were sent back to the perimeter on recon with some Brit' troops, right?

So there we are walkin' through the woods, see? And along comes this Kraut. I mean, right out o' nowhere.

"So me and Jenkins spot him first, and hide behind some trees. I take aim on this guy, and give Jenkins a nod. He calls out to Max, and as soon as he turned around-*POW*! Got 'im right between the peepers," Horton exclaimed ecstatically, poking his forefinger between his eyes.

"Poor slob didn't know what hit 'im," Horton yelled with a laugh. "And got a souvenir to boot. Took it off 'im while he was still twitchin'," Horton added putting a hand in his pocket.

He put the souvenir in Raines' hand. Raines' heart pounded hard in his chest. His stomach tightened as he forced himself to look down. In his hand, he held a piece of cloth. A patch.

The patch of the Iron Wolf.

"That's enough. Give it back," Horton said snatching it off him.

"Shoulda been there, Danny boy," Jenkins added cheerfully.

"Yeah," Raines responded.

"Wait till I show this to the guys back home," Horton laughed as the two of them walked away.

Raines put his hands in his pockets. His mind's eye filled with the vision of a woman and a child in a photograph, only now the man standing with them was no longer there. He then saw the folded paper, scrawled by a child, asking her father to come home.

Raines walked quickly through the snow with his head down, not wanting to look or talk to anyone.

The whole time he walked across the camp, he kept his chin on his chest, not wanting anyone to see the anger they wouldn't understand. He dug his hands deeper into his pockets.

Not wanting anyone to see they had become fists.

But that's war, he reasoned as he sat at his dining room table. That was the price both sides had to pay.

And pay they did.

Holding on to blind hope, Raines tried to find him after the war ended. He spent seven years writing letters to different European agencies, but had gotten nowhere. Finally, he conceded to defeat, and ended his search.

"Well," Closky said, pulling Raines from his memories. "I gotta get home. Dinner'll be ready soon, and my mom hates it when I'm late."

"Can't wait to tell my dad this one," Closky said standing and pushing in his chair. "He'll probably say I'm full of it."

Raines stood up, "Come here, Kevin."

He led Closky into the living room, followed by his family. "Look there," he said to the boy pointing to the tree sparkling in the corner.

Closky looked at the tree with a searching expression. Finally, his eyes fell on what he was intended to see. Among the lights and decorative ornaments, one thing hung alone.

One single crystal.

"Wow," Closky breathed.

Raines laughed at the boy's amazement.

"Come on," Dan Jr. said to his friend. "I'll walk ya' out."

"Merry Christmas everyone," Closky said as he reached the door.

They all returned the sentiment.

11

Raines sat for twenty minutes at his dining room table sipping his wine. The house filled with the aroma of turkey and the rest of Christmas dinner. The children busied themselves setting the table around him. He looked thoughtfully at his glass.

It wasn't Chateau Briard.

He had tried to get some ever since his return, but no stores carried or even heard of it. One store manager told him that it was possible that it was a regional wine, only sold in the area that it was made in.

"Daddy," Kimberly called with a tug on his sleeve.

"What, sweetheart," he answered.

"When's granma and granpa comin'?"

The doorbell rang.

"Honey, could you get that," his wife called from the kitchen.

"Go on and help you mother," Raines told his children as he walked through the living room.

He opened the door to find his parents standing on the stoop, smiles on their faces and snow on their shoulders. Every year, they would make the rounds to their children's homes, and make this the last stop, where they would visit and stay for dinner.

"Come in, we've been waiting for you," Raines greeted stepping to the side.

"Let your mother in," his father said. "I need help bringing in the," his voice lowered to a whisper. "*P-r-e-s-e-n-t-s*."

"Sure, dad," Raines half laughed giving his mother a kiss as she walked by him.

The two men walked down to the curb, where his father had parked his black four-door. Raines' father popped in his key, opened the door and unlocked the back. "Good Christmas weather," he small talked as he reached in and pulled out a large paper bag filled with gifts.

"Sure is," Raines replied looking up at the falling snow as he took the bag.

His father pulled out a second bag, locked both doors with his free hand, and kicked them shut. "Well, come on boy, before we freeze."

Raines trotted up the steps, his father close behind. He turned the knob with his free hand and pushed the door open with his shoulder. "You know, the kids have been waiting for you two all day," he said looking back at his father.

He entered the parlor and turned. As he did, he found a pair of eyes staring at him from across the living room. Older eyes. Wiser eyes.

Eyes that had stayed low and to the left.

"Your mother and I got a call three weeks ago," Raines' father said with a mischievous grin. "Appears this man's been lookin' for you."

Frank Raines closed the door and took the bag from his son who stood with his mouth open. Here, in the doorway to his dining room stood the German he had been searching for.

He now stood dressed in a gray flannel suit and tie over which draped a long gray woolen overcoat. On his head, a matching Fedora sat tilted to one side. Beside him stood a woman wearing a festive red dress, beside her a young girl wearing a purple dress, her platinum hair pulled back. Beside her stood a boy who looked to be around five, dressed like his father, with the fedora and overcoat replaced by a wool hat, a hooded coat and mittens.

Raines tried to speak, but he couldn't bring himself to believe what he was seeing. This couldn't be real. He was sure he was seeing things. The thought of searching for someone over all those years, then having him just *appear* threw him.

The man grinned at Raines' expression and walked up to him. Nonchalantly, he took off his hat and smirked. "Well," he finally said. "Are you going to say hello, or are you just going to stand there and look stupid?"

"Peter," Raines asked, his tone shrouded in disbelief.

"It's been a long time, Daniel," Werner smiled holding out his hand.

"Peter," Raines exclaimed grabbing Werner's hand and pulling him into a hug. "Where have you been," he asked pulling away, a smile on his face. "I sent letters all over Europe looking for you!"

"Chicago," Werner replied laughing.

"Chi*cago,*" Raines repeated incredulously. "I looked all over *Europe*, and you were in Chi*cago*?"

"I'll explain later, but now, I have people for you to meet."

Werner walked him up to his wife. Raines looked behind him at his mother, and family. He looked at the smile on his wife's face. "You knew, didn't you," he asked with a grin.

"Didn't know what to get you, so . . . *surprise*," she replied.

Raines turned his gaze to the face of the woman in the red dress. "You must be Elsbeth," Raines said softly.

The woman kissed him on the cheek and smiled, "We have been waiting to meet you," she told him. "Peter told us of how you helped him get through Christmas."

"We helped each other," Raines answered.

"And this is-," Werner began, pointing to his daughter.

"Elena," Raines grinned shaking her hand.

"Hi," she said shyly shaking his hand.

"You've grown."

"Yes," Werner said proudly. "And she is quite the American now."

Raines felt a tug on his pants leg. He looked down to see the boy looking up at him with a bright smile on his face. Kneeling down on one knee, Raines returned the expression. "And who are you?"

"I'm Teddy," the boy blurted happily.

"He is the shy one of the family," Werner joked.

"Yeah, I noticed."

12

Raines introduced his family and they all settled down for Christmas dinner.

Werner told of how he had packed his family up after the war and headed west to America. After an extensive check into his background, he was finally allowed passage into the country in 1947.

Upon arriving, Werner used the skills he had learned in the military to land a job as a geographical surveyor for a land-developing firm in Boston. As part of his duties, he traveled the country surveying undeveloped properties for various projects.

Werner made it a habit to look in the phone books of every city he had visited. He would sit in his motel room at night, look up "Raines" in the book, and begin dialing. This was a ritual he repeated for four years.

A ritual that had led him nowhere.

In 1951 his firm opened a branch office in Chicago. Werner, along with four other surveyors was sent to the branch on permanent status.

Werner again packed up his family, and again headed west. After five months, Werner was offered a job as head of the department he worked in. To him it was a bittersweet prospect.

The job was stationary, and would keep him in Chicago. Werner liked the idea of not having to be away from home all of the time and the added income to his growing family, but he knew the added work would make his search impossible.

Nonetheless, Werner took the job.

In the fall of 1953, word came from Boston, that they had clients in Evanston interested in a homestead project. The project was naturally handed to Werner to see if it was indeed workable.

Werner in turn delegated the job to a colleague: Matthew Trent.

On November 31, Werner was busy behind his desk studying graphs and photographs of projects slated for ground breaking in the spring when he received a call from Trent.

Trent informed him that he was in bed with the flu, and would be unable to handle the Evanston job. Werner kept his disappointment to himself. He knew what a Chicago flu could do to a person and understood. He also knew that of his four surveyors, Trent was the only one on hand.

"I'll handle it, Matt," Werner said over the phone. "You take care of yourself."

Werner found himself once again kissing his wife and children goodbye as he headed for the Chicago train station.

He arrived to find Evanston being battered with arctic-like winds, and a sky that threatened at least a foot of snow.

He spent the day in the freezing cold, taking photographs of the area and estimating what would be needed for the job and its cost. After three hours, he had enough to bring to the builders.

After his meeting, he got a room a local motel and plopped wearily onto the bed. He rolled over onto his side and found himself looking at a desk against the wall. On it laid the phone, beside it, the directory.

Werner eyed the phone book. "Ah, what's the point," he mumbled rolling over onto his other side. He lay there still for a while, then said, "Ach, why not?"

Werner pulled himself out of bed, walked to the desk, and opened the book. He flipped the pages until he hit the "R" section, then ran his finger down the names.

He stopped when he found "Raines". There were twelve of them in the book, but none were named Daniel. Still, Werner picked up the phone and began to dial.

The fifth number ended his search.

13

Midnight, like the snow outside, fell softly on the Raines home. The hours whiled away quickly filled with accounts of past years, laughter, and idle chatter. The smaller children had fallen asleep on the living room floor, and Dan Jr. was showing Elena his collection of "Swing" records, finding their tastes in music similar.

Daniel Raines sat at his dining room table. It was only Peter, Elsbeth, Anne, and himself now; his parents had long since said their goodbyes. The women laughed over tea about the things their children had done while growing up, and Raines found himself sitting with a dedicated Bears fan.

"Oh," Werner said as though he had forgotten something. "Elsbeth, could you get my bag, please?"

His wife's expression sparked, revealing that she too had forgotten all about something.

As his wife disappeared into the living room, Werner took off his jacket, rolled up his sleeves, and loosened his tie until it hung below the second button. "Ach," Werner exclaimed to Raines and his wife, "I am becoming forgetful in my old age."

"Here, Peter," Elsbeth said, handing a brown paper bag across the table to him.

Werner thanked her, and set the bag in front of him. He put in his hand, and pulled out a large round can. Pulling off the lid, he slid it over in front of Raines. Dan Raines looked in, and beamed a smile. "Fef-Fef-."

"Pfefferkuchen. My mother sent them to us."

Raines pulled one out eagerly and bit into it. His eyes lit up with approval. "Honey," he said smiling, "get the kids, we're defecting."

Werner laughed as he stuck his hand back into the bag. He looked at Raines with a sly smile. "I brought these with me from Europe," he told Raines. "And saved them for when I found you."

He pulled out his hand, and revealed two bottles of Chateau Briard 1912 hanging from between his fingers.

Werner held them out to Raines, who gratefully took one. Together they pulled the corks out, and filled their wives' glasses. They went to pour a glass for themselves then stopped. They looked at each other for a moment, nodded, and each took a big gulp from their bottles.

"Dan," Anne Raines scolded. "Please. We have company."

"Peter," Elsbeth said sternly. "Such manners."

Raines laughed, "Come on, Pete, let's leave these ladies to talk."

The two men walked into the living room, past their children, to the tree. There they stood silently, watching the lights shimmer off the ornaments. "We will have to do this at my house next year," Werner said taking a drink.

"Deal," Raines nodded, not looking away from the tree. He bumped Werner's elbow to get his attention then pointed to the tree. "Do you remember that," he asked.

Werner quietly put his hand in his pants pocket and pulled out a fist. He held his fist up to Raines. Slowly his fingers uncurled. In his palm lay the crystal he had been given ten years ago. "It has had a place on our tree every year," Werner answered.

Gently, almost reverently, Werner took his crystal and hung it on the branch beside its twin.

The two men stood silent, looking at the shimmering glints of color coming from the tiny prisms.

Their minds roamed back to that night so long ago in a house far away in a land now at peace. Back to a night when they wore the clothes of warriors. Warriors brought together by chance.

They thought of how they had gone from being two soldiers, to being two men. Two fathers. Two husbands. Two sons. Two souls a long way from home who somehow found a way to fill the emptiness of separation from all they cared about.

Two souls who now stood side by side as friends, surrounded by the ones they loved, on the night whose universal meaning had somehow formed between them a bond that neither had forgotten.

The night of peace and humanity.

Raines held up his bottle to Werner with a smile of friendship.

"Merry Christmas, Kraut," Raines toasted warmly.

Werner returned the unspoken sentiment with a smile of his own and bumped Raines' bottle.

"Merry Christmas, Amerikaner."

The Gift

1

December 24 th, 11: 21 P.M.

Triangles of falling diamonds . . .

That was what one would see, if one cared to look out their window onto Bartlett Street at the snow falling past the orange streetlights.

The sight was one directly off a Christmas card.

With the softest hush, white silver-speckled blankets covered the pavements and rooftops of the row homes lining either side of the street. Most of the houses were still lit with assorted colored lights, which served as a constant reminder of the approach of the festive holiday.

Even 3086 Bartlett St.

Although the outside of the home was lit with the same lights as the rest, the shine off them was different. It was a sad shine, like a brave smile on a broken heart. It was a shine of a home incomplete.

This was the home of Greg and Sharon Johnson.

Greg Johnson stood quietly in the kitchen of 3086 Bartlett, arms folded, back propped up against the counter. His eyes stared at the ceiling with the glazed look of a mind gone elsewhere. He was waiting. He was waiting for the phone call to come. The phone call he and his wife had been waiting for since Thanksgiving.

The call that would send a knife through their hearts.

His pale, drawn, face sported a week's growth of hair, his normally well-groomed hair now sprouted in every direction. At thirty-three, he now felt like a man in his nineties.

He stood weakened by lack of sleep; fatigued from the constant tension the wait was putting on both he and his wife. It had even become noticeable on their three-year old son Jeremy.

Johnson wanted desperately to change things, to make everything all better, but he knew it was impossible. Things had already taken their course and he had no say as to their outcome. He could only wait. Wait for that one hellish call that he was told would come.

The call that would tell him his six-year old daughter was gone.

He snapped out of his trance to the sounds of shouting. It was Sharon scolding their son. He looked through the doorway, past the dining room and into the parlor.

"Dammit! What did I tell you about touching the Christmas decorations," she screamed down at her son pointing to the shattered remnants of an ornament on the floor. "Now look what you've done," she bellowed as she grabbed the toddler's arm, and shook him.

The three-year old began to cry.

Greg Johnson ran from the kitchen to stop her. He had been waiting for this for the last month. She had been too strong about the whole thing. She had been too quiet.

He knew this behavior wasn't her. He could feel the tension finally being vented. And as it always is, the held in anger had erupted at the wrong time, for the wrong reasons, and on the wrong person.

"Sharon, stop it," he yelled grabbing the arm that held their son.

Taking hold of her shoulders, he found himself looking into a face he didn't know.

Her long platinum hair, which she normally wore in a long ponytail, now hung over blue eyes on fire with anger and pain. He gave her three hard shakes, "Sharon, stop it! Calm down! Yelling at Jerry won't change *anything*!"

After a few moments, the face of the woman he married returned.

Her face filled with shame as she looked at the floor. "Jesus, Greg, I'm sorry," she said in a weak voice running a shaky hand through her hair.

Greg Johnson put his arms around her, and held her tight. He could feel her trembling in his arms. Gently, he gave her a kiss on the crown of her head. "It's okay. You just need some rest. We all do. It's getting late."

Sharon Johnson looked down at her son.

Clad in his red and green pajamas, the three-year old looked up at her with a face filled with confusion and hurt. He had light brown hair like his father and deep aqua eyes.

Eyes now red and puffy.

Sharon knelt down in front of her son and held out her arms to him. Her heart wrenched as he backed away.

"Honey," she said softly to him, "I'm sorry. Could you come here and give me a hug? Please? Mommy could really use one."

The three-year old walked up to her still sobbing. With a small finger, he pointed to the shattered glass on the floor beside her. "Broke," he said lightly.

Sharon scooped him into her arms and squeezed him. "It's okay, baby, mommy'll clean it up. I'm sorry I yelled at you. Do you forgive me?"

The little boy pulled back and nodded.

"You still love me?" She asked.

Smiling, he nodded again

"How much?"

The three-year old stretched out his arms as far as they could go. "Thiiiiiiiis much!"

She pulled him to her again, and gave him another squeeze, "I love you too, sweetheart. Now, I think it's time for you to go to bed, so Santa can come. Do you want Santa to come?"

Jeremy pulled away again with a big smile and nodded.

"Well then, to bed you go."

Greg put a gentle hand on her shoulder, "I'll do that, honey. Why don't you go get ready for bed? It's been a long day for all of us. Tomorrow after Jerry opens what Santa's brought him we can head right over to the-," he stopped short. "We can head right over."

Sharon stood up, "Yeah, maybe I will."

Greg Johnson looked into his wife's face. She was only a year younger than he was, but she still had the face of a girl in her early twenties. She had a little-girl face that never ceased to brighten up his day when it was happy.

And never failed to break his heart when it was sad.

As she stared into his eyes, he could see her face filling with agony. Her eyes began to shimmer as she bit her lower lip. "Greg, I'm so sorry," she pushed out before the tears came again.

He held her tight and gently rocked her. "It's okay," he whispered. "That was stress, it wasn't you. I know that and Jerry knows that. Now, let me put our little man to bed and then I'll join you."

"Okay," she agreed wiping her eyes.

Greg Johnson picked up his youngest and carried him upstairs.

Sharon Johnson walked to the kitchen and looked at the oven. This time last year her daughter, Samantha, had helped her make chocolate chip cookies.

She had hope then.

"Mommy," Her five year-old called walking into the kitchen.

"Yeah, babe," Sharon answered stirring the batter for the long-awaited cookies.

"Can I help?"

Sharon looked down at her little girl, who looked back up at her with bright eyes, her smile warm.

She looked strong then.

"Sure you can," Sharon nodded. "Go get your apron."

The little girl ran from the kitchen and scampered up the stairs to her room.

Sharon listened to the soft footfalls above her head. Her mind wandered back to the first time she had helped her own mother in the kitchen during the holidays.

She was not much older when she first helped her mother with the cookies that sent that heavenly aroma wafting through their house.

Now that memory meant more to her than ever.

She smiled as the sounds of rummaging made its way into the kitchen. She remembered the joy she felt as the doctor laid her screaming child on her stomach.

As the sweat of the labor ran down her face, she looked in awe at the life she had brought into the world. The sounds coming from their second floor was what she had wanted all her life.

That was her little girl up there.

"I got it, mommy." Samantha yelled running into the kitchen holding the pink plastic apron up.

Sharon swung around a smile on her face. "Okay," she said. "Put it on, and then we'll get to work."

Samantha Johnson slipped the apron over her head and pulled the center strings around to her back. She swung her hips, her face filled with concentration as she tried desperately to tie them. Finally, she groaned in frustration, and looked up at her mother. "I can't get it tied," she stated angrily.

Sharon laughed at her angry expression. "Here," she told her daughter, kneeling down in front of her, "let me show you a little trick your grandmother taught me. Turn your apron around."

He daughter looked at her curiously for a moment then did as she was told. She turned the apron around until the ties were in the front.

"Okay, now tie it tight," Sharon instructed.

Samantha tied it, making a grunt as she pulled the initial knot taught, then with nimble fingers, made a bow.

"Okay, now turn it around," Sharon told her with a smile.

Her daughter pulled the apron back around to the front. Giving the plastic a tug, she found it still tight. Samantha looked at Sharon in amazement. "I did it! I did it!" She exclaimed happily.

Sharon grabbed her and pulled her into a hug. "Yes, you did. You're mommy's helper now."

"Yeah," Samantha agreed happily, giving her mother a tight squeeze.

Sharon pulled away to look at her daughter, her little ray of sunshine. Samantha's smile beamed at her from above her pink apron. Her hair shined brightly in the glow of the kitchen's light, and her eyes shined like two deep pools of blue.

She looked so damned strong then.

Sharon Johnson now stood at the threshold of her kitchen, which stood silent and void of the familiar aromas of the holidays. Tears burned her cheeks as she reached over and shut off the lights. Darkness fell over the kitchen brutally erasing the memory.

The oven had stayed cold this year.

Sharon couldn't bring herself to turn its knob to bake the dough that would have been too painful to mix. "We'll make cookies when you come home, baby," she whispered looking through the darkness at the silent oven. "Mommy will wait, and we can make them together." She put a hand over her eyes feeling moist heat beneath her fingers. She leaned against the doorway.

"I can wait."

2

"You get some sleep now," Greg Johnson said softly pulling the covers up over his son. "Tomorrow when you get up, you can see what Santa brought for you."

"And 'Mantha," Jeremy asked.

Greg forced a smile onto his face. "We'll go see 'Mantha tomorrow, okay?"

The boy nodded. His sister had gone away to a big place where all the people wore white and the air smelled funny.

After she left, he had gone upstairs after his mother when she was cleaning one day and watched her walk into his sister's room. She stood in the center of it for a moment, looked around, and began to cry. The sight scared him.

Mommies weren't supposed to cry.

"You sleep now, buddy. I'll see you tomorrow." Greg said giving him a kiss on the forehead.

"'Night, daddy." The boy said with a hug.

Greg stood up and walked to the door. He reached over to the wall socket where a *Smiley Face* nightlight hung. Flicking the switch on its side, the face illuminated. He then flicked off the light, and walked out of the room.

As he entered the hall, he watched his wife make her way wearily up the steps.

"All tucked in," she asked.

"Snug as a bug in a rug," Greg replied giving her a kiss.

"I'm gonna go in and give him a kiss goodnight. I didn't mean to yell at him like that. I just-"

"Hey," Greg Johnson whispered taking her face in his hands. "It's all right. He loves you. You're his mommy. Okay?"

He could feel her heart shatter. "She's coming home soon, isn't she," she asked. "Greg, please tell me she'll be coming home."

He pulled her close and stroked her hair. "Get some rest, honey," he whispered. "Take it easy."

She pulled away, and nodded with a sniffle. "Yeah, good idea. Let me just say goodnight to Jerry then I'll hit the sack. Are you coming?"

"In a minute. I'm going to check the doors. Make sure we're all sealed up for the night."

"Okay," Sharon nodded. "Turn the tree off before you come up."

"Gotcha."

Greg Johnson walked down the steps into the living room lit now only by their tree. He gave the knob on their front door a twist then checked the door's deadbolt. He walked back to the tree and looked into the shimmering lights.

His mind wandered back to the week of Thanksgiving.

He worked as a computer engineer for a company downtown. He spent that Wednesday forcing himself to act naturally. Samantha had been in the hospital for two weeks then and all he wanted to do was be home with his family.

He had ordered plans sent up from Research and Development he needed to go over before leaving for the four-day weekend. He looked around and caught a glimpse of a young man walking through the maze of desks in the office.

"Mitch," he called to him.

Mitch Sheridan, a college student who was interning with the firm until he graduated, walked over to him a smile on his face. "Yeah, Greg," he asked with a brightness that irritated Johnson.

"Mitch, where are the plans for Carmichael's main-frame I asked for?"

"Oh, Jeez, Greg, I forgot them."

"Could you go down and get them please," Johnson asked impatiently.

"Aw, c'mon, Greg, it's almost quittin' ti-." Sheridan started.

"Dammit, Mitch," Johnson roared, sending the college student stumbling back in surprise. Greg shot to his feet sending his chair toppling over. "When I ask you to do something, I don't want an argument and I don't want a debate, I want it *done*! Are you clear on that! *Are you*?"

His anger rushed from him as he looked into the boy's face and was immediately replaced with shame. Greg looked around the room. All work had stopped; all eyes were upon him.

He looked back to Sheridan. "I'm sorry, Mitch. That was uncalled for. I apologize."

"It's okay, Greg. If you still want those plans, I can-"

"No. No, that's all right."

At the end of the room sat the office of Glen Riley, the office supervisor. The door opened and the white-haired man stepped out. "Greg," he called. "Could I see you in my office, please?"

Greg made his way through the sea of curious eyes to the office. Riley put a hand on his shoulder as he entered the office, then turned back to the workers. "Are we finished?" He asked them.

They all turned back to their work.

Riley stepped back into his office and closed the door. "Have a seat, Greg." Riley said as he sat back down behind his desk.

Greg sat down. "Glen, I'm sorry."

"Your daughter," he asked.

"Yeah," Johnson said with a nod. "She had a relapse a couple of weeks back."

"Greg, I'm so sorry." Riley said honestly. "What did the doctors say?"

Greg looked away. "They say her system isn't fighting back anymore." He looked back, tears in his eyes. "They were trying bone marrow transplants, but she just seemed to slip down hill so fast. They say she's gonna die, Glen."

Greg folded his hands in his lap, and looked down. "She's got pneumonia now. They say she's in the final stages."

Johnson looked up with a slight laugh. "Remember when you were a kid, how it seemed your dad could do anything. I mean, it was like there was nothing he couldn't fix. No problem he couldn't solve?"

"Yeah," Glen Riley replied, sending his heart out to the man sitting in front of him. "Yeah, I do."

"I'm her daddy, Glen," Greg forced out, his face red with the strain of holding back sobs that pounded at the back of his teeth like an angry fist. "She's my baby. She's my baby and she's dying. I'm her daddy, I should be able to fix things and make them all better. She's dying and I can't stop it."

He put a shaking hand over his eyes as he lost the battle against the tears. "Glen, my baby's dying."

Riley walked around the desk and laid a soft hand on Johnson's shoulder. "Greg, why don't you take a leave of absence for a while. You should be with Sharon and your boy. I'll tell them upstairs your sick and needed time off so you see some money. Come back when you're ready."

"Thanks, Glen. Sharon and I appreciate it."

"You're on leave as of now. I'll call you later to see how things are going. And if you need someone to talk to you know my number, huh?"

"Yeah," Greg replied standing. "Thanks, Glen."

Greg's eyes now looked over the glittering lights of the tree struggling desperately to find a reason for the events that were taking place. But he could only remember the first time his daughter fell ill.

He remembered the numbing terror that seized his heart when she was diagnosed with leukemia. What had they done to deserve this? When exactly had everything gone wrong?

When had "Don't lose hope," turned into, "It's only a matter of time."

Greg found the switch for the tree and gave it a flick. The lights shut off sending the house's first floor into darkness.

Sharon Johnson slipped into her nightgown and pulled back the covers. She looked at the dresser at the foot of the bed. On top of it stood the statue of Our Lady of Grace.

The Blessed Virgin Mary stood atop a globe, her arms out, her palms up as though she were reaching down to the world.

Staring into the eyes of the statue, Sharon walked to end of the bed and sat. The brown eyes were peaceful, yet somehow sad. Slowly, Sharon Johnson blessed herself and clasped her hands in front of her mouth. Staring into the eyes of the statue, she whispered only one word.

"*Please*?"

One word that echoed through the bedroom and into the cold December night. One word of pleading sent from woman to woman, heart to heart.

Soul to soul.

Mother to Mother.

3

Our Lady of the Archangels Hospital

11:56 P.M.

Kathy Thompson brushed her long auburn hair out of her face as she readied the work schedule for the midnight shift. She liked working the children's ward and the shift was quiet.

"Hey, nurse," a voice called from down the hall.

She looked up to see a man in his late thirties make his way down the hall. He wore a stethoscope slung over his shoulder and a long white coat. His name was Dr. Robert Cafferty, the senior doctor for the wing.

"Hello, Rob. Merry Christmas."

"Yeah, sure, whatever," the doctor said glumly leaning on the counter.

"C'mon, Rob, it's Christmas."

"You know what your husband, the illustrious Doctor Thompson, is doing right now," Cafferty asked her.

"No, what?"

"Right now," Cafferty began. "Gary is down in his ER, trying to revive an O.D. suicide. And why'd the poor slob do it? Because it's Christmas, *that's why*. Then there's that patient of mine in 308-."

"The Johnson girl?"

"That's the one."

"It's a shame for her," Thompson said in a low voice shaking her head.

"It happens." Cafferty said matter-of-factly.

"How can you be so detached from something like that?"

"You'll learn."

Kathy Thompson put down her work roster and checked her watch. "I have to go give Samantha her antibiotics," she told Cafferty. "Listen, why don't you join Gary and I at the end of the shift for some coffee?"

"Can't," Cafferty answered dully. "Pullin' a second shift in ER at seven."

"You're not going home? I know you hate Christmas but what about your family, Rob?"

Cafferty stood up, "Carol's not talking to me. We had a fight when I told her I'd be spending Christmas here. As for the kids - well, I bought them enough stuff to open that they'll never miss me."

"But it's *Christmas*."

"No," Cafferty replied walking away. "It's *Saturday*."

Kathy Thompson watched the doctor make his way down to his office at the end of the hall.

Cafferty opened the door, stepped in then sent thunder roaring through the halls as he slammed the door behind him.

Turning from the desk, she made her way over to a steel medicine cabinet that housed all the medicines needed for the wing. Sliding open the door, she pulled out a bottle of orange liquid labeled: JOHNSON, SAMANTHA C: HALF CUP EVERY SIX HOURS.

Kathy Thompson opened the bottle and grabbed a small plastic medicine cup off the shelf above. Pouring the antibiotic into the cup, she took a deep breath and prepared herself to enter room 308.

It was then she wished she *were* more like Robert Cafferty.

Kathy Thompson loved all the children on her wing. At home with her husband she had always referred to them as "My kids." She and her husband had yet to have children of their own and the children of the wing seemed to fill the void she sometimes felt. To her they were all precious. But the patient in room 308 was different.

All the nurses on the floor agreed that she had a way of stealing your heart.

Kathy Thompson had been there when they brought her in. She had been there when they told her parents that she had developed pneumonia. She had been there when they told her that the bone marrow transplant had failed and the pneumonia had taken over.

The girl's mother had stayed with her day and night while the doctor's tried desperately to deal with the pneumonia. Kathy had pulled strings to have a cot set up in the little girl's room to spare the woman another night on a hard-back chair.

All through the ordeal, the little girl would always look up at her at medication time, even at her weakest moments and smile as though she were telling her not to worry.

Kathy remembered the look of the girl's mother. Before she left, her face held a drawn, pale, look of worry and frustrated agony. On the few occasions Sharon Johnson would tear herself away from her daughter's side to get a cup of coffee, Kathy would stop and talk to her.

Sharon smiled as she told her about the rough labor that had lasted ten hours then she would hurry to say that Samantha had made it worth it. She told her about Samantha's year in Kindergarten, and how she loved to help with things in the kitchen. She told her of how her daughter would spend hours reading to her dolls.

Kathy had stayed with the mother as the orderlies wheeled the little girl into the treatment room to extract the marrow. She had held Sharon Johnson's hand as they waited for her to come out.

She had been there as the doctor's told them of the pneumonia's worsening. She had been there when the doctor's told Sharon Johnson that she should go home and rest.

She had been there when they told them there was nothing more they could do.

She had watched Sharon Johnson fall into a fit of tears as they told her in so many words that her daughter was going to die.

She looked into the father's face that filled with disbelief and pained horror.

At home in her husband's arms, Kathy Thompson cried tears she never thought would end.

Bracing herself, the nurse walked down the hall with the cup. At its end on the right sat Room 308.

Stopping at the closed door, she took a deep breath then entered.

The room was dark, except for a single fluorescent bar over the bed's headboard. In its corner sat a single chair. Next to the bed sat a tank of oxygen.

In the bed laid Samantha Johnson.

Kathy made her way quietly over to the bed and looked down on the sleeping girl who now constantly wore an oxygen mask. Her long golden hair hung down over her chest. Over her eyes laid neatly cut bangs her mother had done for her earlier that day.

Samantha Johnson's chest rose and fell in labored breaths. Her face was now an ashen- grey, her cheeks and eyes had taken on a sunken look. Under her eyes, dark rings formed.

And in her arms, held tightly, was Scruffs.

Scruffs, Samantha told her when they first met, was her best friend. Scruffs, a brown Teddy Bear, who now sported bare patches from years of constant hugging and was missing his right black-button eye, laid contently in her arms, his sewn on smile beaming up at her.

Samantha told Kathy that she and Scruffs had been together for a long, *long* time. Since she was three-years old as a matter of fact. She told the nurse that Scruffs liked to play dress up and always loved a good tea party. She told of how excited Scruffs had been to go to Kindergarten. But now she told the nurse, Scruffs was sick.

Scruffs had leukemia.

Kathy had watched Samantha lie stone still, her eyes aimed at the ceiling as they inserted the needle into the crest of her hip. She watched the girl wince and her grip tighten on the bear as the gunshot pop of the needle breaking through the bone filled the room.

Not once did she cry or utter a sound.

Kathy told her that it was all right to cry when it hurt. The little girl looked up at her from her bed and told her she couldn't do that. She told the nurse that if she cried, then Scruffs would get scared and start crying too.

She told the nurse that sometimes Scruffs would get *real* scared during the treatments, but he wouldn't cry because she was there with him. And when she got scared it was all right, because he was there to keep her company.

And when they felt sad, they would cheer each other up by singing songs from Kindergarten.

They would go through it together.

They were, "The bestest buddies in the whole wide world."

Kathy laid a soft had on the girl's forehead. "Samantha," she called gently. "Samantha, honey, wake up."

The little girl's eyelids fluttered, then opened. Her blue eyes roamed over to the nurse, a thin smile appeared on her lips. "Hi," Samantha greeted sleepily.

"Hi, sweetheart," Kathy Thompson replied. "It's time for your medicine, dear. Could you sit up for me? Do you want some help?"

The little girl shook her head. Holding Scruffs with her left arm, she pushed herself up with her right. "Is it the orange stuff," she asked tiredly.

"Yes," Kathy replied quietly.

"Scruffs don't like it. He says it's icky," Samantha informed her.

"Well," Kathy told her, "maybe if you take yours first, then I let you give him his, he'll drink it. Think so?"

The little girl nodded.

Samantha removed her mask and took the cup from the nurse. Slowly, she put it to her lips and, with a grimace, drained it.

She then put the cup to the bear's lips. "Come on, now it's your turn."

Kathy smiled, as the little girl coaxed the bear to take the medicine.

"If I can drink it," the girl said wheezing. "So can you. I know it's yukky." She tilted the cup and gave it back to the nurse. Her wheezing increased to a thundering rasp, her chest began to heave as she forced air into her lungs.

Kathy Thompson hurriedly put her mask back on. The little girl's face paled. Kathy looked into Samantha's eyes. Deep blue eyes that had once sparkled with the energy of youth, now dulled under the pressure of her disease.

Kathy Thompson felt her throat begin to burn.

"You rest now, sweetie," the nurse said helping her down into the bed and covering her. She leaned over and kissed the little girl on her forehead.

Feeling sobs tugging at the side of her throat, she turned and hurried to the door.

"Nurse Kathy," a small voice called from behind her.

"Yes, baby," she answered, forcing calm into her voice as she turned.

From the bed, Samantha Johnson looked at her through weak eyes, her bear held tightly in her arms.

"Merry Christmas," she said with a slow smile.

"Merry Christmas, honey," Kathy Thompson replied, a river forming in her eyes.

Holding her hand over her mouth, Kathy Thompson rushed back down the hall to the nurse's station. Reaching it, she leaned on the desktop, resting on her elbows, her hands over her eyes.

The sounds of her sobs echoed through the barren corridors.

A hand rested on her shoulder. She turned to see her husband, his brown hair mussed, his brown eyes filled with concern. "Just come from 308," he asked gently stoking her cheek.

She nodded and laid her head on his shoulder.

"We do what we can, babe," Gary Thompson whispered in her ear as he rocked her. "That's all we can expect from ourselves. It's out of our hands."

4

Samantha Johnson lay quietly in her bed, pulling and pushing air in and out of her lungs. Pulling Scruffs up her chest, she nestled his head in the nape of her neck and closed her eyes. She held Scruffs extra tight tonight. Scruffs was afraid.

He couldn't breathe.

As she lay there, she noticed the room becoming steadily warmer. But it was a strange warm. It wasn't like a summer warm, or the kind of warm given off by her house's heater.

It was a different warm.

She opened her eyes. Looking in the corner of the darkened room, she noticed the chair looked funny. Its normally straight lines were now waving. From nowhere a golden light appeared. The baseball-sized light floated there for a moment then began to grow.

The ball became a diamond then disappeared.

In its place stood a man.

The man wore a purple tunic, belted at the waist with a band of silver. Silver bands ran from his wrists to mid-forearm. Flowing behind him, hung a long purple cape, fastened to the shoulders of the tunic by silver amulets. On his feet, he wore silver sandals, their bands crisscrossing up to his knees.

The man looked over to her with a warm smile. Gold hair flowed around his face and down his shoulders.

Samantha looked at the man who was the tallest person she had ever seen.

Slowly, he walked over to her bed. He looked down at her through blue eyes that glowed as though lit from within.

"Are you an *angel*," Samantha asked weakly.

The figure nodded.

"You're here for me and Scruffs, *aren't you*?"

Again, the figure nodded.

5

Samantha watched the man sit on the side of the bed and she noticed that, even though he was big, the mattress didn't sag. In her mind she was afraid of this thing that had come from nowhere, but in her heart, she liked his eyes. After a moment, she found the nerve to speak. "Tommy says you're a monster," she informed the being.

For a moment the thing on the bed looked down at her with a pained expression, then one of question. "And who told you that," the angel asked, his voice was deep and powerful, yet its tone was soft and soothing.

It reminded Samantha of her father's voice the day she had run home crying. She had fallen off her bike, and her daddy had fixed the boo-boo on her knee with a Band-Aid and a kiss.

Before he let her get down from the kitchen chair, he ran a hand through her hair, and told her everything was all better. His voice was strong and full of love.

And the angel's voice sounded the same way.

"Tommy Watkins did," she answered. "He's a lot older than me. He's nine. He had cancer, but now they say he's all better. He's in the room next to mine. He's going home tomorrow, and he told me he's going home because he beat the Grim Reaper. He says the Grim Reaper is a monster that kills people."

The angel's face gave a look of hurt.

The angel lowered his head. He, like all angels, was given a task upon his creation. Tasks for the angels varied. Some were specific duties like those of the Archangels and the Guardians; others were merely free-floating angels, which were meant to spread goodwill.

His duty was different.

His duties were wide and spanning. He had caused great grief as he swept through the kingdom of the Pharaoh, taking the first-born son of every house, except those which had lambs blood smeared on their doorways.

He had taken the old and weak who welcomed him and what he had to offer. He had taken soul after soul into his care and he had loved them all. He was the one who held the blessed task of leading his Creator's children into the Kingdom of Light. He had been given many names over the ages, but he knew who he was. He was Mordius.

The Angel of Death.

"Please do not be afraid of me, little one," the angel said softly as he ran a warm hand across her cheek. "I am Mordius and my name means 'the caretaker of souls,' and it is my job to bring all of the Father's children back to him when it is their time."

"You're not a monster," Samantha asked.

Mordius handed her a smile that made the little girl feel warm all over. "Do I look like a monster, Samantha," he asked.

The little girl's eyes widened, "You know my name?"

"I know all the names of my charges, little one. And this must then be Scruffs," the angel said patting the bear on its head.

"Yeah. He's sick, just like me."

"Well, after tonight, you will be sick no longer. After tonight, the Father shall take care of you, little one."

"Why do you keep calling me that?"

Mordius stood and backed away from the bed. "Before you are remanded back to the Father, you are in my care. You are one of my little ones. And I love all my little ones, for they are the creation of the Father."

Mordius pulled his cape around him until the front of him was covered. "Come, little ones," he called. "Come say hello to Samantha." He pulled back his cape, and a thousand tiny nickel-sized orbs of gold appeared.

Samantha Johnson watched in awe as the orbs left the angel and flew around the room. Taking off the oxygen mask that obstructed her view, she watched the orbs dart back and forth in front of her. Some chased each other around the room; others flew in and out from underneath the bed.

A gold orb shot to the tip of her nose making her jump with a start. The orb flashed. Samantha looked over to the angel, perplexed.

"That is William," the angle smiled. "He is saying hello."

Samantha looked back to the floating object. "Hello, William. I'm Samantha." The orb flashed brightly twice and gave the tip of her nose a gentle tap, then as quickly as it flew to her, it darted away.

Samantha giggled at the sensation the soul gave her when they touched, "That tickles." She looked on in wide-eyed amazement at the tiny lights that filled her room. They were beautiful, and she could feel that all of them felt the same thing.

They were happy.

Mordius looked into the eyes of the child and smiled. He then looked at the floating orbs. "Come, little ones," he called to them, opening his cape. "Come now with you."

The orbs flooded back underneath the purple cape. Mordius closed it gently over them. A second later, he threw the cape behind him, and the orbs were gone.

"There," the angel said returning to the bed and sitting down. "See how happy they are? See, there is no fear."

"But," the little girl began. "I can't go with you, Mr. Mordius. I'm not scared, and I won't cry, but what about mommy? I can't leave mommy. She needs me. When she makes cookies; who will help her?

"If I go, she'll have to make them all alone. Please, Mr. Mordius, I can't do that to her. If I go, she'll cry."

The little girl's eyes filled with tears.

"When she comes to see me, she always cries. She doesn't think I see her. She goes out in the hall, but I can hear her. And I feel bad for making her sad. Please, Mr. Mordius, I don't want her to cry anymore."

Mordius turned his head away from the girl, his eyes betraying his sadness. He turned back to her. "But, Samantha, it is necessary. It is His will. Do you understand?"

The little girl looked up at him with tear-filled eyes, and shook her head.

Mordius stood and walked to the end of the bed. Facing away from Samantha, he bowed his head and spoke softly. "I know it is my duty - but please - on this night of nights, please grant me this one wish. This I beg of you."

Samantha Johnson watched another baseball-sized orb appear beside the angel whose head hung low. The room again warmed. The orb grew into a diamond, and another man appeared.

Samantha looked into the deep brown eyes of the man who had appeared. He looked familiar. He looked like the statue that was in her room just above the light over her bed.

The statue that hung from the cross.

Peacefully, he looked down at her, his long brown hair flowing over a white robe.

"Master," Mordius whispered, not raising his eyes. "I-I-."

Christ laid a soft hand on the shoulder of the angel. "It is all right, Mordius," He said in a soft deep voice. "I thank you for beckoning me. Go now, and bring my Father's children home. I will send for you when it is time."

"Yes, my Lord."

Samantha watched the angel turn back into a ball of light, then disappear.

The little girl began to wheeze and rasp. Her chest began to heave as her lungs again began to feel like lead.

Jesus walked up the side of the bed and sat down. Gently, He laid His hand on the crown of her head and the rasping ceased. Samantha found she could breathe easier. "What is this I hear, Samantha? You do not want to come to see me?"

"No, it's not that," she said lowly. "I can't leave my mommy. She'd be so sad if I went away. If I leave, who'll help her around the house? My little brother's real messy. That's 'cause he's a boy. Boys are messy." She gasped and threw her hands over her mouth, "Oops. Sorry. I didn't mean that *You* were-"

Jesus smiled. "I remember being messy when I was his age."

"You were?" Samantha asked, amazed.

"Yes," Jesus nodded. "When I was a child, I had toy animals made of wood. Toys Joseph had made for me. And I would sit on the ground and play with them, and my clothes would get dirty."

"You had toys?"

"Certainly," Christ answered. "I did not have many, but I had a few. I would play with them all the time. Then, when my Father called upon me to begin my work gathering his flock, I put them away and did what I had to do. But when I did play with them, I made my share of mess. Your brother will learn. He is only young now, as I was then."

Samantha's face saddened.

"I was bad, Jesus," she told Him.

"Were you," He asked.

"Yeah. I hit my little brother once."

"And why did you do that," Jesus asked.

Samantha looked up at Him, "He bit Scruffs' eye off and flushed it down the toilet. So I whacked him right on the head. And I yelled at him too." She looked down at her hands, her face grim. "I'm sorry."

Jesus gently cupped her chin in His hand and raised her face to His. "Do not be sad, Samantha." He leaned over and kissed her on the forehead, "All is forgiven."

"Jesus," the little girl asked.

"Yes."

"Did You know what was going to happen?"

"Yes, little one, I did. I had always known."

"In Kindergarten, Miss Simmons used to read Bible stories to us before nap time. She told us that they hung You on the cross because they didn't like You. Why didn't they like You? If You knew what was going to happen, then how
come-."

"I had to, little one. I had to show them the way to the Father's kingdom. I had to gather the souls that had strayed. And by letting them do to me what they did, I opened the gates of heaven to all who wished to follow. I let them *hate me*, because I *loved them*."

"I'm glad you love me," Samantha told Him.

"Yes, little one, I love you very much."

"I love You too. My mommy says we all should love You, because You love us so much. And she would tell me all the nice things You did. Jesus?"

The messiah looked down into her inquisitive face and smiled. Of all His Father's children He loved the young ones. So exploring; so curious. "Yes, little one."

"What was Your mommy like?"

Christ thought back to a time in Jerusalem, when He had been in the fields helping tend to the sheep. He was eleven then, and old enough to keep an eye on the flock.

The day's sun was setting, and Jesus had spent most of it gathering the baying animals.

"Jesus," He heard echoed over the hills.

The voice was sweet, and the tone was like music to Him. He turned to see His mother standing in the field. Her robe billowed gently in the fading light of the day.

He ran across the field calling out to her. As she saw Him, her face brightened. She spread her arms wide and knelt down. Jesus ran smiling into her arms. She wrapped her arms around Him, and gave him a squeeze.

She held Him out in front of her. "Look at You," she smiled looking into the dirty face of her Son. "It looks like You have been working hard."

Jesus nodded with a smile. It was true. The larger animals were very content to stay in the flock and graze, but the smaller ones loved to wander.

And they had led him on many chases.

"It is time for dinner. Put the animals away for the night and come home."

"Yes momma," He answered while she ruffled his hair.

That night Jesus, Mary, and Joseph sat around the table Joseph had crafted and ate a meal of Menna, bread and lamb. He remembered how lovely His mother looked in the orange flicker of the candles. As they spoke of the events of the day, He remembered the sweet sound of her laughter.

"My mother is beautiful, little one, as is yours; as are they all. Blessed are those who bear the fruit of creation."

"When You went away, did Your mommy cry too?"

"Yes," Jesus replied softly.

He remembered looking down from the great wooden cross; high on a hill they called Golgotha, which meant Place of the Skulls.

A place they now called Mount Calvary.

Pain ebbed through every part of His body, His feet numb, His arms on fire; the blood from the thorns stinging His eyes.

Through the pain, He could see His mother beside her sister Mary of Cleophas, and Mary Magdalene. Her tears ran like a bitter rain down her cheeks as she looked up at her Son. He could hear in the background some weeping others cheering the death of the One they called 'The King of the Jews.'

"If You're really the king of the Jews, come down off that cross," a voice chided from somewhere in the crowd.

As blood dripped from the wounds in His hands and landed in the dirt below, He knew in His heart He was doing what needed to be done. But that knowing didn't help His pain as He looked down into the eyes of the woman who had raised Him.

Her eyes turned up to His, their pain ineffable. Her face contorted with sobs. Her heart had loved Him from birth. Her heart had been with Him as he made his way through the land preaching His Father's Word. Her heart had broken as they tortured her Son for His teachings.

Unknown to the soldiers, they had driven in four nails that day. One in His left wrist, one in His right wrist, one in His feet . . .

And one into the heart of His mother.

Jesus looked down at her tears and His heart broke for her. He couldn't bear to see her tears. He couldn't bear to see her in pain.

He couldn't leave her alone.

Looking to His right, His eyes fell on a disciple whom he loved dearly. His head thundered from the beatings of the night before as He called out to him.

"John," He called to his follower.

The apostle walked forward and stood beside Mary. Jesus looked to his mother,

"Woman"' He said to her, "behold thy son."

Mary looked to the young disciple.

"Son," Jesus then said to John, "Behold thy mother."

From below, Jesus saw the apostle nod. He understood. Putting a consoling arm around Mary, he stayed with her as she wept. The apostle took Mary into his home and cared for her, for she was now of his blood.

Seeing His mother had been put into capable hands, He turned His eyes upward. It was time. It was the moment He had been placed on earth for. Knives ran through his arms and legs. With a final agonized cry, He closed his eyes and His head lowered until His chin rested on His chest. It was time.

Time to open to His Father's children the Gates of Glory.

Jesus now sat on the side of the bed, His head lowered. He thought of those who now used His name and His word for personal gain. He thought of all the violence His Father's children were forcing on each other.

He thought of those who now no longer believed in Him. He thought of those who forced others to live in poverty, so that a chosen few may live in wealth. He thought of how apathetic and uncaring His Father's children were to the plight of their brothers.

"I knock upon their hearts, Father," Jesus whispered. "Why do they turn a deaf ear to me? Why do they not answer?"

And Christ began to weep.

Samantha Johnson watched as Jesus put a hand over His eyes. The sounds of His sobs frightened her. She had heard other people cry, but this was different. It was more than sad.

It held in its tone an indescribable emptiness.

Sitting up, she wrapped her arms around Jesus' neck and squeezed Him. "Don't cry," she whispered laying her head on His shoulder. "Things'll get better, you'll see. My mommy says that sometimes things look really bad, but they always get better. You just have to wait a little while, that's all."

"Thank you, little one," Christ smiled rubbing her back.

Samantha pulled away, with a smile. "Know what me and Scruffs do when we're sad?"

"What do you do?"

"We sing songs. I sang to You last year in Kindergarten."

"You did," Jesus asked, remembering it well.

"Yeah," Samantha nodded.

"And what did you sing," He asked.

"You wanna hear it," she asked.

"Yes, I would like that very much."

Samantha Johnson wrapped an arm around Jesus' neck, laid her head back onto his shoulder, and began to sing. "Away in the manger, no crib for a bed. The little Lord Jesus lay down His sweet head . . ."

Jesus listened with a smile as the little girl serenaded Him, her voice filling the room.

He remembered standing in the middle of the children in the little classroom in St. Charles' Elementary School as they sang the songs of Christmas. They sounded like angels to Him, as the little girl sounded to

Him now. Her voice fell onto His ears like the sacred sound of chiming bells.

Samantha finished the song and pulled back away from Him. She smiled and added, "Then we all said, 'Happy birthday, baby Jesus!' 'Cause Christmas is Your birthday."

"That was beautiful, Samantha," Jesus said hugging her. "Thank you. In my Father's kingdom, the day is also celebrated. And the angels all gather and sing."

"They *do*," Samantha asked, eyes wide.

"Yes," Jesus answered. "The angels gather and sing with joy, and the souls of My Father's children sing with them. It is a joyous time for all in the kingdom."

"That sounds nice," Samantha said.

"Yes. Yes, it is."

Jesus stood and kissed her on the cheek. "I must go now, little one. I must ready for the celebration."

Behind Jesus, Mordius appeared.

Christ turned and walked to the angel. He again laid a gentle hand on the angel's shoulder. The angel looked back at him. In the eyes of the messiah a message came forth.

The angel fell to one knee, sending his cape and hair cascading down over his shoulders. The angel bowed his head, made a fist with his right hand, and laid it on his left breast. "I shall do as You command," the angel said, his eyes closed," in Your name, and by Your word, my Lord."

Christ put His hand on the crown of the angel's head. "You are truly a kind and loyal servant, Mordius," Christ said to the kneeling angel.

"Thank you, my Lord."

Jesus drew His hand away and the angel stood. "I will take my leave of you now, Mordius."

"Yes, my Lord," the angel replied.

"Jesus, wait," Samantha Johnson called.

Jesus turned to find the girl sliding from the bed. Samantha Johnson padded across the room to the two figures. With wide blue eyes, she looked up at Christ.

"Yes, Samantha," Jesus asked.

Samantha Johnson held up her Teddy Bear to Him.

Jesus knelt down on one knee in front of her. Gently, she handed the bear to Him.

"For me," Jesus asked.

"For when You're sad," Samantha told Him. "When You're sad, Scruffs will cheer You up, and You won't cry no more. I don't like to see You cry."

"Thank you, Samantha," Jesus smiled.

Samantha threw her arms around His neck and squeezed Him as tight as she could. "Happy birthday, baby Jesus," she whispered in His ear then kissed Him on the cheek.

Christ held her tight, rocking her back and forth. *Oh, Father,* He thought. *If the world could only feel the love that beats within this child's heart, would it not be a better place?*

Jesus gave the little girl one last kiss on the cheek and stood. He looked over to the angel and nodded.

"Come, little one," the angel said gently, taking her by the hand. Mordius led her back to her bed and watched her climb back in.

Samantha sat in the bed and looked at Jesus, who now cradled the bear to Him. He spoke to her once more then vanished.

"Come now, little one. Lie down," the angel said, helping her nestle back down.

Instinctively, Samantha Johnson reached for the oxygen mask. Mordius stopped her, took the mask, and hung it on the tank. "You no longer need this, little one," he told her.

The angel pulled the blankets up around her neck. "Are you comfortable?"

"Yes," she answered softly, the rasping in her chest returning.

"It is time to do what is commanded, little one. Are you ready?"

Samantha Johnson's lower lip jutted out and her eyes filled with tears. Then slowly, she nodded.

"Good," the angel smiled. "Now close your eyes, and think happy thoughts. For tonight your sickness ends."

Samantha Johnson closed her eyes and let her mind wander to happier times. She thought of the first time she had ridden her bike without its training wheels. She thought of her time in Kindergarten. She thought of the tea parties she had thrown for all her stuffed animals. And as she fought for air . . .

She thought of her mother.

Mordius looked down at the little girl, his face one of compassion, a peaceful smile on his lips. Slowly, he moved his hand over her, and placed it on her chest.

Directly above the heart.

As the hand settled, Samantha Johnson's back arched off the mattress, and from
her lips came a loud gasp.

Six miles away, in the Johnson's master bedroom, Sharon Johnson's body arced, and the gasp, which escaped her lips, filled the room then her body bounced back onto the bed.

Neither her nor her husband awoke.

Sharon Johnson would not awake until morning. She would not remember what had happened. She would only awaken with a feeling.

A feeling that, sometime overnight, something had happened to her little girl.

6

December 25th, 3:30 A.M.

Kathy Thompson flew into the office of Dr. Robert Cafferty. "Rob, you gotta come quick," she blurted. "It's Samantha Johnson."

She stopped and looked at the doctor who sat on his sofa, elbows on his knees, his face in his hands.

He turned and looked up at her, his tie hanging, sweat on his face, his eyes red and puffed.

"I know," he replied shakily.

7

6:00 A.M.

Sharon Johnson's eyes fluttered for a moment, then opened. She sat up and looked around the room. Something felt different. The room looked the same, yet something had changed. She felt odd, and she could have sworn she had heard ringing. Ringing?

The phone.

Sharon looked over to the other side of the bed and found it empty. Terror ripped through her body as she threw off the covers. Jumping out of bed, she ran to the door. Throwing it open, she saw Greg reaching the top of the stairs.

When he saw her, he stopped. "That was the operator at the hospital. Doctor Cafferty wants us to come right away."

"No," Sharon Johnson moaned shaking her head.

Greg walked to her and put his arms around her. "I didn't get to talk to the doctor, maybe-."

"Oh, God, Greg," she cried into his chest. "Not today. Oh, God, *not today*."

"We'll take Jerry to your parents, then we'll go over," Greg Johnson said trying to keep his voice controlled.

8

6:45 A.M.

The ride had been silent all the way to the hospital. Sharon Johnson sat looking out the window the entire way. Freshly fallen snow sparkled back at her as the sun bounced off its tiny crystals. It was bright and cheerful, and she hated the sight of it.

Through damp eyes, she watched the city come to life. The bare branches of the trees glistened with ice, the snow taking the place of their fallen leaves. *She should've been here,* Sharon thought, her heart aching. *She loved the snow.*

She should be here.

Greg Johnson made a left at the intersection and as he drove, Sharon could see Our Lady of the Archangels three blocks in the distance. It had changed now. What once looked like a tower of hope to her, now looked like a monster. A giant, silent, brooding monster that held her daughter.

Sharon Johnson looked up at the large hospital as they entered the large parking lot. Greg Johnson moved the mini van into a parking slot and they stepped out.

They rushed through the large automatic doors of the hospital's reception area to the elevators.

In Sharon Johnson's pain-racked mind, she wondered how she would tell her son that his sister wouldn't be coming home. How would she explain it to him? What would she do now that her little girl was gone?

The elevator doors opened and the two of them stepped in.

The doors opened onto the third floor. Greg and Sharon looked down the hall to their daughter's room. There were doctors huddled outside of it. They stood there talking for a moment, then stepped back inside.

Sharon looked at her husband with confusion as they walked down the hall. *What are they doing to her,* she thought. *Leave her alone. Hasn't she been through enough?*

They reached the door of room 308.

Greg Johnson could feel his chest tighten. His eyes began to burn. Sharon Johnson could feel her throat begin to tighten. They knew they would have to look down at their little girl in her bed.

They knew the fight was over.

Greg and Sharon Johnson walked into the room. They could not see the bed, which was now walled in by poking doctors.

Sharon Johnson looked at them all hunched over her daughter like vultures. Her eyes roamed to the foot of the bed. The nurse who had sat with her during the treatments stood there silent.

Beside the nurse stood a priest.

Sharon Johnson's eyes welled with tears as they slowly wandered back to the bed. Her eyes gazed over the backs of the doctors as though everything were happening in slow motion. Her eyes stopped at the shoulder of one of the doctors and her heart skipped.

Two sparkling blue eyes were peeking over at her.

"*Mommy*!" Samantha Johnson yelled excitedly, shooting to her feet in the center of the bed.

Greg Johnson's eyes widened.

"Baby," Sharon Johnson called leaving her stunned husband's side and rushing over to the bed.

The doctors parted.

"Baby," Sharon Johnson called again, not believing what was happening.

Samantha Johnson jumped into her mother's arms. Sharon Johnson's body shook as the reality set in. She pulled her daughter tight to her and stroked her hair, feeling its silk beneath her fingers.

Samantha Johnson laid her head on her mothers shoulder and closed her eyes with a smile. It was Christmas, and she would be going home. It was Christmas, and as she rocked, she new that hugs were nice, but the best hugs of all were her mother's hugs.

She opened her eyes and looked over to her father. "Daddy," she yelled standing up, holding her arms out with a smile that broke Greg Johnson out of his trance.

Running to the bed, he snatched her up in his arms. As he held her, he felt the same way he had when she was first born: ten fingers, ten toes, and full of energy.

Pulling away, he looked into her smiling face. Her face was now full, the rings under her eyes gone, her skin's ashen gray color, now a bright pink, her breathing deep and steady.

"Mr. Johnson," a voice called.

Greg Johnson turned to see Cafferty, his face showing fatigue.

"Yes," Johnson answered.

"Could I see you outside for a moment?"

"Yeah, sure," Johnson answered, his voice full of question.

Greg Johnson gave his daughter another squeeze, not wanting to let go.

"I'll be right back, sweetheart," he told his daughter with a kiss.

"Okay," she replied with a smile.

As Samantha Johnson lunged back into the waiting arms of her mother, Greg Johnson and Cafferty walked out into the hall.

They waited as the army of doctors filed out past them, followed by the priest and the nurse who had been at the bed. After they all left, Johnson turned back to Cafferty.

"What's going on here? Why the hell didn't they tell us over the phone what was going on here? Do you know what we went through on the way over here?" Johnson asked, infuriated.

Cafferty held up his hands," I'm sorry about that, but things got pretty hectic around here this morning. I barely had enough time to get a message out at all. I just wanted you to get here as soon as possible."

"What's going on here, doc'?"

"It's the leukemia, Mr. Johnson."

"What are we talkin' here, another remission?"

"No, we're talking gone."

"What do you mean gone?"

"I mean *gone*," the doctor repeated, his face showing a childlike joy. "Gone as in we can't find any trace of it *anywhere*. Mr. Johnson we've been running tests on your daughter since four this morning, and she's fine.

"Her white cell count is normal and strong. We threw every virus culture we had at them, and her white cells killed them all. Her lungs are clear and her breathing's fine. We've X-rayed her and can't even find the holes left from where we took the marrow. It's like they healed overnight."

"Are you saying-" Greg asked incredulously.

"I'm saying she's a normal, healthy, six-year old," the doctor laughed.

"Has this kind of thing ever happened before," Greg Johnson asked, his face betraying his confusion.

"No, can't say that it has," Cafferty replied with a shrug.

"Then, what do you think happened, doc'?"

Cafferty put his hands on Johnson's shoulders and shook him with an urgent smile.

"Christmas, Mr. Johnson. Christmas happened."

9

"Okay, honey," Sharon told her daughter as she closed the little girl's suitcase. "I think that's it." She looked around for a moment then looked down at her daughter. "Sweetheart, where's Scruffs?

"I gave him to a friend, mommy," the little girl answered. "For His birthday."

"Are you ready to go," Sharon asked.

The little girl nodded.

Gently, she put on her daughter's white Rabbit-fur bonnet and tied its white strings tight to her chin. Samantha grabbed her white mittens and, with a grunt of effort, pulled them on.

Sharon Johnson looked long at her daughter.

Samantha stood before her in her long, red, coat, dress, and new shoes. She looked at the bangs that sprouted from the front of her fluffy bonnet, and flowed out its bottom. Samantha looked at her mother and gave her a smile that brightened her heart. She looked like a little angel.

A little Christmas angel.

"Let's go find daddy and go home," Sharon said.

"Yeah," Samantha agreed eagerly. She walked over to the bed and pulled the suitcase from it.

"Want me to carry that," Sharon asked.

"No I go it," the little girl said lifting it.

Sharon and Samantha Johnson walked from room 308 and down the hall to where Greg Johnson stood at the nurse's desk filling out forms.

"Hey, Sam!" A young voice called from behind.

Sharon Johnson turned to see a boy walking down the hall, a wool hat over his bald head. She remembered him from her previous visits. He had cancer, and she remembered how happy she was when she heard he was going home.

"You goin' home too," he asked with a wide smile.

"Yeah," the little girl answered, then added, "Hey, Tommy, c'mere."

The boy walked up to her, "Yeah?"

Samantha hauled off and swung her suitcase with all her might, catching Watkins in the arm, almost knocking him over.

"Hey," the boy yelled more surprised than hurt. "What'd ya' do that for?"

Samantha dropped her case and put her hands on her hips. "He's *not* the Grim Reaper," Samantha scolded. "And he's *not* a *monster either,* Tommy Watkins! You, *Yutz*!"

Sharon Johnson looked over to her husband who was also watching. He looked back at her and shrugged. Both felt a chill run the course of their spines.

"Yeah. Merry Christmas to you too," the boy said shaking his head, and walking back to his room.

"Let's go home, mommy," Samantha said picking up her bag.

Greg Johnson finished signing the last of the paperwork and handed it to the nurse. "Nurse Thompson, my wife and I can't thank you enough for your support."

"My pleasure," she smiled initialing the papers.

Robert Cafferty and Gary Thompson walked from the elevator, their hair mussed, their white coats wrinkled.

"Hey, sweetie," Gary Thompson called as they made their way over to the desk.

"Hey there, doc;" Kathy answered giving him a kiss as he leaned over the counter.

"Doctor," Johnson said to Cafferty, "Could we see you again for a moment?"

"Sure thing," Cafferty beamed.

Johnson and the doctor walked over to his wife and daughter. "Doc', we really want to thank you again for all you've done."

"Yeah," Sharon Johnson said giving him a hug and a kiss on the cheek. "Thank you."

"Go on home," he said pulling back. "All of you. Go home and get some rest. You all deserve it."

Cafferty knelt down on one knee in front of the little girl. "Bye, Samantha. You'll never know what a pleasure it was knowing you."

"Merry Christmas, Dr. Cafferty," she said giving him a hug.

"Merry Christmas, Samantha," Cafferty said. Tears in his eyes, he whispered two words in her ear, not knowing if she could hear him. Not caring. Two little words.

Thank you.

Cafferty stood and quickly wiped his eyes as though they were tired. "Go on you three. Go home and enjoy the holiday."

Cafferty accepted one more note of thanks and waved to them as they entered the elevator.

"Hey, Rob," Gary Thompson called over, "Kathy and I are going down to the cafeteria for some coffee before we go. Wanna join us?"

Cafferty shook his head, "No. No, you two go on. I've got a call to make."

Kathy and Gary Thompson gave Cafferty a curious look as he walked down the hall to his office. His voice was distant.

Distracted.

Cafferty turned as he reached the door to his office. "Hey you two," he called down to them, "Merry Christmas."

"What," Kathy called back, sarcastically. "What happened to 'No, it's *Saturday*'?"

Cafferty looked down at his shoes for a moment, a smile on his face, then back. "No," he said. "Not this year. Not ever again. Merry Christmas, guys."

"Merry Christmas, Rob," the Thompsons replied.

Cafferty opened his door and stepped inside.

10

Dr. Robert Cafferty closed the door to his office and hurried to his desk. With a shaking hand, he began to punch in seven digits. He tapped his fingers expectantly on the desk as he listened to the ringing. Finally the other end picked up.

"Hello," a woman's voice answered.

"Carol? It's me."

"Rob? Shouldn't you be in the ER now?"

"I'm on my way," he told her. "But listen, maybe you and the kids could stop over and we could go out for lunch or something," Cafferty said, a quiver in his voice.

"Sure, babe," his wife said, concerned. "Honey, are you all right?"

Cafferty smiled, "Never been better. I'll see you then?"

"Yeah, we'll be over," his wife assured.

"Okay, babe, I gotta go now, but I'll be waiting."

"Alright, see you then."

Cafferty hung up the phone, walked to the sofa and plopped down on it.

When his wife and children came he wouldn't tell them what had happened to him. He wouldn't tell of how he had been in the ER and when he returned to his office, he found Someone standing in front of his desk. The figure stood before him in a white robe, with long flowing hair, and the deepest of brown eyes.

He wouldn't tell her of his shock when this Someone called out to him by name. He wouldn't tell her how he walked to the robed Man, who smiled so warmly at him.

He wouldn't mention the disbelief he had, that soon disappeared when the robed Figure took his face in his hands.

He would not talk of how he dropped to his knees before the One who stood before him and fell into tears. Tears of hopelessness. Tears of despair. Tears of a soul riddled with cynicism.

He would not tell his wife how he felt like a child before this Man. He would not say how he had told the robed One of his feelings of inadequacies as a healer, and the dreams which he had when he left medical school, that now lay in shattered pieces.

He would not tell her how the Man beckoned him to stand. He would not say how the Figure took him into His arms, and told him to have faith, and from faith would spring hope.

And he would not tell of the tears. Tears flowed from him as the Figure cast out the darkness of cynicism from his heart and destroyed its chains around his soul.

He would not tell her of the three words the Figure spoke to him before He left.

Three simple words spoken gently.

Send her home.

He would not tell of how he plopped onto the sofa, dripped in sweat, his eyes filled with tears as the Figure left.

And how it was then that the nurse rushed in to get him.

He would not tell his wife and children that as he looked on the little girl in room 308, who sat in the bed smiling at him, his heart leapt and he felt as though he weighed nothing.

He would not say that looking upon her, he saw more than a little girl who had been touched by something greater than man.

He saw hope.

No, he would tell them none of these things. He would only embrace them, and tell them he loved them.

And wish them a Merry Christmas.

11

The Johnsons had stayed at Sharon's parents for two hours talking and laughing, then went home. Twenty minutes after they arrived, there came the much-awaited event.

Twenty minutes after they arrived, the oven roared into life.

The rest of the day became a menagerie of friends, family, and neighbors who paraded in and out of the house. All came bearing smiles on their faces, and the best of wishes upon hearing the news of the miraculous recovery.

For the Johnson family, this would be a Christmas to remember.

12

December 25th, 10:23 P.M.

Samantha climbed sleepily into her bed, snug in her red flannel Christmas gown with its white lace fringe. She lay down, and her mother pulled her blankets up over her.

"Honey," Sharon Johnson spoke softly.

"Yeah," her daughter asked sleepily.

"Honey, remember today - when you were talking about the Grim Reaper?"

"Uh-huh."

"What were you talking about?"

"Tommy said he was a monster, but he's not. He's an angel. He shows people the way to heaven so they don't get lost. He came into my room last night."

"He came into your," a shiver ran through her body, "into your *room*?"

"Uh-huh," the little girl replied. "And then Jesus came too."

"Jesus came too," Sharon asked with another chill.

"Yeah," the little girl smiled. "He's so nice, mommy. We talked for a while about stuff."

"Like what?"

"Well, we talked about when He was little. He played with little wooden animals. Did *you* know that? I didn't know that. And we talked about His mommy, and when He went to heaven. And when He left, He told me to tell *you* something *too*."

"He did?"

"Uh-huh."

"What did He say, sweetie?"

"He said to tell you, 'She heard you.'"

Sharon Johnson's entire body shook.

"What did He mean, mommy?"

"Well," Sharon Johnson explained, her eyes glistening. "Sometimes when a mommy's in trouble, she calls another mommy for help; a mommy who had the same type of problem. 'Cause when it comes to taking care of our babies, us mommies have to stick together. Give us a hug."

Samantha sat up, wrapped her arms around her mother's waist and squeezed as tight as she could, smiling as she felt her mother do the same.

"You get some sleep now, and I'll see you in the morning," Sharon Johnson said laying her daughter back down and kissing her on the forehead.

Sharon took one last look at her daughter for the night and shut off the light. She stepped into the hall and closed the door behind her.

Sharon Johnson walked to her and her husband's room, sat on the foot of the bed, and looked deep into the eyes of the statue of the Blessed Virgin. Alone, in the dark, she silently made the sign of the cross.

She bowed her head for a moment then looked back to the statue. "Thank you," she whispered softly. Then for the last time, Sharon Johnson's tears came. Tears only happiness could bring. Tears only joy could create.

Tears only a mother would understand.

Samantha Johnson lay quietly in her bed looking out the window at the snow that had again begun to fall. A smile fell over her face. It was Christmas, and she knew that somewhere a joyous celebration was taking place.

Somewhere the Celestial Choir of Angels was singing. Somewhere souls were happy and playing. Somewhere Jesus was smiling. And deep down in her heart, Samantha Johnson knew that somewhere . . .

Somewhere . . .

Scruffs was smiling too.

These Four Walls

1

My name's Sam Hatcher, back then it was Sammy, because my dad was Sam. Why was this Christmas so special to me? I guess because it was the year I learned what Christmas means. It was the Christmas of '48.

I was ten that year, almost a man. Yep, in a year or two, I'd be a full-fledged man. I was certain I'd at least be shaving by spring.

My family had moved to Philly in October, after my dad found a job at the Dodge Steel plant on State Road. We lived in Reading before that. My dad was in the war and when he returned the factory had given his job to someone else. What could they do? They couldn't *fire* the guy; so my dad went looking for a job in the city.

Dad had been in the Army Engineers in Europe; that helped him get the job at Dodge. So, with the money he sent home to my mom that she refused to spend, my dad made the down payment on a small row home on Knorr Street.

It wasn't fancy like my grandmom and grandpop's house in Reading, and my dad said it had more drafts than World War II, but it was home.

There was a park across the street and an avenue with a Woolworth's, a few restaurants and a movie theater close by. My mom liked it because St. Leo's, a church with an adjoining school, was right down the street and I was enrolled when we got down here.

The nuns were strict, but I just chalked that up to their having to wear that starched, hard-as-concrete thing on their heads. I know that if I had that thing digging into *my* forehead, I'd be just a bit cranky with the world, too.

I was a little short for my age. Four-foot-five inches. I had straight black hair like my dad and was skinny like my mom. My height and weight made me an easy target for the bigger kids, but that didn't matter much. After you get beat up a few times, you get used to it.

One day while walking home from school, I passed a group of older kids, sixth-graders, looked like, playing football in the park. I knew better than to look over. I was in my school uniform and my best coat, and didn't want to mess them up by getting beaten up.

Nothing invited a whupping like eye contact.

Keeping my head down hadn't worked. They had seen me.

I was meat.

"Hey, kid," one yelled.

I looked over and saw the tallest of the kids had walked away from the other four. He was wearing jeans, and a jacket that was just a little too big. He had red hair, and his face was freckled. *It would have to be the tallest one that spotted me*, I thought seeing my doom coming like a runaway train. The tall ones were the worst, and this guy looked to be at least five and a half feet. When they set on you, it was like they were everywhere at once.

"Hey, kid," he yelled again.

It was no use. If I ran they would surely catch me. I knew from experience that it was worse if you made them chase you. Bullies hate putting out that extra effort. So, opting to take it like a man, I did what any man would do, I pointed to myself and said, "Who, me?"

"Yeah, you," the boy said rolling his eyes. "Who else am I talking to? C'mere."

"Why?" I asked stupidly.

"We need a sixth man. C'mon let's go."

Hesitantly, I walked over to where the boys stood. All were dressed like the tall one. All wearing ragged hand-me-downs, and here I come in my nice Catholic school uniform. I supposed they liked that. That would keep them from hitting each other by mistake.

Just go for the kid in the tie!

As I reached them, they all just looked at me like a dog wondering which part of the bone to tear up first. I pondered my prospects. They could either take my books and play keep-away with them and *then* pounce on me, or just start pounding from the git-go.

"Gimme your books," the tall one ordered holding out his hand.

Looked like keep-away was the game of choice.

Slowly, I handed my books over to him. Taking the bag, he ran away from us further into the park. He turned and held the bag up.

I guess it was time to chase them.

"Right here is the line," he exclaimed putting the bag down. "The sidewalk is the other one. Anything over them is out of bounds." He didn't actually say, "Out of bounds," it was actually,
"Out of balance," but we didn't realize there was a difference until we

were older.

After he was satisfied that we all understood, he ran back to us. "And from that tree,' he said pointing down into the park, "to that tree," he pointed to the other end of the park, "is the end zones. Got it?"

We all agreed.

I couldn't believe it! They actually wanted me to play! I was going to live!

"What's your name, kid?" the tall one asked.

For a moment, I just looked at him all stupid. The thought of being included had stolen my power of speech.

"Are you retarded?" the tall one asked honestly.

"I-I don't think so," I stammered.

Everyone laughed at that.

"Well then, what's your name," he asked again.

"S-Sammy," I finally got out.

"Sammy?" the heaviest one asked.

"Yeah," I nodded looking over to a husky kid with full face also covered in freckles. "My dad's Sam, so I'm Sammy."

"Oh, I get it," he nodded.

"That's Dave Brewster," the tall kid said pointing to the one I was talking to. "We just call him Bull. And this one," he said pointing to another kid, this one was lanky with blond hair, "is Micky Brockwell. We call him Bean, as in *string*. The one next to him," this one smaller with brown hair, and a bit heavier, "is his brother Adam, we call him Tag Along. And last we got," he pointed to another boy, this one with an elfish face, "is Terry McBride. But we all call him-."

"Don't say it, Billy," McBride warned, shaking his head.

"Lovverrrbooyyyy!" All the boys cooed then laughed.

"C'mon, guys, don't call me that," he whined.

"Amy Martin's got a real case for you, Loverboy," Bull said batting his eyelashes. "Oh, Terry, kiss me you mad, impetuous, fool you," he exclaimed in high-pitched voice.

"Ooooh," all the boys chorused as poor Terry's face turned red.

"Stop it," he pouted.

To this, the rest of them replied by making kissy noises.

"I'll go home," he warned.

"All right, guys," the tall one laughed. "Leave the little baby alone.

And I'm," he said putting a hand on his chest, "am Billy Merill. But everyone calls me Sailor."

"Why, Sailor," I asked.

"You'll see," he assured me.

"What about my nickname," I asked wanting to be part of the gang.

"You ain't got one, Sammeee," Bean taunted.

"All right, let's choose up. I'm captain for my team. Bull, you take the other side. Now, who wants Sammy?"

Everyone stood looking at me in silence. I was up to their shoulders, and I also knew from experience that the shortest kid never got picked for anything.

"Not me," Bull said shaking his head.

I thought I had made friends, but they didn't want me. I had now resigned myself to the fact that soon I would be a man.

A *short* man.

I suppose my disappointment showed, because Billy put a hand on my shoulder and smiled. "All right, you saps," he said. "I'll take Sammy and we're gonna whoop your *butts*."

I couldn't believe it, I was playing with the older guys, and the biggest one of all said that *we* were going to kick butt! What a day this was turning out to be!

Billy looked over to me and asked me what position I wanted to play, and I confidently replied Quarterback.

That caused a few raised eyebrows.

Billy shrugged and handed me the ball. "All right, Sammy, let's see what you can do with it."

When I went to take the ball, I noticed that Billy was wearing old olive-drab Army gloves with the fingers cut out. Gloves with the fingers cut out were so sharp to me then. I would have done it to my own, but the fear of my mother ending my life prevented me from actually carrying out the act.

But they were sharp just the same.

"All right, Sammy, I'm gonna go long, and you give it your best heave, okay," Billy nodded.

"Okay," I nodded back taking the ball and rolling it over in my hands.

Billy gave the others a doubtful look greeted with shrugs then squatted down into running position. "Ready, Sammy," he asked.

"Ready," I replied trying to grip the ball in my right hand.

"Hut one," he bellowed crouching lower. "Hut two! Twenty-three, Twenty-two, Twenty! Hut, hut!"

With that, he was off like a rocket, his legs moving so fast they were blurs beneath him. "Throw it, Sammy," he yelled as he ran.

I just watched him.

"Throw it," he yelled again.

"C'mon," Bull blurted. "Before he runs outta park to run in!"

I waited until he was almost to the end zone. I wasn't much for football. I was more of a baseball, kid, but this was Quarterbacking. And I knew one thing for sure. Even at my age, I had one helluvan arm.

I took two steps forward, then sent her as hard as I could into the sky. For a moment the ball wobbled in the air, then straightened into a smooth spiral.

"Son of a *bitch*," Billy yelled as he forced himself to speed up to meet the ball on its return to earth.

Wow, I thought. *Gloves with the fingers cut out, and he curses, too! What a guy!*

As the thought left my mind, I noticed something. The park was long, and had two paths leading into it, one from my street, and one from Rawle Street a block over.

And on the paths were benches, old wooden ones held together by iron struts and bolts. It was the bench on the Rawle Street path that Billy was heading smack into; his eyes on the ball going for the over-the-shoulder catch.

"Billy, look out!" everyone began to scream

But he wasn't listening. It was just that ball and him, and I could tell by his face that he was going to catch that thing even if he were headed toward a cliff. *Great,* I thought. *My first friend in the neighborhood, and I was going to get him creamed on a park bench*.

He was ten feet from the bench when he made one of the most perfect catches I had ever seen.

We watched as he turned and kept going toward that bench. I wanted to turn away, but I was ten, almost a man. And men don't turn away from disaster.

It was then I realized how he had gotten his nickname.

Without stopping, he lunged high over the bench in a belly-flopping dive, flew three feet across the cement path, five feet across the grass divide, and landed on the second path feet first running himself to a stop.

My jaw resting comfortably on the tips of my shoes, I watched him run in a circle whooping like a madman, holding the ball high in the air.

"The Sailor makes another grandstand play, and the crowd goes wild," he yelled as he ran back.

"Hey, Billy," Bull yelled as Merill reached us, "I changed my mind! I'll take Sammy!"

"Aw, naw," Sailor said shaking his head and tossing me the ball. "I gave you first dibs and you said no."

"I changed my mind," Bull contended.

"Too late," Billy said.

"But it ain't fair, you and him on the same side."

Another boost, I thought. I never had kids fighting over whose side I was on before. And to have it said that having me on a side was an unfair advantage made my chest stick out just a little bit.

Aw hell, it stuck out a *lot*.

"No, no," Sailor said putting his arm around my shoulder. "Sammy stays with me. Now, go on and we'll kick first, just to be fair."

"Yeah, like it would help," Terry grumbled.

"I'll tell you what," Billy said to Terry winking at me. "We'll let you go and get Amy Martin, how's that?"

"Shut *up*," Loverboy pouted angrily, stomping down to the other end of the field.

Sides soon where chosen and we took off our coats and got ready for some serious ball playing.

As the other guys readied to receive the kick, Billy squatted on my right, and Bean readied on my left. I rolled the ball over in my hands one more time.

"Shotgun," Billy said looking over to me.

"What." I asked, looking at him like a dummy.

"Shotgun Sam," He said with a nod.

I swear I grew six inches when he called me that. Not only did I have new friends, I had a nickname.

A neat one at that!

"Well, come on, Shotgun," Billy said, breaking me from my trance.

"Let's give 'em what for."

The game was tackle football, and we played for two hours until Bull finally gave up. We beat them by almost thirty points, and that made for some severe razzing when it was all over.

"Maybe we *shoulda* got Amy Martin," Bull said sarcastically as he shot an accusing eye over to Terry, who had succeeded in dropping four passes.

"I hate you guys," he whined in return.

"Aw, but we *love you*," Billy said all lovey-dovey like. "Kissy kissy, woo woo!"

Then everyone, including myself, made kissy noises.

"Pissants," Terry grumbled folding his arms and jutting out his lip.

That just made it worse. We all broke out laughing, causing Loverboy's face to redden more than it already had.

"Hey, I hope you don't get into trouble," Billy said to me.

I didn't understand what he was talking about, until I followed his gaze down to my shirt. It was covered in mud and grass stains, my tie as no longer a blue plaid, but a solid brown. Aw man, was I gonna be in dutch with my mom when I got home. But I played it cool. After all, I was ten-years old. "Naw," I said fighting the sinking feeling inside. "I'll be okay."

Once again, I was meat.

Why am I telling you all this? Well, the guys are part of the story. They, Billy in particular, played a role in my meeting the witch. Yeah, I know, a witch on Christmas? Just bear with me, and I'll tell you how I met the woman all the kids knew as the Wicked Witch of Knorr Street.

Picking up my bag, I walked with the other guys over to Keystone Street, which ran the length of the park. "Hey, where do you live, Sammy? Tomorrow's Saturday, and we play football all day. We could come knock for ya'," Billy said as we crossed Keystone.

"I live right here on Knorr," I said pointing to the second house off the corner.

All the guys looked at each other.

"What?" I asked looking at them.

"You meet the witch yet?" Billy asked.

"Witch?" I asked. "What witch?"

"C'mere," Billy waved me on to the corner of Keystone and Knorr.

We followed him to the corner, he pointed to the house on the opposite end of the street. The house was brown with an overgrown yard. All the shades were drawn. "She lives in there," Billy whispered as though somehow he would be heard. "Never comes out in the day, only at night. Has a black cat too. They say a kid went in there once and never came back out again."

"Ate 'im up," Bull nodded. "Cooked 'im in a pot and ate 'im like stew."

"Nuh-uh," I said, certain they were pulling my leg.

"It's true," Bean whispered. "Every kid around here knows to stay away from that house."

"Why are we whispering?" I asked.

"So's she don't hear us, that's why," Tag Along answered like I was a stupe for asking.

"But she's allaway down there," I said.

"Don't make no difference," Billy said.

As the words left his mouth, we heard a high snarl behind us. Turning we saw a black cat shoot from under a parked car and up Knorr towards the house on the corner.

"It's her cat," Bull screamed. "Run!"

Then we all screamed and shot off to our respective houses. Billy was right, she heard us. I knew about witches from Hansel and Gretel, so I knew that they came out at Halloween, and they ate little kids, and they always had black cats, and if they wanted to, they could turn into cats themselves.

Out of all the houses we could have moved into, we had to pick the one down the street from a witch.

Is that bad luck, or what?

I ran as fast as I could back down towards Rawle, and into the alley that divided the two sides of the block. I darted to my back gate, almost knocking myself over trying to get through it with the lock still on, and into my back door. I slammed the heavy wooden door behind me, and breathed a sigh of relief.

Ah, safe.

"Daddy, is that you," my little sister yelled from the living room.

My little sister, Tilly, was a cute little thing. She had platinum hair like my mom, kept it in a long ponytail, and always wore dresses with white socks and black strap-over shoes. She looked like a little doll.

Now that I'm older I can say that, but back then she was a Wombat. A lousy whining, tattle-telling little Wombat. A true thorn that God saw fit to plant right into my side.

It was too late. I could hear her running through the dining room into the kitchen. Nowhere to hide, I just gave up and readied myself for the worst. Tilly ran into the kitchen clutching onto her favorite doll, an ugly worn-out thing named Sophie.

Sophie: Daughter of the Wombat.

Tilly's jaw dropped when she saw my uniform and, as she drew in breath, I could hear my mother scolding me. *How humiliating*, I thought dismally. *Almost a man, and I'm gonna get a scolding by my mom*. And, sure enough, the Wombat didn't disappoint me.

"Mom," she screamed as though she had found a severed head on our counter right between the container of sugar and the box of *Bon Ami*. "Come see Sammy! OOOOH! He's all messy!"

I heard my mother coming down the steps from the second floor, and waited for the inevitable. And as I did so, I looked back to the Wombat, who now wore her 'Ah-ha, are you gonna get it' face. My mother had a way of yellin' that made you want to shrink right into the woodwork, but not until *after* she allowed you to go.

My mother walked from the dining room into the kitchen dressed in her favorite white dress with little yellow flowers on it. Her eyes widened along with her mouth as she put her hands up to her cheeks. "Good heavens, Sammy, what happened to your good school clothes?"

Tilly looked over to me with a smile, waiting for the blood to flow.

"I," I stammered again. "I was playing football with some friends, and I guess I got a little dirty."

"Friends," my mother asked, her voice surprisingly light.

"Yeah," I replied still not knowing why the storm hadn't arrived yet. I watched her put her hands on her hips and look me up and down, anger showing on her face. Doom had once again entered my life. The worst kind of doom there was.

Tilly's grin grew wider as she looked from my mother to me.

My heart began to pound.

I looked at Tilly, who in turn gave me that same smug expression she had when she called our
mother. She knew what was coming. I was about to suffer . . .

The Wrath of Mom!

I looked back to my mother and waited. No last meal. No final prayer. It was all going to end on the linoleum in the kitchen.

Then my mother shook her head and smiled wearily. "What am I going to do with you, Sammy," she asked with a light laugh. My mom had the sweetest laugh you'd ever want to hear. It was like music, and whenever she laughed, everyone around her would have to smile at the sound of it.

"You're not gonna yell at me," I asked seeing a light at the end of the tunnel.

"Yeah," my sister demanded. "You're not gonna yell at him, mom?"

"No," she answered shaking her head. "I *should*, but I think we can let it go this time."

"But, mom-," Tilly whined tugging on my mother's skirt.

"You shush now, Tilly," my mother said sternly looking down at her. "Go on and play."

Tilly eyed me.

I eyed her.

The Wombat had been denied its kill.

I would live.

Sammy One, The Wombat Zip!

"Well, go on," my mother shooed her.

Tilly and Sophie stomped away with a disappointed groan leaving my mother and I alone.

"So," my mother said walking to me and kneeling down so that we were eye-to-eye, "You made some friends today, huh?"

"Uh-huh," I began my mouth running faster than my brain as I tried to explain. "A bunch o' fellas asked me if I wanted to play with them, and I did, and that's why I'm dirty, and late, and-
and-."

"I'm glad," she said brushing my mussed hair back off my forehead. "I was beginning to worry about you. You've been here a month and you've never mentioned anything about friends."

"'Cause I didn't have any."

"I know," my mother said in the kind of sympathetic voice that always makes a kid feel warm all over. "Are they nice boys?"

"Yeah," I nodded, happy that the subject had changed. "They're good guys."

"Good," my mother smiled again. "But do your mom a favor next time, will ya', Sammy?"

"Sure," I said. "Anything, mom."

"Next time you play in the park with your friends, come home and *change first*."

"Okay, mom."

"And, Sammy . . .?"

"Yeah, mom?"

"Next time you play in the park," she said giving a gentle tug on my mud-soaked tie. "Leave the park *there* when you come home. Okay?"

"Okay, mom," I nodded with a smile.

"Okay," she grinned ruffling my hair as she stood. "I want you to go get those clothes of right now, and bring them down for me to soak. And don't *dawdle,* I don't want that stuff to dry in any more than it already has."

I ran from the kitchen into the dining room and up the stairs that separated the living room from the dining room. I stopped mid-way up and looked down into the living room where my sister and her ugly little doll where sipping make-believe tea from little plastic cups.

"Hey, Tilly," I called in a hushed voice.

She looked up at me.

"Tonight, when you're asleep, I'm gonna tell the thing under your bed to eat you."

"What thing," she asked in her prissy tone.

"You'll see," I said with a malicious smile. The best part of being a big brother was that you got a blank check to pick on your younger, stupider, siblings.

Sometimes life is good.

"There's *nothing* under my bed, *Sammy*," she said shakily.

"Oh," I explained, "you can't see it . . .but it can *see you*."

"Mom!"

"Up*stairs*, Sammy," my mother yelled from the kitchen.

"Yes, mom," I yelled, giving the horrified Wombat and her ugly little doll one last smirk before I left.

I ran to the third floor and into my bedroom, slipped out of my uniform, and threw on a pair of jeans and sneakers. My bedroom was in the front facing Knorr Street. I looked at the window, and couldn't help myself.

Walking to the window, I looked down the street to the house with the overgrown yard and the drawn yellowed shades. After a few moments of unadulterated staring, my eye caught the black cat running from beneath an old pick-up truck and up the steps onto the porch of the house. I jumped back and pulled down the shade hoping that the cat hadn't seen me.

Witches are tricky. They don't come right after ya'. Oh, no, they wait on ya'. They wait on ya', then when you least expect it, you're in a big pot with potatoes an' carrots. Yeah, they're tricky all right.

In the distance, I heard the clank of our backyard gate closing. I looked over to my wind-up clock and saw that it was five o'clock. And right at five my dad would come home.

I ran to the small landing at the top of the steps. From there I heard the large wooden door open and the, deep, booming, voice of my father as he greeted my mother and the Wombat.

I ran down to meet him.

We all had heroes growing up; everyone had someone different. Some of the guys liked Jimmy Cagney, some liked Bogart and John Wayne, but not me.

No, my hero never walked across the Silver Screen.

My hero never wore a tuxedo. My hero never even got his picture in the papers. But I was luckier than my friends. You see, my friends would have to go pay money to see *their* heroes, and all I had to do was go home. . .

Because my hero was my dad.

I ran down to the first floor and found my dad in the dining room sliding his worn brown suede coat over the back of one of the dining room chairs. He was a big man, my dad. He was as tall as the ceiling, and his arms were big as tree stumps, and his shoulders went for a mile in each direction. Sometimes in the summer, he would just walk around in a tee-shirt, and I'd say, "Dad, make your veins stick out."

He'd laugh, lean over so his bicep was right in front of my face, then he'd make a fist and curl that forearm up. His muscle would grow so big it looked like it was gonna pop right out of him. Then I'd put my hand on it, and it was like rock.

And I knew that, when I was a man, I would have muscles like that, too.

My dad was dressed in his work clothes; a green work shirt and pants, and scuffed up black shoes.

And on his head sat his big wide-brimmed brown Fedora.

That was a magic hat, I'm tellin' ya'. When my dad wore it to work, it looked just as ratty as his coat did, but on Sunday when we all went to church, he would brush it off, and comb it with the lint brush, and when he dressed in his suit and put that hat on, it looked like the crown of a king.

And I knew that, when I was a man, I would have a hat like that too.

"Hey there, Sammy," he said with a smile as he took off his hat and laid it on the dining room table, "Whaddaya know, whaddaya say, son?"

"Hey, dad," I said walking over to him. "How's work today?"

"Hard and heavy," he replied pulling a pack of cigarettes from his pocket.

"But you can handle it, huh, dad," I said confidently.

"Your dad can handle anything they wanna dish out, Sammy boy," he said with a wink and a
smile as he slid a cigarette into his mouth.

"Yeah," I smiled.

"Yeah," he laughed pulling me into a bear hug and ruffling my hair.

"Daddy," Tilly called pulling his pant leg.

My dad let me go and looked down at her. "And how's my girl today," he asked.

"Pick me up," she said putting Sophie on the table and holding her arms up.

My dad took the cigarette out of his mouth, laid it on the table, rolled up his right shirt-sleeve and held his hand just above my sister's head. "Go on, Tilly Girl, hop on," he winked again.

My sister's face brightened as she took his hand with both of hers. Slowly my dad lifted her off the floor. She screamed and giggled all the way until they were looking each other dead in the eye. "Hold on," he warned.

"Okay," she nodded.

"Ready?"

"Uh-huh,"

My dad yelled, "Whoa," and Tilly screamed again as he swung her around and threw her onto his back. Tilly immediately wrapped her legs around his waist and her arms around his neck. "You on," my dad asked turning his head to the left where Tilly had laid her head on his shoulder.

"Uh-huh," she answered.

"Who's my little girl?"

"I am?"

"*Who's* my little girl," he asked again with a smile.

"I am!" Tilly yelled happily.

"Good," my dad nodded. "And who's my number one boy!"

"I am," I yelled just as happily.

My dad turned to my mother, who was leaning against the side of the doorway leading into the kitchen smiling at the commotion that always greeted my dad when he came through the door after work. "Now, let's go see my *other girl*."

My mom laughed as he trotted over with my sister bouncing on his back and me close behind.

"Did I ever tell you how I met you mother, kids," he asked smiling at my mom.

Tilly and I shook our heads.

"Well," my dad began never taking his eyes off my mother. "When I was back in Reading, there were a lot of pretty girls there. A lot of them. And one day the most beautiful girl in Reading came walking down the street, and I saw her and she saw me. And, I mean, she was *beautiful*."

My mother smiled and looked at the floor.

"And one day," my dad continued. "This beautiful girl comes over and says hello, and we get to talkin', see? And she says, 'When are you gonna ask me to marry you, Sam Hatcher?' And I say, 'Never.' And she says, 'But I'm the most beautiful girl in town.'

My mother looked at him a bit confused.

My dad went on taking no notice. "And I said, 'I don't want to marry the most beautiful girl in town, I wanted to marry your mother."

Then *we* looked at him confused, and my mother's mouth fell open.

My dad walked right up to her until their noses were almost touching. "Because," he finished with a smile, "if I couldn't have gorgeous, I wasn't gettin' married at all."

My mother's eyes widened. She had the prettiest blue eyes, my mom. And her face turned red.

"How's my big girl today," my dad asked kissing her on the tip of her nose.

"Busy," she answered tiredly.

"Come on, give us a kiss," my dad said.

"Sam," my mom said shocked. "The *children*."

"Yeah, I noticed 'em too," my dad said then kissed her anyway.

It wasn't no little one either, it was one o' them *movie kisses*.

That succeeded in a long 'Ooooooh," from my sister and I.

My parents laughed, and my dad said, "Uh-oh, we've been caught!"

It was Friday night, and on Friday nights, my dad took us all to Linton's Diner for dinner. It was our one big night out a week. My mother would get dressed up, and I would watch my dad at the sink shaving off his five o'clock shadow so when I had to shave I would know how to do it.

Then he would slap some aftershave on both our faces and we'd all pile into the car.

Linton's diner was one of the better-sized diners. Next to Horn and Hardardts it was one of the biggest in the neighborhood. As you walked in, there were booths lining the right hand wall, and the back, and on the left was the counter.

My dad walked us down the aisle between the counter and the booths stopping to say hello and introduce us to a few men he knew from work, then we sat down at a booth in the back. The booths were almost all filled that Friday night with other families out for the evening.

The booths were where the parents sat with their kids, and the counter was where the truckers and the factory men sat and talked sports or politics, and other men stuff.

We had wonderful times in that place, my family and I.

Why am I telling you all this? You'll see.

Hope you're not getting bored.

Let me jump ahead now.

Let me jump ahead to December of 1948.

That was the month I was as rich as a king.

Then poor as a pauper.

And that was the month I came face to face with the Witch.

2

It was a cold one, that December, but that didn't stop me from doing my job. What was my job? Well, I'll tell ya'. A year ago, when I was just a kid, not nearly as close to being a man as I am now, my dad took me over Pottstown with him. And while I was there, I saw this kid shining shoes on the corner.

And he was making some pretty decent dough at it, too.

So, when I got home, I told my dad about it, and asked him if I could have a shoeshine box of my own. He looked at me over his paper with one eyebrow cocked. "Your own shoeshine box," he asked.

"Yeah," I answered.

A smile ran across his face as he laid his paper on his lap.

"What's wrong, dad," I asked not understanding why he was smiling.

"Guess 'cause you're growin' up faster than I thought," he answered. "Want some moolah of your own, eh Sammy."

"Yeah," I said thinking about what I could do with all those nickels.

"I'll see what I can do for ya, how's that?"

"Thanks, dad."

And that Saturday, my dad went down into the basement and took some old wood, and built me one. It was a real beauty too. It was a deep box, deep enough to hold rags and polish and a couple of brushes.

The lid had a flip-up lock on each side, and bolted to the lid was the stand my dad had made out of an old sewing machine pedal. And let me tell you, it was fancier than the one that kid from Pottstown had. And when I was done for the day, I just flipped the lid over and there was a handle on the other side so I could pick the whole thing up and carry it home.

After my dad finished it, he painted it red, using yellow paint left over from doing my grandpa's shutters, he painted *Sammy's Shoeshine Co. 5¢* on the side. It was the most beautiful thing I've ever seen.

I was gonna be a gazillionaire by next year.

For the first two weeks, I sat on the corner every day after school, and after a month, I had made fifty cents. It turned out that there was another shoes shiner at the Reading train station, and all the men went to him.

My dreams of being a gazillionaire were fading.

One night we, me, my family and my grandma and grandpa were sitting at the dinner table when my dad asked how my shoe shining was going.

I sat there playing dismally with my vegetables and told him that all the men were going to another shoe shiner at the train station and hardly anyone was coming to me.

My dad thought about it for a moment then told me to stop playing with my food, and after dinner we were going to the train station.

My mother asked why, and my grandfather looked over to my dad with a grin. "Goin' back to the enemy camp, eh, son?"

"Gotta know what they're up to, pop," my dad said with a wink.

Both of them laugh.

After dinner, my father and I got on our coats, he slipped on his Fedora, and out to the car we went. My dad didn't say anything the whole drive there, not even when I asked him why we were going. Then I wondered what my grandfather meant by 'enemy camp'.

My dad wasn't gonna *shoot him,* was he?

The Reading train station was just a small one with an outside platform, which was now filled with people waiting for the train into the city. My dad and I walked up onto the platform, and into the station house.

Wooden benches lined the wall, and at the end closest to the door were the ticket booths. And in the far corner sat the shoeshine boy, his Jeff hat on backwards, his knickers stained with polish.

My dad and I walked up to him as he finished a customer, and my dad said, "How much, son?"

"Two bits, sir," the kid replied.

"Square deal," my dad agreed putting his foot on the wooden stand of the box.

I'll tell ya', I've never seen a rag fly so fast. It was a blur over my dad's shoe, and after the kid finished my dad's other shoe, he sent that rag cracking like a whip onto its tip, looked up and said, "Done."

My dad looked over the shoes and nodded. "Fine job, son. Fine job." He pulled out a quarter and handed it over. Giving the shoes another look, he reached into his pocket, pulled out a dime, and rested it on his thumb. "For you," he said flipping it into the air.

The kid snatched it out of the air with his hand and it immediately disappeared into his pocket.

"Thank you, sir," he said with a nod.

Then, without a word, my dad and I left.

When we got home, my dad sat at the kitchen table, and I sat next to him just as disheartened as when we left.

"How was your trip," my mother asked setting a cup of coffee in front of my dad.

My dad didn't answer; he just stared straight ahead drinking his coffee. He set the cup down, put a cigarette in his mouth, took a drag then blew out the smoke. "Go and get your box, Sammy," he said finally.

I slid off my chair, ran to my room, got my box and brought it back to my kitchen.

In the living room, I could hear my grandfather turn on the radio, and familiar music began to play. I knew I was in low spirits then. It was time for Edgar Bergen and Charlie McCarthy, and I didn't even feel like listening to it. He was my favorite, but I liked Mortimer better than Charlie. But I don't even think Mortimer could have cheered me up then.

My mom, grandma, and Tilly, who had not yet reached full Wombathood but was getting there, were in the living room now, leaving just my dad and I in the kitchen.

"Set 'er up, Sammy," my dad said drinking his coffee.

I set up my box on the linoleum, and pulled out my rags and polish.

"He did a real fine job on these," my dad said looking over his shoes, which only made me feel worse. "But they're not A-1. Understand?"

"A-1, dad," I asked. "What's A-1?"

"A-1 is what ya' wear when you have a weekend pass and you're headed to town," he said looking up, a smile covering his face.

I followed his gaze to where my mother now stood watching us.

"Or if its Friday night and your callin' on your best girl."

That made my mom smile and leave.

"What now, dad," I asked turning back to him.

"Hold on, Sammy. Hey, pop," he yelled into the living room.

"Yeah!"

"Where're your Sunday shoes?"

The mention of touching my grandpa's Sunday shoes got his immediate attention. I could hear him get up and make his way out to the kitchen. "And what do you want with my Sunday shoes?"

"Sammy's gonna shine 'em," my dad said.

"He *is*?"

"I *am*?" I asked feeling a squadron of butterflies dart around in my belly.

"You *are*," my dad said with a confident nod.

"I am," I told my grandpa halfheartedly.

My grandpa looked at me for a moment then stuck a thumb over his shoulder. "Well, you know where they are, Sammy. Go fetch 'em."

You see, many of you may be too young to remember exactly what Sunday shoes were. Sunday shoes were not regular shoes, no sirree. Sunday shoes were for church and special occasions *only*. They were fancy shoes. They either had buckles, or fancy laces that never seemed to soften because they were only worn once a week.

Sunday shoes cost money, and were not to be trifled with.

My grandpa's especially. His were black with a strap across the top held down by a shiny gold buckle. He only wore them to church, the rest of the time they sat in the bottom of his closet wrapped in cloth, in the same box they came in. Real careful with his Sunday shoes, my grandpa was. And I had to shine them.

My life passed before my eyes.

I ran into my grandparent's room, a room that was off-limits to us kids anyway, and got the box with my grandpa's shoes. *Don't pull a snafu on this one, Sammy*, I thought as I brought the box back down to my father.

I ran into the kitchen where my dad and grandpa were talking over coffee and laid the box on the table.

My grandpa stood up with his coffee and walked to the doorway leading to the living room.

"Well, I'll let you boys get to work. I'm missing my Edgar Bergen."

"Call ya when they're done, pop," my dad said lighting another cigarette.

"You do that," my grandpa said leaving.

My dad went to the sink, filled a glass with water then sat back down. "Go on and put a shoe up there, Sammy."

I opened the box and picked up a shoe like it was made of fine crystal. Gently, I set it on the stand and waited for my dad to tell me what to do next.

"Now get your rag, and let me see how it's done," my dad said.

With dad kneeling over me telling me what to do, I worked and worked on those shoes, and I didn't stop until my dad *told me* to stop.

"Hey, pop," my dad called into the living room.

My grandpa came out and I handed him his shoes. He looked them over once then looked them over twice then he looked at me. "Well, I won't be walking through the church doors with these come Sunday," he said flatly.

My heart sank.

They were my grandpa's Sunday shoes, and I had botched them. My life was over. I was a failure at nine.

"Oh, no," my grandpa went on. "I'll be *high-steppin'* come *this* Sunday!"

"Really," I asked with a pounding heart.

"You betcha, m'boy," he exclaimed looking over his shoes, only now he was smiling.

I knew that whenever my grandpa called me 'm'boy', I had made him proud. I could feel the buttons getting ready to pop off my shirt. "I polished them myself," I said proudly.

"You did?" my grandpa asked looking over to my dad.

"All by himself, pop," my dad confirmed.

"Well, then," grandpa said digging into his pocket. "How much do I owe ya'?"

"A nick-," I began, but my dad cut me off.

"A *dime*," he said.

A *dime,* I thought. *Wow! A dime for one pair of shoes?* Now there was some serious money! But was it worth a dime?

Grandpa pulled out a dime and handed it to me. I took it with amazement, but that amazement paled compared to what came next.

"Sammy," grandpa said.

"Yes, grandpa?"

"From now on, every Saturday whether they need it or not, I want you to go upstairs and shine these shoes for church on Sunday, and I'll leave a dime out for ya' in the morning."

"Yes, sir, grandpa!" I couldn't believe it! I was actually in charge of shining my grandpa's Sunday shoes.

What a job!

As for my shoe shining business, well, it boomed like you wouldn't believe. Yeah, the kid at the train station was good, but my dad showed me a better way. The trick was to put on a layer of polish, then a layer of water, and keep doing it until the shoes shined like mirrors. And I always made sure they did.

And once word got around town that yours truly could pull off an A-1

Spit Shine, and do it for a dime, I had lines waiting for me. And since I was fifteen cents cheaper than the kid at the train station, it was nothing to get my dime, and another nickel on top of that!

I was rich!

One Saturday afternoon, I saw that kid on the street while I was working. He was with his parents. If looks could kill, I'd've been dead a thousand times over. By the looks of their clothes, they didn't have much money, and looking back, I'm sure that kid never got to keep what he made shining those shoes.

I felt bad for taking away his business. Yeah, I wanted money, but not that way. But before I knew it, we were on our way to Philadelphia. Before I left, I told my dad about the kid in the train station, and I asked him if he would take me there before we left.

So the day before we left for Philly, my dad drove me and my shoeshine box to the train station. We walked inside, and I immediately caught a glimpse of the kid in the corner sitting on his crate, his rag flying in his hands as a well-dressed gentlemen looked down at him patiently.

After the man left, I walked over to him.

"How's it goin'?" I asked him.

"Oh, it's *you,*" he huffed pulling out a fresh rag. "Whaddaya want?"

I set my box down beside him on the crate.

"You ever hear of an A-1 shine," I asked.

"A what," he asked looking at me like I was speaking Latin.

He was good just like my dad said, and before I left, he had the spit shine down to an art form. In return for showing him my little trick, he showed me his.

The trick to cracking a rag when you shine.

He told me, to wind it up three or four times, then snap it with a flick of the wrist. And most importantly he pointed out to me was never hit the shoe with the used end. Always use the soft, finishing end so as not to scuff the surface.

He was a real pro.

Now, here I was in Philadelphia with my shine box at the bank on the corner of Tulip and Longshore Streets. It took a while to get customers because, unlike Reading, shoe shining was not a rare trade here. It seemed like every kid had a shine box.

And to make things worse, I had to take Tilly with me while I worked.

She'd sit there with her ugly little doll and pester me to no end while I worked. Then to top it all off, sometimes a customer would give her a nickel for nothing.

For *nothing!*

One Thursday, as the sun was setting and the winter's first snow was beginning, I was packing up my box while Tilly yammered endlessly in my ear about how cold it was when Russ Parker and his crew came walking down Longshore from Torresdale Avenue, Tacony's main strip of stores.

Russ and his cronies were bad news all right.

He and his friends were in the same school as me, and were two grades ahead. I spotted Russ's swagger halfway down the block and immediately began to pack my stuff faster.

Knorr Street was one block over. I knew if I had to, I could outrun them even if I did have to drag Tilly and her ugly doll with me.

I hitched the lid on and told Tilly we had to move it. She hemmed and hawed like she always did, and before I knew it Russ and his boys were at the corner.

"Hey, Hatcher," he yelled over in a voice that always made my blood run cold.

"Y-yeah," I asked knowing where the conversation was leading.

"Hey look, boys," Russ said to his friends. "Little Sammy has a shoeshine box."

They all laughed at me.

"Lemme see it," Russ said holding out his hand.

"N-no," I mumbled.

"What," he asked putting his hand up behind his ear and leaning in closer. "What did you say, runt?"

"I said no," I repeated not knowing why my mouth was insisting on getting me into hot water.

"Yeah," Tilly said indignantly stepping in between us. "Are you *deaf*!"

I began to pray for the both of us.

"You leave us a*lone*," Till yelled in mom-like fashion.

"Outta the way, shorty," Russ grunted. He took his right hand and shoved Tilly onto the ground.

I looked down at my little sister who lay there crying, still holding onto her ugly little doll then I looked at Russ who stared at me like I was dinner. Yes, he was bigger than me. Yes, he was stronger than me. Yes, he could break me in two without really trying.

But all that didn't matter now . . .

'Cause *nobody* hit the Wombat but *me*.

I closed my eyes and swung as hard as I could. I felt my hand hit something hard and the pain was unbelievable. When I opened my eyes Russ was on the ground with a bloody nose. Yeah, I guess he didn't realize I was almost a man. Rage covered his face as he stood up.

I had knocked him down in front of his friends, and that just wasn't done to Russ.

I was gonna die.

"Fight, fight, get 'im," his buddies yelled.

Before I knew it, Russ was charging. He hit me square in the chest and we both went down. He punched me in the face, then in the chest. My mouth bleeding, my breathing next to nothing, I socked him square in the jaw. And to my surprise, he fell back off of me.

I was trying to get up when I saw he was taking three steps back. I knew what a drop kick looked like, and old Russ was winding up for a doozie. "Let's see how tough ya' are with a few busted ribs, runt," he hissed.

Russ broke into a run and hauled off with his right foot.

A scream filled the air, and before I knew it, Sailor was flying over me just like he had done with that bench. He body-tackled Russ and drove him right into the cement, and that was when I found out something about Sailor I'd never known.

He was a great guy and he'd do anything for you, even give ya' the shirt right off his back. But when he was fighting, he was fighting like nobody's business.

He hammered on Russ like he was driving in a nail with his fist.

I stood up and turned to see Bull, Bean, Tag Along and Loverboy running up the sidewalk from
Keystone Street.

"You're meat," Bull yelled. "Especially *you,* Baxter!" I turned back to Russ' friends. One of them was shaking his head and in seconds he was off and running down the block.

And right behind him went the rest of Russ' friends.

Billy pulled Russ to his feet, and threw him back. "You want some more, Russ," Billy asked with his dukes up fully prepared to give it to him.

Russ looked over to me, "I'll see *you* in school, runt!"

"Yeah," Billy warned, "and *I'll* see you right *after*, *Ruuussseeelll*."

"Yeah, and you better watch yourself, Merill," Russell blurted.

"Get on back to your side of the avenue, 'fore I whup ya' s'more," Billy replied.

Russ looked around and saw that his friends had gone, and that took a lot of cockiness out of him. He swiped the blood off his lip and ran back down Longshore.

"Thanks," I said as Billy walked over to me.

"Ah," he said shrugging it off. "Nobody hits Shotgun Sam and gets away with it, right guys!"

"Yeah," they all agreed.

That was when I heard the crying.

Billy walked over to Tilly who sat on that cold cement in her nice little dress, tears running down her face and knelt down in front of her. "Tilly, right," he asked.

"Uh-huh," she sniffled.

"My name's Billy. Are you hurt?"

"A little."

Billy looked her over then smiled. "Ah," he said, "don't look so bad."

"And *Sophie,"* Tilly said shoving that ugly little doll into Billy's face.

Billy took the doll, looked it over then handed it back. "Sophie looks okay too. Come on," he said taking her hand. "Let me help you up."

Yeah, I remembered that first day when I came into the house all muddied up and told my mom that I had met some good guys. But until now, I didn't know how true that was.

The guys walked back to my house with Tilly and I, and we all made sure to cross the street when passing the witch's house. We couldn't help but look over. All the shades were still drawn, and unlike all the other houses, no lights were on inside.

The guys walked us to the front gate of our house, and I told them I would be out after dinner to throw the ball around. Tilly walked up to Billy and waved him closer. Billy knelt down, and that's when the Wombat struck. That's when my sister did the most embarrassing thing to me she'd ever done.

She kissed him on the cheek.

And of course all the guys went "Oooooooh!"

How humiliating.

Billy stood up not saying a word, although his face was a bit red. But what do you want? He'd just been kissed by a girl for cryin' out loud.

Yeeeeecccckkk!

"Looks like we got another loverboy," Bull joked.

"Shut up, ya' mug," Billy said holding a fist up to his face.

Bull took the hint and decided to end the razzing right there.

I told the guys I'd see them in a half hour, but I wolfed down my pot roast and made it in fifteen.

The snow fell hard as we played rough-touch football on Knorr Street, using telephone poles as End-Zone markers. For an hour and a half we laughed, yelled, and slammed each other as hard as we could into parked cars. If you were real good, you could slam a guy head first into a car door hard enough so he'd have to lie there for a while.

Ah, childhood.

After the game, which turned into street-tackle after the snow had deepened enough, we decided to have a snowball fight. It was great! I got hit in the head so hard with an ice ball that my vision blurred for ten whole minutes!

And my ears popped too!

We ended up at the corner, all of us hiding behind cars, chucking snowballs as fast as we could make them. I got brave and ran out into the street, and heaved one at Billy catching him in the back.

"Aw, you're dead now, Sammy," he laughed picking up and balling another clump of snow.

Billy wound up and threw it right at my head. I ducked and could hear it whiz over me. Then I heard the slam of sheet metal. I turned to see it had hit the witch's door smack in the center of the metal part under the glass.

We all froze in terror.

No lights turned on, but the inside door opened. The reflection of the streetlights on the glass of the storm door obscured her face, but her voice was raspy. "Hey, you kids, get outta here!" She screeched.

"Ah, stow it, ya' old witch," Billy yelled.

"Yeah, ya' old witch," I chimed in feeling my oats.

The storm door began to open. She was coming to get us!

We all screamed and ran like our lives depended on it back to our houses. I bolted up onto my porch, threw open my door and dashed inside slamming it behind me.

"That you, Sammy," my dad yelled from the kitchen.

"Yeah, dad," I yelled shooting up the steps and into my room.

I looked out the window and could see her silhouette in her front yard. She was out! She was out and coming to get us! I jumped into my bed and threw the covers over my head. It seems odd, but as a kid I always did that when I thought the monsters were coming to get me. I always pulled my blanket up over my head, like for some reason that would stop them. Silver bullets . . .Hah! A wooden stake . . .Hah! A crucifix . . .Hah! A wool blanket . . .No!

Getting to sleep that night wasn't easy. It was my first encounter with the witch, and she had seen me. I was a goner for sure. That was the first time I met the witch.

Now, let me tell ya' about the second.

3

December 14th was freezing, but all of us, the Wombat included, went up to Torresdale Avenue to sneak a peak into Woolworth's window to see what kind of toys they had. Yeah, soon Christmas would be here, and the house would smell like turkey, and my mom would make cookies and cakes.

It was a good time but, and I know it sounds funny, not my most-favorite time, but I'll get to that later.

"Whadja ask for for Christmas, Sammy," Bull asked as we walked from Woolworth's, which was at the Longshore-Torresdale intersection down the avenue to Knorr.

"Nothin' much," I shrugged. Like I said, I was ten, almost a man, and sad but true, I had already figured out who Santa Claus was, and right now Santa Claus had just gotten a new job and had to put clothes on our backs. So whenever Santa would ask me what I wanted for Christmas, I'd just shrug.

But not Tilly.

Oh, no, Tilly had a list a mile long, and if Santa had brought her everything she wanted, we'd need another house to fit it all.

"I asked Santa for a doll house," Tilly said walking beside us.

"What," Bull said. "There ain't no Santa, stupid."

Billy whacked him in the chest and gave him a hard look. Bull looked at him confused then looked down at Tilly who looked up at him with wide eyes.

"I-uh," Bull fumbled.

"Don't pay him no mind, Tilly," Billy said. "He just gets stupid sometimes."

"Uh, yeah," Bull agreed looking warily over to Billy. "I just go all stupid is all. I didn't know what I was sayin'. Must be the cold."

"Yeah," Billy agreed. "Musta frozen your brains."

"Yeah, frozen my brains."

"Anyway," Billy said, looking down at my sister who still had a shocked look on her face, "what did you ask Santa for?"

We all looked at her, especially Bull, who knew that if his little slip of the tongue blew it for my sister, he'd be in trouble with Billy deep.

For a moment, Billy and my sister looked at each other, then she smiled. I suppose she thought that if Billy, who by now had become her hero, believed in Santa Claus then he must be real. "I asked Santa for a doll house, and a new dress, and clothes for Sophie, and . . ."

And blah blah blah all the way home.

Later that evening, we played ball, and after all the guys left for dinner, I thanked Billy for making pretend for my sister. She may be a Wombat, but she's still my sister, y'know?

Billy told me it was no problem.

That night, I found out that Billy, the oldest of five kids, lived in a house on Keystone between Longshore and Disston. His 'old man' as he referred to his father had two problems. One was the inability to hold onto a job, and the other was the bottle.

Standing at the gate leading to my front yard, we both stood there in our soaked-through shoes talking. "My old man," he said rolling his tattered football back and forth in his hands. "He's sick, y'know? A real boozer. I remember when I was about your sister's age, my old man took all our Christmas money to the bar."

"Christmas morning I got up and looked under the tree and there wasn't nothin' there. I told my old man Santa musta missed me, and my old man got up and looked at me with his eyes all red and said, 'That's 'cause there ain't no Santa. Never was. And the sooner you get that into your head, the better off you'll be. Now leave me the hell alone.'

"I don't know, Sammy," Billy said quietly. "It's like when I found that out, I wasn't no kid anymore, y'know? I know it sounds corny, but it was like when the belief in Santa Claus left, it took something with it, y'know? Something inside. I mean, what's wrong with believing, right?"

"Right," I nodded. And that's why I suppose Billy and I were such good friends. It wasn't like the other guys weren't good friends, but Billy and I could always talk about serious stuff without the fear of being razzed about it.

We were buddies.

Billy looked down at the football, whose bladder was threatening to bulge through. "Sure would be nice to have a new ball, though." Then he looked up and smiled a smile that was much too old for a kid his age. "Maybe next year, eh Shotgun?"

"Yeah," I answered sadly. "Maybe."

Billy and I said our goodbyes, and he headed off for home.

The sweet aroma of baking swirled around me as I opened the door of our house. Pound cake, it had to be. My mom made the best pound cake in the whole, wide, world.

I walked out into the kitchen and our kitchen table was full of little pound cakes. Tilly and my mother were at the stove, and my father was closing in quietly on the table of unsuspecting cakes.

My dad had a will of iron, a regular Rock of Gibraltar. That was until it came to my mom's pound cakes.

I watched his eyes scan the cakes until they fell on one in particular. Target spotted. He looked up at my mother who was busy mixing batter, then back. He looked at me and put a silencing finger up to his lips.

I nodded.

He took a step toward the table.

My mother and Tilly laughed and joked as Tilly helped stir.

My father reached the table.

Oh, he was good . . .

He reached.

"Sam Hatcher," my mother said swinging around and slapping his hand.

But my mother had eyes in the back of her head.

It's a mother thing.

"Just a little bit," my dad begged.

"No, they're for the neighbors."

"The neighbors," my dad blurted. "But I'm your husband!"

"It's a good way to get to know your neighbors, and I already *know you*," she countered.

"Well," my dad said giving me a wink. "Couldn't you pretend we were strangers for about five minutes?"

"Sam Hatcher," my mother said trying not to laugh. "Out!"

"Sammy," my mother said turning to me. "I want you to deliver these for me."

"Okay," I said. "I'll be right back."

I went upstairs to my room and turned on the light. Sliding open the closet door, I reached back into the corner behind my shoeshine box and pulled out an old shoebox. This was where I kept my stash of loot.

I told ya' I was rich.

I opened the box and looked at my stash of nickels, dimes, quarters, and even five dollars in ones. All totaled with tips, I had almost fifteen dollars. I would have had more, but spit shining takes a lot of polish. But thanks to a trait I got from my mom, I managed to squirrel it all away. Fifteen dollars in a year and a half, I would be a gazillionaire in no time.

But I had plans for this money, that's why I never touched it.

Remember when I said Christmas wasn't my favorite time of year? Well it wasn't. My favorite time of year was spring. Not because it gets warmer, not because the trees and flowers bloom, not even because it signals summer vacation's near.

It was because spring was when baseball started.

Yeah, I liked playing football with the guys, but I *loved* baseball. I remember sitting out on the porch in Reading drinking lemonade with my dad and grandpa, listening to the games on our radio. I remember us cheering when our team whacked one out of the park.

That was what my money was for.

My dad taught me everything I know, from tying my shoes, to spit-shining them. He taught me how to think before I acted, and to put myself in other people's shoes before I treated them harshly. Maybe it was his upbringing, maybe it was seeing a war up close, but my dad was a great believer in compassion.

And I wanted to thank him just for being there.

Yeah, come this summer, I was gonna take my dad to a ball game. Just the two of us. Between polishing shoes, and returning pop bottles, I'd have the money to get us tickets and hot dogs, and pennants, and we could sit there and watch the whole thing, not just imagine it.

Yeah, this summer, we'd be in Connie Mack for sure.

And maybe, just maybe, if I worked extra hard, I could get Billy that football too.

"Sammy," my mom yelled up the steps.

"Coming mom," I yelled putting my box back.

"Whatcha doin', Sammy," Tilly asked walking into my room.

"Nothin'," I huffed.

"Nuh-uh," she said walking over to me.

"All right," I admitted. "I was thinking about what to get you for Christmas."

"Really," she asked all enthusiastic.

"Yeah."

"What're ya gettin' me," she asked jumping up and down.

"Ain't tellin'."

"Aw, come on, Sammy, please?"

"Nope."

"Pleeeeeeeeaaaaasssse?"

"Uh-uh," I said shaking my head.

"Saaaammmeeeeeee!" She whined jumping up and down ready to explode.

"Okay," I gave in. "Come here and I'll tell ya'."

Tilly came closer brushing her hair back from her ear so she wouldn't miss anything I said.

I leaned over to her ear and whispered, "I got you a," I stuck my finger in my mouth, swished it around, then jammed it in her ear, "Wet Willie Wet Willie!"

On the line, in the boat, cleaned, cooked and on the plate with a lemon wedge.

Hook, line, and *sinker.*

Tilly shrieked and jumped away from me holding her ear. "Ewwwww," she yelled in disgust.

"Now, *get outta my room,* ya' Wombat," I grumbled.

"You're a *pig,* Sammy," she yelled following me out the door and down the steps.

"*I'm* a pig," I asked. "*I'm* not the one with someone else's *spit* in my ear."

"Ewwwww," she groaned rubbing her ear again. "I *hate you*, Sammy."

"Wombat."

"Stop calling me that!"

"Wombat! Wombat! Pig-nosed Wombat," I sang.

"I'm tellin' dad!"

I turned around and Tilly stopped short. "You tell dad," I warned. "And I'm gonna tell the thing under your bed to kill you in your sleep."

"You wouldn't," she gasped with fear in her eyes.

"Oh, no," I asked. "You just tell dad and see if you live through the night."

I walked downstairs, confident the Wombat would keep her mouth shut. Every kid had something that lived in their room. Something no grown-up could see. Something, that came out only after the lights were off. Something only covering your head with the blanket could stop.

For my sister, it was the thing under the bed.

I walked downstairs and into the kitchen where my mother was busy wrapping cakes in foil. "Okay, Sammy," she said putting five cakes in a bag, "Go on and deliver these, and don't forget to wish our neighbors a merry Christmas."

"Yes, mom," I said taking the bag.

My mom was like that. She'd go out of her way to make friends, 'cause she said you could never have too many of 'em. And at Christmas time, even in Reading, she'd make cakes for our neighbors.

I put on my brown corduroy coat and took the bag. It took a while, but I finally finished doing my side of the street. Our neighbors got one whiff of that cake, and took them thankfully, and patted me on my head when I wished them a merry Christmas from our family.

I went back to our house and my mother had another bag waiting for me to do the other side of the street. The witch's side. Needless to say, I started at the other end of the block.

Knocking on doors, ringing on bells, I went from house to house handing over my mom's cakes. And let me tell ya', they were accepted just as eagerly as on my side of the street. I went to the house next to the witch's and looked in the bag. Miracle of miracles, I only had one left.

Saved!

I knocked on the door, delivered the cake and took off like a rocket. I shot the witch's house one last wary glance before I flew inside the house.

I walked into the kitchen and found my dad munching on a hunk of cake. My eyes widened with amazement. He'd done it. He'd flown in low and got one! "You got one," I asked truly shocked.

"Mom burned it," my dad said popping another piece into his mouth.

"Some one dis*tracted* me on purpose," my mother said looking over at him.

"Not me," my dad said in his own defense. "And *surely* not on *purpose*."

"The Lord hates a liar," my mother warned.

"But I bet he loves pound cake," my dad winked taking some more of the burnt cake.

"Get the last one out of the fridge, Sam," my mother asked my dad.

Last one?

No, it couldn't be.

No, I delivered them all.

I watched my dad pull out the cake.

"Still a little warm," he said putting it down on the table.

"It's all right," my mother said wrapping it. "It's cool enough to stand."

"Who-who's this for," I asked hoping for an answer other than the one I had suspected.

"It's for the woman in the end house on the other side of the street," my mother said giving my dad a look. "You see your father's *eating* hers."

"But, mom," I started.

"Yes, Sammy?"

"I can't go over there."

"Why?"

I had to find a good answer, and I had to make it believable.

"She's a witch," I blurted, mentally slapping myself the second after I said it.

"A what," my dad asked laughing.

"Sammy," my mother said flabbergasted.

It was too late; I'd really stuck my foot in it this time. I had to tell them. "She is, mom," I said with all the conviction in my soul. "And if I go there, she'll eat me. Witches eat kids! Eats 'em with potatoes and carrots! Don't make me go there, mom!"

My mother looked over to my father, who looked thoroughly amused by the whole scene.

The Wombat just looked bug-eyed, at everybody.

"Sam," my mother said. "Say something."

"C'mon, give a guy a break," my dad grinned. "I mean, if she's gonna *eat 'im . . .*"

"*Sam!*"

"All right," my dad said holding up his hand. "Sammy, do like you mom tells you."

"But, dad-."

"No, buts, Sammy," my dad said taking the cake from my mom and handing it to me. "Go on."

"All right," I moaned. "But remember, I'm your *only son*."

My dad, in later years, told me that after he heard me say that, he had to keep the laugh in until I was out the door. And keeping that laugh in, he said, had almost herniated him.

But, at the time, I didn't see the humor.

It was the longest walk I had ever taken. The dark house on the corner came closer with every step, and as it did, the wind blew harder, and the air got colder.

I opened the rusted metal gate leading into the overgrown front yard, and the grinding creak from it echoed up and down the block. Like a doomed man walking to the chair, I made my way up to that old metal storm door.

I gave the metal two quick raps.

Well, nobody home.

Oh well, guess I live.

The lights in the living room went on.

Oh well, guess I die.

The door opened, there she was.

The witch.

Her hair was scraggly and fell over her eyes so I couldn't really see them and her dress was gray with flowers, and her hands were gnarled like claws.

"Whaddayou want," she asked, and even her voice sounded odd.

"M-my mom sent me here to give you this," I said holding up the cake.

"What is it," she demanded.

"It's a cake," I said.

"Well, bring it on in, I'm busy," she said walking into the house and disappearing into the
kitchen.

Oh, no, I thought as I stood there. She's cooking!

I froze.

After a few minutes, she poked her head out of the kitchen doorway. "You comin' in or not? I'm not paying to heat the whole neighborhood!"

I opened the door, struggled to remember how to say the Our Father, but it escaped me, and went in.

The living room was dingy with peeling wallpaper and stuffing coming out of the furniture. I walked from the living room to the dining room that had an old chandelier hanging from the ceiling over an old beat up dining room set.

Yeah, this was a witch's house for sure.

I walked into the kitchen and found her standing there with her hand on the door of her oven.

Oh, no, not the oven! My mind screamed. At least I could *try* to climb out of a pot!

"Well," she said pointing to a lop-sided old Formica-topped table. "Put it over there."

Her voice was so odd.

She opened the oven door.

I stepped back.

She took a dishtowel, wrapped her hand in it and reached into the oven. *She's already got a kid in there*, I thought. *Maybe that one'll fill 'er up, and she won't have room for me!*

But it wasn't a kid. Through all the fear, I guess my beak stopped working, 'cause I could smell it now.

It was cookies.

She pulled out a pan, and on it laid the biggest chocolate chip cookies I'd ever seen.

"Look out," she warned as she walked past me into the dining room and flipped on the light. She laid the cookie pan on a wooden block in the center of the table, and shook the towel off her hand.

It was then that I saw it.

It was a picture on her wall. A big one. It was a black and white of a B-52 bomber sitting on an airstrip.

"Wow," I said unable to help myself.

She looked at me then followed my gaze to the picture. "That was taken in France," she told me.

Then I noticed a model of the same plane on a buffet that sat beneath the picture. The top of it was full of war stuff.

I walked over and looked over the model.

"My fianc sent me those from overseas," the witch told me.

I walked to the end of the buffet where a picture in a gold frame sat. The picture was of a man in a flight jacket sitting on the wing of a plane, his back propped up against the side of the fuselage. He was a big man like my dad, and had a movie star's face with clean-cut blond hair, and a big white smile.

"That him," I said picking up the picture.

"Gimme that," she snapped, whipping the picture from my hand.

I looked at her stunned by the outburst, and she looked right back at me as angry as could be. But the minute she looked at that picture, her face went sad. She walked over to a chair at the dining room table and sat down, staring longingly at that picture.

"He was a tail-gunner in the war," she said even though I didn't ask. "He was from Marlton, Pennsylvania. I met him when he was in basic training in Biloxi. He sent me the money to come up here and live with his folks until he got back. Said when he did, we'd get married.

"He sent me the money for the down payment on this house while he was in Europe and said as soon as he got back, we'd raise a family here." She looked around the house with its cracked ceiling and peeling wallpaper and her eyes shined. "Now look at this place. Paper's peeling, plumbing leaks, ceiling's cracked."

"Well, where is he," I asked. "Is he-is he dead?"

"No," she said shaking her head, looking back at the picture. "A few months after the war, I got a letter from him. He was in England," and as she said that, her eyes got all watery. "Turns out he met somebody else over there and decided to stay. I didn't hear from him, or his family, again after that."

She ran her hand over the front of the photograph. "You said you loved me," she said to the picture with tears beginning to run down her face. "You said you'd come back."

And then she started to *really* cry. It was an empty sound, a sound I didn't like at all. And she didn't look mean anymore. She looked helpless and lost. And she didn't look old at all, either. Looking back on it now at my age, I realized she wasn't old. As a matter of fact, she was just a baby.

Sometimes when I think about her sitting there sobbing, I just want to run back into that memory and put my arms around her and tell her everything would be all right. But I was only ten. Only ten, and here I was with this poor girl who was a long way from home, with nothing to keep her company but dingy walls and a broken promise.

Then I began to cry too.

Yeah, it wasn't the most-manly thing to do, but I just couldn't help myself. I was mean to her and she didn't deserve it. That's not something a man does.

She looked up at me questioningly.

"I'm-," I choked out walking over to her. "I'm sorry I called you a witch. I'm sorry. I really a-."

And that was about all I could say before my throat lumped up on me.

Then she surprised me. She didn't yell or get mad, instead she put her arms around me and gave me a hug. "It's all right," she said rubbing my back just like my mom does when I feel bad. "Maybe I was acting like one."

"Hey," she said softly just like my mom. "How about some cookies, huh?"

I nodded, feeling stupid.

There we sat, at her dining room table, eating cookies with milk and talking. And I'll tell ya', she could bake a cookie, boy! Chocolate chips everywhere with walnuts. That was some good eatin', there!

Her name was Clara Harper from Biloxi, Mississippi, that's why her voice sounded funny. And the reason her shades were always drawn and she never came out during the day was because she was the night operator for the phone company and kept the shades down 'cause she slept in the living room on because the ceiling in the bedroom was coming down. That was why she looked so mussed up when we hit her door with that snowball. We woke her up. Guess I woulda been angry too.

She worked hard to keep up the mortgage on the house, and found little left over to fix it up, but she said she worked on it little by little.

As I looked over my glass of milk at her as she talked, I realized something else. Something, that until then, I had only realized about my mom.

Clara was beautiful.

She had black hair that shined like silk, and deep brown eyes, and a little-girl face like Tilly. And when she laughed it was musical. Clara was only twenty-three. Twenty-three and living alone in this big house. Twenty-three and trying to hold her life together on an operator's salary.

Twenty-three.

She was just a baby.

"Why don't you go home to your mom and dad," I asked.

"All my money's in *this place*," she told me. "It takes a lot to keep a house runnin'."

"Can I come back and visit again, Miss Harper," I asked.

"Why, sure you can, Sammy," she smiled.

She had a pretty smile too, just like my mom.

A knock came at the door.

Clara got up with a curious look on her face.

I watched her go into the living room as I wolfed down another cookie.

"Hello," it was my dad's voice. "Is our son in there?"

"Yes," Clara said letting him in. "Come on in."

"My," she said following my dad to the dining room. "This is the most company I've had in three years."

"Hope he was no trouble, ma'am," my dad said taking off his Fedora.

"No," Clara smiled. "No trouble at all."

"Gettin' late, Sammy," my dad said. "It's gettin' past your bedtime."

"Hey, dad," I said jumping off the chair. "Miss Harper needs help with her plumbing."

My dad's eyebrow went up, and Clara laughed into her hand.

"He means it leaks, Mr.-."

"Hatcher," my dad said shaking her hand. "Sam."

"My dad can fix it," I said proudly. "My dad can fix *anything*."

"Well, I don't want to be a bother," Clara said feeling a little bit on the spot.

"No," my dad said. "I can take a look at it for ya'."

Clara walked into the kitchen with my dad and me behind her and opened the doors under the sink revealing a half-full bucket of water. My dad knelt down and looked inside. Poking his head in, he grabbed the pipe and wiggled it around.

"Got a loose fitting on the elbow joint, Miss Harper," he said standing. "Looks like it loosened then rusted that way. I'll be right back, I can get her tightened up with a wrench. Got one in the toolbox. Sammy," my dad said looking down at me. "You remember what our water shut-off valve looks like at home?"

"Yeah," I nodded.

"Go on downstairs and shut the water off, just in case that pipe's older than it looks."

"Yes, sir," I said gladly. Next to listening to baseball, helping my dad was my favorite thing.

It was *men stuff*.

After my dad left, Clara looked down at me, put a hand on my shoulder and said, "Well, Sammy, seems like it's a good thing I met you."

"Sure does," I agreed. "I'm glad I met you too, Miss Harper."

Clara led me down to the basement warning me to watch my step. Once we got down there, I had a pretty good idea where that valve was, but there was so much junk. I mean piled floor to ceiling and I didn't quite know how to get to it.

"Where'd all this stuff come from?"

"Left behind by the people who owned the house."

"Why don't you throw it out," I asked looking over the mess.

"Too heavy to do all by myself," she admitted.

I spotted the valve line in the back and began to climb over old chairs and a dresser, and some rocking chairs and other assorted junk.

"Be careful," I heard Clara say behind me as I climbed to the back of the basement.

I worked my way over to the back wall, and I don't think Clara would have been so worried if she knew how much fun I was having climbing over all that stuff.

Finally, I reached the back wall, and like my dad taught me, I followed the pipes until I found the hot and cold ones leading to the sink.

Once found, cranking them off was a breeze.

I stayed down there until my dad told me to turn the lines back on, and when I did, I heard my dad yell, "Attaboy, Sammy! She's workin' now!"

My dad and me were one helluva team.

Clara thanked us all the way to the door, and to top it off, she gave us the rest of those cookies to take home too! Just for fixin' a pipe!

"Guess she wasn't a witch after all, eh, Sammy," my dad said digging his hands into his pockets.

"No," I said feeling bad again for the things I had said to her. "But it was odd, dad. She looked like one when I first saw her, but then when I talked to her, she didn't."

"Maybe she's just lonely, son," my dad said as snow covered the brim of his hat. "Ya' see sometimes when people get lonely, they get angry. And with nobody to talk to they keep it all bottled up inside. And sooner or later, that anger and loneliness starts to show."

"Yeah," I said feeling a bit down again.

"But all that's changed now, right?"

"How," I asked.

My dad put his big arm around my shoulder and gave me a light shake. "'Cause now she has a friend."

"Yeah," I said feeling a little bit better.

"My boy," my dad said proudly.

The snow was coming down hard, and the bright orange of the sky made it look like the middle of the day in the middle of the night. I tossed and turned in my bed, unable to sleep.

Quietly, I got out of bed and walked across the cold room to my wind-up clock. It was late, almost quarter after ten.

I walked to my door and closed it quietly so the Wombat wouldn't awaken, then went to my book bag at the bottom of my bed.

Pulling my Social Studies book from it, I opened it directly to the back where the maps of the United States and Europe were.

How far away was Mississippi?

I walked to the window and, not wanting to risk my parents knowing I was awake, decided to use the light from the street to look for it. It took some time, but I found it. I found it way down between Alabama and Louisiana.

It was a long way from Philadelphia.

I closed the book and placed it back in my bag. As I redid the straps, I heard the distant creak of an old metal gate.

Walking back to my window, pressing my cheek against the cold windowpane, I saw a long-coated silhouette scurry from Clara's house and down Tulip street.

She was on her way to work now, I thought.

She was on her way to work leaving behind the silence that would greet her when she returned from her hard night. No one would ask how her day had gone like my mom did with me. No one would sit and listen to the radio with her like my dad did.

I could see her in my mind, hurrying up Knorr Street to catch the 56 Trolley at Torresdale, bundling her collar around her neck to keep out the cold. I could picture her standing alone in the snow on the empty avenue waiting, stamping her feet to keep warm.

Snow filled my head with thoughts of sledding and snowball fights making me happy and excited at the thought of playing in it when day broke. Now, I felt neither happy nor excited.

I wondered what it would be like to be sitting in this house alone.

My parents were down on the first floor and Tilly had been asleep for hours, the silence made that picture easy to paint.

I imagined myself the only living thing in this house, that seemed so small when we were all milling about, how big it would be if it were only me. I imagined walking from room to room, expecting to see someone and finding nothing but emptiness.

I imagined what it would be like without my mom and dad here with me. I imagined they were far away.

Far away in a place I couldn't get to.

I put the palms of my hands against the pane and laid my forehead on the frosted glass. I had never felt this way before. My *heart hurt*. A bad hurt, like when somebody punches you hard right in the middle of your chest.

I ran to open the door of my room. Poking my head out, I listened as hard as I could, straining to catch the slightest sound. The hollowness I felt as I stood there in the dark got worse as I found there was nothing to hear. I waited for what seemed like an eternity, my heart pounding.

I heard my dad talking then he and my mom laughed.

I breathed a slight sigh of relief, walked back into my room and closed the door. I walked back
to my bed and lay down slowly so the springs in the mattress wouldn't creak too much, and slid my blankets around my neck.

I lay there on my side feeling a sad kind of relief. No I wasn't alone. My mom and dad were still here. But Clara *was* alone, and her mom and dad *weren't* here. The picture of her running across the street filled my mind as my eyelids became heavy.

"I'll be your friend, Miss Harper," I assured the picture in my mind as I drifted off to sleep.

4

As I expected, the snow was deep and school was closed.

Billy knocked for me bright and early, around seven o'clock, football under arm. "Hey, Sammy," he yelled happily, "guess what! Went to school this morning, nobody was home, same at Leo's! Let's go play some ball!"

"What," I asked, half asleep, standing at the door with only pants and a tee-shirt on.

My mom walked up behind me, and smiled. "Good morning, Billy," she greeted.

"Morning, Mrs. Hatcher. Can Sammy come out?"

"Well," she said. "We're just sitting down to breakfast. Have you eaten yet?"

"No, ma'am."

Wow, such manner's from a guy who cursed and wore gloves with the fingers cut out.

"Well, c'mon in," my mom waved. "Do you like flapjacks?"

"Boy*, do I*!"

Billy came in, took off his worn coat, wool cap, and my mother set another place for him at he table.

"Good morning, Billy," my father greeted cheerfully looking over his paper.

"Morning, Mr. Hatcher," Billy said sitting down.

"Good morning, Billeee," the Wombat greeted.

"Hey, Tilly," Billy said as we both rolled our eyes at each other.

It was great having Billy around. He could always make us laugh with the stories of what his brothers and sisters did. It was the kind of stories that could only come from big families.

He told us about his little brother Ernie who was only five, and his other brother George who was four.

One day while Billy was stuck babysitting his brothers and sisters, Ernie wanted Billy to play soldiers with him, but Billy was busy fixing his bike in the yard while he watched his two little sisters. For an hour his little brother stood behind him begging, pleading, whining, until finally Billy screamed at him.

Ernie pouted, walked away, and Billy thought no more of it.

Unable to sway Billy, Ernie grabbed George, who was playing with building blocks. Sneaking into the kitchen, the five-year old grabbed two pots for helmets and ran into the living room. Grabbing his little brother, he yanked him upstairs to play soldiers with his two wooden guns.

Ernie put on his pot then stuck the other on Gorge.

It went down to his shoulders.

Ernie took the pot back off and told George to stay there while he got a smaller pot.

Dashing back to the kitchen, Ernie exchanged the pot for a smaller one, then ran back. The pot was a little small, but bound and determined to play soldiers, Ernie pushed down on it.

George's head slid all the way in and got stuck.

Billy finished working on his bike, righted it, rolled it back and forth to make sure the chain he had salvaged from a bike he found in the trash, would hold. It did. Feeling a sense of accomplishment, he decided to go in and get a glass of milk.

When he went into the kitchen, he found Ernie sitting at the table looking at the ceiling, swinging his feet, and wearing his best angelic face.

"What did you do," Billy asked.

"Nothin'," Ernie answered.

Ernie, in his infinite wisdom, knew he would get a whuppin' for taking his mother's best pots to play with, so he figured he just wouldn't tell anybody. Maybe if he just acted natural, nobody would notice George walking around with his head jammed in a pot.

"Don't tell *me* nothing, Ernie," Billy demanded. "What did you do!"

"Nothin', I'm tellin' ya'!"

"Where's, George," Billy asked looking around.

"I don't know," Ernie shrugged.

"What did you do with, George!"

Ernie was about to answer when a bang followed by a thump came from upstairs.

Billy said he ran upstairs with Ernie right behind him. As he got half way up, he heard the noise again. Bang-Uh! Clang-Uh! Thump!

Billy said he ran to the top of the steps and turned the corner to see little George pulling himself to his feet, his head transformed into a large metal cylinder.

George, being the genius he was, decided not to cry or scream, or yell for help. Oh, no, he *liked* walking around with his head crammed into a pot. And by the sounds of him laughing under it, he was having a good ol' time, too.

George got up, felt for the wall, turned away from Billy, and began walking.

"George," Billy called.

Slowly, George turned, the weight of the pot making him wobble like a drunk.

"What," a voice answered from under the pot.

"Get over here," Billy yelled.

His little brother walked toward him, his hand sliding along the wall. He reached the wood-framed doorjamb of the bathroom and stopped. "Billy, look," the muffled voice said.

With wide, disbelieving, eyes, Billy watched George crane his head back and slam it right into the doorjamb as hard as he could.

CLANG!

UH!

THUMP!

"Don't *do that*," Billy screamed, running over to his brother who again was laughing wildly. "You dent mom's pot an' she'll have a bird!"

"Didn't hurt," George informed him as Billy pulled him to his feet.

"Not at *all*," Ernie asked utterly amazed. "Not a little bit?"

"Nuh-uh," George replied shaking his pot.

"Wow," Ernie breathed.

"Shut up and get downstairs, Ernie," Billy growled.

Billy said he tried and tried to get that pot off, but it wouldn't budge. Finally, he got an idea. He pulled his little brother out into the back yard and he said once his sisters saw George, it only made matters worse.

"Hey, look," Billy's seven-year old sister Sandy said running over, "Georgie's head's caught in mom's pot! Hey, Georgie, why you got your head in mom's *pot*!"

Billy's other sister, Margaret, who was Tilly's age, ran over and rapped on the top of the pot with her knuckles. "Hey, Georgie, knock, knock!"

"Who's there," the four-year old answered.

"Wisyer."

"Wisyer who?"

"Wisyer head in *that pot*!" She yelled laughing wildly.

George, who had no idea what she had just said, laughed just the same.

Ernie disappeared.

Billy told George to stand there while he unraveled the garden hose. Billy said he turned just in time to see Ernie creeping up behind George with a hunk of old wood.

"Hey, Georgie," he called.

The four-year old turned and Ernie slammed him right in the face like a batter swinging on a fastball.

CLAAAANNNNGG!

UUUUUGGGGHHHH!

WHUMP!

"That hurt, Georgie," Ernie asked enthusiastically, wanting to find out how much pain could be reduced by the donning of your average cooking pot.

George just lay there, sprawled out on the ground like a lump.

"Jeeeez, ya' *killed'im*," Billy yelled running back to his fallen brother. "Hey, Georgie," he called shaking him. "Georgie, you okay?"

From beneath the pot he heard, "Uhhhhhhhh."

"Gimme that," Billy hissed, snatching the board away from his brother. "Now, get in the house, before I *brain ya'*!"

As Ernie stomped his way into the house, Billy shook George back into consciousness. He jammed the garden hose into the pot as far as it would go, then told the four-year old to hold his breath.

My mom winced at that point of the story.

Then he turned the hose on full blast and pulled the pot off.

By the time he finished my mother was holding her head in her hands, and Billy, my father and I were laughing so hard our faces were red.

"What did you ask Santa for, Billy," Tilly asked.

That was when Billy's laughing slowed to a chuckle, then stopped altogether.

"Nothin'," he answered as brightly as he could. "I don't need nothin'."

"Not even toys," she asked.

"Maybe a football," he half smiled.

"That's all," my sister asked astonished.

"Yeah, that's about it," he smiled. "Hey," he said in a brighter voice to me. "You ready, Sammy? The guys should be out soon."

"Can I go, mom," I asked.

She nodded.

Billy stood up, "Thanks for the flapjacks, Mrs. Hatcher. They were great."

"Thank you, Billy."

"I'll wait for ya' on the porch," Billy said leaving the room.

"So," my mom said. "What about our neighbor up the street, Sammy?"

"She's nice," I said. "I feel bad for her. She's up there all by herself."

"Yeah," my dad agreed. "But what can ya' do?"

My mother's face brightened and she smiled at my dad.

My dad in turn looked at her apprehensively. "Oh, no, Molly," he said shaking his head. "You get that smile right off your face."

"What smile," she asked innocently.

"I know what you're thinkin'." My dad said standing and putting on his coat.

"What?"

"*You know what*," my dad answered putting his Fedora on.

"I'm not thinking anything."

"Yeah," my dad said grabbing his lunch pail as chances for escape were dwindling, "that's what scares me. Whenever you're not thinking anything, you're thinking *something*."

"Why don't you ask Eddie over for dinner Saturday," my mom said matter-of-factly.

"*Molly*!"

"*What*!"

"Y'see, Sammy," my dad said making his way to the door. "When a woman says she's not thinking of anything, that's the best time in the world for a man to worry."

My mother gasped in shock as she followed my dad to the door.

"Sam," she called.

"Yes, dear," he answered turning.

"Aren't you forgetting something," she asked offering him her cheek.

"Why yes, I am," my dad said. Then he leaned down and kissed Tilly on the top of her head.

"Sam Hatcher," my mother yelled.

My dad gave her a kiss on the cheek.

"Now, go on," she shooed him.

"See you tonight," he winked as he left.

"Don't forget," my mother yelled after him. "Saturday night!"

"Yesssss, deeeaaar," my dad droned back.

My mom blew him a kiss and closed the door.

"Sammy," my mother said turning to me. "I want you to invite Miss Harper to dinner Saturday night, all right?"

"Okay, mom," I agreed a bit confused.

5

The ball playing was good that morning. We must have "washed-out" each others faces in the snow about a zillion times in that game. Cause when ya' had a guy on the ground in eight inches of freshly fallen show, it was almost a moral imperative to jam his face in it. The only thing missing was Bull who, for some unknown reason, couldn't come out.

Which meant I had to steady quarterback for both sides.

There was nothing like back-lot football in the snow. Cold, slippery, and the ball's leather covering frozen so hard, it became almost impossible to hold or throw. If it weren't for that bladder sticking out, I wouldn't have been able to hold onto it at all.

After the last touchdown, we all gathered in a huddle in the center of the park, all of us shivering, our throats raw from sucking in freezing air. Despite the cold, despite the three coats of packed snow on our clothes we grinned anyway. It didn't bother me at all.

A man can take the cold.

"Hey, guys," I began a bit hesitantly.

"Yeah," they answered breathing into their hands.

"I was wondering if you could give me a hand doin' somethin'?"

"Whazzat," they asked.

"Miss Harper needs her basement cleared out, and the stuff is too heavy for her to lift. But we could do it."

"Who's Miss Harper," Billy asked.

I didn't want to say. I knew how they would react.

"She's," I said slowly. "She's the lady in the end house."

""The *witch*," Tag Along blurted his face filling with fear. "I ain't goin' in no witch's house!"

"It's not like that, she's-," I tried to explain.

"Nix on that, Sammy, witches *eat kids,* ya' dummy," Bean said with a shake of his head.

"But, guys, she's no-."

"No way, uh-uh, not me, boy!" Loverboy said backing up his hands in the air.

I bit my lip and my face got hot.

"Not me, Sammy," Billy said. "I ain't goin' into the house o' no wi-."

"She's not a *witch*," I screamed, my breath blowing out in clouds like a bull.

All the guys got quiet and looked at me surprised. I guess they weren't expecting such an outburst. I even shocked myself. I was never one for losing my temper, not really. And when I did, it was only at the Wombat.

"Hey, Sammy, take it easy," Billy said putting a hand on my shoulder.

"Get off me," I shouted shrugging his hand away. "She's not a witch," I yelled looking at them. "She's just lonely! She got nobody; she ain't even from around here! She's from all the way down South, an' she's up here all by herself!

"She met some guy in the Army, and he said he loved her, and he was gonna marry her. And he brought her all the way up here, and he left her all by herself in that big ol' house! That no good-no good-Billy, you say it, I'm not allowed!"

"No good son of a *bitch*," Billy snorted.

"Thank you," I yelled still riding the adrenaline wave.

I looked around at all the guys who just stared at the ground. My breathing was still hard, but my anger was subsiding.

Billy walked over to me and put and his arm around my shoulders. "Hey, Shotgun," he asked. "Whatcha doin' for the rest o' the day?"

"Nothin'," I huffed.

"Wanna clean out a basement?"

All the guys, myself included, looked at him in shock.

"Hey," he reasoned to the fellas, "if she's Jake with Shotgun, she's Jake with us, right?"

Bean, Tag Along, and Loverboy just gawked at us.

"Right," Billy asked again, his voice firmer.

"Yeah, right," they answered with no enthusiasm whatsoever. "Sure."

"Good," Billy smiled. "Now stop standin' around with yer' yaps open, ya' look like a bunch o' stupes."

It was around ten o'clock when I knocked on Clara's door, hoping not to wake her. She didn't answer. I turned and looked at the guys. All of them, Billy included, still held expressions of reservation on their faces.

I knocked again.

From behind the large wooden door, with its cracked and peeling paint, I heard the deadbolt turn. From behind me, I could hear the guys take a step back.

Clara opened the door, dressed in a gray dress, her hair pinned back. "Oh," she said as she looked down and saw me. "Sammy. What is it?"

"I didn't wake ya', did I, Miss Harper," I asked.

"No, no, not at all," she replied with a dismissing hand. "And who are these boys? Your friends?"

"Yes, ma'am," I nodded gesturing to them each respectively. "This is Bean, his little brother Tag Along, and this is Sailor. They're my buddies."

"Nice to meet you boys," Clara smiled.

And I suppose her smile had the same effect on them as it had on me, because they all smiled back, and I could see the tension ease out of them. "Hello, ma'am," they all said. All except Loverboy.

He walked right up to her, whipped off his wool hat and shook her hand. "My real name's Terry McBride, Miss Harper."

"Ooooooh, Lovvverrrboyyyy," Billy, Bean, and Tag Along crooned.

That made Clara laugh that musical laugh of hers and Loverboy went all shades of red.

"Shut up, guys," he yelled turning on them.

"Oh, Amy Martin's gonna have a cow when she finds out about this!" Billy warned.

"C'mon, guys," Loverboy pouted. "*Stop*!"

"What can I do for you boys," Clara asked, her laugh turning to a smile.

"We come to haul your stuff outta the basement, Miss Harper," I said. "Tomorrow's trash day."

"Well, I don't know," she said. "Some of that stuff's pretty heavy. Do you think you boys can handle it?"

"Sure we can," we all said putting on our deep man voices.

All but Loverboy, who just stood there looking at her with a big, dumb, smile on his kisser.

"Well come on in," Clara said stepping into the house.

We all walked in behind her, except for Loverboy, who just stood there looking like a love- struck puppy, a smile on his face and his cap in both hands.

Billy walked back to get him. He stood there with his arms folded for a moment then smacked Terry right in the forehead.

"Hey," Loverboy yelled snapping out of his trance and rubbing his forehead. "Whadja do that for?"

"'Cause ya' look like a mook, that's why," Billy replied impatiently. "C'mon, ya' mug," he said grabbing Loverboy by the collar and pulling him inside.

It took two hours of pushing, pulling, hefting and hauling, and a lot of sweat to get all that stuff up those steps and out that door, but we did it.

Billy, who was good at planning ahead, ran home, grabbed his dad's hatchet and we all took turns hacking up the larger pieces of furniture so the trash men would take it. Bean and Tag Along, in the meantime, had run home for a big ball of twine to tie the debris.

By one o'clock, we all sat red-faced and sweating on Clara's porch. As for the other guys I can't say, but I ached all over and then some. But it felt good. It was the ache of labor.

It was a man's ache.

"Good heavens," Clara exclaimed walking out onto the porch. "You boy's did all this?"

We all nodded, out of breath and proud as peacocks.

"Mercy," she said shaking her head. "I've made some hot cocoa and some sandwiches. Are you hungry?"

"I'm starving," I nodded.

"Brother, you said a mouthful," Billy said pulling himself to his feet.

We all, Clara included, sat at her dining room table and talked about everything from football, to the Mississippi River. It took a while, but she finally taught us all how to spell it with that old song, *MISS-ISS-IPPI!*

She was in better spirits than last night; I suppose that was proof of what my dad had told me. Maybe Clara *was* just lonely and needed some company. And maybe she was right, too. Maybe she had acted like a witch because of it, but not anymore. Now two things were certain: one, she had friends now, and two . . .

The witch was dead.

The only time her face seemed to darken a bit was when we talked about our families; Clara showed us a picture of hers. It was a photo of her standing with her mother and father, and little sister. She smiled and said someday she would go back.

With apologies, she said she had to go to bed by three to get some sleep for work.

We said our goodbyes.

"Oh, Miss Harper," I said as I walked out.

"Yes?"

"My mom wants to know if you want to come over for dinner on Saturday night?"

"That would be lovely," she said brightly. "Ask her if she'd like me to bring something?"

"Yeah," I nodded. I figured it was worth a try. "More cookies."

She looked at me with scrutinizing eyes.

Aw nuts.

"Okay," she finally said with a smile, "I'll do that."

Hot dog!

We walked out onto the sidewalk and promised to return tonight to put all the junk out on the curb for the trash man. There we stood, five guys with nothing to do. I reached into my pocket and took inventory: I had a marble, a lens off a magnifying glass, two shiny rocks I found, and after some searching I found what I was looking for.

"Whaddaya wanna do now," Billy asked.

Bean, Loverboy and Tag Along shrugged.

"Well, men," I said in my deep voice. "We did a good job today. I think we deserve some reward."

"Like what," Billy asked.

I held up a quarter.

"Penny candy?" I asked looking at their faces. They all looked at me like I was J.D. Rockerfeller himself.

"Whoa, Mr. Moneybags," Billy gasped.

Normally I didn't spend my money from shoe shining, but I figured I could blow a quarter and still have enough to get dad and me to a ball game, and get Billy that football.

"Licorice whips," Tag Along cooed.

"Gum drops," Bean added.

"Peppermint sticks," Loverboy offered.

Then we all looked at Billy, who had not expressed his choice.

"Gentlemen," he said cocking an eyebrow.

We all hushed in anticipation.

"Jaw breakers," he said at last.

"JAW BREAKERS," we all yelled in agreement, then took off like rockets to the avenue screaming like, to quote my mom, "A bunch of banshees."

Within fifteen minutes, we were standing on the corner of Torresdale Avenue and Knorr, our faces swelled with the bulk of candy lodged in our cheeks. Everyone, that is, but Tag Along whose mouth was a bit too small for his.

He looked more like a dog rasslin' with a bone.

"Hey, guys," Bull yelled running up Knorr. "What's doin'? Aw wow, ya' got jawbreakers! Can I have one! Can I can I?"

"Well, I don't know," Billy said as Bull slid his bulk to a stop in front of us. "We was workin' all day while you was loafin'. Ain't that right, Shotgun?"

"Yeah," I agreed, knowing full well that I had his in my coat pocket. But, hey, if ya' can't razz yer' buddy, who can ya' razz, right?"

"Aw, c'mon, guys," he begged. "Ain't my fault. Had to go with my dad to pick up my aunt Gert at the bus station. I was haulin' bags all mornin'. You think *you* was workin'? Shoulda been with me! My aunt Gert's only here till after Christmas, an' she brought her whole house with her! Then I had to listen to how her feet hurt, and how her leg's actin' up!"

"Well," Billy said folding his arms trying not to laugh at poor Bull's predicament. "I still don't know . . . What about you, Shotgun?"

"Ah, it's a toughie, all right," I said rubbing my chin.

"Bean," Billy asked.

"I don't know."

"Loverboy?"

"Hard call, Billy."

"Tag Along?"

No answer.

We all looked down at Tag Along who was looking in cross-eyed concentration at his mouth as he worked on his jawbreaker. Mouth working, jaw bulging, Tag Along rattled his skull trying to break that thing.

Poor kid.

After a few moments he looked up, realized we were all staring at him, and said, "Huh?"

"Should we give Bull a jawbreaker or not," Billy asked again.

Tag Along's jaw stopped moving. He looked at Bull, then us. Then he answered in a voice that dripped with conviction . . .

"Puh-wuh-wuh," he answered, the pink candy ball peeking out through his teeth, then immediately went back to work on his jawbreaker.

"He's not sure either," Billy translated.

"Aw, c'mon, guys," Bull groaned. "All right, I saved the worst for last. Listen up," he said looking like a lawyer about to spring surprise evidence on an unsuspecting prosecutor. "She's a cheek pincher."

We all winced.

Every family has one, and if you were under eighteen, you were fair game for them. Yeah, sure, they'd lure you in with something innocent like: "Come here and give auntie a hug," or, "Come give grandma a kiss," and, of course, if you didn't want a lickin' from your parent's, ya' did it. And when ya' got close enough . . .

WHAMO!

That's when they got ya'!

Then as they tried their best to disfigure ya' by pulling on your face so hard you could stick your tongue out through your eye hole, they would say stuff like: "Oh, you're so cute!" or, "You look more and more like your father every time I see you!" At which point I would look at my dad to see if half of *his* face was hanging off.

Yeah, next to dentists, cheek pinchers were a kid's worst nightmare.

"For real," Billy asked sympathetically.

"Yeah," Bull nodded ruefully grabbing a fistful o' cheek, pinching it, then wriggling it around. "Just like this."

"Ewwww," we all moaned, visions of personal experiences flashing through our minds.

I handed over the candy without so much as a word.

Poor Bull earned it.

He had a lot of cheek.

Poor guy.

"Oh, Terreeeee," a girl's voice mooed.

"Aw, naw," Loverboy grimaced pulling us into a wall in front of him and squatting down.

I looked in the direction of the voice.

Running toward us in a brown coat with white rabbit fur collar and cuffs, and wearing a white hat made of the same was a girl I had never seen before. She was a large girl, who, if the truth be told, bounded more than ran. Red hair stuck out in bangs in front and flowed down her back.

She waved wildly with one white-mittened hand.

"Who's that," I asked watching her bear down on us like a runaway train.

"*That's* Amy Martin," Billy grinned.

"*That's* Amy Martin," I asked.

"All three tons of 'er, brother."

I looked back at Loverboy, and understood now why he was cowering.

Amy ran up to Billy, who folded his arms, his smile brightening. I, mean, why shouldn't he smile? She wasn't *after him*!

"Where's Terry," she asked.

"Why, Amy," Billy said sidestepping with such speed and grace that Loverboy was left alone crouching in the snow covering his eyes. "Why, he's right here. Look, Terence, you have company."

Loverboy took his hands away from his face and, upon looking around, realized he was out in the open. He looked up at the beaming gargantuan specimen of adolescence that was Amy Martin.

All the blood ran from his face.

"Hi, Terreee," Amy said shifting on one foot.

"Hi, Amy," Loverboy said with a tone of resignation as he stood up.

"I'm having a tea party later," she said. "Wanna come?"

"Heck, no," Loverboy said indignantly. "What do I wanna go to some dumb ol' tea party for?"

"Aw, c'mon," Amy answered. "It'll be fun. It'll be just you . . .and meeeeeee."

"No way," Loverboy blurted, horror covering his face. "Not me. No siree Bob."

"You should be a little nicer to me, Terence McBride," Amy scolded.

"And why's that, blubberface," Loverboy answered slightly more than irritated.

"Because, one day, we're gonna get married," Amy yelled happily.

Before Loverboy could rebut the threat, Amy had him in a hug. Not a normal hug. Oh, no, this was a bear hug.

Hell, his feet were off the ground!

Now, you gotta understand, Amy was a big girl. I mean, not only weight-wise, she was almost as tall as Billy, even though she was Loverboy's age. And I mean to tell ya', even though my manhood was just months away, even I would have run in terror at the sight of that bearing down on me.

I'd never seen such a horrendous exhibit of thrashing and shaking in all my life. Loverboy's head disappeared for a while, overwhelmed by Amy's massive arms. Every once in a while we'd hear an "Ack," or an "Umph," but that was about it.

And all the time poor Loverboy was fighting for oxygen, Amy was going on and on about a nice house, and how many kids they were gonna have, and where they were gonna live. She was so caught up in her dreams of their future I honestly believe that she didn't realize she was crushing him to death.

"Hey, Amy," Billy finally said. "Let 'im go, will ya'!"

Amy stopped, looked at Billy, then looked down at Loverboy who looked back at her with pleading, watery, eyes set in a purple face.

"Oh my, are you okay," she asked forgetting to release her hold.

Loverboy answered with a gurgling noise.

Without warning, Amy let go and our pal collapsed into a gasping heap.

"Are you okay, Terry," she asked again.

"Ya' wanna kill me," Loverboy forced out rubbing his ribs.

"You're such a silly," Amy said waving her hands in the air. "Why would I do that if we're gonna get married?"

"Stop *sayin' that*, will ya'?"

Amy took no notice of his implied refusal of matrimonial bliss, instead, she informed us all that she had to go and toddled her way up to the avenue.

We helped Loverboy to his feet.

"That true, Loverboy," Billy asked.

"What," he asked rubbing his chest.

"Five kids?"

"Shut up, Billy!"

We spent the rest of the day playing rough-and-tumble in the park sprinkled with a snowball fight here and there. Then we all split up for dinner.

As promised, we all returned to Miss Harper's that night to take out her trash.

That night, like the night before, I lay awake staring at my ceiling. For some reason, this seemed like a lonely time, quiet and somber. *I could take my rubber snake and go dangle it in Tilly's face until she wakes up and scare the bejiggers out of her*, I thought.

But then I'd get yelled at.

Even though I decided not to do it, the sheer thought of the Wombat's face twisted in terror made me smile a bit.

Instead, I thought of Connie Mack stadium, and my dad and I in the stands trading stats, screaming at the Umps and eating roasted peanuts. It was a warm spring day in my dreams, and the Phillies were playing the Brooklyn Dodger's.

And what a game it was.

After my mental seventh inning, I looked at my wind-up clock. It was time. I got out of bed and walked to the window.

Pressing my face against the glass, I looked down the street.

After a few minutes, Clara came out, walked down her steps, and out the gate onto the snow-covered sidewalk. She stopped for a moment and looked at the pile of trash that had been pulled out of the basement then walked across the street to go to work.

After she disappeared from view, I stood there listening to the silence, feeling that same emptiness I had felt the night before. I looked beyond her house to the other houses, some of which were already decorated with colored lights. That seemed to only make the emptiness grow.

No one should be alone on Christmas.

My eyes wandered over to the pile of broken wood lying in front of Clara's house. What a job *that* was, my arms ached at the mere thought of hauling all that furniture. It sure would have been easier if Bull had been there, I thought.

But, no, he spent his day with his aunt getting his face ripped off.
That was when I smiled.
That was when the emptiness went away.

6

To my disappointment, we had school the next day. Despite the lack of sleep, I fidgeted in my seat the entire day. To make matters worse, it was Friday, and Friday was Arts and Crafts day.

Kid stuff.

Some kids were drawing Christmas scenes with crayons, other made snowmen on paper, filling in the outlines with cotton balls. Others made Santa's using cotton balls for beards.

I tried to create something, but instead doodled aimlessly on a piece of paper.

After an eternity, the bell rang. I flew up out of my seat, only to stand in line to get my coat out of the cloakroom. One thing I couldn't understand, since none of us owned, let alone knew what a cloak was, why was it called a cloakroom?

It was one of those many intriguing kid questions. But being our class teacher was Sister Agnes Patrice, the fastest yardstick in the West, I decided it was a question best kept to myself.

Prudent decisions make great men.

We were all herded like uniformed cattle into the second floor hallway, and were led out by our respective teachers.

Once outside the great red brick building and in its massive schoolyard, we all burst in different directions like a blossoming human fireworks display. Some of the none-to-bright kids couldn't wait until they were out of sight of the nuns to pick up snowballs. Some got a chance to heave them at unsuspecting classmates, some didn't before they were all rounded up by the nuns and pulled back in for detention.

I flew through the yard toward two sets of double wrought-iron gates, which blocked off ramps leading onto Keystone Street. Running through the gates closest to Unruh Street I grabbed the iron railing and swung myself onto the pavement.

Then I stopped cold.

There was Russ and his buddies facing me like a great, angry, wall I would have to hurl through. I was pulp, I thought looking into their eyes.

I had to think fast.

"I'm on my way to Billy's house," I said matter-of-factly. "Any messages?"

Begrudgingly, they stood aside and I bolted down the street.

It was a block and a half to my house, and I sprinted the distance paying no attention to the bouncing bag of books on my back. I remember nearly killing myself on a couple ice patches along the way, though.

I ran across Rawle Street and up the alley to my back gate. Throwing it open, I shot up the path, and nearly flattened myself against the hard wood of our door.

"Sammy," my mother said opening the door. "Are you okay?"

"Yeah, mom," I blurted running past her and into the living room doing a ninety-degree turn up the steps.

I rounded the corner at the top of the steps and ran to the steps leading to the third floor. I hit the bottom of the steps and stopped short.

Tilly was on her way down the steps.

"Outta my way, Wombat," I growled reaching her.

"Promise not to call me that, an' I'll move," she said.

"No."

"Then I'm not movin'," she said smugly folding her arms.

"I said outta my way!"

"Promise?"

"No!"

She stood silent, her jaw stiffened.

My jaw stiffened.

It was war.

I dodged to the left.

She dodged to the left.

I dodged to the right.

She dodged to the right.

"All right," I said. "You asked for it." I put my finger in my mouth, swished it around, and pulled it out slow with a string of saliva running from my fingertip to my mouth. I took a step toward her.

She screamed, threw her hands over her ears and ran past me down the steps.

The Wombat, once again, had fallen.

I ran into my room, slammed the door behind me, whipped off my clothes and got changed. Going to the closet, I pulled out my shoebox of moolah, pulled out a dime, and ran downstairs.

"I'm goin' out, mom," I yelled grabbing my coat and hat from the wall-hooks of our dining room closet.

"Okay," my mother yelled as she ironed clothes in the kitchen, "but be back by dinner time!"

"Okay," I yelled running out the front door.

Once out on the street, I took off toward the avenue, a smile popped onto my face as I passed Miss Harper's house.

There was a pay phone at the corner of Torresdale and Longshore, I could call from there, I thought as I ran across Tulip street, high-hurdling mounds of shoveled snow.

I reached Torresdale, skidded to a stop in front of the phone booth, and ran in.

Miss Harper was my friend. . .

I dialed "O".

"Operator," a voice answered.

And she was all alone. . .

"Connect me to the terminal in town, please, ma'am."

The phone rang, then another woman answered. "Reading Terminal."

And I had to do something for her. . .

"How much for a bus ticket to Mississippi?"

Because, no one should be alone for Christmas.

"Where in Mississippi, sir? Jackson? Greenville?"

"Biloxi, please."

"One-way, or, round trip?"

"Round trip."

"One minute, please, while I check."

"Sir," the woman called after a few moments.

"Yeah?"

"Round trip to Biloxi, Mississippi is twenty-five dollars."

"Twenty-five dollars," I asked feeling my sense of joy fade.

"Yes, sir."

"Thanks."

"Thank you for calling," the operator said hanging up.

What was I gonna do now, I thought digging my hands into my

pockets. When I ran up to the avenue, I was ten dollars ahead, now with one phone call, I was ten dollars in the hole!

I looked up and down the avenue at the storefront decorations and the wreaths on the utility poles lining the two-way street. PTC's 56 Trolley rattled its way down toward Cottman Avenue, sparks flashing from the rod tethered to the cable that ran the length of Torresdale. As I watched it roll by, I noticed the sign in Woolworth's window.

9 MORE SHOPPING DAYS 'TIL CHRISTMAS!

My heart sank lower in my chest. Ten dollars was a lot of money.

Then something struck me. That lady called me *sir*! I was almost a man, right? I was gonna be big, and have a Fedora, and drive a car soon. Yeah, I was almost a man!

And men don't give up!

I looked down the avenue and spied Mr. Benner's barbershop. My dad and I go there for our haircuts. I figured maybe I could work something out with him.

Mr. Benner was a nice old guy, who'd been in the same shop for twenty years. He knew a lot of jokes, and always let me pick out the kind of smelly stuff I wanted on my hair when I was done.

I ran into the shop, all four chairs were full. The first three had men reading papers waiting their turn.

Mr. Benner was busy with a man in the last chair.

The minute I flew through the door everyone looked at me. I knew most of these men. They would walk through the park on their way home from work at Disston Metal Works.

"Hey, there, Mr. Hatcher," Mr. Benner smiled. "What can I do for ya'?"

I cleared my throat, and puffed out my chest. After all, I was among men, and men don't get intimidated. "Mr. Benner," I said walking down the row of customers, "I'd like to make a deal with ya'."

That made all the papers drop, and all eyes fell on me.

Mr. Benner's eyebrows went up. "A deal, y'say," he said, putting his scissors down. "And what might that be?"

"Well, Mr. Benner," I said deepening my voice. "I need some extra money, and I was wondering, if maybe I could shine shoes in your shop, and I could pay you a dollar a week for lettin' me."

First they started to chuckle.

Then they started to laugh.

Then it became a mild kind of roar.

I felt like crawling into a hole. Here I was, this kid standing in front of all these men, and they were all laughing at me.

"A dollar, you say," Mr. Benner said still laughing.

"Y-yes, sir," I mumbled.

"Aw, go on, Marty," the man on the end yelled slapping his knees. "Give the kid a chance. You'll go far with this one!"

Mr. Benner was laughing so hard he began to cough. He slowed down just enough to hold out his hand. "All right, Mr. Hatcher," he said taking my hand and shaking it. "I'll take it!"

"You will?"

"Yes, sirree," he laughed. "You got moxy. I like that in a partner. When d'ya' wanna start?"

"What time is it?"

"Almost four," wiping his eyes to look at his watch.

"I can start now. I don't have to be home for dinner till six!"

Then the roar got louder.

"You go get yer box, then, Mr. Hatcher, an' I'll get ya' a stool from the back room."

"Yes, sir!" I replied brightly.

"Gentlemen," Mr. Benner said to the other men, "meet Sammy Hatcher, world's youngest businessman! A real tycoon!"

"You go to it, kid," the man in the chair said with a wink.

That made me feel better.

I walked toward the door.

"Go get 'em, Sammy," the next man said slapping me on the back.

"Yes, sir," I said, my back straightening a bit.

"You're goin' places, kid," the next man said putting down his paper to shake my hand.

"Thanks," I smiled, my chest puffing out just a bit.

"Now there goes a workin' man for ya's, boys," the one closest to the door grinned.

I was so close to being a man I could feel it!

"Uh-Mr. Hatcher," the man Mr. Benner was working on called.

"Yeah," I was beginning to like this ' Mr. Hatcher' stuff.

"How much do you charge for your service, sir?"

"Two bits," I answered before I knew what I was saying.

"Two bits," he asked. "You must be pretty good."

"Best spit shiner in Philadelphia," I answered confidently.

"Spit shiner," they all said looking at each other.

"I haven't had a spit shine since I was in the Army," the man closest to me said looking at the others.

"Yeah, me neither," the one next to him said.

"Well, you hurry up then, Mr. Hatcher," Mr. Benner chuckled. "Looks like you got customers!"

"Yes, sir!"

I ran home like I had never run before to get my shoeshine box.

I shot through the house not hearing my mother's warnings to slow down, grabbed my box, and headed out the front door.

As I took off back to the avenue, I ran into Billy walking toward my house.

"Hey, Shotgun, what's the rush?"

"I got a job," I said out of breath.

"No kiddin'," he asked.

"Yeah," I nodded. "At Mr. Benner's barber shop shinin' shoes."

"Daddy Warbucks," Billy exclaimed. "Hey, guess what?"

"What?"

"The old man went for a job today?"

"Yeah? Where?"

"Down Dodge. Starts Monday."

"That's great!"

"Yeah, if he *keeps it*."

"Maybe things'll be different now," I said.

"Maybe," Billy agreed out of politeness. "You on for football tomorrow?"

"Maybe later. I wanna work tomorrow."

"Okay, I'll knock around four."

"Okay."

We split up, and I took off to the barbershop.

For the rest of the day, I shined shoes like I had never shined before. It was important. I had two weeks to make ten dollars if I was gonna get Miss Harper a ticket home for Christmas.

At six o'clock, I packed up my box and handed Mr. Benner his dollar.

"Here ya' go, Mr. Benner."

"Pleasure doin' business with ya', Sammy," he said putting the quarters in the register. "You gonna be in tomorrow?"

"Yes, sir," I nodded. "First thing."

"Good deal," Mr. Benner grinned. "Hey, Sammy, get me a piece o' paper off the counter will ya'?"

I walked to where Mr. Benner had his scrap paper, and grabbed a sheet. I handed it over, and he began to write on it with a pencil.

"There," he said finishing. "Whaddaya think," he asked holding it up to me. It read: *Spit Shines 25¢*.

"Good deal," I smiled.

"Good deal," Mr. Benner nodded. "If ya' like, ya' can leave your box under the counter."

"No thank you, Mr. Benner," I said hefting it. "My dad made it for me, and-."

"I understand," Mr. Benner said holding up his hand. "It's a fine one too. I'll see you tomorrow."

"See you tomorrow," I nodded then left.

Boy, that box seemed a lot heavier walking home. My arms were as sore as could be from all that rag work. Spit shining was no easy job, but it was worth it. I had reached Hegerman and Knorr and my arm felt like it was going to fall off. But then something hit me. It was Friday!

Diner night!

I walked as fast as I could with my box, the melted snow beginning to ice under my feet.

I walked down our alley and through the gate. I could see my dad through the window with the Wombat on his back talking to my mom. I hauled the box up the walk and opened the door.

"Hey there, Sammy," my dad greeted me. "Whaddaya know, whaddaya say?"

"Hey, dad," I smiled."Guess what?"

"What?"

"I got a job!"

"A *what*?" My dad asked.

"A job," I beamed.

"Doing what?"

"Shinin' shoes at Mr. Benner's barber shop," I explained. "He let's me shine shoes in the shop, and I give him a dollar a week."

My father threw out a loud laugh that shook the house just like the men in the shop, and my mother joined him. "Well, whaddaya know, mom," he said to my mother. "We have a businessman on our hands!"

"Yes indeed," my mom nodded.

"I'm more than *that*," I shined. "I'm a real *typhoon*!"

"That you are, Sammy," my dad roared. "Well, come on," he went on. "Get ready. Time to go to dinner. Us workin' men gotta eat, eh, Sammy?"

"Yes, sir!"

Workin' men!

Yeah!

7

We drove into the parking lot of Linton's Diner, my mom and dad listening to how my day went, and the Wombat sitting there, silently hating me for all the attention I was getting.

We walked into the diner, past the counter lined with the factory men and the booths filled with screaming kids competing with their screaming parents, to the booths in the back. We talked and laughed all through dinner, and my dad bought Tilly and I extra scoops of ice cream for dessert to celebrate my new job.

After dinner we talked about the day's events, and as always, I eyed my dad. My mom and Tilly sat opposite my dad and me, and my dad would sit there, his arms stretched along the back of the bench.

He would put his Fedora on after dinner and sit there with his cigarette hanging from the corner of his mouth making it bob whenever he talked. Then I'd look up inconspicuously at that great brown felt hat that sat tilted to one side on his head topping off the picture. I was gonna be just like my dad when I grew up.

He was somethin' to see.

My mother got quiet all of a sudden and ran her finger around the lip of her coffee cup. "Well, Sam," she asked.

"Well, what," my dad asked.

"Did you ask Eddie about tomorrow night?"

"You know," he said snapping his finger with a loud pop. "I clear forgot about that."

"Sam!"

"Honey," my dad explained. "It was hectic today. I barely had time to look around."

"Sam, you promised," my mom huffed.

"Well, honey," my dad began, shaking his head. Then he looked down the aisle. "Oh, no."

We all looked down the aisle to where a burly man was walking through the door shaking off the cold.

"Eddie," my mother called waving her hand in the air.

My dad put a hand over his face as he walked over.

Eddie McReedy worked with my dad. He was a bear of a man, almost as tall as my dad, and a little bit heavier. We met him when he came to our house to help my dad with some repairs.

It turned out that Mr. McReedy was in the same European area in WWII at the same time as my dad. He was in demolitions. He and my father laughed about that, saying that it was Mr. McReedy's job to blow up everything my dad built.

"Hiya, folks," Eddie greeted in his easy-going way.

"Eddie, what are you doing tomorrow night," my mom asked ignoring my dad's faces.

"Hmm," Mr. McReedy Pondered, rubbing his chin. "Saturday. Let's see . . . laundry's gotta be done. Apartment's gotta be cleaned. Dishes gotta get washed." Then he shrugged, "I'm not doing anything tomorrow night, why?"

Then he and my mom and dad laughed.

"Well," my mom said. "I thought you might like to come over for dinner."

"Ooh," Mr. McReedy cooed. "What's cookin'?"

"Pot roast, sweet potatoes, cranberry sauce . . ."

"Enough," Mr. McReedy said. "Sold American."

"Then you'll come?"

"I'll be there. Never let it be said Edward R. McReedy passed up free eats."

"Good," my mom smiled. "Well," my mom said getting up. "I think it's time to freshen up. If you men will excuse us?"

My mom and the Wombat left.

Mr. McReedy sat down; he and my dad stared at each other for a moment.

"Pot roast," Mr. McReedy asked.

"Yep," my dad answered.

"Sweet potatoes?"

"Uh-huh," my dad grinned.

"*Cranberry sauce*?"

My dad started laughing.

"What does she look like, Sam?"

"You don't have to come, Eddie. You know how Molly is. Hates to see a good man go to waste."

"What does she *look like,* Sam?"

"Honestly," my dad asked.

"No," Mr. McReedy said sarcastically. "Lie to me."

"Okay," my dad shrugged. "She has a hunched back and one dead eye."

"Sam!"

My dad started laughing again.

"C'mon now, I'm serious," Mr. McReedy said. "My sister does this to me all the time."

"All right," my dad conceded. "She's a looker, Eddie."

"Really?"

"Whaddayou say, Sammy," my dad asked.

"Yeah," I agreed. "She's pretty, Mr. McReedy, you'd like her. I, mean, I like her, and she's a *girl*."

And at ten, that was saying something.

"Guess, I'd better get gussied up then, huh," Mr. McReedy asked a bit awkwardly.

"Why," my dad asked.

"Well, I'm not exactly Prince Charming over here, y'know? What if she sees me and thinks-."

"Eddie," my dad said leaning on the table. "You blew up tank divisions while their ground forces were sending bullets over your head and *that* didn't bother you, why should this?"

"That was different," Mr. McReedy contended. "That coulda just got me killed. Ain't like gettin' rejected. I mean, that was just the German War Machine, this is a *woman*."

"Then just pretend she's a Nazi," my dad laughed.

"Ha ha."

"Well," my mother said returning to the table with the Wombat and her ugly doll in tow. "And what were you boys talking about while we were gone?"

"Nazis," my dad answered, handing Mr. McReedy a wink.

"You boys and your war stories," my mom said as Mr. McReedy slid out of the booth.

"Well, I gotta get going," Mr. McReedy said.

"But you didn't even *eat yet*," my dad said.

"I gotta do laundry."

That made my dad laugh again.

"See you tomorrow."

"See you tomorrow, Ed," my dad waved.

Mr. McReedy turned and walked rather spryly out of the diner.

8

Three people.

Seventy-five cents.

Six o'clock.

Closing time.

I sat in the corner of Mr. Benner's barbershop feeling depressed. This should have been a gold mine. But, instead, it turned out to be a bust. My first day as a typhoon, and I failed.

"Don't look so down, Sammy," Mr. Benner said as he walked from the back room with a cup of coffee in one hand and cocoa in the other. He handed me the cocoa and sat in the barber chair closest to me. "We all have our bad days."

"Yeah, I know," I mumbled putting my polish back in the box.

"It's not you, boy," Mr. Benner said looking toward the window. "It's that."

I looked out the window, and surprised that I'd not noticed it before, but snow was falling in buckets on the street.

"Sure, snow's pretty. Gets you in the holiday mood, but it's bad for business, Sammy," Mr. Benner said drinking his coffee. "The business stays home in weather like this."

And he was right.

Later in life I realized that snow was a great gauge by which to tell if you're getting older. When the sight of heavy snow turns the joy at the thought of snowball fights and sledding into the dread of driving conditions and shoveling; you're getting older.

But I was ten, and couldn't see the problem with the white stuff.

"I'm open from noon till two tomorrow, Sammy. I'll be here right after church," Mr. Benner said grabbing his push broom and sweeping up what little hair there was on the floor. "Why don't we give it a try tomorrow? Maybe it'll be better."

"I sure hope so, Mr. Benner. I need the money fast," I said walking to the door.

"Sammy," he asked me in a concerned way. "Is everything all right? I mean, your family hittin' on hard times, boy?"

"Oh, no, sir," I said. "I need the money to buy a bus ticket."

"A bus ticket," he asked. "Gonna go to Hollywood and become a star, are ya'?"

"No, sir. Nothin' like that," I answered with a shake of the head. "It's for a lady on my block. Miss Harper. She lives down the street from me. Her whole family's in Mississippi and she's up here by herself. And she ain't got the money to go home, so I figured-well-."

"Figured it'd be nice to send her home for the holidays, that it?"

"I guess so. I'm her friend. That's what a friend would do, right?"

"I'm of a mind to say so, Sammy," he nodded. "Come back again tomorrow. Maybe this blasted snow'll let up a little, and we can do some work."

"Yes, sir," I agreed opening the door. "G'night, Mr. Benner."

"G'night, Sammy."

I walked outside; the snow was over my ankles. Snow was bad for business. Snow over your ankles was *fatal* for business. My hopes for a prosperous Sunday were fading fast.

As I walked down toward Knorr and Torresdale, I heard a bump behind one of the parked cars. I looked around but didn't see anybody. I started walking again. I heard the sounds of feet scurrying in the fresh snow.

"Who's there," I called stopping again. I looked around and still didn't see anyone. Then I realized that Russ and his friends lived only a few blocks off the avenue, and maybe they had spotted me. I turned and walked faster towards the corner trying to figure out the fastest way to run with this box in my hand.

"Hey, Hatcher," a voice screamed.

I turned and something came whizzing through the air at me. I dropped my box and caught it. Looking down, I realized it was Billy's football.

Billy's football?

Ankle-deep snow?

Then it all clicked.

Aw, nuts!

"Rough and tummm*bullll*," Bull screamed running out from behind a car and catching me in the mid-drift. We both went down hard into the snow.

"You're it, Sammy," Bull yelled hopping off me.

"I think ya' busted my lungs," I groaned.

Billy and the other guys came running over.

I stood up, shoved the ball into Bull's stomach and down we went again.

"No fair," Bull said as we got up. "I didn't even get a chance to run."

"Okay," Billy said picking up the ball and jamming it into his stomach again. "Run."

Bull looked at us.

We looked at him.

He took off screaming.

I grabbed my box.

We took off after him.

We played all the way down Knorr Street. The best one was Tag Along, who after complaining he never got to play, had the ball thrown to him. He promptly caught it with his forehead and laid there like a beached whale informing us he saw colors.

Poor kid.

We ran down the alley to my house, piled through the back gate, and stormed into my kitchen.

"That you, Sammy," my dad called from the living room where he was listening to the radio.

"Yeah, dad," I called as we all stomped our feet on the rug in front of the door.

The Wombat ran into the kitchen, her ugly little doll in tow.

"Hi, Billeeee," she smiled.

"Hi, Tilly," he grinned then shot the evilest glare at Bull I'd ever seen.

"What," Bull asked.

"What's what, *that's what*," Billy said.

"Hello, boys," my dad greeted walking into the kitchen. "Billy, I saw your father at work the
other day. Looks like we'll be working together."

"For a while, anyway," Billy said under his breath.

"Hey, dad," I asked trying to change the subject. "Where's mom."

"Up Miss Harper's house. Been up there all day. Took some fabric with her, and said she was going to help her with the house."

We all ran through the house, out the front door and up the street.

Miss Harper's house looked different now. All the lights were lit, and for once, it actually looked like someone lived there.

We all ran up onto the porch, and I banged on the storm door. My mom answered, her hair up in a kerchief. "Sammy, Billy," my mom said. "You boys are just in time."

"In time for what, mom," I asked.

"In time for *work,* Shotgun," Billy answered for her.

"I knew you were a smart boy, Billy," my mother grinned letting us in.

All of us walked in, and couldn't believe our eyes. My mom had taken the same stuff she made our curtains out of, and had sewn Miss Harper new curtains for her living room, and the both of them had succeeded in scraping off all the wallpaper.in the living and dining rooms.

"Hello, boys," Clara said walking from the kitchen with two cups of tea.

"Hi, Miss Harper," we greeted.

"Well, Clara," my mom said surveying the room. "We gals really did some work today."

"Molly, I can't thank you enough for this," Clara said. "You and your family have been so nice to me. I don't know what I would've done without you boys cleaning out my basement. That was quite a job."

"It was nothing," we said putting on our deepest voices.

After all, we were almost men.

"Well, I have to get going," my mom said finishing her tea. "I have a dinner to make."

"When's Mr. McReedy comin', mom?"

"Who," Clara asked.

"Oh," my mother answered. "One of my husband's friends from work."

"Molly, I-," Clara began with an uncertain shake of her head.

"Oh, come now, Clara," my mother said. "It's only dinner. Ed's a very nice man."

Clara put a hand on her head, realized her hair was also mussed under a kerchief, and her jaw dropped. "Oh, my," she exclaimed. "I must look a mess. I have to get ready. What should I wear, I don't have anything to wear."

"Relax, Clara," my mom laughed. "It's just dinner."

"I know, but, I don't want to look like a rag-picker," Clara said.

"All right," my mom nodded. "We'll be on our way then so you can get ready. Come on, boys," my mom said to us gesturing to three bags full of wallpaper shavings, "Take those bags out to the porch, please."

After we lugged the bags out onto the porch, we all walked down to the sidewalk, where we said our goodbyes.

Billy walked down to my house with me.

"So our dads'll be working together, huh?"

"Yeah, looks that way."

"Hey, maybe things'll change, y'know." I offered. "Maybe this year'll be different."

"I'll believe it when it happens, Sammy," he said stopping at the gate.

"Yeah," I nodded.

"Well, knock for ya' tomorrow?"

"Sure, around three?"

"Great. See ya', Shotgun."

"See ya, Billy."

9

Mr. McReedy was the first to show up that night. He wore a real nice suit, too. At first I thought he'd gone to church, but he had worn it just to eat pot roast.

He musta really thought highly of pot roast.

He, my father and I, sat at the dining room table while my mom and the Wombat made dinner. Mr. McReedy was moving around in his seat, and messing with his tie, and sweatin'. Then my dad finally found something to make him feel at ease.

"So, whaddaya think about that new press they put in down at the plant."

"No good, Sam," Mr. McReedy said with a shake of his head. "Calibrating system is off. They had me looking at it yesterday. I might be able to get it within a sixteenth of an inch, but she'll never slam 'em right on the money. Design flaw, I'd say. But, hey, who am I, right? They're the big bosses, I'm just a mechanic."

"When it starts costin' 'em, they'll listen," my dad said.

"You know it," Mr. McReedy agreed. "Right, Sammy?"

"Right, Mr. McReedy," I nodded. I liked Mr. McReedy. He never treated me like a kid. And when he and my dad would talk, he'd always find a way to let me into the conversation.

A knock came at the door and Mr. McReedy's whole body went stiff.

"I'll get it," my mom said setting the platter of pot roast on the table.

"Well, Sam," Mr. McReedy said standing. "I gotta be goi-."

"Siddown," my dad said grabbing his shoulder and pulling him back into his seat.

In the other room we could hear my mother talking with Clara. I looked back across the table and saw that Mr. McReedy was sweating again.

My mother walked back into the room holding Clara's black coat. Then Clara walked in. She looked beautiful. She had on a blue dress, and her hair was now flowing down over her shoulders.

"Ed," my mom said to Mr. McReedy. "This is Clara Harper. Clara, Ed McReedy."

Mr. McReedy and my dad stood.

"It's-it's-uh," Mr. McReedy said with his mouth hanging open.

"It's a pleasure," my dad coached out of the corner of his mouth.

"It's a pleasure," Mr. McReedy repeated.

"To meet you."

"To meet you."

"Miss Harper," my dad finished.

"Yeah," Mr. McReedy agreed.

"It's a pleasure," Clara said holding out her hand.

Mr. McReedy shook it with a smile.

"Sammy," she said looking at me. "I left the tray of cookies on the chair in the living room. Could you get them please?"

"Boy, *could I*," I yelled running into the living room.

"Miss Harper said *get them,* not *eat them*," my mom yelled after me.

The night went well, I thought. Mr. McReedy and Miss Harper would shoot each other glances, but didn't say much, until Mr. McReedy mentioned he had spent six months in Jackson, Mississippi.

The conversation lightened and flowed freely after that, and at times, I thought Miss Harper would laugh so hard at Mr. McReedy's stories that she would burst.

At ten o'clock, Miss Harper sadly said that she had to be leaving for work.

"Hey, it's snowing again," the Wombat yelled happily running from the living room back into the dining room.

"Oh, no," Clara moaned.

We all walked out onto the porch to see snow falling in white sheets onto the streets.

Mr. McReedy looked over to Clara who was shaking her head.

"I could drive you to work, Miss Harper," then he blurted. "I mean, if you like. This is no night to be waiting on trolley's."

"Oh, no," Clara replied. "I couldn't ask you to do that.'

"Really," Mr. McReedy said. "It's no problem. A cold, dark, avenue is no place for a lady."

Miss Harper smiled at that and nodded. "Well, if you're sure it's no problem, Mr. McReedy."

"Not at all," Mr. McReedy said. "And you can call me Ed, if you like."

"All right, Ed," she smiled. "Thank you."

We all walked back inside, Miss Harper and Mr. McReedy put on their coats.

"What time do you work till, Miss Harper?" Mr. McReedy said putting on his coat.

"Eleven to seven," She answered. "And, please, call me Clara."

"Well, Clara," Mr. McReedy began hesitantly. "It looks like it might be a bad one. I could pick you up from work and drive you back."

"Oh, no," Clara said. "That would be too much trouble. I wouldn't dream of putting you out like that."

"No trouble at all. I'm up by six anyway," Mr. McReedy said. "And if you're in the mood, maybe we could stop and have some breakfast. I go to Linton's every Sunday for breakfast, and if you wanted to join me-."

"There's nothing quite like eating alone, is there, Ed," Miss Harper asked.

"No, Clara," Mr. McReedy agreed, his voice a little less jovial. "No there's not."

"Breakfast sounds nice."

"I believe I may not sleep tonight," Mr. McReedy laughed.

Clara smiled and turned red.

"Did I ever tell you about the bridge I blew up outside of Italy, Clara?"

"Why, no."

"Well our Captain got orders to-."

"Wait a minute," my dad broke in. "Was it double-bolted, with cross beams, high struts?"

"Yeah," Mr. McReedy said snapping his fingers.

"I built that bridge, Ed," my dad said lightly irritated.

"Oh, and a fine one it was too, Sam. A helluva job. Took me two sets of charges to send it into the water. Damn fine work. It was a pleasure to blow it to smithereens."

"Thanks."

We all laughed as my dad shook his head.

That night, I lay in bed staring at the ceiling hoping that tomorrow's business would be better. Last night's emptiness was gone. Tonight, Clara wouldn't be alone on that cold avenue.

And tomorrow, she would have someone to talk to after work.

She would have someone to ask her how her night went.

10

I sat glumly in the corner of Mr. Benner's barbershop. We had three customers and only one needed his shoes shined.

Mr. Benner walked out of the back room with a cup of cocoa for me, and a coffee for himself. "Not a very good day today, eh, Sammy?"

"No, sir."

Mr. Benner groaned as he sat in his barber chair. "How far off from that ticket are ya' now, son?"

"Eight dollars" I replied, the mere sound of the amount making me wince.

"Tell ya' what, Sammy. This time I got a deal for you."

"Yeah," I asked.

"Yep," he nodded. "You straighten up after closin', and take out the trash, and you can keep the dollar you was gonna give me, and I'll give ya' fifty cents a day on top o' that. How's that sound?"

"Really," I asked feeling a bit of hope peek through the clouds.

"Really. Deal?"

I ran over and shook his hand, 'cause that's what men do when they make deals. "Square deal."

I didn't get to see much of the guys after that. I went right home, did my homework then went right up to Mr. Benner's shop.

Mr. Benner showed me how to arrange his counter, and where the rags were to clean the large mirror behind it.

Business was slow, but Mr. Benner let me clean up nonetheless, then he would give me fifty cents. I washed the windows, swept the floors, made sure all the combs were clean, and carried out the trash. For the first week, business was slow.

Then, customers showed up from nowhere.

11

"How's it goin', Sammy," Mr. Benner yelled over his shoulder as he rang up a sale.

The shop was full with men waiting for haircuts. It was December 23, and every man in the neighborhood was making sure that his hair was neatly cut for Christmas mass.

"Fine, Mr. Benner," I said as I finished shining the shoes of the man in the chair.

"Hey, kid," the man in the chair next to us called.

"Yes, sir," I asked.

"You done with him?"

"Not yet," I said. Then I grabbed that rag, gave her a twist, and flung 'er at the tip of that shoe.

SNAP!

"Now, I'm done," I answered.

"Not bad, kid," the man said looking at his shoes and flipping me a quarter.

The place was mobbed the entire day, and my arms felt as though they were going to fall off. Some men went home while they were waiting and brought back extra pairs of shoes for me to shine.

I ran it like my own little production line going from one chair to the next, catching the quarters as they were flipped to me. If a man waved me off, and didn't want a shine, I would ask the men waiting if they wanted a shine so as not to waste time.

I made my way to the last chair, and a familiar voice said, "Give 'er a special shine, Sammy."

I looked up to see Mr. McReedy sitting in the chair. "Hi, Mr. McReedy," I smiled pulling my stool closer.

"Hey, there, Sammy," he grinned. "I need 'em shinin', m'boy. I got me a date tonight."

"With Miss Harper," I asked making conversation.

"Yes sirree Bob," he grinned.

"She's nice, ain't she?"

"Yes, Sammy, she is."

"Yeah, I'm glad we're friends," I said out loud, but it was mostly to myself.

"She's glad too. She's quite fond of you. Says you helped her out a lot."

"Wasn't nothin'," I said shrugging it off.

"I need you to do something for me, Sammy."

"What's that, Mr. McReedy," I asked putting on the polish.

"Are you good at keepin' secrets. A secret just between us men?"

"Yes, sir," I beamed at the sound of 'just between us men'.

"I wanna do something for her, and I need your help, Sammy."

"Sure, Mr. McReedy. You just name it," I said finishing the first coat of water.

"I need you to get her out of her house on Christmas Eve, and keep her out of it for a while."

"How long?"

" ' Bout an hour or so."

"Will do," I agreed.

"Now, when you come to get her, I'll already be there. I'm working on some wiring in the house. So I'll pretend like we never talked. Okay?"

"Never talked about what," I said slyly, giving his shoes a finishing snap.

"Good man," Mr. McReedy smiled reaching into his pocket. "For you, Sammy."

"A whole dollar." I said excitedly.

"Merry Christmas, Sammy," Mr. McReedy winked.

"Merry Christmas, Mr. McReedy." I breathed putting the dollar in my pocket.

12

"Oh, and may the good Lord bless my feet," Mr. Benner groaned plopping down into his barber chair after the last of his customers had gone. "I'm tellin' ya, Sammy, the last days before Christmas and Easter are killers. Just *killers*."

"Yes, sir," I agreed pushing the broom with two dead arms. "They sure are."

"So," he asked. "How much doe-re-me, did ya' pull in today?"

"Four dollars and tips," I said dumping hair into the flip-top trash can. "I'm still a buck-fifty in the hole. But, I should be able to make that tomorrow."

"Not tomorrow, Sammy," Mr. Benner informed me.

"What," I asked. I was so close. All I needed was one more day.

"Nope, we're closed till after Christmas. It's the Lord's time. Gotta close outta respect. That's why we had so much business today. Last chance for a cut till December twenty-sixth."

"But Mr. Benner, I-."

"I'm sorry, son," Mr. Benner said shaking his head. "Them's the rules. I'm sorry."

"Yes, sir," I said trying not to sound disappointed. "Well, I guess I'll see you after Christmas," I said picking up my box.

"Yep."

"Well," I said shaking his hand. "Merry Christmas, Mr. Benner.'

"Merry Christmas, Sammy."

I hefted my box and hauled it to the door.

"Hey, Sammy," Mr. Benner called.

"Yes, sir."

"Forgot somethin'?"

"I don't think so."

"You work for free now, son?"

Work for free, I thought. What did he mean work for free? Two-fifty! It's the end of the week. I get two-fifty! "No, sir," I yelled, my skies again brightening.

"Didn't think so. Won't be a Rockefeller operatin' like that," he said getting up and opening the register. "Here ya' go, Sammy," he smiled handing over my money. "Now you go on, and I'll see ya' after the holidays."

"Yes, sir," I said pocketing the money.

"Give my best to your folks, Sammy," Mr. Benner yelled after me as I threw open the door.

"I will," I yelled running out onto the street.

I ran all the way home. I was in the final stretch. I had the money; I had the plan. I was looking good.

I shot down Knorr Street, bolted down the alley, and ripped through our back gate.

"Mom, I'm home," I yelled running into the kitchen.

"I see," my mom said while making dinner.

"Where's dad?"

"Out front putting up the lights."

I ran into the dining room, put my box in the corner, and took off out the front door.

My dad was on his ladder sinking Molly Bolts into the ledge of the porch, a string of lights sitting on the ladder's wooden fold-down tray.

"Well, hey there, Sammy," my dad said screwing in the last of the bolts. "Whaddaya know, whaddaya say?"

"Whaddaya know, whaddaya say, dad," I replied.

"Wanna give yer old dad a hand here?"

"Sure," I said. "Whaddaya want me to do?"

"Well," my dad said handing me a roll of electrical tape. "You take them lights there, see? And ya' start 'em at the end of the railing near the steps and tape 'em up good along the top. Then I'll run 'em up the pole and string 'em along the top. Deal?"

"Deal."

It took all of ten minutes to put the lights up, but that didn't matter. It was the fact that my dad had asked for my help that meant a lot. When you're little, it's kinda like ya' don't exist when it comes to the important stuff.

"We gotta get the tree tonight, Sammy," my dad said folding up the ladder and putting it against the wall. "Ask your mom how long it'll be till dinner's ready."

I did like my dad asked, and ran back out. "An hour," I told him.

"More than enough time. Tell your mom we're gonna go pick up a tree, and we'll be back."

I ran in, told my mother we'd be back, and ran out.

My dad and I climbed into our old four-door and off we went. My dad never bought a tree before the twenty-third, because he said they were cut too early and wouldn't last through the season. He didn't buy trees in the city either, because he said the exhaust from the cars made the trees look sick.

So we drove out Route 73, to a small stand just outside of Philadelphia.

"What about this one, Sammy," my dad asked holding up a six foot spruce which was tied tightly with baling rope.

"She looks like a fine one," I said.

"Sure does," my dad said. He paid the man and helped him heft it onto the car roof and tie it down.

On the way home we sang *Jingle Bells*, and *God Rest Ye Merry Gentlemen*. I didn't know a lot of the words, so I just hummed while my dad sang. My dad had a good voice.

We drove down Cottman Avenue and turned onto Torresdale. We reached Woolworth's when my dad said. "Hey, isn't that Billy?"

I looked over, and sure enough, there was Billy staring in the window of the store, his hands in his pockets, a bag at his feet.

My dad parked and we walked over.

"Hey, Billy," my dad said as we reached him. "Need a ride home, son?"

"Yeah, thanks," Billy answered not looking away from the window.

I followed his gaze and looked through the frosted glass.

In the center of the Christmas display filled with running trains, dolls in all shapes and sizes, and toy cars, sat a football."

"Christmas shopping," my dad asked.

"Yeah," Billy nodded not looking back. "For my brothers and sisters. Saved up money from pop bottles all year." Billy put his gloved hands on the glass. "Santa's comin' to our house this year whether he likes it or not."

Billy turned and looked up at my dad. "Mr. Hatcher, could you do me a favor?"

"Sure," my dad nodded.

"Could you keep this stuff at your house, an' I'll get it tomorrow. I don't want my brothers and sisters to see it. They still believe in this stuff, y'know?"

"And you don't," my dad asked.

"Naw," Billy answered picking up his bag. "It's kid stuff. And the sooner ya' learn that, the better off you'll be."

We all walked back to the car, turned onto Keystone and up to Longshore.

"Well, I'll see youse later," Billy said hopping out of the car.

"Okay, Billy," my dad said. "You take care now. And you can pick up those things whenever you like."

"Thanks, Mr. Hatcher," he said. "See ya' tomorrow, Sammy."

"See ya', Billy." I said feeling sad for my friend.

My dad pulled away up to Tulip Street, and circled back to Knorr.

"They don't have Christmas at Billy's house, Sammy?" my dad asked.

"Well," I said. "His dad's kinda sick, and that's why he loses his jobs. And they're kinda tight on money."

"I see," my dad said. "Well," he said in a lighter tone. "You ready for Christmas, Sammy?"

"Yes, sir," I brightened, thinking of all the things my mother would be baking tomorrow.

I helped my dad set up the tree in the corner of our living room, and with a series of loud pops, he cut the ropes. "There ya' go big fella," he said to it stepping back. "Now you just let your branches fall over night, and we'll decorate ya' tomorrow. Sound good, kids," he asked my sister and I.

"Yeah," we shouted.

After dinner, filled with the Wombat going over her Christmas list again and again. I ran upstairs and grabbed my box of loot. Dumping it on the bed with a series of *chings*, I proceeded to count it over and over.

Each time, it came to twenty-six dollars.

Bingo!

But in all the excitement of Miss Harper seeing her family, I had clean forgot about what I had originally been saving for. What about Connie Mack in the spring? What about my dad and I in the stands with roasted peanuts and pop? Then my heart sank even lower.

What about Billy's football?

I thought of how happy my dad would be watching a real live baseball game. I thought of how happy Billy would be with a new football. I thought of how happy Miss Harper would be seeing her mom and dad.

But I couldn't make all of them happy at once.

I did like my dad always told me when I had a problem. I took a better look at it, and weighed my priorities as to which I would like to come first, and what in reality should be done first. It was tough.

Being a man is tough.

Finally, after chewing on it for a while, I decided that Miss Harper should come first. And I don't mind tellin' ya' the decision wasn't easy. Now I had another problem.

How do I get to the terminal?

I mean it was all the way downtown.

I realized I would have to ask my dad. *That* made me feel even *lousier* than I already did. It was like saying, "Hey, dad, I was gonna take us to a ball game, but then I decided not too. By the way, could you drive me all the way downtown so I could spend the money on somebody else? Please? Huh?"

I felt like a schmuck, but I had to do it. It was the only way.

I gathered all my money and put it back into the box, then walked back downstairs with my head hanging a bit.

I found the Wombat was looking through decorations while my mom helped my dad turn the tree so that its bald spot was against the wall. I thought about what to say, and thought about it, and thought about it. Then in the end, I just said it.

"Hey, dad," I called walking up to my parents.

"Yeah, Sammy," my dad answered turning around.

I looked up at my dad, knowing I was going to let him down, and felt like dirt.

"Dad, could you drive me downtown tomorrow?"

"Downtown," he asked surprised. "Why?"

"Well," now came the hard part. "I have to go to the bus terminal."

"The bus terminal?"

"Yeah," I nodded. "I had this idea that maybe it would be nice if Miss Harper could maybe go home to see her folks for the holidays, so I figured, maybe I could get her a ticket."

"Tickets cost money, son," my dad smiled.

"I have the money," I opened the box and showed him. "See?"

"Good heavens," my mom gasped.

"Sammy," my dad gawked. "Where'd you get all that?"

"I saved it," I said then I figured I might as well tell him. "I was saving it for us, dad."

"For us," he asked looking from me to my mom, who shrugged in wonder.

"Well, yeah," I said hesitantly. It wasn't every day you let your dad down. "I was gonna take us to a ball game this year, and we could spend the day together. Y'know, just us. I mean, just to say thanks for teaching me how to shine shoes and stuff, y'know? I mean-if it wasn't for you, I wouldn't know how to do any of it. I just wanted to say thanks-y'know, just for bein' around and showing me stuff." I prayed he would understand. "Y'know?"

My dad looked at me for a moment, his face softened and he turned away from me. He stood there with his hands on his hips, his head down. My mom walked over to him, whispered something in his ear then rubbed his back.

I knew it. I made him feel bad, and that made me feel worse. I felt like crawling away and hiding under a rock until I was a zillion years old.

"I'm sorry, dad," I muttered.

My dad cleared his throat then turned his head to the left. "Nothing to be sorry for, son. You take your money upstairs and keep it safe till tomorrow. I'll take you down first thing. Now, go on and let your dad finish the tree."

"Okay, dad," I said walking back upstairs with my money in my hands and my heart in my shoe.

13

The next morning I awoke to something pounding on my window. I walked across the cold room and pulled up the shade. It was vile outside. Rain mixed with sleet was knifing down on the roofs of the cars, and the walls of the houses.

I had a feeling the pinging of the sleet was the death knoll for our trip downtown.

I dressed and went downstairs where my mom was making breakfast, and the Wombat was feeding her ugly little doll.

"Where's dad, mom," I asked walking into the kitchen.

"He's out on the porch," my mother said.

I walked to the front door, and opened it to see my dad standing at the top of the steps wearing his Fedora, red plaid wool coat, and drinking coffee.

I walked up beside him, and for the first time, I didn't know what to say to him. So I just said, "Looks bad, huh?"

"Yep," he answered taking a gulp of his coffee. "Radio says it's gonna turn over to snow by noon and go on till tomorrow morning."

"Guess we better stay home, huh," I asked.

"Nonsense," my dad said putting a cigarette in his mouth. "That Chevy o' ours weighs about two tons. She'll plow right through this stuff."

"Really?"

My dad looked down at me and handed me a wink and a smile. "You go on and get your money and your coat, and we'll head out."

"Yes, sir," I yelled running into the house. He couldn't have been too mad at me. He winked! That was always a good sign!

Driving on Delaware avenue was slow going, and my dad took care not to drive fast. But after about an hour, we made it to the terminal.

The cavernous room was packed with people waiting to board outbound, or picking up arrivals. It was chaos.

My dad and I got into line at the ticket window and, after twenty minutes, finally reached the front.

"And what can I do for you," the man behind the counter asked.

"Go on, Sammy," my dad said looking down at me.

"I'd like a round-trip ticket to Biloxi Mississippi, please," I said putting my box on the counter.

The clerk counted the money then set it to the side. "All right, young man," he said. "Now what date do you want it marked for?"

"Huh," I asked.

"Well," he explained. "I stamp the ticket, and its good to return within thirty days after the stamp date."

"Well, I don't know, sir," I replied looking at my dad.

"Could we get it blank," my dad asked.

"Certainly," the clerk nodded. "I'll just sign it, then when you're ready to use it, you just come back and have the clerk stamp it."

"That'll be fine," my dad said. "We'll do it that way. Perhaps Miss Harper would like to go home when the weather's nicer, eh, Sammy?"

"Yeah," I agreed.

Smart man my dad.

The clerk wrote out a ticket and slid it across the counter, "There ya' go. Have a nice holiday."

"You too," my dad and I replied.

14

Miss Harper's ticket firmly in hand, my dad and I walked out onto the sidewalk. The snow was now nothing more than gray-brown slush in the streets.

My dad looked down at me, sleet bouncing off the brim of his hat. "I think we should run."

"Me too."

We ran down the street and jumped into our car.

On the way home, my dad and I talked baseball. We traded stats, and made predictions for the coming season.

My dad drove up to Frankford and Bridge, and down.

"You eat breakfast, son," he asked.

"No. You?"

"Uh-uh," he replied. "What say we head over to Linton's for some?"

"Really," I asked. "Just us?"

"Just us."

Wow, and it wasn't even *Friday*!

My dad pulled up against the curb opposite the diner, because the lot was full of cars and banked snow, and we sloshed across the avenue.

Entering I scoped out the booths and spotted a vacant one in the rear. I ran to it, sliding onto the bench.

"Hey, Sammy," my dad called.

I looked up to see him standing by two empty stools at the counter. "C'mon," he said. "Let's sit up here."

The counter, I thought amazed.

I slid out of the booth, and sauntered up the aisle, passing families with screaming kids. *Children*. Yeah, I was gonna sit at the *counter*.

I was a *man* now.

I hopped up onto the stool and swiveled it a few times just for fun. Aw, c'mon, a man's gotta have fun sometimes.

My dad sat down next to me and leaned on the counter.

Then I leaned on the counter.

My dad raised his hand, and the waitress came down. "I'd like a coffee please," my dad said. "How 'bout you, Sammy?"

"Hot cocoa," I said.

"And a cocoa for m'boy here."

"Anything else," she asked.

"Still makin' up our minds," my dad said.

"Okay," she smiled. "Let me get you your drinks while you're decidin'."

The waitress set down our drinks, said to call her when we were ready, then walked on to other customers.

"That was a big thing you did for Miss Harper, Sammy," my dad said looking down at me.

"Then you're not mad at me," I asked.

"No," my dad said with a quizzical grin. "Can't make a father anything but proud to see his boy turnin' into a man, and a fine one at that."

Then my dad took off his Fedora, regarded it with a smile and, gently, placed it on my head.

"For me," I asked.

"For you," he smiled. "You're gonna make a fine man, son."

I proudly straightened the Fedora on my head. I got taller! I swear I did! Just by putting it on, I got taller!

"Thanks, dad," I said looking up at him from under the wide brown rim.

My dad put his huge arm around me and gave me a squeeze, "Merry Christmas, Sammy."

I put my arm across his back that had broadened from laboring to support his family.

"Merry Christmas, dad."

Outside, the rain and sleet came down hard, but that didn't matter. The sky was gray and heavy, but that didn't matter. No, nothing mattered but that moment. That moment I sat at the counter of Linton's diner Christmas Eve day 1948. The world disappeared and it was just me and my father.

Just me and my hero.

15

That night I stood in my bedroom wondering how I was going to get Miss Harper out of her house for Mr. McReedy. I paced back and forth, the Fedora, which I had to pack with newspaper to keep it from sliding down over my eyes, bouncing on my head. Then my mother called up to me.

"Sammy, are you coming?"

"Coming where," I asked walking to the top of the steps.

"St. Leo's is having Christmas caroling. Your father and your sister and I are going. Are you coming?"

Christmas caroling?

That's it!

I ran down to my mom. "Wait here, mom," I blurted urgently. "I'll be right back!"

I ran down to the closet in the dining room, grabbed my coat, and took off out the front door. The snow was coming down hard again, and the cars were already covered. It was a perfect night for caroling.

I just hoped Miss Harper thought so too.

I ran up onto her porch and banged on the door.

"Why, Sammy, hello," Clara said opening the door. "What is it?"

Mr. McReedy walked up behind her grinning.

"We're going Christmas caroling. Do you wanna come with us?"

"Who's going," Clara asked.

"My whole family."

"You know, Ed, I haven't been Christmas caroling in ages. Let's go."

"You go," he replied. "I have to finish snaking that new wire to the second floor."

"It can wait, can't it?"

"Not unless you want your fuses to blow out every time you flick a switch," he answered. "But you go on, and I'll finish it up. Okay?"

"Are you sure," she asked. "I could stay and help."

"No, no," he shook his head. "You go on and have fun."

"Well, if you're sure."

"Clara, I'm positive."

"Okay, let me get my coat."

She walked away and Mr. McReedy handed me a wink and a thumbs-up.

I did the same back.

"All right, I'll be back in an hour or so," Clara said as she pulled on her coat.

"You have fun, now," Mr. McReedy said. "I'll see you when you get back."

Clara and I walked down to my house where my family stood on the porch. From there we walked down to the church.

The pastor met us all at the steps of the rectory, and handed out white candles to the grown-ups who promptly lit them. Then one of the sisters from the convent handed out the books of carols.

In one long procession, we paraded down Keystone Street, stopping at houses and singing carols.

We sang everything from the *Ave Maria,* to *We Three Kings of the Orient*. It was a good time. The snow was falling, the candles were burning brightly behind shielding hands, and Christmas at last was in the air.

"Hey, Sammy," I heard a voice call.

I looked around and saw the guys running down the block.

"Hey, Sammy," Bull called skidding to a halt. "Carolin', huh?"

"Yeah," I nodded. "Youse guys wanna come along?"

"Ah, I don't know," Bean said.

"Oh, come on, boys," Clara said. "You can even share my book."

"I'll sing," Loverboy beamed running over to her and looking into her book.

We all rolled our eyes.

We marched down Keystone to Longshore, then up to Torresdale Avenue, where we stopped on the corner and sang to passers-by who, in turn, smiled and wished us a merry Christmas.

My dad handed me his book and the guys and I used it, even Billy seemed to be enjoying himself.

We walked down Torresdale to Unruh Street, then down to the church, stopping at each house along the trip.

Finally we made it back to the church, and went into the school's basement, where the Ladies Auxiliary had made hot cocoa and cookies for all the carolers.

There we sang more songs and drank cocoa and talked to neighbors we had only seen before in passing.

"Hey," Bull said, his mouth crammed with cookies. "These eats ain't bad."

"Yeah, it's pretty good," Bean added.

Tag Along said something, but all that came out of his clogged mouth were crumbs.

I swear, that kid thought his mouth was twice the size it really was.

Loverboy walked up to Clara, who was drinking a cup of hot chocolate. "These cookies
are good, but not as good as *yours,* Miss Harper."

"Why, thank you kindly, Terry," Clara smiled. "The very next time I make them I'll be sure to send some over to yo-."

Terry backed away from her, his eyes bugging out of their sockets.

"Terence, what is wrong with you," she asked.

Loverboy's mouth dropped open spilling crumbs and half-eaten cookie onto the floor.

Then Loverboy took in a deep breath, screamed bloody murder, and ran.

Amy Martin flew past us.

"Get away from me," Loverboy screamed running the length of the hall.

"Terreeeeee," she cooed following his every step.

"Ooooooh, Lovvvvverrrrrboyyyyy," we all yelled.

"No," Loverboy screamed dodging her and darting up the steps.

"Terreeee, waaaaiiiitt!" Amy yelled bounding up the steps after him.

"Oh, my," Clara chuckled with wide eyes. "Is he going to be all right?"

"Sure," Billy said drinking his cocoa. "If he don't stop runnin'."

Then all us guys burst out laughing.

Forty-five minutes later, we walked down Keystone Street toward Knorr.

The guys said their goodbyes at the corner of Knorr, all except Billy, who retrieved his brothers and sisters presents from our house

"What's going on up there," Clara asked standing at our gate looking up at her house.

We all looked up at the end of the block and found that Clara's house was completely dark.

"I don't know," my dad said.

"Wasn't Ed up there," my mom asked.

"Yes," Clara nodded sounding a bit concerned. "I hope he's all right."

"What was he working on, Clara," my dad asked.

"He was replacing wiring going to the second floor."

"If he touched the wrong wires . . ." my dad said to himself.

"Sam, that's not funny," my mom said sounding a bit concerned herself.

"I'm not laughing," my dad said beginning to walk up to the house, Clara, my mom, the Wombat and myself followed close behind.

We walked to the end of Knorr Street and looked at the house, which now stood like a dark husk, the only thing moving was the falling snow.

"Ed," my dad yelled over. "Ed, you in there!"

"Molly, this is scaring me," Clara whispered to my mom.

"I'm sure he's all right," my mom said, more to convince herself than Miss Harper.

After a few moments we heard the creak of the metal storm door, and Mr. McReedy stepped out onto the porch. "Hi, folks," he yelled. "Have fun caroling, did we?"

"Ed," Clara said taking a few steps forward. "What are you doing in there?"

"Stay there, Clara," Mr. McReedy said then he turned and went back into the house.

"What is he doing," Clara asked.

"No idea," my mom said shaking her head. "You know how men get."

"Clara," Mr. McReedy yelled through the storm door.

"Yes, Ed!"

"Merry Christmas!"

In an instant, the entire outside of the house exploded in colored bursts of light. They framed the roof, down the sides, across the porch, and down the support poles. It was spectacular, the brightest house on the block.

"Oh, my," my mom and Clara gasped.

"Ed, ya' outdid yerself," my dad laughed.

"Wow," Tilly gasped. "Sammy, you see that?"

"Whoa," was all I could say.

Mr. McReedy ran across the street to us and put his arm around Clara. "Ya' said you haven't had a real Christmas since you got here, so . . ."

"Ed," Clara said a little teary. "It's beautiful."

Then she kissed him.

Normally I would have thought that kissing a girl was disgusting, but not this time. This time it was all right.

"It's wonderful, Ed," my mom said.

"Thanks," Mr. McReedy grinned.

"Helluva light show, buddy," my dad agreed.

"Like to kill myself putting up the ones on the roof."

"Y'know something, Miss Harper," I said.

"What's that, Sammy?"

"Your house kinda looks. . . *happy*."

"It does," she glowed. "Doesn't it?"

"Yeah."

"Come inside, and see what else," Mr. McReedy said excitedly.

"There's more," Clara asked.

"Sure thing," Mr. McReedy nodded.

We all walked inside to find a Christmas tree fully lit, but still not decorated standing in the corner. "What would Christmas be without a tree," Mr.McReedy said gesturing to it.

"It's beautiful," Clara said walking over to it and touching the branches.

"I bought it for my apartment," Mr. McReedy said. "But a Christmas tree always looks better in a house, I think."

Miss Harper ran over to him and put her arms around his waist. "Thank you, Ed."

"Merry Christmas, Clara," Mr. McReedy smiled. "Oh, and I think you've got something on your dining room table too."

Clara stepped back and looked at him sideways.

"Hey, I'm just sayin'. . ." Mr. McReedy shrugged.

Clara walked into her dining room and turned on the light.

In the center of the dining room table sat three boxes wrapped in bright paper. One was large and rectangular, the other a smaller rectangle, and the last a small square one.

"Ed, what did you do," Clara asked.

"Wasn't me," Mr. McReedy protested. "I hear a knock at the door, I open it, and there's this fat guy in a red suit. He comes and leaves it. I just figured you knew him."

Clara and my mom laughed.

"You mean Santa was here," Tilly asked, her eyes wide.

"Sure was," Mr. McReedy said. "But he said he wasn't coming to your house until you were asleep."

"Aw," the Wombat moaned.

"Well, go on, Clara," Mr. McReedy said. "Let's see what you got."

Clara looked at us all with hesitant embarrassment.

"Oh, go on," my mom nudged.

Clara gave Mr. McReedy another timid glance then picked up the smaller of the oblong boxes. She tore open the wrap revealing a white box underneath. She pulled open the lid, and her eyes turned to saucers. "Ed," she gasped. "It's beautiful."

"Do you like it? Really?"

"Yes," she nodded. "Yes, I do. Molly, look at this," she said pulling a long blue evening gown from the box.

"Good heavens," my mom said. "Ed, is that real silk?"

"Sure is," Mr. McReedy nodded. "Picked it out myself. Well, go on," he nudged again. "That's only number *one*."

Clara opened the large box, and her eyes widened again. "Ed, this is the coat we saw at
Wanamaker's."

"Yeah, ya' said ya' liked it."

Clara slowly removed the coat from its tissue paper bed. It was a long black wool coat with fur around the collar and shiny black buttons. Clara immediately put it on, cuddling the fur around her neck. Then she took it off and gave it to my mom. "Molly, try this."

My mom put it on and pulled the collar tight. "Ooh, this is *nice*," she agreed. Then she turned to my dad. "Sam, I think next year, you should go shopping with Ed.'

"Thanks, Ed," my dad huffed good-naturedly.

"Think nothing of it," Mr. McReedy beamed. "One more, Clara. Ya' can't stop now, I'm battin' two for two."

Clara smiled and picked up the small box. She unwrapped it, and her jaw dropped. "Ed, they're beautiful."

In the box was a pair of earrings with a small diamond that dangled from a thin gold chain. "Ed, you shouldn't have."

"No, I had to," Mr. McReedy replied. "The church has a New Year's Eve party every year, but I never went because I had no one to take. And I was wonderin', If ya' weren't busy-that maybe you and me could-well, y'know."

"Yes, I know," Clara smiled. "I would love to go."

"You'll be the prettiest one there, Clara."

Mr. McReedy glanced to his left, then the glance became a stare, then his smile faltered and disappeared.

We all followed his stare over to the wall of the dining room. We looked at the wall with the picture of the bomber on it. Our eyes then fell to the buffet buffet with the war stuff and the picture of Clara's fianc on it. Our eyes stopped at the picture of a guy who looked like he belonged in the movies, right up there beside George Raft and Gary Cooper.

A real leading man type.

He looked back from the wall to Clara, then to his shoes, then back to her. "I know we haven't known each other that long," he began. "And I know I'm not as handsome as yer old fella was. All I can say is, I like you a lot. And If you'll' just give me a chance, I promise I'll never hurt ya', Clara. And-well-before ya' say anything . . . Clara, I can't compete with a ghost."

Mr. McReedy got quiet after that and looked down at his shoes again before looking back to her.

A tear ran down Clara's face as she looked at Mr. McReedy. Then her lips began to shake. Then she looked angrier than a hornet.

She stormed out of the room and into the kitchen. The back door slammed against the wall as she threw it open and went outside.

A few minutes later, she came back in with a metal trashcan.

Throwing it up against her buffet with a loud crash, she began to throw the war mementos into it.

The scene was so violent we didn't know what to do. We just stood there and watched her heave piece after piece into that can.

Later, I realized she was doing more than just throwing away pictures. She was throwing away *him*. She was refusing to sit in the dark any longer, crying over a man who had left her. She was standing up against him and what he'd done.

She was taking her life back.

Clara picked up the photo of the smiling flyer and slammed it so hard into that can that the glass shattered. She grabbed the picture of the bomber and smashed it down over the back of the dining room chair shredding it right up the center.

"No more," she panted looking at us with tears rolling down her cheeks. "No more sitting here alone. No more letting the past eat at me. No more bad memories. It's time for a new life," she said then she smiled. "Time for new friends."

She walked over to Mr. McReedy' wrapped her arms around his neck, and as soon as he put his arms around her she went limp as the weight on her vanished.

She buried her face in her chest for a moment then looked up into his eyes. "Time for new memories."

Then Mr. McReedy kissed her. A big one, like my dad gives my mom when he comes home from work.

Clara rested her head on his chest a while longer, looked back at the buffet. There was one more thing on it.

The model of the B-52.

She walked over to it, picked it up, and handed it to me. "Sammy, I remember you liked this. I don't want it, do you?"

I took the plane, and looked it over.

The B-52 was a fine war machine.

"He gave this to you," I asked.

"Uh-huh."

"Then I don't want it either," I said slamming it into the can.

Then Clara and I smiled at each other.

"Oh, Ed, darlin'," she said in a musical Southern Belle accent.

"Yes, dear," Mr. McReedy answered with a slight grin.

"Why, I declare, I do believe it's time to take out the *trash*. Would you be so kind, sir?"

"My pleasure, Miss Harper," Mr. McReedy said hefting the trashcan and carrying it from the room.

"Let me give you a hand, Ed," my dad said taking the picture of the B-52.

"Thank you, Sam."

"Ed?" my dad asked as they walked through the kitchen.

"Yeah?"

"You really blow up my bridge?"

"'Fraid so."

"I really liked that bridge, Ed."

"She was a beauty all right."

Clara and my mom laughed. Then my mom turned to her. "Clara, are you all right?"

"I'm fine," Clara said as my dad and Mr. McReedy came back. "I really am. And I do think this is the best Christmas I've ever had."

"Ain't over yet," my dad said.

"What?" Clara asked.

"Sammy has something for you too."

"Holy cow," I yelled. "I almost forgot!"

I felt like such a lunk head.

Reaching into the pocket of my coat, I handed the envelope over to her.

"What is it?" she asked.

"Open it," I said with a smile I couldn't help.

"Why, I just don't know what to do with all this attention," Clara said as she opened the envelope and pulling out the ticket. "This is all just so-," she stopped and gasped.

"What is it, Clara," Mr. McReedy asked.

"It's a ticket," Clara breathed, looking from it to me. "It's a ticket to Mississippi. Sammy," tears welling in her eyes. "I-I don't know what to say."

And to tell you the truth, at that point, neither did I.

"It's so you can go see your mom and dad," I said finally.

Clara knelt down and looked at me.

"It don't have a date on it, so you can go whenever ya' want. Ya' just have to get it stamped first," I told her. "Ya' gotta see the ticket clerk for that, then it's good for thirty da-."

Clara grabbed me and hugged me so hard I thought my lungs were gonna pop.

"Thank you, Sammy," she sobbed. "This is one of the best presents I've ever gotten."

"Merry Christmas, Miss Harper," I said hugging her back.

"Yes it is," she sniffled. "Merry Christmas, Sammy."

Then something struck me. Maybe this whole girl-thing wasn't so bad after all. I mean, they smelled kinda nice, and when ya' held 'em, they were kinda soft and mushy.

Yeah, I knew I was gonna like bein' a man.

We all sat in Clara's living room around the tree. The grown-ups had coffee, and Clara made cocoa for Tilly and me.

It was about eleven o'clock when my dad stood up and yawned. "We better get goin', or Santa might get tired o' waitin' for these kids to go to sleep and not come at all."

"And you two still have to finish decorating this tree," my mom said standing.

Clara and Mr. McReedy walked us to the door where my parents spent another fifteen minutes saying goodbye while my sister and I froze on the porch.

That night, I lay in bed awake again, only this time everything seemed right with the world. Snow fell softly outside my window, the bulky quilts kept me warm under their comfortable weight.

My door opened.

I watched Tilly walk over to my bed, her ugly little doll in her arms. Her eyes were full of concern. Quietly she sat on the edge of the bed. "Sammy, you sleepin'?"

"No," I answered. "Whaddaya want?"

"I didn't hear Santa yet," she said mournfully. "Maybe we stayed up too long like daddy said, and he ain't comin'. Y'think?"

"Nah," I answered. "He'll come. Ya' just can't hear 'im is all. He walks real light like. He's real good at it. He's been doin' it for a long time y'know."

"Well, what if he thought I was bad, and didn't come?"

"He won't think you were bad," I said. "Don't worry. He'll be here.

You wait an' see."

"Okay," she said standing up. "Merry Christmas, Sammy."

"Merry Christmas, Tilly."

Tilly held out her ugly little doll.

"Merry Christmas, *Sophie*," I added.

Tilly smiled and walked to the door.

"G'night, Sammy."

"G'night, Tilly."

16

The next morning, paper littered the floor of our living room as Tilly and I opened our presents. Mom and dad sat on the sofa having coffee, smiling as they watched us gleefully open our gifts.

In the future, when I had children of my own, I realized that was a 'Parents' Christmas', watching the looks on their children's faces as they opened their gifts. The oohs and aaahs, and wows seemed to make the lengthy chore of shopping all worthwhile.

Tilly got some new dolls, and some dresses, and a new pair of shoes, and a baby coach. I got a new baseball glove, and some shoes, and some clothes, and some other toys.

I sat there, my wide-brimmed Fedora propped back on my head looking that glove over like it was made of gold. This summer, I would be playing in style, boy!

A knock came at the door.

"Who could that be," my dad asked out loud as he went to the door and opened it. "Billy," he said festively. "Merry Christmas."

"Merry Christmas, Mr. Hatcher," he answered as my dad let him in.

"Merry Christmas, Billy," my mom smiled.

"Merry Christmas," he said with a nod.

"Billy, look what I got," Tilly yelled excitedly, running over and showing him her new doll.

"She's a pretty one, Tilly," Billy smiled.

"Merry Christmas, Billy," I said walking over.

"New glove, huh," Billy said.

I looked down and realized I was still wearing it. "Oh, yeah."

"Nice one," he said digging into the pocket of his coat. He pulled out a wrapped box and handed it to me. "Here, Shotgun. Merry Christmas."

I looked at him feeling like a sap then I took it. I unwrapped the box and opened it. My eyes went wide, and my jaws dropped. "Wow," I breathed. "Gloves with the fingers cut out!"

"Cut 'em off myself," Billy said proudly. "Just like mine."

"Billy," dad called from the dining room.

"Yes," he answered.

My dad walked into the living room with a wrapped box of his own. "Here," he said handing it over. "Santa must've left this here by accident. Y'know, since our houses are so close and all."

Billy and I looked at the box, then to each other and shrugged.

"Must've," Billy agreed a little surprised.

"Well open it," I said.

Billy opened it to reveal a brown box that was folded shut. He pulled open the flaps and looked at my dad with his mouth wide open.

"Merry Christmas, Billy," dad smiled.

"Sammy," he breathed. "Sammy, look," he said pulling out the football we had seen in Woolworth's window. "Mr. Hatcher, I-," he began.

"Billy could I talk to you for a minute," my dad asked, nodding toward the kitchen.

"Sure."

My dad took Billy into the kitchen and they stood at the table. I couldn't hear what they were saying.

My dad looked down at Billy and said something. Billy looked down at the floor and nodded. Dad said something else, and Billy gave another nod and swiped at his eyes with his sleeve.

Then Billy looked up and my dad put a hand on his shoulder and said something else.

Billy nodded and smiled as he swiped at his eyes again.

Then dad put an arm around his shoulder and they walked back into the living room.

Billy looked at me kind of embarrassed. He'd been crying. He knew it, and he knew that I knew it, too. But we were friends. And friends know when not to make fun.

"Hey, Billy," I said. "Bet that thing'll fly a country mile, huh?"

"And if it can't, I bet you could make it, Sammy," he laughed.

I took off my mit and slipped on the green wool gloves Billy gave me. Then I held out my hand. "Merry Christmas, Sailor.'

"Merry Christmas, Shotgun."

Then we shook hands like men.

"Hey," Billy said in a bright tone. "Ya' wanna go throw the ball around!"

"Sure," I nodded, just as anxious as he was to try it out.

"Oh, no you don't, Samuel Hatcher," my mother said. "We still have to eat breakfast and go to church."

"Aw," we both moaned.

"Hey, Billy," my dad said. "You wanna stay for breakfast and go with us?"

"Yeah, sure," Billy nodded. "Let my folks wrestle with Ernie for a while.'

Both my parents laugh.

17

What happened after that?

Well, Clara did go to Mississippi, but not until spring, and Mr. McReedy went with her. From what she told my mom, unlike the flier, Mr. McReedy and Mr. Harper had hit it off just fine.

A year later, they were engaged, six months after that, they were married, and I was in the wedding. A year after that, after fixing it up, they sold the house on Knorr Street, and bought one on Rawle, just around the corner.

And the summer after that December . . .

Oh, what a summer it was. I worked like a dog at Mr. Benner's barber shop all winter, and come summer, My dad, Mr. McReedy, and all us guys were in the stands of Connie Mack, screaming till our faces were red.

I'm sixty-five now, with children and grandchildren of my own

I live not too far from my old house on Knorr Street, and every once in a while, on the way home from work I'll drive by just to look at it.

All us guys stayed close through the years, Tag Along lives just a block away from me; his brother Bean lives up in Lawncrest.

Bull lives on Levick Street and is in charge of security for Philadelphia's new ballpark. Which means, opening day . . . we're there.

Loverboy? Well, let me tell ya' about Loverboy. The greatest day of his life was the day Amy Martin went off to college for four years. It looked like it actually added ten years to his life.

But wait, there's more . . .

When she came back, she was something else again. She had gone to NYU and when she returned none of us recognized her. She looked like a model out of a magazine.

She actually caused a guy to slam his car into a pole when she was crossing the street.

The funny part was, Loverboy finally fell for her. She put that poor guy through the wringer. He begged and pleaded for her to go out with him. He bought her flowers, he bought her candy, and she still wouldn't look twice at him.

She made him get down on his knees and beg her to go out with him right in front of all of us. And he did it. Unbelievable.

What a stupe.

They live over in Castor Gardens now, Loverboy is a State Representative, and Amy practices law for a firm downtown.

And I'll tell ya', she could still cause an accident or two.

Then there's Billy . . .

Billy hung around our house a lot after that Christmas, and became part of the family.

His father kept his job at Dodge Steel, but his problem with booze lasted for five years after that, until the bosses threatened to can him if he didn't get help.

Billy sat his father down one night, and they talked for hours. Billy stayed close to him while he kicked the habit, and said it wasn't easy for either of them. But he hastens to add that the friendship that developed after it was over was worth it.

Billy went to Father Judge, same as me, and we both landed on the football team, even though baseball was still my favorite sport.

We made quite a name for ourselves there. Yep, Billy "The Sailor" Merrill and "Shotgun" Sammy Hatcher tore up a lot of playing fields together. We even had our nicknames stenciled on the backs of our jerseys.

And when Billy put on the moves, the stands went wild.

Billy and I did everything together from the time we were kids. Inseparable, we were. We were almost like brothers. Now, I guess we're closer.

Now he's my brother-in-law.

The Wombat had struck again.

I was the best man at their wedding, with the other guys as ushers. It was a good time.

I danced with my sister, who now insisted on being called Matty instead of Tilly. She looked like an angel in that long white dress.

"You look beautiful, Matty," I said as we danced.

"Thank you, Sam," she smiled.

"Well, looks like you got to marry your hero, huh?"

"Yeah," she nodded. "But he wasn't my first hero."

"No?"

She shook her head, tears formed in her eyes and she gave me a hug. "Thank you for all the times you were there for me, Sammy."

It was then I realized why my father turned away from me that day. And to be honest, I felt like turning away myself. Instead, I gave her a squeeze. "That's what big brothers are for, Tilly."

"Sammy?"

"Yeah?"

She stuck her finger in her mouth, swished it around, and jammed it in my ear.

"Wet Willie, Wet Willie!" She screamed.

"Oh, gross," I laughed slapping a hand over my ear.

We both stood there laughing at each other. It was then I knew I wouldn't have to keep such a close eye on my little sister anymore.

The Wombat had learned the art of timing.

My wife and I drop in on Billy and Matty often. While there, we laugh about the tauntings, and bring up the most intriguing question. . .

Exactly what *was* the thing under the bed?

I mean, every kid had one, but no one ever really knew exactly what it was. All that was ever known about the thing was that it only came out when the lights were off. One night while we were sitting in their kitchen, Tilly finally figured out what the thing under the bed was.

It was the second cousin of the thing in the closet.

I spent a lot of time at the kitchen table of our old house talking with my dad. We could spend hours just talking about nothing. And nothing was just fine with us. It's a wonderful thing, growing up.

First we talked father to son.

Then we talked man to man.

Then we talked friend to friend.

Reminiscing together would fill an evening for us.

Y'know, looking back on my younger days, I don't know how we managed those little Friday night excursions. We were like most Tacony families, blue-collar, working hard for what we had. And after long talks with my dad, I found that the times I thought we were rich, we were actually living literally from pay check to pay check.

But our parents, through scrimping and saving, never let us feel it.

And at two in the morning, after my mother was in bed, we'd sit over two Stegmeir's and I'd say, "But I remember those times to be the happiest, dad."

My dad would fold his arms, shrunken a bit with age, and look around at the silent house, then back. "This house never had a lot of money in it, son, but it had a lot of love. And if ya' really think about it; which would you rather have?"

A smart man my dad.

Well, I've taken up enough of your time, and I know you have things to do, it bein' the holidays and all. So, I'm gonna let you get going. Sorry about rambling so. Well, Merry Christmas, and a Happy New Year to you all. Hope you weren't bored. Thanks for list'nin'.

I think I'll call Billy.

Suddenly I'm in the mood for a snowball fight.

The
Long Road Home

1

Christmas Eve.
30 Miles East of Bangor, Maine
6:00 P.M.

Dear Mr. Middleton . . .

The words that began letters like these never ceased to strike fear into Harvey Middleton's heart. They were the words that came in the official brown envelopes with the little window in the front so he could clearly see that the letter was for him and him alone.

"Dear Mr. Middleton," the mere sound of them inferred affection, but the words that followed had no affection in them. No, the words that laid between the beginning capital letters to the ending periods were cold.

Cold and businesslike.

Harvey Middleton sat in his red plaid shirt and worn jeans at the kitchen table, his eyes reluctantly running over the words that the bank had been kind enough to make sure had been delivered today. No, they couldn't have waited for *next week*. That would have indeed been a sign of affection, or at least compassion. No, these words had to be delivered today.

He supposed they thought the words would have more of an impact on Christmas Eve.

Middleton took a sip of his beer as he finished the letter. His brown eyes set firmly in his weathered face, a face that looked older than its forty-two years, looked solemnly at the bubbling and peeling wallpaper. The wallpaper looked shabby in the sunlight, but the sun had decided not to shine today, and the light of the fluorescent circle in the center of the ceiling made it look worse.

"Harve," a woman in a flowered dress called walking into the kitchen, "The kids were wondering when they could start decoratin' the tree. I told 'em it was up to you."

"Decorate it for what," Middleton huffed bitterly taking another drink of his beer.

"Harve, what's wrong," she asked sitting in the worn chair at the other side of the table.

"This," he answered holding up the paper. "It's a letter from the bank. They say we're three months behind on the mortgage and unless we cough something up come Monday, they're gonna put it on the block. Oh, yeah, and by the way, they said merry Christmas."

"But, they *know* you were outta work all that time, it's not like we just weren't payin'. They should at least-."

"They don't *care*, Bev'," Middleton roared loud enough to make her jump. "All my life I've worked. All my life I've struggled," he bellowed his face reddening. "For what! For what," he screamed balling up the paper and hurling it angrily at the wall. "For what, Bev!" So we could live like rats in an overpriced shack that's fallin' down around our ears! Is that it! Is that what I got arthritis and a bad back for!"

"Shush, Harve," Beverly Middleton blurted. "The children'll hear y-."

"Hear what, Bev," he shot back. "Hear that their old man's a failure! That all his life he's been a failure!"

"You're not a *failure*," Beverly shot back, her voice rising.

"I'm not," he asked angrily. "Look at this," he said rocking the kitchen table on its one bad leg. "Look at this," he rumbled grabbing a piece of hanging wallpaper and tearing off a huge patch.

"Harvey stop it," Beverly screamed standing.

"We got a heater that ya' gotta kick to keep started, we got a damn stove that could blow up at any time, we got drafts so bad, we might as well not have any damn windows at *all*! No, I'm not a failure! I'm just on o' your run-of-the-mill goddamn success stories!"

Middleton heard the floorboards creek and turned to see his twelve-year old son, Ethan, and his eight-year old daughter, Marie, standing in the doorway, their eyes wide. He looked at his son who stood there in his worn jeans and tee-shirt, then to his daughter who stood like a statue in a pair of old hand-me-down clothes and tattered sneakers.

"You two go decorate the tree," Beverly Middleton said shooing them into the living room. "Everything's all right."

"It's not all right," Harvey said to her as their children left the room.

"Harvey," she said softly. "Things'll get better."

"Oh, sure they will," he grunted. "Look at you, Bev'."

"What," she asked looking herself over.

"Look at that dress you got on," he said bitterly. "When was the last time you had a new dress?"

"Harvey, I don't *need* a new dress," she answered.

"I know you don't *need* a new dress," he rumbled back his face shaking. "It's just that you should-," he stopped. In the center of the hurricane that was his face, his eyes filled with rage. "I should be able to give y-." He lowered his head, turned to the counter and sent his fist down on it hard enough to shake the dishes that sat on its top. "Dammit!"

Beverly Middleton stood motionless as her husband lowered his head, his body still his voice silent. She could feel it ebbing off him like a hot tide. Frustration. Frustration that comes from a willing back no one will put to use. Frustration at watching his family struggling to get by. Frustration at having to grovel to keep what he had worked for his entire life.

Frustration of a strong soul made to feel weak and broken.

"Honey," she said calmly as she wrapped her arms around his waist and laid her head on his back. "You just be still now. Things will get better. We just gotta keep the faith is all."

"I don't know, Bev'," Middleton said staring blankly at the wall. "The rich spend their money, the poor collect the welfare, and we eat garbage 'cause we just wanna work for a better life. I mean, when this country's in trouble, who do they come to, Bev'? They come to us.

"They take us for wars, they raise our taxes. They tell us we gotta tighten our belts just a little bit more. And we do it, and what do we get? I'm tellin' ya', it's like the Middle Class is the crutch this country walks on when it's hurt, and it's the first thing it throws away when it's mended. And what did we get for it?"

"Wallpaper that's real easy to peel off?"

Despite himself, Middleton had to laugh; behind him he could hear his wife laugh with him. Turning around he put his large arms around her and pulled her close. "I think I'd go crazy if I didn't have you, girl. Y'know that don't you?"

"I haven't been a girl in a long time, Harvey."

"You'll always be a girl to me, Bev'. My girl."

Beverly Middleton grinned closing her eyes like she always did when he held her like this. The arms she felt around her weren't rich. The arms around her weren't connected to a big-city big shot in fancy-pants clothes.

In these arms she felt safe. In these arms, no matter how bad things seemed, she could run within their grasp and feel that nothing could touch her. In these arms she could find comfort. These arms were connected to something more valuable than gold, and in her opinion, something that in these days was becoming more rare.

These arms were connected to a man.

In her eyes, from the day she had first met Harvey Middleton, she knew he was just that. He didn't complain when he had to work sixteen-hour days when the plant told him to. He didn't whine when he lost his job, he merely went out and found another one. But when the last one folded, jobs had become hard to come by. And in the mind of her husband, a man who couldn't work to support his family was no man at all. And to him, taking assistance would mean the loss of dignity and honor.

The loss of that would have killed him.

"Harvey," Beverly Middleton called softly.

"Yeah?"

"Why don't you come to church with the children and me tomorrow? Every Sunday you just drop us off. Why don't you come in for a while?"

"'Cause me and God got nothin' to say to each other," he answered flatly.

Beverly Middleton stepped back and looked up at him shocked. "Harvey," she gasped. "You shouldn't be talkin' like that. It's sinful"

"What do you think He feels is worse, Bev'," Middleton asked walking from her and picking up his beer. "Some one who doesn't talk to Him at all, or someone who gets down on their knees and prays to Him every Sunday and doesn't mean it? Which do you think He hates more? A sinner or a hypocrite?"

"God doesn't *hate* anyone," she answered flabbergasted as he walked to the kitchen doorway.

"You're wrong, Bev'," he answered looking around the kitchen then back to her. "God hates."

After he left the room, Beverly Middleton cast her eyes upward. "He's a good man. He didn't mean it. Please . . . He didn't *mean it*."

2

Beckman and Son's Trucking Co.
Bangor.
6:10 P.M.

"No, dad, it just arrived *now*, " Bert Beckman Jr. explained anxiously over the phone. Beckman was a scrawny little man in his mid-thirties dressed in a cardigan sweater and loafers. His father Bert Sr. had built the company from the dirt it sat on to what it was today. He was a trucker and the men who worked for him respected him for that. But "Junior", as the truckers referred to the younger Beckman was what they liked to call him behind his back a "College Puke."

"*Now*," his father repeated. "That damn shipment should be in Augusta by *now*!"

"I know dad," Junior replied walking to the window of the small trailer office. "But the weather slowed him down." Junior looked out into the yard at the heavy snowfall. Outside, fifteen yards from the window, sat a twenty-foot trailer with floodlights on it, and painted red no less, and from where he stood, he could see none of it.

"The trucker said it got bad at the Canadian border and got nothin' but worse on the way down."

"Son, this is the biggest account we've ever had. If we keep it, we got it made," the father explained. "But that load *has* to be in Augusta my mornin'!"

"Dad, I *know that,* but-."

"But, *nothing,* " his father roared. "You get a man in a rig and get that damn truck to Augusta! If that shipment isn't in Augusta unloaded, sorted, and ready to go out by the twenty-sixth, we lose it! Do you understand me?"

"But how," his son asked. "You can't see your hand in front of your face out there."

"No, kiddin'," Beckman Sr. replied. "I got windows, Junior. You start callin' around. Go by seniority. You give em time and a half under the table, and a two grand bonus if they take it. That oughta force one of em outdoors. If I was still truckin', I'd take it. You got any ground help still there?"

"Morris and Scheafer are out back yet."

"Unhook that Canadian piece o' crap and rig up the Silver Streak."

"But, dad," Junior protested. "We just *bought* that. That thing cost us-."

"Do it," Bert Sr. rumbled. "She's big, fast, and oughta rip through this stuff with no problem."

"Yes, sir. But what if I can't find anyone to take it?"

"Then you'd better learn how to drive a stick," Bert Sr. snorted.

The color drained from Junior's face.

"Yes, sir."

Bert Beckman Jr. began to place the calls.

6:15 P.M.

"Forget it, *Junior*."

Click.

"Two grand? For what, my old lady to bury me with? Beat it, *Junior*. "

Click.

"No way. You got a problem with that, tell it to the union."

Click.

"Oh, sure. That time and a half will do me a lot of good in the boneyard, *Junior.* "

Click.

3

6:20 P.M.

"Harvey, please," Beverly pleaded kneeling down beside the torn chair her husband sat in. "Just this one time? What could it hurt?"

"And what could it help," he asked.

The phone rang.

Harvey watched his son drop the tinsel and run to the small end table. "Prob'ly the dentist wantin' his damn fillings back."

"Dad, it's for you."

"Who is it, Ethan?"

"Mr. Beckman."

Middleton's face held a confused expression as he walked to the phone.

"Hello?"

"Harve, this is Bert."

"Yeah, what do you want, Bert?"

"We got a problem down here."

"And that is . . .?"

"We got a shipment of supplies from Ottawa that's gotta get to Augusta tonight"

"Good luck to ya', Bert," Middleton said looking out the window.

"Harvey, we need you."

"You looked out your window lately, Junior?"

"Yes."

"Then you know you don't need *me*. What *you need* is the mercury to jump about sixty degrees."

"Harvey, we're prepared to give you time and a half under the table. A full day's worth."

"Ooh. I make what, nine an hour. No dice, Junior."

"Harve, there's a two thousand dollar bonus in it for you for your troubles."

Middleton stopped and turned to his son. "Ethan, there's a crumpled up piece of paper on the counter. Get it for me, will you?"

"Harvey, I'm waiting."

"Give me a minute."

"Harvey, I-."

"You know how to drive a truck, Junior?"

"No."

"Then hold your damn water a minute."

Ethan ran back with the balled up note from the bank. Middleton smoothed it out on the end table and looked it over. Fifteen hundred in the rears. The bonus would cover that, and the five hundred plus his wage for the haul could cover new clothes for the kids, a new dress for his wife, and a new heater.

"What would I be drivin'?"

The question made Beverly rush to his side. "Harvey Middleton, you're not going out in this are you?"

"Bev', please."

"The new rig we got in last week."

"The *Silver Streak*? "

"Yeah."

"Morris still there?"

"Yeah."

"Tell 'im to stay put till I get there."

"See you when you get here."

Middleton hung up the phone and walked to the closet, his wife close behind. "Harvey, this is insane," she reasoned. "The plows are barely keeping up with what's coming down out there." In any other state, that wouldn't mean much, but in the great state of Maine, a place where summer only really owned one month out of the year, that was saying a lot.

"Bev'," Middleton said, "we need this."

"No, we don't. We need *you*."

"I ain't arguing this with you, honey," he said in a soft tone as he put on his old brown suede coat. "I'll be back sometime in the AM."

On his way to the front door, his eyes fell on his son who was looking out the window. Ethan turned from the storm and ran up to his father as he reached the door. "You goin' to work, dad?"

"Yep," Middleton answered. "Got a load hasta be in Augusta by mornin'."

"But the snow ain't lookin' so good."

Middleton looked down into his face and could see the apprehension. With a smile, he knelt down in front of him. "Ethan, sometimes a man's gotta do things he'd rather not do. He does these things to keep care o' his own. Understand?"

The boy nodded.

"Good," Middleton smiled. "Now you look after your mom and sister. You're the man of the house till I get back."

An invisible weight dropped onto Middleton's shoulders as his words came from his mouth. The words stabbed at him like a million knives. "I mean," he grinned. "I'll be back come mornin'. You make sure the windows are tight, and the doors are locked. Deal?"

"Deal," Ethan nodded.

"Now give the old man a hug."

"Aw, dad," he moaned.

"Come on, I won't tell no one."

Reluctantly, Ethan put his arms around his father's large neck. Harvey Middleton gave him a squeeze. "Ethan," he whispered.

"Yeah, dad," his son whispered back.

"You stay young as long as you can, boy."

"OK."

"Promise me?"

"I promise."

"Good," Middleton whispered with a smile giving his son a peck on the cheek before standing.

"I'll say prayers for you," Beverly assured as her husband opened the door to howling winds.

"Good," Middleton said pulling his gloves from his pocket and slipping them on. "While you're talkin' to Him, see if He can't do something about the plumbing. He could part the Red Sea, maybe He could get us some hot water too."

"I'll see you when you get back," Beverly said with a tinge of anger in her voice.

"Will do," Middleton replied ignoring it.

Opening the storm door that lead out onto the long driveway, Middleton stepped out. Immediately the property lit up with a blinding white light from the motion sensor activated floods he had put on the garage. "Jeeze,' he muttered covering his eyes as he walked to the garage door.

With a hard pull the door broke free of the snow and rattled its way up the tracks. Middleton looked down at where the snow had packed against its wood frame. Looked to be around seven inches, he figured. Kneeling down, he grabbed a handful of it and crunched in his fist. Opening his hand, he found it still in a powder. *Dry snow, too,* he thought to himself. *No damn good*.

Turning to his old '86 Suburban that now sat with its hood up and its battery connected to the heavy-duty charger mounted to the wall, he groaned. Pulling the alligator clips from the terminal and fender, he threw them out of the way and slammed the hood down.

Getting behind the wheel, he started the engine and gave it a few revs. Looking out at the snow, he gritted his teeth and slowly backed the Chevy up to the rear wall of the garage. Some cars, he figured, knew how to look pretty. Some cars knew how to go fast. Some cars knew how to save gas.

But Chevy Suburbans . . .

He switched to four-wheel drive and hit the gas.

Chevy Suburbans knew how to get ugly.

The Chevy hit the snow running sending white clumps into the air. Its grill hammered its way through like a plow as its tires dug like teeth into packing snow. Harvey laid his weight on the gas knowing what would happen if he stopped. A swerve here, slide there, and a brief threat to go sideways, and he was out onto the road where the plows had lowered the snow enough for him to regain traction.

Beverly Middleton watched with a pounding heart as the Chevy drove from the light's reach, into the darkness, then out of sight.

4

Beckman and Son's Trucking Co.
7:39 PM

"All right," a man in a red plaid wool coat and hunter's hat yelled hooking up the last of the hydraulic lines. "That'll do 'er!"

On the other side a man in a parka gave a thumbs-up with one gloved hand. "This one too! Now, let's get the hell home!"

Running at full speed, the two men bolted toward the trailer, the one in red slipping, flying into the air and landing with a grunt.

"Morris," the one in the parka called stopping. "Will you quit foolin' around!"

With an angry groan, Morris dragged himself to his feet and began running again.

The two men shot into the trailer where Junior sat at the desk slamming the door behind them.

"Whoa," Morris exclaimed whipping off his hat. "Mama Nature is *pissed* to*night*."

"You noticed that, too," Scheafer grinned handing him a cup of coffee.

"Thanks," he nodded taking the cup more to warm his hands than to drink. "Hey, Junior," he asked.

Beckman shot him an angry glare.

"Oh, excuse me, sir. Mr. Beckman, sir."

"What," Junior asked looking back to the trucking manifests.

"Who'd you get to take the haul?"

"Middleton's coming in."

Morris and Scheafer looked warily at each other.

"Something wrong, gentlemen," Beckman asked looking from one to the other.

"Middleton lives a half mile from me," Morris said. "He got a wife and two kids. Couldn't you've found somebody else?"

"I know he has a wife and two kids," Beckman replied. "I suppose that's why he's taking this haul."

"But he's got family."

"Yeah," Scheafer chimed in. "Couldn't you've got Myer to do it."

"Yeah, what an ass *he is*," Morris added.

"Yeah," Scheafer agreed. "If anyone deserves to ride this pony it's *him*."

"Myer has seniority, Middleton just started. It's his ride."

"That and you know he needed the money, right?"

"He could've refused:" Beckman contended.

"Tain't right," Scheafer said under his breath.

Beckman shot him another glare shutting up his protest.

"Where is it," Middleton blurted coming through the door, snow flying in around him.

"Close the damn door," Beckman yelled.

"Mike," Middleton nodded as he slammed the door.

Morris nodded.

"Glen."

Scheafer nodded.

"Where is it," Middleton asked turning to Beckman.

Beckman picked up the manifest and pulled a set of keys from a rack behind him. "Loading bay one."

"You two ride in together this mornin'," Middleton asked Morris and Scheafer as he took the keys and papers.

"Yeah," Scheafer nodded.

:"Good, I need a favor, Mike," Middleton said slipping the trucks keys into his pocket.

"Anything, Harve."

Middleton pulled out his key ring, slid off the smaller ring that held his car keys and held them out to Morris. "I want you to drive the Chevy back to my place and give the keys to my wife. Just in case I ain't home by tomorrow. She'd hate to miss church, y'know?"

"Yeah, Harve," Morris said taking the keys. "Sure thing."

"Well, take care, guys," Middleton said looking back as he opened the door.

"You too, Harvey," Scheafer and Morris replied.

"Morris, Scheafer," Beckman said as the door shut. "Get the Canadian rig into bay two and lock it down for the night. Make sure all the bays are secure and the rigs hooked up to their chargers."

"Sure," they answered walking out the door.

As the two men reached the center of the yard a horn blared making them jump.

"There he goes," Morris said as the huge blue, silver striped, semi pulled its haul out of the gate.

"Tain't right," Scheafer repeated as they headed to the bays.

8:03 P.M.

Beckman sighed as he put on his overcoat and slipped the last of the manifests into the desk drawer. A burst of biting wind and snow flew through the door as Morris threw it open.

"Close that damn door," Beckman bellowed.

"Sorry, Jun-Mr. Beckman, sir," Morris said closing the door after Scheafer.

"Everything locked up," Beckman asked slipping on his leather gloves.

"Yes, sir."

"Then you two can go on home."

The phone rang.

"Beckman and Son's Trucking," Junior answered.

"Did that load for Augusta leave yet," Beckman Sr. asked.

"Sure did, dad," Junior answered proudly. "Be there by mornin'."

"Call it back."

"What," Junior answered incredulously. "But you said if we didn't get it there-."

"I don't give a good goddamn what I said," Beckman replied loud enough for Morris and Scheafer to hear. "Call that damn truck back! Who's drivin it and does he have the Silver Streak?"

"Middleton's driving, and yes he has it, like you said."

"Good, that thing's got a spare generator and a cabin back. Get on the box and tell him to stop wherever the hell he is and shut it down for the night. I don't want any of my people on the road now."

"But you said earlier-."

"That was earlier," Beckman Sr. bellowed. "Thing's have changed. Haven't you been watchin' TV or been listening to the radio!"

"No, I've been getting the manifests in order," Junior answered.

"Just get a hold of Middleton and tell him to shut 'er down till tomorrow morning."

"Yes, sir," Beckman said then hung up.

"What was that all about," Scheafer asked.

"Turn on the television," Beckman ordered as he walked to the CB on top of the filing cabinet behind his desk. "Put on the Weather Channel."

While Morris flipped on the small thirteen-inch television, Beckman turned on the CB hearing nothing but static. "Middleton," Beckman called into the handset as he flipped frequencies. "Harvey, come in."

Morris and Scheafer sat in silence, their eyes widening. Beckman turned to the TV, his jaw dropping. "Morris, turn the volume up."

"It's lookin' like a real humdinger for the states along the Canadian/American border tonight," the cheerful voice of the weatherman dressed in his festive red and green sweater echoed in the office. "As you can see from our Doppler Radar shot," he said motioning to two white blobs one coming down from Canada, the other coming in from the Atlantic, "that this storm means business. Up into Canada we have one front moving South, and from the Atlantic we have yet
a*nother* front moving west.

"These two *very precipitous* fronts have already merged to form one nasty storm which is now pummeling the upper New England states and a good part of Canada. The good new is, albeit small," the weatherman laughed.

"Yuk it up, chuckles," Morris said angrily.

"Shut up," Scheafer said.

The weatherman pointed to the front coming from the Atlantic. "The good news is; the more dominant of the two fronts coming in from the Atlantic is carrying with it some very high winds which should *push* the joining systems out to the Midwest. But unfortunately for those states already hit, that movement should not be taking place until sometime in the wee hours of the morning. Possibly these states could see some clearing by two or three AM, but by then these states could see up to three feet of snowfall.

"A Severe Storm Advisory has been posted for Maine, Vermont, New Hampshire, Rhode Island, and Upper New York. Just in from Maine; the governor is now considering placing a State of Emergency, but is yet undecided. We'll update you folks on that as it develops."

"Jeeze Louise," Morris breathed.

"Middleton, come in," Beckman called into the microphone, his voice now urgent.

"You ain't gonna get him on that thing in this weather," Scheafer said grimly.

"If you took one of our rigs, do you think you could catch him?"

"You kiddin'," Morris said. "He's had a twenty minute head start, and he ain't stupid. He's probably cannonballin' it all the way to 202. We ain't gonna catch him now."

"Well, listen," Beckman said trying to sound positive. "I'm sure he'll pull it over if it gets too bad. No sense in us hanging around here tonight. He'll probably spend the night in Augusta. Let's just go home and I'll try to raise him tomorrow morning when the weather breaks. He'll pull over, right? Right?"

"Don't try an' clear your conscience on me," Scheafer replied. "Told ya' it wasn't right sendin' a man out in this. Hell, I wouldn't send a *dog* out in this."

Southbound 202
8:17 P.M.

"Come on, baby," Middleton coaxed lowering his foot on the gas. "This ain't nothin'," he told the truck. "This ain't nothin'. We've had worse."

Middleton looked anxiously out the windshield his eyes searching the darkness beyond his fifty-feet of visibility.

Along the road, cars littered the highway. Some were now only white humps, others partially covered. Still others lay by the roadside in twisted heaps, their windshields blown out. They were the carcasses left by the animal of winter.

Middleton eased up on the gas.

You're the man of the house till I get back.

The words echoed through his head as he watched heap after heap go by.

Shoulda never said that to him, his mind burned. *It's too much pressure on a boy.*

Now you look after your mom and sister.

DAMMIT, I SHOULDA NEVER SAID THAT!

5

9: 00 P.M.

"Come on, now," Beverly Middleton said walking over to her children who sat complacently in front of the television, "time for bed."

"Do I gotta," Marie protested.

"Yes, you gotta," Beverly answered.

Ethan stood up and turned off the TV. He looked up at her, his face serious. "I'm gonna go check the windows and doors before I go."

"You do that," Beverly smiled.

As she watched her son walk into the kitchen a rapping came at the door. She rushed over breathing a sigh of relief. "Harve," she said opening the door. "You didn't go after a-."

"No, Bev'," Morris said. "Just come by to drop off the Chevy."

"Why," she asked, her voice rising. "Did something happen?"

Behind her, she could hear Ethan walk back into the living room.

"No. Good gosh *no*," Morris blurted. "Harve wanted me to bring it back in case he had to lay over so's you could get to church. I already pulled it into the garage for ya'."

"Oh," she answered forcing a smile and taking the keys.

In the light of the floods, he could see a dark cloud cover her face as she looked at them.

"Bev', he'll be fine," Morris said.

"I hope so," she said looking around wildly, her eyes shining. "They say even the plows are getting stuck out there. If anything happened to him, I don't know what I'd do."

"He'll be fine," Morris said again forcing a commanding tone.

From behind a horn blared.

"I gotta go, Bev', Glen's waitin on me. If ya' need anything . . ."

"Thank you, Mike," she nodded.

Morris gave a weak grin, then headed back down the driveway.

Beverly Middleton closed the door, walked to the chair her husband had been sitting in and looked down at the keys in her hand.

"Mom, are you all right," Ethan asked taking her hand.

"I'm fine, honey," she answered with a sniffle.

"You goin' to bed?"

"No, I'm gonna wait here until your dad gets home."

"You want me to stay with you," he asked concerned.

"Oh, no," she said with a smile rubbing a hand over his cheek. "You go on to bed. Daddy'll be here soon."

Reluctantly, Ethan Middleton agreed. Giving his mother a peck on the cheek, he walked slowly up the steps.

Beverly Middleton sat alone in the silence of their living room looking solemnly at the keys. She couldn't go to bed. She and her husband hadn't slept apart in fourteen years, even when she had given birth to their children he had been there overnight. No, she would rather sit alone in the light and hope, than lie alone in the dark and wait.

6

Route 202 southbound
Augusta Exit
10:30 P.M.

WELCOME TO AUGUSTA

Middleton breathed a sigh of relief at the sight of the sign. "It's good to be here," he said to the sign as he passed it on his way off 202. "Ah, Maine," he said to himself. "The Pine Tree state, where you'll find beautiful coast lines, friendly people, picturesque countryside, an' idiots like me on the highway in a blizzard on Christmas Eve. Harvey Middleton," he said easing the semi around onto a deserted street, "you are a real yahoo. One for the All-Time Yahoos Book all right."

Making a left, he eased the tractor down another deserted stretch of street taking care not to hit any of the cars that littered its sides. Dry snow and a good-sized semi with a full load is a bad combination and he knew it. Gotta keep it moving at a steady pace, no slowing down, no speeding up, especially when it came to the tight spots. One good hump buried under fresh snow would be good enough to send the trailer swaying, and with a heavy load, bounce-back time was slow.

Yep, one good swat by a semi could play holy hell with a car for sure.

Fifteen minutes of breath holding, palm-sweating maneuvering, and he was there. In front of him sat two large double-gates, on them a sign that read: MONROE AGRICULTURAL SUPPLIES. "Praise the Lord and pass the bottle, here we are," Middleton hollered sending two horn blasts out into the night.

A few minutes later, a man in a yellow poncho and a security guard's hat appeared at the gate and quickly swung them open. Holding onto his hat, he ran to the cab waving his free arm.

Middleton rolled down the window.

"You the shipment from Bangor," the guard asked climbing up to the window.

"Yeah," Middleton answered.

"Damn," the guard breathed. "We'd given up on ya'. Figgered you'd bedded down for the night."

"Naw," Middleton said with a shake of his head. "I gotta get back by mornin'. My family's waitin' on me."

"You sure," the guard asked. "We got room for your rig. You can bed down in your cabin here tonight."

"No thanks," Middleton replied politely.

"Be safer. We got five truckers parked in here already."

"No, I really gotta get back."

"Well, in that case, we'll try to get ya' outta here as quickly as possible," the guard conceded. "Take 'er over to bay five and we'll unload as fast as we can."

"Much obliged," Middleton grinned throwing the tractor into gear.

"Don't mention it."

The scream of the hydraulic brakes filled the air followed by the rumble of the diesel engine as the Silver Streak pulled her load into the yard.

Before the rig, like small bugs, old pickups fitted with plow blades worked feverishly to keep the open lot cleared. To the left in the big yard, Middleton could see the lights of the loading docks. Easing his truck to the last one, he backed up and half drove, half slid, into the padded bumper beneath the bay door where three men waited anxiously with tow-motors.

Middleton cut the engine and hopped out of the truck. "Here ya' go, fellas," Harvey said jumping up onto the dock and pulling out the manifest. "Do me a favor and get me on the road by eleven, huh?"

"Will do," one worker nodded. "Break room's in there on yer right. Coffee machines an' the like."

"Thanks."

Middleton walked into the bays filled with stacks of chemical fertilizer, seed, tractor and combine parts, and anything else a farmer or lumber man would find a need for. Pulling off his gloves, he headed into the truckers break room.

The small room consisted of vending machines with everything from Little Debbie Cakes to coffee and cigarettes lining the right wall. In the center, three men sat at a beaten-up table playing cards.

"You just in," the haggard looking man at the end of the table asked putting a cigarette in his mouth.

"Yeah," Middleton nodded plugging a quarter into the coffee machine. "Down from Bangor."

"A real mess out there tonight," another trucker commented.

"That's for sure," Middleton agreed pulling his coffee out of the machine. "They got a phone around here?"

"Phone's out," the first trucker answered. "Been out since nine."

"Tastes like mud," the third trucker warned as Middleton sat on the bench beside him.

"Just as long as it's *hot mud*," Middleton replied taking a sip.

"Amen to that, brother," the first trucker nodded holding his cup up in a toast.

"Where you boys from," Middleton asked pulling out a cigarette and popping it into his mouth.

"Name's Chuck Furley, outta Tulsa," the first trucker said shaking Middleton's hand.

"Mick Davis, outta Pennsylvania," the second trucker replied shaking his hand.

"Stan Black, come in outta Buffalo," the third trucker said shaking hands.

"Rough ride," Middleton asked. "Been here long?"

"'Bout an hour for me," Davis replied. Came in on 95. Wrecks all over the place. Seen a few stuck plows, too. Hell, even came up on a wreck right in the middle of the inside lane. Rolled right up on it."

"What'd ya' do," Middleton asked.

"Plowed that sucker right off the road," Davis said laughing. "I figured, hey, it's already banged all to hell, so a few more dents ain't gonna do nothin' but increase what the driver gets from the insurance company, right? Them bloodsuckers get enough o' our money anyway. Besides, it was one o' them little foreign jobs. You know, the ones made out o' plastic? Flew off real easy. No sweat. Sent it off onto the shoulder. Did other drivers a favor."

"You sure it was empty," Furley asked.

"Sure, I'm sure." Davis replied getting up and going to the coffee machine. "I ain't stupid. Thing was all cut up and open. Whoever was in it was long gone. By ambulance probably. Good thing, too. With that visibility out there, I was on top of it before I knew it. And you boys know what happens when you gotta do a tight swerve on packed-down wet snow."

The three nodded.

"Yeah," Davis agreed. "Next thing you know your butt's racin' your nose down the highway an' you're dealin' with sparks an' busted glass. No thanks. I don't need to go down *that road*. "

"Hear, hear," Middleton chorused with the others as they raised their cups of mud.

"Nah, I'll bed down here tonight, an' head back tomorrow," Davis said sitting back down. "Besides, Christmas day my kids come over with the grandkids and all that. What a screaming mess. I like to sit down, a little TV, a beer. Leave me alone it's my day off, y'know? I'll let my wife field it. She loves it when the house gets torn apart by the kids. She's real into the holidays like that. Besides, how many times can you get underwear and say, 'Ohh, this is great! Just what I wanted!'

"Whoever says, 'Ya' remember that big-screen TV that was on sale, kids, and that nice reclining chair with the back massager and heater built into it? Well, forget those. What I'd really like is a bunch of economy six-packs of tighty whities. Or, perhaps, a nice tie that I'll only wear to funerals and weddings.' Which in my opinion are *almost* the same thing *anyway*."

All the men burst into laughter.

Middleton liked Davis. The Pennsylvanian had a slick, dry, wit that a man from Maine could appreciate, and his humor calmed the tightness in his chest he had left over from the drive down 202. Davis lit up a cigarette, shuffled the cards, and began to deal.

Nothing like cards to pass the time, Middleton thought.

7

10:56 P.M.

"So what did ya' do then," Furley asked Davis, who was busy studying his cards, his cigarette dangling.

"Well," Davis replied throwing down two cards and picking two out of the deck. "Here I am at this toll booth, right? I got no quarters, no dimes, no bills till I hit a machine, right? And here's this schmoe at the tollbooth telling me it's two-fifty. I tell him I ain't got it. He tells me, he don't care. I tell him I got fish in the back that'll get up and do the hokie-pokie if I don't get this truck to Reading soon, but he don't care."

"And . . .," Middleton asked.

"So," Davis continued. "I act like I'm fishin', excuse the pun, for change, right? I'm goin' in the glove compartment, under the seat, on the visor, you name it and I looked there. And the whole time, this mutt's waitin'. Well what he ain't seein' is the line formin' behind me."

"Oh, no," Black groaned.

"Oh, yeah," Davis nodded with a sly grin. "So, I look in my side mirror, and the lines going up the ramp and out onto the Turnpike. There were some pretty ticked off yuppies in them cars let me tell ya'. They're honkin', screamin', the whole bit.

"Finally, I let the schmuck have it. I look at him and say, 'Two-fifty was it?' And he says, 'Yeah.' I get outta my cab and dig into my pocket. And I start givin' him pennies."

"You didn't," Furley laughed.

"Yeah," Davis nodded. "Counted them off too. One penny, two pennies, three pennies, felt like the vampire on Sesame Street. One penny, hahaha, two pennies, hahaha, three pennies, hahaha! I get up to ten and he finally says, 'Go on, get the hell out of here.' And I said real innocent like, 'You sure? I got more.'"

"And he let ya' go," Harvey asked.

"Yeah. Good thing too," Davis laughed. "I was runnin' out o' pennies."

"Damn that was good," Furley howled nearly falling off the bench.

"Mr. Middleton," a man called into the break room.

"Yeah?"

"Your rigs ready to go."

"Thanks," Harvey said getting up.

"You ain't goin' back out in this are ya'," Furley asked.

"Gotta," Middleton said buttoning his coat. "Family's expectin' me back come sun up."

"I wouldn't," Furley added.

"I wanna be there when my kids get up," Harvey said slipping on his gloves.

"Hey, Harvey," Davis said.

"Yeah, Mick."

"You come up on any wrecks, you hammer it a good one for me," he grinned.

"Will do."

"Made damn good time, boys," Middleton said to the workers as he walked out onto the dock. "Appreciate it."

"No problem," they yelled back. "Drive safe now."

"You know it," Middleton answered climbing into the cab.

8

Route 202 northbound
11: 59 P.M.

The ride had been treacherous, the snow falling in blankets now mixed with hail. Middleton had counted three abandoned plows on the roadside, their yellow lights still flashing to avoid collisions. Middleton searched the road, his eyes moving with the slapping beat of the frozen-over windshield wipers. He had seen no one for the last ten miles.

Then he saw the flashing red and blue glow in the distance.

As he neared, he could see the State Patrol had cars lined end to end across the roadway. Slipping into low gear, Middleton brought the truck to a halt. A trooper got out of his car and walked over to the cab gesturing for him to roll down the window.

"What's the problem, officer," Middleton asked not seeing any wrecks or ambulances.

"Governor declared a State of Emergency around eleven-thirty. Route's closed till daybreak."

"Closed," Middleton asked in disbelief.

"Hard to believe," the troop agreed with a shake of his head, "but that damn storm ain't goin' away like they said. It's just hoverin'. They say it should move on by four AM. Oughta have the roads movin' by six. All depends on when we can free up those plows back there. Hell, we got damn near four feet already. We got orders to send everyone into Waterville until daybreak. They got the diner open and the school's set up for one big pajama party."

"But, I gotta get home *tonight*."

"Yep," the trooper nodded. "You an' ev'rybody else. Nothin' we can do. It just ain't safe tonight."

"All right," Middleton conceded his shoulders slumping. "Thanks."

"Sure thing," the trooper said stepping back. "Just stay right and follow the signs."

The Silver Streak pulled out and followed the line of bundled troopers who had appeared with orange cone-covered flashlights to wave him onto the exit.

"This is great," Middleton huffed. "This is just *great*."

There was a diner in the center of town and Middleton figured he would hold up there until the roads opened. Pulling the semi onto Main Street, he slowed the semi. The diner was at the other end right on its boundary where the town gave way to part of Maine's wooded region, a region that took up ninety percent of the state.

As he drove under frozen traffic lights that now flashed all three of their colors, he could make out the glow of truck lights and a large sign for Benny's Diner. "Here we go, Harve," he said to himself. "Good luck findin' a booth tonight."

Pulling over beside the diner on the street so he could move out first, he hopped out of the cab. He locked up the truck, waded through the drifts in the parking lot, and finally reached the door.

Middleton opened it to find a sea of faces looking at him. He nodded his hellos as he walked through the crowd looking for a seat.

"Hey," he heard a voice call.

Harvey turned to see four men sitting in a booth. One wearing a flannel shirt over long johns and a dirty red ball cap waved. "You a trucker," he called, the other three men watched.

"Yeah," he called back. "Comin' up from Augusta on my way to Bangor."

"You union?"

"Just got my card last week."

"Well, then," he said cheerily as he moved over. "Grab some wood, brother."

Middleton nodded his thanks as he walked over and sat down. "Where you boys from," he asked.

"We're half a convoy headed to Quebec, the other ha-."

"Can I get you something, sir," a waitress broke in.

"Just a coffee, thanks," Middleton said.

The other truckers shook their heads obligingly.

The waitress forced a smile and walked away.

"I was hopin' to make it to Bangor tonight," Middleton said sadly. "Got a wife and two young ones waitin' on me. Phones are out, can't call. My Bev' must be goin' nuts."

Middleton looked up from his hands to see the other men looking at each other solemnly, as if they had something to say, but weren't sure if it was right.

"What," Middleton asked. "What's up?"

For a moment, the men said nothing, then the ball cap shrugged and lit a cigarette.

"How bad you wanna get home, brother," he asked exhaling smoke.

"What do you mean?"

"I mean," he began again, "how much of a risk would you take to get home tonight?"

"Tell me," Middleton asked not hesitating.

"Well," the ball cap said pulling a map from the bench between him and his partner. "This is what I'm talkin' about," he said unfolding the map and laying it on the table. "Lookey here, brother," he said pointing at the map. "Here's 202, and here's us. Now, like I was tellin' ya, we're half a convoy. The leader of the other half decided to try to make it tonight. Ain't sayin' it was smart, ain't sayin' it was stupid, just sayin' he did it.

"He rolled 'em out right over here," he said poking a thumb at the wall, "on Waterville Rd. He back roaded it, brother. Took 'em for a walk in the woods. And by the sounds of it they was high-ballin' it too. There ain't no lights, and there ain't no moon, but there ain't no *troopers* either. Get m'meaning?"

"Yeah."

"Now, he figured he would back road it smack into Bangor, and try his luck from there. All I'm sayin' is, you got four semi's flyin' ahead o' ya', and they left no more'n twenty minutes ago. If you head out now, you can follow their tracks. They're plowin' the way for ya'. But, like I said, it's dark, and it's back roads, and you ain't even got the moon on yer side. That's why I asked ya' how bad ya' wanted to get home."

Middleton looked over the map apprehensively. Maine back roads were winding, and if this guy didn't know which ones to take, it could mean a four-truck pile up, and he didn't want to be the fifth. The back roads were marked off in pencil, some with names written along them. Whoever this trucker was, he had a working knowledge of the area.

Middleton nodded as he ran his finger along the route, knowing most of the roads. Then his finger stopped at the last one leading into Bangor. The road was named Pineview. Middleton grinned at the name. He knew the road well. After all these years he should.

He drove out his driveway onto it every day.

"Waitress, make that coffee to go," Middleton yelled. "Thank you," he said standing and pulling his collar up around his neck.

The ball cap folded the map and held it out. "Keep it, brother. We ain't goin' nowhere until 202 reopens. But before you go, I gotta tell ya' this. . ."

"What?"

"If you're serious about makin' that run, you're gonna have to do no less than forty, and that's pretty damn fast for navigatin' woods in the dark on a night like this. But, I'll tell ya', you go any slower and give that rig time to sink in, you'll be stuck out there until spring thaw and that don't happen 'round here till *July*."

"I'll remember that."

"How long you been truckin'," the ball cap asked.

"'Bout a month now," Middleton admitted.

"Well, this may sound crazy," the ball cap said, "but I ain't lyin'. I been haulin' fifteen years, and I'm tellin' ya', there are times when it's best to leave yer keys in yer pocket. And there are roads that don't want people on 'em. Them's killin' roads."

Middleton tried to smile, but the ball cap's eyes were dead and serious.

"Tonight's one o' them nights," ball cap warned. "And on a night like tonight, those are killin' roads. And that's why I'm keepin' my boys right here till dawn. You ain't lived until you've rolled twenty tons o' steel, brother. It's like havin' the gates o' Hell open up and the devil scream right into yer soul."

"Thanks for the warnin'," Middleton nodded chills racing up his spine.

"An' yer goin anyway," the ball cap asked.

"I have to."

"Well, in that case," the ball cap said standing and holding out a friendly hand. "May God go with ya', and may the sun find you safe at home, brother."

"Thank you," Middleton smiled feeling a bit eased by the well wishing as he shook the ball cap's hand.

"Good luck to ya'."

Middleton picked up the coffee and walked back out into the whipping storm. He ran the route over in his mind as he fired up the Silver Streak's engine. There were some bends and sharp turns, especially toward the end near Pineview where the road made a sharp right onto a steel bridge that crossed a creek.

He could make it.

Middleton threw the truck into gear and headed off down Waterville Road. The tracks were like the ball cap had said, there were four sets, and they overlapped one another. The traction was good. Harvey hit the high beams, then pressed down on the gas.

Within minutes, he was in sight of the woods, their great trees standing like wooden soldiers at attention. He looked down at the speedometer checking his speed. With a rumble of the engine, and a swish of snow, he found himself enveloped in thick trees, with nothing but snowed-over tracks moving in the arc of the headlights.

It was time to take a walk in the woods.

9

Christmas Morning
12:01 A.M.

Beverly Middleton stared blankly at the glimmering lights on the tree. It was past midnight and still no word from him. She forced herself to think of better times, which seemed sadly enough for the two of them, few and far between.

She caught a glimpse of motion from the corner of her eye and turned.

Ethan stood on the steps dressed in his long johns, his face filled with worry. "Dad ain't home yet," he asked walking over to her.

"No, sweetie," she grinned. "Soon. What are you doin' up?"

"Couldn't sleep," he shrugged. "Can I stay down here and wait with you?"

"Sure you can," Beverly smiled laying a hand on his shoulder.

"Ya' want some tea, momma? I could make ya some."

"How 'bout y'make some o' that hot chocolate with those little marshmallows."

She could see Ethan's face brighten. Hot chocolate in the Middleton household was a treat. It just wasn't a necessity. But on Christmas, Harvey was certain to buy it for the kids to warm them when the shoveling and the sledding were done. But, it had to be asked for, and it wasn't always given. Moderation was a way of life in this house.

"Yeah," Ethan asked.

"Yeah," Beverly smiled. "You go on and heat the water."

"Okay," he smiled running into the kitchen.

Outside the wind howled savagely enough to make her jump.

"Lord, keep him safe," she whispered. "He spoke out of turn, I know, but he's trying. He only wants what's best for us. Please bring him home." She lowered her head, a tear running down her cheek. "Please," she begged. "He's good man."

She looked at the tree fighting for better thoughts. In their shimmering lights she lost herself so completely, Ethan had to shake her.

"Yes," she asked, startled.

"Here, momma," he said holding out a mug.

"Thank you, sweetie," she smiled as she took it.

Ethan sat down in front of her and looked at the tree.

"Where's yours, honey," she asked.

"I'm gonna save it for dad when he gets home. It's cold out there," he said laying his head against her leg.

"I'm sure he'll appreciate it," Beverly said forcing the words through the red-hot lump in her throat.

Ethan Middleton could feel his mother run a gentle hand through his mussed brown hair. He closed his eyes and concentrated on that feeling. He was young, but he'd seen enough winter storms blow through Maine to know this was the worst in his lifetime.

He knew he had to stay here.

If his father walked though the door, he could show him that he had done his duty.

And if he didn't . . .

Ethan Middleton shut his eyes as hard as he could.

He knew he had to stay here.

He was the man of the house now.

10

The Maine Backwoods
1:08 A.M.

"Whoooooeeee," Harvey Middleton hollered as he shot the Silver Streak toward Pineview. "Come on, Mother Nature," he screamed out the windshield at the falling snow. "I got something for ya'! Oh, yes I do! I'm comin' home to ya', Bev'! Harvey Middleton's luck is about to change, girl! It's gonna be a great Christmas!"

The road widened before him and he knew the sharp right and the steel bridge would be coming up shortly. From there it was just three short miles to his driveway. He would park the truck, kiss his wife, hug his kids then have a beer.

He stepped on the gas.

The truck dipped then rose as it hit the snow that had packed under the weight of the trucks from Quebec, but the Silver Streak took them in stride. Harvey lit a cigarette and took a celebration puff.

Up the road to his right, he saw an orange glow in the woods, flickering in the darkness. As he passed it, he looked out the window, but couldn't make out where it was coming from. *A fire,* he thought. *On a night like this? Better call the troopers when I get home.*

Then from nowhere chills shot up his spine as the words of the ball cap came back to him. *You ain't lived until you've rolled twenty tons o' steel, brother. It's like havin' the gates o' Hell open up and the devil scream right into yer soul.* Middleton forced the words from his mind and turned back to the road.

That was when he saw the eyes in the darkness.

The devil's eyes.

Red and myopic just beyond the light in the darkness they stared into his eyes. "What the-," Harvey blurted. Then it came into the light. A buck. The largest he had ever seen. It had to be at least two hundred pounds and had no less than fifteen points on it. And there it stood dead in the lights of the Silver Streak.

Hypnotized.

"Damn," Middleton screamed swerving the truck to the left. Beneath him, he could hear the wheels slip. The tree line headed straight for his windshield. He turned into the slide and brought it out just as the trees slammed the front left fender bouncing him across the road.

Furiously, he spun the wheel trying to steady the tractor. From behind, he could hear slamming. Looking to the side mirror, he could see the trailer beginning to rock. "Oh, God, no," he breathed as the truck again grazed the trees, bouncing back off only to be thrown into the trees on the other side.

The trailer began to fishtail. Behind him, Harvey could feel the thunder as the trailer ripped into the trees. The front end began to tilt.

A yellow sign whipped by.

"Oh no," Middleton yelled spotting the guardrail for the right turn. Grabbing white-knuckled onto the wheel, he sent the truck hard right. The horizon began to tilt again. He looked into his side mirror and watched in horror as the trailer began to tip. He could hear the whine of the right tires as they left the ground.

The world tipped on its side.

Harvey hit the door with a heavy thud as the semi rolled, the speed not decreasing. He looked on in horror as the large steel supports of the bridge shot toward his windshield. His mind now ran a thousand miles a minute, his thoughts confused.

Pictures flashed before his eyes.

Ethan looking up at him.

You're the man of the house until I get home.

No! His mind screamed. *He's just a boy!*

An old man in a hospital bed with a half-mobile face and sandpaper-covered scars for hands.

You're the man of the house till I get home, boy.

No! It's too much pressure on a boy that age!

I should've never said that!

Ethan . . .

Now you look after your mom and sister till I get back.

The old man in the bed. . .

You look after you brother and sister and your momma till I get home.

Middleton covered his face as the girder flew at the front of the truck.

I should've never said that to you!

ETHAN!

Large steel double doors.

FORGIVE ME!

Middleton heard the world come alive as the gates of Hell opened.

Glass exploding.

Ethan, I didn't mean it!

Pain searing into his legs.

Stay young for as long as you can!

Metal crushing.

Beverly, girl, I love you!

The warmth of blood on his face.

You should've had more!

The devil screaming.

You deserved better than me!

Darkness.

God hates.

From the darkness a picture faded in, and with it the nauseating smell of antiseptics. Harvey found himself in the hall of St. Matthew's Hospital in Portland. He could feel a hand holding his, and looked up to see his mother, her face full of worry.

"Over there, Harvey," she said walking him to the admissions desk.

"Can I help you," a nurse at the desk asked.

"I'm looking for Ethan Middleton, he's my husband. The workers at the dock said they took him here."

"I believe he's still in emergency. The doctor will come out to talk to you as soon as they're done with him."

"Done with him," she blurted. "What are they doing to him!"

"Mrs. Middleton," the nurse said quietly. "Please calm down. The doctor will explain everything."

"But-."

"Please, just have a seat right over there. Doctor Brentner should be with you shortly."

It was summer, and it was hot in the hospital, Harvey thought. His dad had fallen down, and that was why he was here. That was what his mother had told him. He sat quietly in his worn jeans, his beat-up shoes, and his old 4-H tee shirt waiting with his mother for what seemed to him to be an eternity.

Soon a doctor emerged from the large steel double doors.

"You wait here, Harvey," his mother said as she walked across to meet him.

Harvey couldn't hear what he was saying, but whatever it was, his mother didn't want to hear it. She shook her head and turned around, the doctor moved back in front of her again, his mouth still moving. Finally, the doctor ushered her though the large double doors.

After fifteen minutes she came back.

She walked over to him and knelt down. "Harvey, your dad wants to talk to you. I want you to go in there and talk to him like you always do. You hear me?"

"Sure, mom," he shrugged not understanding what she was telling him.

"You go on then, and I'll wait for you out here."

"Okay," he said getting up and walking to the doctor that waited at the doors.

The doctor ushered him into a room of beds surrounded by curtains. Once they were inside, the
doctor stopped him and knelt down. "Now . . . Harvey is it," he asked.

He nodded.

"Now, Harvey, your dad's gonna look a little bit different, all right," the doctor told him. "But he's still your dad. I want you to go talk with him. It would be good for him right now. Okay? Can you do that?"

He nodded again.

"Okay," the doctor smiled. "He's right over there."

Harvey followed the doctor's finger with his eyes and walked to a curtain at the end.

He walked behind the curtain to where his father lay on the bed staring at the ceiling. Slowly, he walked over beside him. "Dad," he called quietly.

His father rolled his head to face him.

The right side of Ethan Middleton's face was taut as though every muscle had contracted at once and pulled. Harvey could see the right corner of his mouth had curled into a smirk of a grin, and from the very corner a bit of saliva had worked its way down his chin.

Harvey looked solemnly into his father's face.

Ethan Middleton was a fisherman. He was a Maine fisherman. You can look into the face of a Maine fisherman and see the seasons etched in his skin. With every weather-beaten crease and sun-baked valley, the seasons made themselves evident.

Their hands were hard and rough like the seas they worked. They were rocklike from years of working the nets while salt water seeped into their cuts. To call yourself a fisherman, to Ethan Middleton, was a proud thing.

But to call yourself a Maine fisherman was to hold a special place of honor.

"They-," Harvey began, "They said you fell down."

"Yeah," Ethan Middleton replied weakly, only half of his mouth moving. "I s'pose I did."

Harvey swore to himself he would be strong for his father, but at twelve, strength only reached so far. Red-hot tears began to run down his cheeks as he looked at the destroyed seasons on his father's face. "Daddy, what happened to you," he wailed.

"Oh," his father said softly reaching over with his left hand and patting his son's head, "be still, boy."

The words did Harvey no good, nor did they succeed in damming up the rivers pouring from his eyes.

Ethan Middleton wrapped his arm around his oldest son and pulled him into a hug. "Be calm, son. I need you to do something for me, now. I want you to take care of your brother and sister and your momma till I get home. You're the man of the house now."

"I can't," Harvey answered in a high-pitched tone that pushed past the lump in his throat.

"I need you to be a man for me, Harvey," his father said with a tear running out of his good eye.

"I don't know how," Harvey cried into his father's chest.

"You'll know how, boy," his father assured him. "You'll know. You be a righteous man for your momma."

"Daddy, I can't."

"You can," his father answered trying to nod. "There ain't no age to becoming a man, son. It just happens. And your time is now, Harvey. In life, boy, you're gonna get choices, one'll be easy, the other'll be hard. The hard one will always be the right one, boy. You remember that, Harvey. It's time for you to be a man, son. And a righteous man you'll be."

Harvey wrapped his arms around the rock that was his father and held on as tight as he could. He figured that if he held on tight enough, his father wouldn't go anywhere. If he just wished hard enough, they would fish together off the docks again.

But life had made other plans.

"No," Middleton roared bolting into a sitting position. For a moment, he didn't know where he was. Then he remembered the crash. But where was he now? He looked down and found himself inside a large sleeping bag.

He lay in a large circle surrounded by four-foot walls made of iced-over snow. In the center of the circle in a pit, a fire burned. Over him, covering the circle was a canvas cloth with a hole in the center right above the flames to let out the heat. On the other side of the fire lay a large black leather over-the-shoulder travel bag.

Outside, he heard the chomping of footsteps in the snow, then the scraping along the other side of the canvas. The footfalls circled back to a little square doorway cut out of the snow walls.

A man in his early thirties poked his head in the doorway. "Oh," he smiled. "You're awake. I thought you were gonna sleep clear through to the summer. You hungry," he asked crawling in and going over to the leather bag. I have sardines and bread, if ya' like."

Harvey looked at him with confusion.

The man was clean cut, with dark hair and brown eyes. He wore a parka and a black sweatshirt, blue jeans and worn hiking boots. "You sure did take a tumble out there. Sounded like thunder from here. I ran down to see what was the matter and found you in the cab of your truck. You weren't lookin' so good then, but you cleaned up all right. Got a nice knot on your noggin though."

Harvey put his hand up to his head feeling a bump under a bandage.

"You were unconscious when I found you, so I dragged you back here."

"Thank you."

"You're very welcome," the man smiled pouring coffee from a Thermos bottle into a cup and handing it to him.

Middleton took it appreciatively.

The man pulled out a can of sardines and rolled the top open, then grabbed a loaf of bread and ripping off a hunk. "Here ya' go," he said handing it over. "No mustard. Sorry."

"Thank you," Harvey said taking it.

"No problem," the man said sitting down.

"Who are you," Middleton asked.

"Name's Sheppard," the man said holding out his hand. "Chris Sheppard."

"Harvey. Harvey Middleton," Harvey said shaking his hand. "What are ya' doin' out here?"

"Hikin'," Sheppard smiled. "Snow got too bad, so I set up here for the night."

"This is nice," Harvey said appreciatively as he looked around. "What is it?"

"It's a snow tent," Sheppard said looking it over.

"A what," Harvey asked.

"You dig out a circle and use the snow to build a wall around it," Sheppard explained. "The walls have to be around a foot and a half thick. Then you put in eight poles around the walls, and light a fire in the center. The fire begins to melt the walls, and you keep stacking snow on it as it does. Every five minutes you cover the fire to let the ice harden until it holds the poles firm, then you put the canvas on. A snow tent."

"Where'd ya' learn that," Middleton asked.

"Made it up myself," Sheppard grinned pouring himself some coffee.

"Smart."

"Ah, I'm used to livin' outdoors."

"What do you do."

"I wander."

"Wander?"

"Yeah," he nodded. "I like to go different places, meet different people, hear different stories. I wander."

"How do you get by?"

"I depend on the kindness of strangers."

"Run into that much," Middleton huffed.

"Yeah," Sheppard nodded with a bright smile. "I do. It's always good to see that people are still basically good."

Harvey pointed to the hiker's belt buckle, an old sixties peace sign made of steel.

"You a hippie," he asked.

"I don't really know," Sheppard answered honestly. "But I like what it represents."

"Well, hippie or no, I'm glad I bumped into you."

"Didn't bump into me," Sheppard smiled. "But ya' did bump into a whole lot o' trees out there."

"Jeeze Louise," Middleton screamed. "My truck!"

Middleton dropped his food, scurried out of the bag, and shot through the hole in the snow tent. Ignoring the dull throbbing in his legs, he moved rapidly through the woods and out onto the road.

"No," he repeated over and over as he came up onto the shredded remains of the trailer. He ran to the bridge his eyes widening as he saw the twisted girder. Beside the girder, trees lay in splintered pieces on the embankment. He ran onto the bridge and looked down.

There in the moonlight, he could see what remained of the Silver Streak. By the looks of it, it must have hit a hump in the road, taking the girder with its radiator grill instead of the windshield. It was now completely spun around facing the direction it had come from and lying on its side. What was once the flagship of Beckman's fleet was now only a twisted hunk of snow-covered metal.

"Oh, dear God, no," Middleton groaned turning away and sliding down the rail onto the ground.

"Hey, Harvey, you all right," Sheppard yelled running up the road. He skidded to a halt and knelt down in front of Middleton. "Hey, Harvey, take it easy. It's only a truck."

"Only a truck," he seethed looking up at the stranger filled with white-hot anger. "If I would've gotten that truck back in one piece, I could've kept my house! I could've bought my wife a new dress! I could've gotten my kids some decent clothing! That's not a truck laying down there destroyed," he roared grabbing the stranger by the collar and shaking him. "That's my *life*!"

Sheppard looked into the wild eyes of Harvey Middleton and waited. Soon Middleton's eyes cleared, then they looked ashamed. He let his hands drop lifelessly into the snow. "I'm sorry," Harvey moaned putting a hand over his face.

"No harm done," Sheppard said helping him up. "It's good to get things out."

"Yeah," Middleton nodded. "Look," he said holding out his hand. "I gotta get home. Thanks for everything, but I've gotta go."

Middleton shook Sheppard's hand and walked away. He took ten steps when his world began to spin around him. The next thing he knew, his face was in the snow.

"Harvey," Sheppard yelled running over and falling down beside him. "You all right?"

"Just a little dizzy is all," Middleton said sitting up. "Must be that bump."

"Harvey, you should really come back with me," Sheppard said.

"No," Middleton said shaking his head. "I gotta get home."

"How far do you live from here."

"Three," he stopped and shook the fog from his head. "Three miles."

"I'll tell you what," Sheppard offered. "You come back with me so I can douse the fire, and I'll walk with you."

"Why," Middleton asked honestly.

"Because." Sheppard smiled. "All right?"

"Yeah," Middleton conceded. "All right."

The two men walked back toward the glow. Middleton looked down and grimaced.

"What," Sheppard asked.

"There," Middleton seethed pointing to deer tracks going off into the woods. "Merry Christmas, you lousy, flea-covered *hat rack*," he bellowed into the trees.

"Feel better," Sheppard asked.

"A little," Middleton grumbled.

Within minutes, the glow of the fire faded and died and the two men were off. "It's a good night for walkin'," Sheppard said pointing up to the sky, which was now clear and full of stars.

"Yeah, great," Middleton said putting on his gloves.

11

Mile One
3:00 A.M.

The winds were incredibly calm, Middleton thought, but he wasn't complaining. It made the walk easier. Beside him, Sheppard silently walked with his hands in his pockets.

"Musta been nice, huh," Sheppard asked.

"What's that?"

"Growin' up around here."

"What makes you say that?"

"Fresh air, beautiful scenery . . ."

"That's for the tourists," Middleton said lighting up a cigarette then digging his hands into his pockets.

"What happened to your dad," Sheppard asked.

The question was like a lightning bolt out of a clear blue sky. Middleton shot a look over to him. "What about my dad?"

"You were calling to him over and over when you were out of it," Sheppard shrugged. "I was just wondering what happened to him."

"My old man slaved his whole life and got squat," Middleton said.

"What do you mean?"

"What do you care," Middleton asked.

"You just sounded hurt when you were calling to him is all."

Middleton looked around agitated.

"He run off on ya'," Sheppard asked.

"No," Middleton yelled offended.

"Hey, I'm sorry," Sheppard apologized. "Just talking to pass the time."

"You wanna hear about my old man," Middleton said whipping his cigarette out of his mouth.

"Sure," the hiker shrugged.

"My old man," Middleton said angrily, "Worked hard every day of his life. He ran the nets off the boats. He went out no matter what. He went out when the surface of the ocean looked like glass, and he went out when the swells were as big as mountains! He had his fingers pulled from their sockets three times trying to hold the line in rough seas.

"He had arthritis in his hands so bad that in the morning when we were all sitting at the kitchen table for breakfast, he'd have to put them under the table top and crack the joints into place. Sounded like gunfire. And the whole time he did it, I looked at his face, and not *once* did he show the pain! And you know why! Huh, you know why!"

"Why," Sheppard asked.

"He did it to feed and clothe us, *that's why*. He took everything that damn ocean had to give him and he *spit it* right back in her face! He was a great man!"

"Then why do you sound so angry," Sheppard asked.

"One afternoon, he comes in off the boats and is wranglin' the nets, and he drops like a rock. Legs just went out from under him,"

Middleton said in a low angry voice that came close to a growl.

Sheppard watched Middleton's face darken with hate.

"What happened," he asked.

"Stroke," Middleton hissed. "Took out his whole right side. He slaved all his life to do right by his family, and what did he get for it?"

"They say God works in mysterious ways, Harvey," Sheppard shrugged.

"Don't tell me that," Middleton roared. "My wife tells me that! My mother told me that! My old man went to church every Sunday, and what did he get? He got a stroke to land him in the hospital, and two more to land him in the boneyard!

"My dad was a righteous man," Middleton screamed bolting head long at the nearest tree. He hauled off and sent a fist driving into its bark.

"And he died . . .!"

Another savage hit sending the hollow sound of bone into the air.

"Drooling . . .!"

Another hit resounded into the night.

"Harvey," Sheppard yelled. "You'll break your hand!"

"Onto his goddamn . . .!"

Another furious hit landed into the bark peeling away the outer layer.

"*PILLOW*!"

"Harvey," Sheppard yelled grabbing the balled, blood-soaked, glove in mid-flight. "Stop!"

"Get away from me," he rumbled, pushing Sheppard back.

Middleton stumbled to the center of the path and looked up at the stars. He outstretched his arms, the ragged, bloody, glove hanging in tattered shreds. "Is that how You take down a righteous man," he screamed. "After all he'd been through, was that the best You had to give him!"

Middleton's knees disappeared and he found himself crashing to the ground.

Sheppard ran over and knelt down in front of him. "Harvey," he called gently.

Middleton looked up, tears streaming down his face. "My dad was a righteous man."

"I know," Sheppard said putting a hand on his shoulder.

"He didn't deserve to go like he did," Harvey said hanging his head.

Middleton felt the tears coming and found himself unable to hold them back. It took a solid fifteen minutes to regain control. He looked up at the hiker, who only looked down at him patiently, his hand still on his shoulder. "I'm sorry about that," he finally said.

"About what," Sheppard asked.

"'Bout bawlin' like a woman," he replied with a tone of embarrassment.

"Y'know, Harvey," Sheppard said, "I went to the circus once, and there was this lion tamer. He was tellin' this lion to bow, and whackin' it with a whip. He whacked it and whacked it, until it finally bowed. But the tamer still kept his distance. You know why?"

"Why?"

"Because even though the lion bowed, it was still a lion," the hiker said with a smile.

"Thanks," Middleton said with a weak smile. "You don't have to walk with me, y'know. You can leave. I can make it."

"I like walkin' with ya', Harvey," Sheppard said pulling off his bag and unzipping it. "Here, give me your hand."

Middleton held out the bleeding hand and winced as Sheppard pulled off the glove. "Of course," Sheppard said pulling gauze from the bag and wrapping the hand, "if ya' want me to go, that's up to you. I can't force you to let me walk with you. But I'd rather know ya' got home safe. And besides, I like talking to you. Helps pass the time."

"Yeah, it does." Middleton agreed as Sheppard helped him to his feet. "Y'know I don't even know why I just told you all that."

"Sometimes it's easier to talk to strangers," Sheppard said hefting his bag back over his shoulder.

"Yeah," Middleton agreed. "I guess it is at that. I just mean if you got somewhere you gotta be, don't let me hold you up."

"Harvey," Sheppard said slapping him on the back. "I got all night."

The two men again began walking down the road.

"Harvey," Sheppard asked.

"Yeah."

"Mind if I ask you another question?"

"Sure," Middleton grinned still a bit embarrassed putting another cigarette in his mouth.

"What happened after your father died?"

"Well, he made me the man of the house, and that's exactly what I was. Against my mother's wishes, I quit school at fourteen and went to work on the docks under the table until I was old enough for papers. Then I went full time."

"Sounds like hard work," Sheppard said.

"Yeah," Middleton agreed. "But I had my brother and sister to think about. Patrick was nine, and Sissy was five when my dad died, and my mother was killing herself trying to make ends meet. I had to do something. So when I was old enough to work on the docks, I did it. We had mouths to feed. At times, when I could, I'd work the docks cutting catch during the day, then stay the night getting the nets ready for the next morning, mending them and the like."

"Sounds like a lot for a young boy to handle," Sheppard said.

"I didn't really think about it then," Middleton said taking a puff of his cigarette. "All I knew was that my brother and sister needed shoes and clothes and hot food in their bellies. Any extras I could fit in for myself was just icing on the cake. A Coke here, licorice whips there. I'd keep a penny a week and save it up."

"Sounds like it was hard on you," Sheppard said sympathetically.

"I did what I had to do," Middleton said matter-of-factly. "My father told me I had to be a man. That it was time. But, I'll never be half the man Ethan Middleton was."

12

Mile Two
3:36 A.M.

Sheppard looked up again into the night sky. "Stars sure are bright tonight," he said.

"Sure are," Middleton agreed.

"So, what was it like growing up here," Sheppard asked.

"For me," Middleton asked looking into the darkness of the trees then back.

"Yeah," Sheppard shrugged with that friendly good-natured smile of his. "For Harvey Middleton."

"Not much," Middleton shrugged. "I didn't go to school, and I worked with people older'n me. I didn't have many friends. It seemed like feedin' my family was all I had to think about. I didn't go to proms or church dances. I was always workin' on keepin' the heat on, or the lights on, or the car runnin' so my mother could get to her job. There was a lot to take care of."

"You sound regretful," Sheppard said.

"Yeah," Middleton shrugged, "I suppose I am a bit. I don't care what my father told me, no matter how true it was about life. Life should leave you alone until you're old enough to deal with it."

"That'd be nice," Sheppard agreed. "But we all have our own road to travel, and some start sooner than others."

"Amen to that, brother," Middleton said lighting another cigarette.

"What about your brother and sister? Did they work," Sheppard asked.

"Oh, no," Middleton replied. "It was bad enough we had one dropout in the family. We didn't need any more. No, I made them stay in school. Pat was real good, and I was tough on him." Middleton looked down at his shoes, his face growing sad. "Maybe a little *too tough*."

"Why do you say that," Sheppard asked.

"Pat was smart, see," Middleton explained. "I mean he had a brain on him you wouldn't believe. I stayed on his case all the way through school. In high school, he got a partial grant for Harvard. I worked two jobs to pay for the other half.

"He went, and I worked my fingers to the bone while he was away, sending whatever extra I could to him so he could have some kind of life. He graduated with honors from law school. He was a good kid," Middleton said stopping and putting his bandaged hand over his eyes. "He was a real good kid."

"What's wrong, Harvey," Sheppard asked stopping with him.

Middleton pulled the cigarette from his mouth and blew smoke into the air. "When I saw that he had a way out, I forced him to take it. It was like *I* was getting out *through him,* y'know? He would write us, and tell us about all the parties and dances he was going to, and the people he was meeting, and it was like *I* was there with him. It was like I was doing those things *through him*. It was like I had finally gotten out.

"And I was hard on him, Chris," Middleton said in a voice soaked with self-loathing, "I was hard as nails with him. He wasn't going to fail. He wasn't going to come back here. He wasn't going to end up like my dad and me. He wasn't going to break his back for next to nothing. He was going to be somebody.

"The day he graduated," Middleton said taking a hard puff on his cigarette. "He looked so important in that cap and gown surrounded by one of the greatest institutions in the world. I looked at him, and I was so proud, but for some reason, I just couldn't say it to him.

"After graduation, he moved out," Middleton said, his shining eyes looking at the stars. "He's a big attorney in Connecticut now. His wife sent me pictures of their kids." Middleton looked over to the hiker, pain in his eyes. "I got a niece and nephew I ain't ever seen.

"I shouldn't have driven him so hard," Middleton said taking another drag on his cigarette. "And no matter how hard I drove him, he took it. Yeah, my brother-my brother was a good kid. I shoulda told him I was proud of him," Middleton said beginning to

walk again. "He shoulda heard
it from me."

"I'm sure he knows," Sheppard said walking up beside him.

"Don't make a lick o' difference," Middleton replied. "I shoulda told him."

"What about your sister," Sheppard asked.

"Sissy," Middleton asked. "She turned into one beautiful woman, she did. I bloodied quite a few noses over her back in the day, let me tell ya'. She was a looker. I *hawked* over *her,* and you ask any man on the shoreline; anyone stepped outta line with her dealt directly with *me*.

"She got married right out of high school. Nice enough fella. He even came to me and asked for her hand real proper like. Guess he figured better safe than sorry. They struggled for a while, but he finally landed a god job and they live in Ogunquit with three kids. They normally stop down over the holidays for a visit. It's good to see she's doing so well. She's happy."

"And your mother," Sheppard asked.

"My mother and I lived in our old house on the coast until I landed work inland. I rented a house and brought her with me. After I married my wife, we bought the house, and my mother lived with us. She lived with us up until two years ago, then I got laid off, and the work wasn't steady. My sister took my mother to live with her. She calls all the time, it's like she never left. My sister's got a big house, and her kids love havin' my mother there. My mother loves kids. She says they keep her young."

The two men trudged through the hills and the valleys of the tracks left by the Quebec trucks as the wind rushed through the trees. Middleton let out a shiver.

Sheppard pulled his pack off, rooted through it, found the Thermos bottle, and poured some coffee. He handed it to Middleton, then pulled out a second cup and filled it for himself.

"Thanks," Middleton nodded.

"No problem," Sheppard said in his pleasant tone.

13

Mile Three
4:01 A.M.

Middleton and Sheppard walked in silence for some time, each trying to stabilize themselves on the mounds of snow. The wind was now beginning to blow hard through the trees causing a howling noise in the woods. Harvey looked into the darkness beyond the trees, deep into the shadows. "Eerie sound, ain't it," he asked looking over to Sheppard.

Sheppard looked into the woods, his eyes, like Middleton's peering deep into the shadows. "Doesn't bother me," he shrugged. "You?"

"No," Harvey answered. "Besides we're almost out of the woods."

"Almost," Sheppard repeated. "So, what about your family, Harvey?"

"Yeah," Middleton said his face brightening. "Wanna see?"

Sheppard laughed at the obvious tone of pride in his voice. "Yeah, I'd like that."

Middleton reached back under his coat and pulled out his wallet. "Lookey, here," he said walking closer to Sheppard holding up the picture fold. "This here is my boy Ethan," he said with a wide smile."

"Inherited his dad's good looks I see." Sheppard grinned holding the picture up into the moonlight.

"Naw," Middleton said embarrassed. "I think all the looks in the family came from their momma. He's got the smarts too. He ain't no dummy like his old man. I keep tellin' him that someday his old man may be workin' for *him*."

"And who's this," Sheppard asked flipping the folder.

"That's my little girl, Marie," Middleton smiled looking over Sheppard's shoulder.

"She's beautiful, Harvey," Sheppard smiled.

"That's my angel," Harvey nodded. "Pretty like her momma. Oh," Middleton pointed. "Turn it."

"Hey," Sheppard said, "she's beautiful."

"That's my Beverly," Middleton said with bright smile. "That's my girl."

"If I didn't know better," Sheppard smiled. "I'd say you were a man in love, Harvey."

"From the first day I saw her," Middleton nodded. "I was working in a machine shop in Portland when I first saw her. I was on the docks loadin' and unloadin' parts when I met her. Well, didn't actually *meet* her, I just kind of saw her. She worked in the office, and had come down to pick up paperwork from the dock supervisor.

"She was somethin'," Harvey said in a reminiscent voice. "From the moment I saw her, I couldn't stop thinkin' about her. At work I would find ways to catch a glimpse of her, and when I was home, I moped around like a beat puppy. Once I bumped into her on the docks and she asked
me where she could find my boss, and all I could say was I-I-I."

Sheppard let out a deep hearty laugh that seemed to fill the night.

"No," Middleton laughed. "That was just the way it came out. The other guys looked at me like I was a fool. They all had no trouble talking to her. And I know each of them had asked her out at least once."

"You're joshin' me," Sheppard said.

"Honest truth," Middleton said holding up his hand like a boy scout.

"Well, how'd you finally meet her then," Sheppard laughed.

"I was on my way out the gate in my old truck when I saw her standing there. She waved her arm and I stopped. I asked her what she wanted, and she said her girlfriend had gone home with the flu and she needed a lift and if I couldn't give her one. I said sure, got out of the truck, opened the door for her and let her in."

"Nice touch, Harvey," Sheppard said proudly.

"My mother'd beat me with a switch if I'd done any less," Harvey grinned.

"Then what happened?"

"Well I drive her 'cross town, and I can't think of anything to say, right? So I'm just drivin' like a numbskull sayin' nothin', and the whole time she's just sittin' there with her hands in her lap lookin' out the window.

"I drive her to her parents' house, and say, 'Well, here ya' go, Miss Sutter.' And I look over and she's mad. I mean, not just *mad,* she's *snortin' mad*. I'm thinkin', what did I do? As far as I could figure, I didn't do nothin'.

"'Here we are,' she yells at me. 'Here we are! Is that all you have to say to me! We drive clear across Portland, and all you have to say is here we are!' I didn't know what to do.

"The whole time I'm thinkin', she's just lookin' at me waiting for me to say something. Then she finally let out this real big sigh and yells, 'Are you ever going to ask me out, so I can stop coming down to those dirty docks. You're buddies *smell,* Harvey! I've ruined more dresses with motor grease coming down to see you! Well, say something!'

"I just looked at her. I couldn't believe what I was hearing. She was the most beautiful thing I'd ever seen, and she's yelling at me for not asking her out. Here I was, this uneducated hump from the shores, and she got the eyes for *me*! I just said, real slow and cautious like, 'How 'bout the movies on Saturday?' and she yells, 'Fine! Pick me up around seven-thirty! And I said, 'Okay.' And she got out of my truck, slammed the door, and stormed into her house." Middleton's face painted over with a warm smile. "Bev's been my girl ever since."

"She sounds nice," Sheppard said giving Middleton a soft pat on the back.

"She's my girl," Harvey said putting his wallet back into his pocket. "I gotta get home," he said with a tone of urgency. "Gotta get to church come daybreak."

"You a church goin' man, Harvey," Sheppard asked.

"Was once. Not anymore. Just drop Bev' and the kids off now," Middleton answered.

"Why don't you go," Sheppard asked.

"You sure like preachin', don't ya'," Middleton said slightly angered.

"You don't believe," the hiker asked rubbing his hands together.

"Did once," Middleton said lighting another cigarette.

"Not anymore?"

"I went," Middleton said taking a puff on his cigarette. "I went, and I went, and I went, and I said all the prayers, and I sang all the hymns, and I listened to all the sermons, and for what? For what? Where did it get me? Nowhere. I still worked two jobs, I still had to break my back, I still had to scrape and scrounge. Prayin' did me a *world* o' good. I just stopped goin'. I ain't prayin' if no one's listenin'.

"All my life, I fought for a better life," Middleton rumbled angrily. "Every mornin' I gotta get up and watch my wife try and find somethin' to feed my kids for breakfast in cupboards that are never full! I gotta watch other guys, guys I grew up with, give their families everything they need, and what do I got! I got a falling down shack, a car that leaks more oil than the Exxon Valdez, and a heater you have to beat on t'keep runnin'!

"My wife goes to church every Sunday, and look what she got stuck with." Middleton stopped and looked down his lips narrowing to ribbons, his eyes turning to slits in a taut face. "She got stuck with a man who can barely feed and clothe his family. I got nothin' to say to God. If she wants to pray, that's fine. Me? I'm done talkin'," Middleton seethed beginning to walk at a faster pace.

"Ever hear of Job," Sheppard asked running up beside him.

"Read it when I was a kid," Middleton rumbled digging his hands in his pocket.

"His life was hard as I recall, too," Sheppard said matter-of-factly. "But in the end, God gave him everything he needed."

"Hooray for Job," Middleton said taking a drag of his cigarette.

"Job had it tough, but God never left him," Sheppard said.

"Don't you tell me that," Middleton said poking a finger in Sheppard's chest. "Don't even *hand me* that! Don't you tell me God don't leave! I haven't seen hide nor hair of Him since I was *twelve*!"

"From what you've told me," Sheppard shrugged. "I'd have to say you were wrong on that, Harvey."

"Wrong," Middleton roared. "Exactly where am I wrong! I busted my ass all my life, and I got nothin'! I had *one* chance to turn things around, and that chance is lying crushed in a *creek bed* three miles back! Tell me how great God is now! Go on," Middleton bellowed. "You tell me!"

"Harvey, you had a hard childhood, and you bore it," Sheppard replied calmly. "You were given a responsibility and you rose to meet it. When you needed money, I don't mean, when you *wanted* money, but when you *needed it,* was it there? You talked about your cupboards that were never full. Were they ever empty, Harvey? Did you ever ask for the strength to go on another day and not get it?

"It sounds as if God has already given you the greatest gift of all, Harvey. You carry pictures of them in your wallet. He won't give you a mansion, or a sports car. Those are things of Man. But He can give you love, Harvey. The gift of love. A house can stand beside a mountain, and even when the house crumbles and falls, the mountain still stands. Man made that house, God made that mountain. Man can give you riches, only God can give you love."

Middleton turned away and walked to the edge of the trees, his head down. "I felt so alone, sometimes," he muttered taking another drag of his cigarette. "Like the world was crushing down on me."

Middleton thought back over his life. He looked through all the old memories and could think of no time his family of brother and sister and mother had gone without food. He could think of no time they had gone without a roof over their heads, or heat when the jaws of the Maine winters clamped down. And, although they were not the best, they always had shoes on their feet, and shirts on their backs.

Harvey's gut clenched. He was taught to believe from the time he was a child. He was taught God would stand beside him no matter how rough the seas, no matter how strong the winds. He had ridden those waves, he had stood in those winds, and he had survived.

Then came Bev'.

Even now, when he thought the seas would drown him, and the winds would blow him to pieces, he knew he could turn around and she would be standing there with him. He had been given someone to erase the loneliness from his heart and the despair in his soul. He had been given a gift from God.

The same God he cursed.

Tears formed in his eyes.

Then came the realization of exactly who had abandoned whom.

"I'm sorry," he whispered into the shadows.

"What," Sheppard asked.

"Nothing," Middleton replied swiping at his eyes.

"Maybe, it's time you talked to Him again," Sheppard said.

"He wouldn't listen," Middleton said.

"Why not?"

"'Cause I know if I were Him, I wouldn't," Harvey said looking down at his feet. "I've said some evil things to Him in my day. If someone'd said the things I'd said to me, I wouldn't want anything to do with them at all."

"Then you talk to his Son. That's what He's there for. He knows what it's like. He understands what you're feeling. I'm sure if there're any rough edges, He could smooth 'em over for ya'. Close your eyes, Harvey."

"What? Why," Middleton asked.

"Go on," Sheppard coaxed. "I wanna show ya' something."

Middleton closed his eyes.

"Now," Sheppard went on. "Take all your troubles, and put a name to em. Put a face to 'em so you can see 'em in your head."

"Okay," Middleton said. His mind walked back through his life. With every picture his shoulders sank as if lead had been set upon them. It was the world crushing down on him. He went through picture after picture until his back was almost hunched from their weight. A deadening weight.

A black weight.

"Now give 'em to Him," Sheppard said.

Middleton's mind spun with regrets of a youth cut short, of a life derailed. Behind the swirling pictures of his past, he could feel his temples tighten as his teeth clenched. *Lord,* his mind screamed. *I'm just a man! I just wanna do right by my family! I can't do it alone anymore! Help me! For my family's sake, help me!*

Warm winds blew.

Warm winds with subtle strengths. They swirled through the halls of his soul, pushing through the darkness. In his mind the pictures began to spin; his body felt as though it weighed no more than a feather.

A feather carried on the warm winds.

The warm winds that lifted him rushed into the pictures, shattering them, breaking their hold, pushing them out like dead leaves on a winters day. . .

Until they were gone.

Harvey opened his eyes and looked at Sheppard.

"I do it all the time," Sheppard smiled.

"You do," Middleton asked, a calm rushing through his body.

"Feels good, doesn't it?"

"Yeah," Middleton replied honestly. "Yeah, it does."

"Now, just remember," Sheppard said with a smile, pointing a well-meaning finger in Middleton's face. "You can give your back to Man, but you save your soul for God."

"You shoulda been a preacher," Middleton grinned.

"I've had my share of hard times too, Harvey," Sheppard said honestly. "I've had times when I wanted to give up. And when I had those times, I did just like you did now. 'Cause I know whatever happened to me happened for a reason. I've had dark times when I felt alone, just like you. But I went through 'em knowin' there was a reason. I was never alone, Harvey. And I just wanted to show you that you weren't either, y'know?"

"Yeah," Middleton nodded.

"How ya' feeling," Sheppard asked putting a hand on his shoulder. "You okay?"

"Uh-huh," Middleton nodded.

"Good," Sheppard smiled. "Cause it looks like you're almost home."

Middleton watched the hiker nod down the path. He looked and saw the opening of the woods was less than a hundred yards away."

"Let's go," Middleton smiled. "I wanna see my wife and kids."

"Sounds good," Sheppard smiled adjusting his bag.

"You'll have to meet my wife," Middleton said as they walked to the forest's end. "You'd like her."

"I'm sure I would."

The two men emerged from the forest to see the skies open before them. "It is a beautiful night tonight," Sheppard breathed."

"Yeah," Middleton agreed. "Yeah, it is."

"Oh," the hiker said holding out his hand. "Merry Christmas, Mr. Middleton."

Harvey laughed and shook the hiker's hand, "Merry Christmas, Mr. Sheppard."

The snow became thigh-high in spots as the two men waded down Pineview, passing dark houses as they went.

"Hey, Chris," Middleton called.

"Yeah, Harvey?"

"I'm sorry, I lost my temper with you back there. I really am."

"No problem," the hiker shrugged. "You're a fisherman's son. I think it runs in the genes. My best friend was a fisherman, and you should've seen the temper on him. He had a roar on him that could raise the *roof!"*

"No, kidding?" Middleton laughed.

"Honest Injun," Sheppard laughed.

The two men trudged down the road, each commenting how cold it had gotten. Middleton stopped at a house with a long driveway. "That's my buddy Mike's house," he said. "Ain't far from here. Hope he put the Chevy on the charger."

Middleton led Sheppard down past three houses then stopped. "That's me over there," Harvey said pointing a small home on the right off in the distance.

"Not a bad looking house at all, Harvey," Sheppard said.

"Needs a boodle o' work though," Middleton grunted as they began walking again.

Reaching the end of the driveway, Middleton stopped and put an arm up to Sheppard's chest to halt him.

"What's wrong, Harvey," Sheppard asked.

"Cover yer eyes," Middleton said.

"Why?"

"Trust me," Harvey nodded. "This time you take *my* advice."

"Okay," Sheppard agreed putting a hand over his eyes.

Middleton walked over to the end of the driveway, and stamped his foot down.

The world lit up with solid, blinding, white as the four Halogen floodlights kicked on.

"Whoa," Sheppard said squinting as he put his hand down.

"Keeps the critters off the lawn," Middleton grinned.

"I'll bet."

"C'mon," Middleton said with a nod towards the house. "I want ya' to meet Bev'."

The two men high-stepped through the calf-high snow that now blanketed the driveway, and up to the front door.

"I wanna thank ya' again," Harvey said as they stopped at the door.

"Like I said," Sheppard smiled. "Not a problem."

"You know, you were right."

"'Bout what, Harvey?"

"It is easier to talk to a stranger."

"We're not strangers anymore, Harvey," Sheppard smiled extending his hand.

"No, I guess we ain't," Harvey grinned shaking it, "I just wish I knew how I was going to explain what happened to that truck."

"Put it in God's hands, Harvey," Sheppard shrugged. "He'll do as He sees fit."

"Ya' think His Boy could put in a good word for me," Middleton asked, one eyebrow cocked.

Sheppard burst out laughing and clapped his hands and shook his head. "Harvey," he said slapping Middleton on his shoulder, "I'm sure He will."

"Say, listen," Middleton said seriously. "It's Christmas. Why don't you spend it with us? Nobody should be alone on Christmas. We don't have much, but what we have, you're welcome to it."

"You're inviting me into your home, Harvey," Sheppard asked.

"As humble as it is, yes sir," Middleton smiled.

"Are you sure you want me to come in?"

"Yeah, I'm sure."

"You're positive you want me to come in?"

"I'm positive."

"You're definitely *certain* you want me to come in?"

"Yes, I'm definitely certain." Middleton laughed.

Middleton watched the hiker's face light up, a big smile extending nearly ear to ear. For a moment, he thought for sure his invitation would be taken up on. Then Sheppard's smile faded into a smaller smile of contentment.

Then slowly, he shook his head.

"No, Harvey," Sheppard said putting a hand on Middleton's shoulder. "You spend the day with your family."

"Are you sure," Middleton asked with a bit disappointment.

"The mere fact you invited me in is enough for me, Harvey," Sheppard smiled with a slight nod. "Today is Christmas Day, Harvey. Today, is a beginning of a whole new life for you, I can feel it. You love your family today."

"I will," Middleton nodded.

"You *are* a righteous man, Harvey," Sheppard said holding out his hand again.

"Thank you," Middleton said with a wide smile shaking his hand.

"A *righteous man,* " Sheppard repeated with a wink.

"Could you at *least* stay and meet my wife," Middleton asked.

Sheppard shrugged, hung his head, and gave it a shake.

"Great," Middleton smiled. "Won't take but a minute."

Harvey turned, opened the storm door and knocked. After a few moments, the door swung open. Beverly stood smiling, her eyes filled with sleep.

"Harvey," she yelled throwing her arms around his neck and kissing him. "Harvey don't you ever do anything like that again," she cried burying her face in his chest. "Please, promise me."

Harvey wrapped his arms around her kissing her on the crown of her head. "I won't leave you like that again, girl. Never again. Things'll be different for us now, I promise."

"Harvey, what happened," she asked looking wide-eyed at the bandage on his head.

"Had a little fender bender with the truck, I-."

"Dad," Ethan called running to the door.

"Ethan," Harvey yelled dropping to his knees and holding out his arms. The minute he was close enough, Middleton pulled him into a bear hug.

"We were worried," Ethan said sleepily, wrapping his arms around his father's neck.

"I know," Harvey said. "I'm sorry for makin' ya' worry."

"I was the man of the house till ya' got back, just like ya' said, dad," Ethan assured him.

Middleton bit his lip, tears formed in his eyes. "I'll bet you were, boy," he said as they ran down his face. "I'll bet you were a fine one too. But you be a boy for just a little while longer, huh? Dad's home now. He's gonna be here for ya' a good long time. You have all the time in the world to be a man," Middleton nodded. "When your time comes, you'll know. And when that time comes, a righteous man you'll be too. A *righteous man*."

"Harvey," Beverly called. "What *fender bender*,"

"I'll explain it all to ya' later," Middleton said squeezing her hand in his. "Right now, I got someone want you to meet."

Middleton turned behind him. He looked and found Sheppard was gone. He searched the darkness up the street, but saw no one. Then his eyes fell on the freshly laid snow on the driveway. And in the snow . . .

Only one set of footprints.

"Harvey," Beverly Middleton asked. "Are you all right."

Middleton didn't answer. He walked down the driveway, out of the light's arc and looked up at the stars. How beautiful they were, he thought as he watched them shimmer against the purple velvet of the morning sky. How new they looked. How new everything looked.

How new he felt.

14

5::01 A.M.

Harvey carried Ethan, who had fallen asleep ten minutes after his father arrived, up the stairs to his room. Gently, he laid him on the mattress and pulled the quilts over him. He rustled then forced open his eyes.

"I was gonna have hot chocolate with you when you got home," he muttered.

"I'll tell ya' what," Harvey said putting the blankets against his son's neck. "Tomorrow after church, we'll go sleddin', then we can have it. How's that sound?"

"Good," Ethan answered already falling back to sleep.

"Okay."

Middleton walked from the room and down the steps where Beverly was busy setting the few Christmas presents they could afford under the tree. "Harvey," she asked following him into the kitchen. "What happened to you?"

"Bev'," Harvey said sitting at the table, "I wouldn't know where to start. All I can say is I'm home now, darlin'. I'm right where I wanna be."

Beverly smiled, sat on his lap and laid her head on his shoulder. "You gonna drop me off at church tomorrow?"

"No," Harvey answered.

"No," she repeated looking at him. "Now, Harvey, don't you start that talk aga-."

"Tomorrow we're *all* goin;" Harvey nodded. "You, the kids, *and* me."

"You mean it?"

"I mean it."

"We gotta leave early. I gotta go see Beckman."

"Why?"

"To tell him about the truck."

"What about it?"

"It went out of control on Pineview back in the woods," Harvey explained. "It's totaled. The trailer too."

"It's a miracle you weren't killed," Beverly gasped.

"It surely is, Bev'," Middleton said rubbing her back. "I gotta warn ya', girl."

"What?"

"Silver Streak was a brand new truck, star of the fleet. And that trailer wasn't even ours," Middleton groaned. "I'm gonna lose my job over this, Bev'. No doubts there. I lose *that job,* we lose *this house*."

"We've never gone without a roof, Harvey," Beverly said.

"I know, but-."

"And we'll get by this time too," she said confidently. "You've always taken good care of us."

"I told you lately, I love you, girl," Harvey said kissing her on the cheek.

"Only a million times," she laughed.

"Well, you just go on an' make it a million and one."

"I'm goin' up," Beverly said standing up. "You comin'?"

"In a bit," Harvey smiled.

"All right."

The phone rang.

Middleton's heart jumped in his chest. It didn't take a wizard to know that it was Beckman wondering where his truck was. Beverly looked over at Harvey. Middleton handed her a peaceful smile.

God will do as He sees fit.

"You go on, honey," Middleton said calmly. "I'll handle this."

"You sure," she asked anxiously. "I could-."

"I'm sure," Middleton smiled. "You go on."

Hesitantly, Beverly Middleton turned and walked upstairs.

Harvey took a deep breath, walked to the wall phone, and picked it up.

"Hello," he answered.

"Harvey," the voice asked.

"Yeah," Middleton answered a bit confused.

"Harvey, it's Patrick."

"Pat," Harvey said flabbergasted. "What has you ringin' my phone at five in the mornin? Is everything all right?"

"I'm sorry," his brother apologized. "Did I wake you? What a stupid question. I'm sorry."

"No," Middleton blurted. "No, I was up. I'm just surprised is all."

"I was thinking about you today."

"Were you?"

"Yeah," Patrick Middleton laughed. "My son found your fishing pole."

"Fishing pole?"

"Yeah, don't you remember it?"

"No."

"Remember that time you took me fishing when we were kids. I was around six. And you made us both fishing poles. You baited up my line, and the fish took it and pulled the pole in cause I wasn't holding onto it. And I started bawlin', and you told me if I stopped cryin' I could have yours. Remember?"

"Yeah," Middleton nodded. "You *kept* that thing?"

"Sure I did," Pat said. "You gave it to me."

After that there was a long pause.

"I didn't call because of that," Pat finally said breaking the silence. "I called to say I'm sorry."

"For what," Harvey asked honestly.

"For a lot of things," his brother sighed. "I should've never left the way I did."

"I shouldn't have pushed you so hard," Harvey said.

"Harvey, if it weren't for you, I wouldn't be where I am today," Patrick Middleton said. "And by the time I realized that, I was ashamed to call you and say so. It must've been hell on you after dad died. I know that now, but I was too selfish to see it then. I look back now, and realize how young you were. I just wanted to say thank you for everything, Harvey."

"I did," Middleton said swallowing hard. "I did what dad told me to do. Pat?"

"Yeah."

"Pat," Harvey said swiping at his eyes with his sleeve. "I just want to say, I'm proud of you, boy. You did me proud, you did momma proud, you did all of us proud, you did . . . you did your father proud. I want - I want you to know that."

"Thank you, Har-," he cut off into silence. "Thank you."

"I love you, little brother," Harvey said, his face wrinkling. "Never forget that, okay?"

"I love you too," Pat replied. "I'd like to bring the family out to see you."

"That'd be grand," Harvey smiled. "That'd be real fine."

"Hey, Harvey, you got any beer?"

"Yeah, why?"

"We never had a beer together," Pat said. "Maybe we could have one over the phone."

"Maybe we could."

Middleton walked to his refrigerator, pulled out a bottle of beer and twisted off the cap. On the other end, he could hear a snap then a hiss.

"You got beer in a *can*, Pat," Harvey asked.

"Yeah. Why?"

"Looks like I still got more to teach ya'."

"But I recycle," Patrick Middleton contested.

"God bless ya'."

The two men burst out laughing.

"Merry Christmas, Harvey."

"Merry Christmas, little brother."

15

Bangor, Maine
7:00 AM
Christmas morning

The plows ran like an army of huge metallic ants ripping and pushing snow off the streets of Bangor. Harvey maneuvered the

Suburban carefully though the streets, as people jumped over drifts on their way to Christmas Services.

"Do you want me to come with you, Harvey," Beverly Middleton asked concerned.

"Naw, Bev'," Harvey answered. "I'll drop you and the kids off in front of church and meet you before the services. I'll handle this on my own."

"You sure?"

"I'm sure."

Middleton pulled up in front of the church and got out. Walking around to the other side, he opened the passenger side door and helped his wife and children out and over the plowed snow.

"We'll get by," she said blowing him a kiss.

"Always have," he answered with a smile as he walked around the Chevy and got in.

The ride to Beckman's was a long one. It was only ten blocks, but they had been ten of the longest blocks Harvey had ever ridden. All the way, he tried to figure out exactly how you tell a man you've just destroyed a hundred-thousand dollars worth of his property and another eighty-thousand dollars of someone else's property that *he's* going to have to pay for?

Middleton drove up to the gates of Beckman Trucking and saw the line of cars behind the fence. It looked like everyone had come in today. He supposed they were all here for the Harvey Bar-B-Q. His chest really tightened when he saw the black Blazer at the end of the line. That was the old man's. Junior he could deal with, a veteran trucker like the old man could be a different story.

"Dear, Lord," he muttered getting out of the Chevy. "If I ever needed you . . ."

No sooner had he entered the gate than Junior walked out of the trailer. He stopped the minute he saw Harvey.

"Here we go," Middleton grumbled.

"My father wants to talk to you," Junior yelled.

"I'll just bet he does," Middleton said under his breath.

"He's over at the truck dock," Junior said pointing to the wall to Middleton's right. "He's been waiting for you since six." Junior turned in the direction of the dock. "Hey, dad, Middleton's here!"

Harvey straightened his back, clamped his teeth, and walked to the wall of the truck dock. If he were going to get blasted, he would take it like a man.

"Where is he," Beckman Sr. yelled appearing from around the corner. Beckman was a short stocky man with a gray buzz-cut that was now covered by an oil stained cap. He always wore a goose-down vest and faded jeans, and when he walked he looked like a five-foot five-inch bulldog with a cheek full of chewing tobacco.

"I'm right here," Middleton yelled walking up to meet him.

"How the hell'd ya' do it, is all I wanna know," Beckman said in his notorious growl.

"It's a long story," Middleton said walking right up to him.

"Oh, I'll bet it is, Middleton, I'll bet it is," Beckman growled spitting out tobacco juice and walking away back to the docks. "And I can't wait to hear this one! This one's gonna be damn good!"

Middleton followed him around the wall. If he was going to fire him, he could at least have the courtesy not to make him follow him all around the yard before he did it. Middleton's face reddened as he rounded the corner.

Then he saw her.

She sat in the center of the yard all by herself, her paint catching all the light the sun had to give her. The silver striping glared, and her chrome gleamed. Behind her, the trailer sat like an obedient dog on the leash of a great master. Neither one bore even a scratch.

There she stood in all her glory.

The Silver Streak.

Middleton stood there in a daze, his mouth open and his mind blank. It took him a few minutes to hear that somewhere there was a dog barking. It took him a few more minutes to realize that it was Beckman.

"What," Middleton asked.

"I said," Beckman said in his hyper way. "I'm sorry, son. I wanted to call you back. I wouldn't've ridden it, and if I wouldn't, then none o' my people should either. But, ooowee damn, son, you pulled it off!

"I'll tell ya', son," Beckman went on standing in front of him with his hands on his hips, his two little eyes peeking out from under his cap, "I did a haul through Kansas in the late spring in my twenties. Know what late spring is in Kansas, boy! Tornadoes! You ever outrun a tornado in an eighteen wheeler, son," Beckman asked poking a stubby little finger into Harvey's chest.

"No, sir," Harvey answered.

"Me neither," Beckman growled. "Son o' bitch picked up my whole rig and chucked it clear into a corn field! Scrambled me like an *egg*! "

Beckman turned to the men who were now walking out onto the docks. He grabbed Harvey by the collar. "You see this man," Beckman growled. "This is a trucker! Only a trucker coulda blown through that storm last night, and this is a trucker right here! This trucker held onto a contract that'll keep all your sorry carcasses in a job for the next twenty years and put us on the map! Junior!"

"Harvey," Morris and Scheafer yelled jumping off the docks and walking over with their hands out. "We thought you'd given up the ghost."

"No, not me, Harvey said shaking their hands.

"Morris," Beckman barked.

"Yes, sir," Morris jumped.

"You see that truck," the old man growled pointing to the Silver Streak.

"Yes, sir."

"From now on, the Silver Streak's Middleton's truck, you got me?"

"Yes, sir."

"Good. *Junior*!"

"Yes, dad," Junior replied running up.

"Where's this trucker's money?"

"Got it right here, dad," Junior said pulling out a thick envelope and showing it to him.

"Well give it to him," Beckman barked.

"Thank you, sir," Middleton said taking the envelope.

"Junior," Beckman growled again.

"Yes, dad."

"Who's our highest paid driver?"

"Myer, dad. Fifteen an hour."

"Middleton gets sixteen!"

"Hey," A man in pressed jeans, cowboy hat and boots, and a sheepskin vest protested walking over. "I been here longer'n him."

"Shut up," Beckman snapped spitting a wad of juice onto his right boot tip.

"Hey," Myer yelled jumping back.

"I've seen your layover slips," Beckman rumbled. "Where were *you* last night, Myer! You think you coulda done what Middleton did! Hah! You couldn't drive a golf ball in a sun shower!"

Morris and Scheafer snickered.

"Now, shut up and be glad you got a job!" Beckman turned back to Middleton. "All right," he said. "You go on home and spend Christmas with the family, Middleton, and I'll see you back here tomorrow morning bright and early!"

"I'd like tomorrow off, sir," Middleton said hesitantly.

"What," Beckman blasted. "You goin' soft on me already!"

"No, sir," Middleton blurted. "But I gotta get a new heater and stove for my house, and-."

"Go see Jack Greene over in Ellsworth," Beckman barked, then stopped and shook his head. "No, no, nix that. Son o' bitch uses second-hand parts!" Then he snapped his fingers with a pop, "I know! Go see Davey LeMay, owns a plumbing and appliance outlet on the other side of town. Drove for that son o' bitch ten years. Tell 'im ol' Bert Beckman sent ya', he'll steer ya' in the right direction!"

"Then I'm gonna get my wife a new dress."

"Can't help ya' there, son; don't wear dresses!" Beckman barked.

"No, sir," Harvey grinned. "Me neither."

"Damn good thing too," Beckman laughed. "You just ain't got the build for it, son! All right," Beckman rumbled. "Get this place locked down so's I can get outta here! Middleton, I'll see you the day after tomorrow!"

"Yes, sir," Harvey smiled.

"You wanna pull her into her dock," Morris asked holding up the keys to the Silver Streak.

"No, I gotta get to services. Bev' and the kids are waitin' on me. You can have the honors."

"She's a good luck truck, Harve," Morris smiled. "You can tell. Probably saved your life last night."

"I had more than my life saved last night, Mike," Harvey replied.

"Huh?"

Harvey simply gave him a smile. A peaceful smile. What happened in the dark early morning hours in the backwoods of Maine was for him and him alone to know.

"Merry Christmas, Mike," Harvey smiled.

"Merry Christmas, Harvey."

16

Butte, Montana
Christmas Morning
5:09 AM Eastern Standard Time

At the same time Harvey Middleton was opening his bottle of beer with his brother, Father Timothy Vandenberg, the pastor of the Holy Innocents Church was sitting on the side of his bed rubbing the sleep from his eyes.

Vandenberg, at age sixty-eight, had been pastor here for the last thirty years, and made it a point to be the one to say the first mass on Christmas morning. He looked at the clock by his bed, let out a yawn, and began to get dressed.

Holy Innocents was one of the last remaining old-wooden churches, and its simple atmosphere seemed to fit the feeling of Christmas. But, as Vandenburg knew all too well, it was full of drafts that at times were strong enough to blow out candles. That was why he now found himself slipping on his coat and boots so early in the morning.

The furnace would need a good three hours head start just to get the church to a bearable temperature.

Vandenberg put on his coat and walked to the door of the rectory. He opened it up to find the weather reports had been right. The storm from the Rockies had hit, and by the looks of it, had been here for quite some time. And to make things worse, the new snow was now adding to the near-blizzard they had had two days prior.

With a tired shake of his head, Vandenberg ran out the door, across the street, slipping along the way, to the front doors of the church. Shivering uncontrollably, he ran in, closed the door behind him leaving himself in the dark. He could feel it was colder than usual this morning, and the drafts were blowing stronger. He was glad now that he decided to fire up the furnace early.

Feeling around in the darkness, he flipped the light switch. Light bathed the inside of the church. Vandenberg pulled his collar up around his neck and turned to walk to the altar. As soon as he turned, he stopped short.

"Oh my sweet Lord in heaven," he gasped.

Large chunks of hardened snow from the last snowfall covered the altar, directly beneath the hole where part of the ceiling had caved in from the weight. Vandenberg walked open-mouthed to the half-buried altar. He stood facing the crucifix behind the altar, and his heart sank.

"What a mess," a voice echoed though the church.

Vandenberg jumped and turned.

Walking down the center aisle was a young man in a parka, a black sweatshirt, worn hiking boots, and jeans held up by a belt with a peace sign buckle. Over his shoulder, he hefted a black leather travel bag.

The smile on his face turned to embarrassment. "Oh, I'm sorry, father," he apologized. "I didn't mean to startle you. I was passing through and saw the light shining straight up in the air. I came by to see what was the matter. The door was open."

"That's quite all right, my boy," Vandenberg smiled weakly. "Come in, come in, all are welcome in here."

"Thank you, father," the man said walking up and shaking the priest's hand.

"I'm afraid you are right, though," Vandenberg said grimly. "This is quite a mess."

The man surveyed the altar, then looked up at the ceiling. He looked back at Father Vandenberg with a confident smile. "I can fix it," he said.

"You can?" Vandenberg asked.

"Sure," the man said. "Got everything I need in my truck right outside. When's mass, father?"

"Eight o'clock."

"No problem," the man said with a shake of his hand. "I got a wheelbarrow to haul out those big chunks. I can sweep up the rest. I got canvas big enough to cover that hole good enough for you to say services. When you're done, I got some real nice pine strapped to the carrier of my pickup I can use to patch that hole."

"Son, I can't ask you to do all that on Christmas day," Vandenberg said honestly.

"Not a problem, father," the man replied.

"What's you name," Vandenberg asked.

"Chris," the man smiled holding out his hand.

"I'm Father Timothy Vandenberg. Everyone just calls me Father Tim."

"Pleased to meet you, Father Tim," Chris said as they shook hands.

"I insist you have breakfast with me," Vandenberg said.

"Oh, that isn't necessary."

"No, I insist," Vandenberg said waving his hand. "The least I can do to show you my thanks and that of my parishioners is to feed you. Eggs and sausage and some toast."

"Well, thank you, father," Chris smiled. "It sounds good."

The two men walked side by side back down the aisle towards the door. As they neared the entrance, Vandenberg looked back to the hole in the ceiling and sighed. "Do you really know how to fix that?"

The man in the parka looked up at the ceiling and studied it sternly, then smiled again. He looked over to Vandenberg. "Yes, father, I do," he said putting a hand on the priest's shoulder.

"I was raised by a carpenter."

Afterword

Well, there you have it, approximately 90,000 words later, the first of my novels. Thank you for taking the time to let me tell you a story. This book was a collection of stories written over a period of eight years, and it's not all of them.

Two stories didn't make it.

To keep the "feel" of the book, I had to omit one story. That story was named *Santa's Little Helpers*. I hated to do it, because it was one of my three favorites. When I sat down and wrote it, I could only see Denis Leary as the main character. It was humorous, and had a lot of depth and heart to it, but still, it did not fit the feel of this book.

But, if I release another collection, I will be sure to tack it on.

The second of my favorites didn't make it in because it was an extension of another novel I'd written called *Souls of Fire*. The story was called *A Room at the Inn*. That one was removed because without reading the novel, the Christmas story, albeit entertaining, would have had a confusing ending.

As you can tell from my subject matter, I'm a blue-collar person who likes to write about blue-collar people. They are the backbone of this country. From the man working double shifts in the factory to clothe his family, to the woman who works nights to feed her child because her man wasn't man enough to stick around, they are the true fabric of this country.

You'll see more books out of me in the future. Not all of them will be like this one. Some will be horror, others drama and suspense, but I wrote them all for one reason . . .

To give people a little bit of an escape.

To take them away, even if for a short time, from the things everyday life throws at them.

Keep an eye out in the online bookstores for me. I hope to see you again. I don't quite know what road I'll take you down next time, but I'll do my best to make sure it's a ride and a half.

Now, I'm heading to the AMVETS to buy a round for some of America's true heroes.

Before I head out, I just want to thank the people who helped this project along.

Book layout and formatting:

Sean Gallagher
Grip Designs
Sean@ GripDeasigns.com

Cover Art:
Tim Krueger
Lime Light Images
LimeLightImages@aol.com

Photography:
Anthony J. Heisler

If you want to know when the next book will be coming out or have any comments:

W.A.Heisler@comcast.net

Behind The Words

As is always my practice, after I finish a story, I give it to a few choice people to read. People I deemed the "Inner Circle". They weren't chosen because I know they would tell me it was good. Doing that would be a useless gesture. I chose them because they differ in age, tastes, and gender. They give me a feel of how the book would sell and who would be the key audience. Every time I hand a story off to them, it is an exciting experience for me. It's what I call the " Great Challenge".

One question I encounter over and over is, " Where do you get your ideas. How do you put all of this together?" So, I've decided to put in this little thing called *Behind The Words* to give an idea of where a story comes from and how it comes about.

Here is where they came from:

THE TRADITION: My mother had been gone for three years when December 1991 rolled around. She had suffered from Alzheimer's disease, a horrible disease that steals your life from you little by little.

We had watched her disappear little by little for eleven years, and now three years after she'd finally found peace, the stress left in the wake of the disease was still there. It was my second Christmas in my new apartment. It was the first year I had decided to take on writing with full force.

Through the darkness of those years my mother was ill, one bright shining thing came of it. My father and I had become more than father and son, we had become good friends. It was a bond between two soldiers who had just walked away from a war that had left neither of us them same.

And in the end, it was her that planted the seed for this story.

During the first week of December, I went back to our little row home in Tacony just to visit, as I was prone to do. Walking into our little kitchen, I called for my father. He yelled back that he was in the living room.

I opened our refrigerator, grabbed a beer and walked through our small dining room to the equally small living room. I still can't imagine a couple raising six kids in that house.

He had already put up the lighted garland spanning the wall leading from the dining room to the living room and looking at the glow in the parlor, I could tell he had already put up the tree.

Seeing that he was still decorating for the holidays even though he was now alone in the house made me feel better about him being there by himself.

He asked me how work was going. At that time, I was still busting my hump in the meat house. What else could I say, "Same old, same old, dad." He grinned and nodded as I plopped down on the sofa, "Yeah, it gets that way."

I nodded glumly as I looked at the three-foot tree sitting on a table beside the couch. "Looks good," I nodded.

My dad took a drink from his mug of beer and nodded, "Put it up this week."

I kept a close eye on him now. He had just recently retired, and now he had something he didn't have when my mother was sick. He had time to think. Time to dwell. We talked a bit then I asked, "How are you doing?"

I remember my father looking across the softly lit room to a portrait that sat on top of our entertainment center. It was a picture my brother Anthony had taken of my father and mother. She was a bit better then, and wore her familiar smile.

"She should be here," my father said. "Worked all my life for the day I could retire. Had plans for your mother and I. Go places. Do things. Visit people"

My father had lived through the Great Depression. He had survived World War II. Now, he was working his way through another war. He had to say goodbye to a part of his soul. The part that had given him six children. The part that kept the house running as he worked at the container factory to keep food on our table and clothes on our backs.

The part he kissed goodnight before he went to sleep.

My gut wrenched as I looked at him. I looked for words and found none. This was his war now. As much as I hated to admit it to myself, this was a war I would have to leave him to fight on his own, and in his own time.

I looked over to the picture, then down at my beer and nodded, "Yeah, dad. I know."

" So, what've you been up too," he asked in brighter tone.

I looked up and saw him eying me. Now, he knew *I* was dwelling. The Old Soldier was pulling me out of the trench and telling me it was time to move on. He was telling me he was all right. He was telling me the war was over and it was okay to go on with life.

We spent the rest of the time talking odds-and-end talk. Didn't matter to me a little bit.

To this day any time spent with him over a beer is time well spent.

After the visit, I drove back to my apartment, made yet another pot of coffee and fired up the old *Macintosh Plus*.

I was nursing a horror story at that time.

Sitting there looking at the screen, I thought back on the time I had just spent with my father. I thought of how fortunate I was to have the family I have. I thought of how that feeling, especially around Christmas had gotten lost somewhere between the commercials for jewelry and the ads for toys.

God, that ticked me off.

" Show your love for her with this really expensive ring!"

No, show your love for her by always *being there*.

" Get your kid this great new toy! They'll love you for it!"

No, read them bedtime stories and spend time with them, they'll love you for *that*.

The greatest gift one person could ever give to another is the gift of their time, a gift of themselves.

Then an idea came to me. When I was in High School and had no money, I had written a Christmas story to give to my brothers and sisters and parents as a present. It was raw and crude in style, but it was something personal.

Something with no price tag or fancy box.

Then it struck me. I was working in a meat house, I was still poor, what could I do? I could write a Christmas story. I had people reading my stories, each with their favorite ones; some wanting copies to keep so they could read it again. That was not an option. My policy was always no floating copies. But, this would be different. I would write a story for my family and readers every year. Something they could keep.

Something of myself.

I lit a cigarette, closed my horror story, and opened a new document. I sat there puffing away, staring at this blank page and wondered what I would write about.

She should be here.

My thoughts ran back to our house on Knorr Street and my father's words. Words that echoed the sentiments I'm sure all of my family, myself included, were feeling but didn't want to say.

The idea began to form then the great question was asked.

" What if. . .?"

What if the main character had suffered a great loss? What if it was someone he loved dearly? What if it had happened at an age where he could not fully comprehend what had happened? What if it had festered and had become a hatred that masked his longing to see this loved one again?

What if the main character had that chance?

The story fell into place.

Now, what was I going to call it? I'd decided that the main character would go to his father's grave every Christmas Eve, and as most families do, they have their own way of celebrating Christmas every year. I was going to write a new Christmas story every year. So, what is something you do at a set time every year?

It's a tradition.

I crushed out my cigarette, took a gulp of coffee, lit another one, popped it into my mouth, and began hammering away.

In two days, *The Tradition* was done, and the Christmas story chain had started.

In the end, I was pleased with it. It, I had hoped, conveyed the message I was trying to get out: If you care about someone let them know. Tell them how much they mean to you. Never take it for granted that it's understood. Kiss your wife, kiss your husband or boyfriend or girlfriend, hug your kids. Never go to bed angry with your spouse. Keep close with your family; tell them you love them. Life isn't a game. When it's over there is no RESET button.

The stories lasted for eight years. I finally stopped when I no longer believed I could write a Christmas story good enough to pass muster, let alone show to people. If I don't think it's good, I won't put my name on it, and it's off to the Deletion Abyss for it.

Will there ever be more?

I never say never.

As for my father, he eventually got remarried a spitfire named Eleanor and they're happy.

STILLE NACHT: On the first Christmas Eve Day of World War I the German and British field officers called an informal truce that was to last Christmas Eve day through Midnight Christmas day.

Ignoring orders of fraternization with the enemy by British High Command, cease-fires were called all along the Western Front. Christmas Eve night saw British troops trading Christmas Carols between foxholes;

Christmas Day saw the two sides meeting, unarmed, in the center of the battlefield near Lille, where each side helped bury the other side's dead.

After an informal service for their fallen comrades, both sides exchanged meager gifts, food for the most part. It is also said that both sides took to the woods in a joint-hunt for small game to cook for the holiday feast.

As midnight neared, the men were ordered back to their lines.

In the spirit of honor, a signal was agreed on by the officers of both armies to give the men time to return to their trenches. A flare would be shot into the air.

At midnight the flare blazed its way into the night sky.

Shortly after, the ground rocked with British artillery.

Christmas was over.

The war began again.

The story of the Cease Fire of 1914 was an amazing one to me. It showed how the humanity represented on this one day could stop the bloodiest of battles even if it was for just a short time.

I took the two armies and made them two men. Why? It was more intimate that way, and it allowed me to delve deeper into their personal lives and feelings. It's much easier to show how a person is feeling than how an entire regiment is feeling.

Since all of my uncles and my father were in World War II, I changed it from World War I.

THE GIFT: I had done *The Tradition*, which was a story basically about a father and son. I had done *Stille Nacht*, a story about two men thrown together by war. Now, I wanted to something for the mothers and daughters out there.

And I was stuck for an idea.

I walked into the living room of my apartment, put a tape of Christmas Carols in my stereo, turned it on, and dimmed the lights. I grabbed a few bottles of beer and sat down in front of the speakers. I lit a cigarette, drank my beer, and let myself drift into the Imagination Pool.

I began thinking of this woman. As I thought about her more, I realized she was upset. Now, all I had to do was find out why. I saw her husband, her son, but no daughter. I came to the conclusion that she was sick. That had to be it. She must be hospitalized, that would be the only explanation as to why she wasn't home for Christms. And whatever she's hospitalized with, it must be bad judging by the look I was seeing on this woman's face.

Now, I had to take this problem and fix it.

Once I had found the illness, it was time to get some facts. The next day, I called my sister Mary, who is a nurse, and asked her about Leukemia. With her vast knowledge of medicine, she was able to give me the information I needed to make the story authentic. Her input was monumental in my writing of this.

But, still, how do I fix this?

I was brought up in a Catholic household. You know, no meat on Fridays during Lent. Egg soup. Yeeeech! And, God forbid, you accidentally eat a piece of ham during that time, if you did you were on the express train to Hell!

> You there with the face full of meat! This is the Lent Police! Put the sandwich down and back away slowly! Spit out what is in your mouth and put your hands above your head! Do it now! Now, get on the ground and say an Act of Contrition! If you're lucky, you'll only get purgatory for this!
>
> *And then there was going to church with your parents.*

Church every Sunday, peppered with elbows from your folks for fidgeting in the pew. And if you fidgeted too much, you got swatted on the back of the head. Man, if your mom did it right, you could feel it all the way to the back of your eyeballs.

Clip-on ties for school and uncomfortable uniforms. You know, all that good Catholic stuff. To all you guys who droned through twelve years of Catholic schooling and still refuse to wear a tie, I feel your pain.

What do all Catholics do when someone is gravely ill or times are rough? They pray. I've been through my share of it, and I'm sure I'll be there again.

I then realized I'd never put Jesus in any of the stories. After all, whether the idiots who believe Political Correctness like it or not, Christmas is *His* day. Not *Santa's* day. *His day.*

What if . . . ?

What if someone prayed to Jesus for his or her sick loved one and He actually showed up? What if He showed up to any of us face to face? I mean, not through signs, but BAM, " Here I am!"

What would you say?

I, myself, would need a year just to explain my way out of my twenties. Personally, I'm hoping He leaves that decade out when my time rolls around.

But, really, what would you say?

So, I decided that was the route I was going to take. I had delved deeply into the Bible for story research, and was already familiar with much of if from my upbringing. And I have a spiritual side to draw on. Then I thought; who better, who more deserving, to have that opportunity than a child? An innocent. Who better than someone who hasn't been hardened by life yet?

I took what I had, mixed it all together, and let the story develop on its own. In the end, I changed the main character's last name from Findley to Johnson in honor of my buddy Don, and left her at that.

THESE FOUR WALLS: This is one of the stories that I actually hated to see end. I had an enormous amount of fun with this one, second only to *Santa's Little Helpers*.

I wanted something that wasn't quite as heavy as the previous stories. I wanted something that was just as heart-felt, but not sappy. I wanted something that would pull a grin out of the reader. A laugh here and there would be all the better.

I had wanted to do a story featuring mostly kids, but wasn't sure how I wanted to do it. One day while working at the meat house, an idea came to me about a boy who was transplanted from his hometown to Philadelphia. I figured; since they were from Philadelphia, why not make it Tacony? I grew up there. I lived most of my life there. It would be cool.

So, from there, I decided to put the gang together. All of them were made up except for Loverboy and Billy. They were both drawn from my best friend as a kid. His name was Timmy McHugh. Man, we were inseparable as kids. Then I went back to the football games we would have up and down Knorr Street. You know, the one-on-ones with the steady quarterback.

Tackle football in the street in the snow.

What a fun, but stupid, idea *that was*.

Man, we would send each other off of those cars like pinballs then we'd slam onto that street. It's a wonder we never paralyzed ourselves. Any kid reading this, don't try it. It's fun, but the cars today won't be able to take it.

Rough and Tumble was always a good choice when the proper amount of players couldn't be found. Man, we would spend hours across the street in that park just beating the snot out of each other. Stick Ball, Step Ball, Wiffle Ball, Wall Ball, Wire Ball, and when the pimple or pinkie ball popped: Half Ball.

And in all of them Timmy was the best. He was a wiry little kid with speed and agility. There wasn't a bike he couldn't ride faster, and there wasn't a game he couldn't play better when we were kids.

Not only was he thin and wiry, he was Irish. Fair complexion, black hair cut in a sugar-bowl haircut, I swear the kid looked like a little elf. Really! You just looked at him and said, " That kid's *Irish*." With that face, that kid could get away with murder. Me on the other hand had the German face.

I *always* looked guilty.

All the girls always had a thing for Timmy, and that's where Loverboy came from, because when it came to girls he was as shy as a politician at election time and as subtle as a brick to the forehead. He was an amazing kid. He's now a Philadelphia policeman.

I'm sure he's great at that too.

Stay safe, man.

The brother and sister relationship was inspired by my own family's stories and the stories that came from my friends. Tacony had a lot of big families. If you didn't grow up in a big family, you don't know what you're missing. Yeah, a lot of stuff goes down with your siblings that are annoying at the time and you contemplate killing them, but when you're older they are a laugh to relive.

Every story needs a dilemma. Without dilemma there is no need for the reader to turn the page to see how the characters resolve it.

In comes Clara.

We had a woman in our neighborhood named Grace. She lived on Rawle Street. Grace was a little *off*. She was dubbed the infamous title of, "Cat Lady." Man, she had cats everywhere. And you gotta remember, this is back in the early seventies too. There was no scented clumpable stuff back then.

That house must have *reeked*!

I didn't want Clara to be a " Cat Lady", so I made her a witch. Every neighborhood has a scary looking house when you're a kid. This was hers.

From there, with all the characters in place, I let the story grow to what we have now.

THE LONG ROAD HOME: I was shooting for something earthy. I've always loved the pictures I'd seen of Maine, and the people there are salt-of-the-earth. If they like you, they like you. If they don't, they have no problems telling you that to your face. They're hard workers and straight shooters. You never have to worry where they stand on something.

I like that.

So, Maine it was. I wanted a modern day parable, so I chose to go with a Job feel. But what would his trial be? I decided to make him a man who was given great responsibility, a youth cut short, a family in financial straits, and a crisis of faith.

I had always known the crux of the story would take place in the woods on the walk home, but the problem was; how do I get him there? Harvey, from the beginning was a family man. What would pull a devout family man away from his family on Christmas Eve?

Hard times and a way to make them easier was my solution.

I chose to make *The Silver Streak* the symbol of both Harvey Middleton's soul and hope. I made it brand new and shining, as when he was a child. Then, to match the state Harvey was in now, I destroyed it. I left it in the same crumpled mess his soul was in.

The three-mile walk came from the three falls of Christ. It was there I wanted to send the main character back to what had sent his life on this course. I wanted him to revisit it now so that he could see things through the eyes of an adult, not the child he had been.

Harvey Middleton is one of my favorite characters. He's like most of us. He's a hard working person with simple dreams and goals. The only trap he had fallen into was that now he was concentrating so much on what he didn't have, he'd lost sight of what he did have.

That had to be rectified.

Thus, I trashed his truck, sent him for a walk in the woods, and forced him to take inventory of his life.

I'm the writer.

I'm allowed.

Everyone can tell that he was walking with Christ. The name of the character made that pretty clear. I decided to put in hidden references to Christ's life such as having a friend who was a fisherman with a bad temper, referring to Peter.

I chose to symbolize Harvey asking Christ to enter his heart by his invitation to Him to come into his home. I always feel honored when people invite me into their homes. That's who they are. That's where they live. That's they're little piece of the world.

When Peter denied Christ three times, Christ came back to him. Peter fell to his knees and begged forgiveness. Christ asked Peter, " Do you love me," three time and three times Peter answered, " Yes."

That is why Chris asks Harvey three times if he was sure he wanted him to enter his home.

The part where the floodlights flash on showing only one set of footprints was done because I didn't want any tangible evidence that Chris had ever been there. I wanted Harvey to realize what had just happened to him.

One person said to me after reading it, " I like the reference to that poem *Footsteps*. That was really good." I just grinned and thought, *Didn't mean it that way, but it does kind of go with the gist of things. Well, if you think it makes me look smarter . . .*

So, don't tell anyone, okay?

It'll be just between us.

I then had Harvey's brother call to tie up the loose ends.

Then to symbolize Harvey's rejuvenated soul now filled with faith and hope, I resurrected *The Silver Streak* back to mint condition.

I'm the writer.

I'm allowed.

The chapter with Father Vandenberg at the end was just to give Chris' character a more omnipotent feel. I did it to show that he had shown up in Montana only a few moments after He had left Harvey in Maine.

Well, that's how the book was born. It's easier to mosey around the mind of a writer if you have a guide. There's so much crap up there. A flat bicycle tire here, clothes no one wears anymore there.

Just a mess.

In the end: it's all about faith, gang.

Now, don't get me wrong, I'm not the preacher type, and I'm far from being a saint. I'm sure many people who know me will read this and look at me with their jaws hanging and say, "This came from *you*?"

Heh, heh, I love it when *that* happens.

Yes, it did come from me. It's a side of me. It's the side that comes out only when the coffee's hot, the smoke is lit, the apartment is quiet, and the keys are hammering away.

I guess, after all these years, I'm still a dreamer. And I'm glad: for a world without dreams is a world without hope; and a world without hope is truly no place in which to live.

Before we head on over to the Acknowledgments, I just want to say:

If you've ever had a dream of doing something, go for it. Yeah, sure, you may fail, but to succeed, you must first open yourself up to failure. If you don't, you'll never know. Don't give yourself a reason to wish there was a RESET button. Life is a dare.

Dare to dream.

Dare to love.

Dare to live.

Dare to be.

Printed in the United States
1392100001B/58-171

9 780974 554808